THE GAME YOU PLAY

A RIXON RAIDERS NOVEL

L A COTTON

Published by Delesty Books

THE GAME YOU PLAY
Copyright © L A Cotton 2019

Edited by Andrea M Long

RIXON RAIDERS

The Trouble With You
The Game You Play
The Harder You Fall
The Endgame Is You

To Nina
Thank you for believing in this story

PROLOGUE

"Stupid girl," I muttered to myself as I flushed the toilet and left the stall to wash my hands. The music pulsed through the walls, mimicking the thud of my heart against my ribcage.

He's doing it to get under your skin. Ignore him and he'll stop.

Easier said than done.

Jason 'asshole' Ford was the bane of my existence. Arrogant. Conceited. A total manwhore.

And the guy my heart had apparently decided it wanted.

Stupid, *stupid* heart.

Pressing my hands against the cool marble counter, I stared at myself in the wall-length mirror. I looked good. My hair was curled to perfection, hanging in long loose waves down my back; my makeup was smoky and seductive; and the black dress clung to my curves like a second skin.

I didn't only look good.

I looked downright hot.

"Get it together, Giles," I commanded to the girl staring back at me in the mirror. "He only has power over you if you let him."

And right now, the asshole was out there all over another girl.

1

A girl who wasn't me.

The knot in my stomach tightened as I inhaled a deep breath. "You've got this," I whispered.

Just then, a group of giggling girls spilled into the restroom, pausing to glance me over. I offered them a tight smile and hurried out of there. The New York club Asher's cousins had brought us to was something else. Nothing like the bars we had back home in our small town of Rixon. It was moody and dark, the furnishings sleek and sexy. Frequented by young, rich New Yorkers all looking to let loose and have fun.

I slipped into the hall connecting the cloakroom and restroom to the rest of the club, determined to enjoy the night. So what if Jason was practically dry fucking Asher's cousin? My body—and stupid foolish heart—might have wanted him, but my head knew better.

My head knew Jason Ford was a *really* bad idea.

What I needed was to find a nice guy who wanted to buy me a drink and dance the night away with me. And who knew, maybe I'd get to tick another thing off my list. After all, we were in New York. New freaking York. It was a small miracle my parents had ever agreed to let me take the trip for my best friend's birthday. Of course they only knew about the art exhibition we planned to visit and the sightseeing we wanted to do. But what they didn't know, wouldn't hurt them.

The thought made me smile, putting an extra bounce in my step, as I rounded the corner... and smacked straight into a hard, muscular chest. "I know you want me, Giles, but throwing yourself at me is kind of desperate."

"Fuck you, Jason." I glowered at him, stepping back to

put a safe distance between us. Of course he took that as a challenge, the glint in his eye obvious as he inched closer.

"Jason," I warned, but he kept coming until my back hit the wall, knocking the air from my lungs.

"I know what you're doing," he whispered against my ear, his warm breath dancing over my skin. I gulped, my eyes fluttering closed. His voice was low, husky even, and if I didn't know him the way I did, it would have been easy to mistake his tone for seduction.

But I did know him.

And this was all a game to him.

"I'm not doing anything, Jason," I sighed, ignoring the little voice in my head whispering 'liar'.

He erased the sliver of space between us, plastering his body against mine in the dimly lit hall. "It won't work," he added, his tongue swiping my damp skin before nipping my earlobe. My knees buckled as a full-body shiver rolled through me.

"Jason." It was supposed to be another warning, but my voice betrayed me, his name falling from my lips on a breathy sigh.

One of his hands glided up my body. I fought the urge to lean into his touch, to seek more. He didn't care that he squeezed my breast a little too hard or that his fingers wrapped around my throat a little too tight. Because a guy like Jason Ford did what he wanted, took what he wanted, when he wanted it.

But I did care.

I cared that his rough touch lit up my body in a way it never had before. I cared that I wanted to let him do unspeakable things to me.

I cared that I cared.

Tears pricked the corners of my eyes, but I blinked them away, my gaze hard when he finally lifted his head to mine.

"Keep this up and you're going to get hurt," he said coolly. But the air around us was anything but cool.

It was blistering, crackling with tension, burning with anticipation.

"You're playing with fire, Felicity." God, even the way he said my name did things to me. "And do you know what happens when you play with fire?"

His liquor-scented breath caressed my face; his lips hovering dangerously close to mine. "You end up getting burned."

I should have told him to get the hell away from me. Or slapped his panty-melting face and walked away. Or even kneed him in the balls and run. But I did none of those things. Instead, I said, "Maybe I want to get burned."

Because I was Felicity Giles, a girl with a list and a serious case of the crazies.

Jason's brow lifted, his dark eyes studying me. Although looking into my soul better described the way I felt whenever his dark, intense gaze aimed in my direction.

Why couldn't I have wanted someone else, *anyone* else?

Seconds passed as we stared at one another. The music reverberated around us. Laughter and chatter lingering on the periphery of our dark corner of the hall.

"Jason?" I asked, finally breaking the silence, unable to bear it for a second longer.

"Fuck it," he breathed and then his lips were on mine, hard and demanding. Jason didn't just kiss me, he devoured me. His hands clawed at my dress, scraping the material up my legs until his fingers found the soft flesh of my thighs.

"Oh God," I moaned against his unyielding lips. My hands wound into his unruly brown hair as our tongues tangled together. It was messy and dirty and quite possibly the best kiss I'd ever have.

But nothing good lasted forever, and this was Jason. He wasn't a white knight swooping in to win the damsel's heart. He was the evil Prince out to wreck and ruin and leave a trail of broken hearts in his wake.

"Fuck." He tore himself away from me, his body literally jerking back.

Disappointment swelled in my chest as I watched his expression morph into sheer anger. "That was a mistake." His lip curled in disgust.

"Okay." I managed to choke out, smoothing down my wrinkled dress.

"I need to go; Vaughn is waiting for me."

My heart sank.

I could handle his taunts. I could even handle being called a mistake. But hearing him say he was going back to another girl after kissing me like that... it made me want to puke.

"You should probably hurry," I bit out. "Wouldn't want to keep her waiting."

"Shit, Felicity, I—" Something flashed in his eyes but I cut him off.

"Go Jason, just go." I stared at the patterns in the plush carpet.

His heavy gaze lingered on me for another second and then, like always, he was gone.

———

I woke startled, my eyes straining against the darkness. Crap, my head hurt after one too many drinks. But I'd needed all the liquid courage I could get after spending the night watching Jason and Vaughn. His hand on her waist, her lips on his neck. The sexual energy rolling off them, infecting everyone in close proximity.

My stomach lurched and I pushed up on one elbow, waiting for the waves of nausea to pass. Just then, a creak out in the hall cut through the silence.

"Hailee?" I whispered.

Nothing.

Lying back down, I stared up at the ceiling, my eyes chasing shadows, when I heard the sound again. Ready to go out there and see who was up, I grabbed the covers. But my door swung open and Jason stepped inside.

"What are you—"

"Ssh," he hissed, stalking further into the room.

"You can't be in here," I said, curling my hands into the sheet, keeping them pulled up around my body. His eyes pierced the darkness. Watching me.

Stalking my every move.

Not that I dared breathe with him so close.

"Where's Vaughn? Shouldn't you—"

"Do you ever stop talking?"

"You're in my room in the middle of the night. You don't get to say what I can and can't do."

His lip curved deviously. "Wanna bet?" He edged closer, taking the air with him.

"Jason, this isn't funny..."

"You naked under there, Giles?"

Oh God.

Heat pooled in my stomach when it should have been fear. Because Jason didn't play nice, he played dirty.

Deadly.

Dangerously.

"You're drunk," I said, finding my voice again. "You should go."

"You sure about that?" He was at the foot of the bed now, looking over me like a dark prince.

"I..."

He needed to leave.

I needed to tell him to leave right now.

Jason liked this game too much. A game I should never have gotten tangled up in.

It had all started with a list.

My list.

My foolish little list.

It was supposed to help me rock senior year. To encourage me to do all those things I'd always dreamed of but never been brave enough to do. To shed my wallflower existence.

What I didn't count on was *him*.

I thought I was strong enough to play his game; to engage in war with an expert strategist.

I thought I could protect my heart and have some fun.

I should have known better.

I should have retreated instead of surrendering. But I handed over my heart without even realizing.

And now he owned me.

All of me.

Even if he said he didn't want me.

But now he was standing there, looking at me with hunger in his eyes. A hunger that matched my own.

He did want me.

Jason Ford wanted *me*.

And I knew, the rules had just changed.

1

Felicity

"Are you going to ignore me forever?" I asked my best friend as we stopped at our lockers. She gave me some serious stink eye as she traded out textbooks.

"Hails, come on. It was a mistake. I made a mistake."

Slamming her locker shut, her eyes fixed on mine clouded with disappointment. "You slept with him," she hissed, lowering her voice. "You had *sex* with Jason. Have you lost your goddamn mind?"

"It was one time." *Barely one time when you really thought about it.* "And I was drunk; it was a mistake." One I wouldn't be repeating in a hurry. Not that the aforementioned asshole would want a second round. *Get a grip, Felicity.*

"And you think that's okay? You were drunk. Not to mention a virgin," her voice lowered dangerously, indignation flaming her cheeks. "And you let him—"

"It's done now." I gave her a tight smile, ignoring the knot in my stomach. "It will never happen again. But at least I can check another thing off my list." Strained laughter spilled from my lips, but Hails wasn't laughing.

She wasn't even smiling.

"This isn't funny, Flick." She let out an exasperated sigh. "I can't... I don't even know what to say right now."

"So don't." I shrugged. "Let's pretend it never even happened, okay. Jason who?"

But Hailee wasn't looking at me anymore. She was staring over my shoulder, her eyes narrowed with contempt. I didn't need to turn around to know who it was. I felt him. Felt his lips on my skin, his hands on my body.

A shiver rolled up my spine, quickly morphing into lightning bolts shooting around my body as I turned and met Jason Ford's arrogant smirk.

"Fee, baby, I missed you."

Silently groaning to myself, I forced a smile at Asher, Jason's best friend.

"It's only been a day, Asher. You might need to go see Miss Hampstead about your neediness. It's getting worse." My smile grew, but when I peeked over at Jason and saw his indifference my spine stiffened.

Asher glanced between the two of us, frowning. "What's—"

"So big game Friday?" Hailee cut him off, already tucked into her boyfriend Cameron's side.

Jason Ford, Cameron Chase, and Asher Bennet. The three of them were Rixon Raider royalty and they were hoping to take our football team all the way to State this year.

It was a big deal for our small town. An even bigger deal for Jason and his plan to go off and dominate college football at UPenn next year, hopefully earning him a place in the NFL draft.

"Really, Hails?" Asher mocked. "You're a fan now?"

She glared at him, earning her a low rumble of chuckles from him and Cameron. Jason watched on; his expression devoid of emotion. If anything, he looked... bored. My stomach dipped as I looked away.

Jason was complicated. Cold. Callous. And a complete asshole. Even if he was wrapped up in a frustratingly yummy package. Dark unruly hair, even darker eyes. The kind you got lost in, pulled so far under there was no hope of ever crawling back out. Broad shoulders and muscular arms and cut abs that were entirely lickable. I knew first-hand because I'd—

Don't *go there!*

Jason lived and breathed football. His commitment was borderline obsessive. But then, I guess if you wanted to be the best you had to give your all. Soul included.

"It's kind of hard not to be a fan when your boyfriend is the star wide receiver for the team." Hailee grinned up at Cameron. My best friend had done a real one-eighty since senior year began a couple months back. She had always hated the game. Hated her step-brother Jason even more. He, along with Asher and Cameron, had made her life hell ever since she moved to Rixon. But something changed this year. Cameron started looking at her with lust in his eyes and although she tried to ignore his charms, it didn't take long for him to break down her walls.

Our twosome soon became a threesome; a fivesome if you counted Asher and Jason. Although from the scowl Jason wore whenever he was around us, it was no secret he was tolerating his best friend's and step-sister's new relationship at best.

"Yeah, well, we need to be getting to practice so..." Jason's insinuation hung in the air.

"What's the rush?" Asher said, "We still have—" His mouth snapped shut when his best friend levelled him with an icy stare. "Ladies, it's been a pleasure." He trailed after Jason who failed to say goodbye, but then, he hadn't said hello either.

Cameron lingered, crowding Hailee against the locker and kissing her. I glanced away, giving them some privacy. I'd grown used to their PDA's over the last couple of weeks, but it didn't make them any easier to stomach.

After a minute or so, I peeked over at them. Faces pressed close together, Cameron whispered something to Hailee that made her giggle. Jealousy clawed its way up my throat, but I stuffed it down. After everything they'd put her through over the last few years, she deserved this. The fairy tale romance. The happily-ever-after.

Cameron and Hailee were couple goals and I was so happy for them.

Not at all green.

Nope.

Not even a little bit.

———

My day didn't get much better. Hailee was barely talking to me, and all everyone else was talking about was the Raiders upcoming game against Millington. Which meant all day his name followed me, a whisper on the wind, taunting me.

But it was fine.

I was fine.

I'd wanted to lose my v-card and I had. Okay, so I hadn't anticipated giving it up to one of the most arrogant and conceited jerks I knew, but what was senior year if not a chance to try new things ... and then quickly regret *ever* going there.

Images flooded my mind as I pushed the sandwich around my plate. His hurried and needy and oh so hot kisses. His big strong hands splayed around my hip, my throat, possessive and dominant. The sting of him filling me... the almost tears.

"Flick?" Hailee narrowed her eyes at me. "Where'd you go just now?"

"Huh, I..."

"Forget it." She went back to her fries, and guilt coiled around my heart. I hated that things were awkward between us. But she had walked in on me and Jason doing it, so I knew I had to give her time to come around. My best moment it was not.

"You know, you can go and sit with him." I flicked my head over to where Cameron sat with the rest of the football team.

"I know. But we're not attached at the hip. Besides, he needs this." She glanced over at him. "After everything with his mom, he needs the team."

"How is she?"

"Dealing the best she can. But she's a fighter, and she really wants Cameron to focus on school and the team."

I nodded. "So if he's over there to bond with the team, why is it he hasn't taken his eyes off you?" My brow arched, and Hailee fought a smile.

"He wanted me to sit with them."

Swinging my leg over the bench, I stood up. "Come on, let's go," I said, prepared to take one for our team of two.

Hailee frowned. "What are you doing?"

"We're going over there. He might need the team, but he needs you too. And to be quite honest, I can't eat my lunch with him making moon eyes at you."

"Flick," she groaned, peeking over at the team. "I'm not sure..."

"Fine. I'll go by myself." I shrugged, grabbing my tray and moving around the table.

"Oh my god," Hailee breathed out. "You're serious, you're really going to sit over—"

But her words rolled off me as I made my way over to their table. A few of the guys glanced up when I reached them.

"Fee, baby." Asher's eyes lit up when he noticed me. "And to what do we owe this pleasure?"

"Room for one more?"

"Oh, sweetheart," one of the sophomore players, Joel Mackey, smirked. "You can sit right here." He glanced down at his crotch and I rolled my eyes.

"Back the fuck up, Mackey." Asher nudged the guy next to him and dropped his eyes to the space at his side.

Just as I went around to sit by him, Hailee approached the table. "I wondered how long it was going to take for you to give in," I heard Cameron say to her, quietly. He swung his leg over the end of the bench and pulled her down, slipping his arms around her waist. "Hi."

"Hi."

I sat down, trying to look at anything but Cam brushing

his lips over hers. God, they were so in love. So happy. So freaking perfect. Something inside me twisted.

"You okay over there?" Asher whispered.

"Who me?" I flashed him a warm smile. Asher was... well he was like a stray who followed you around; cute and annoying. But he'd never been anything but nice to me.

"You don't need to do that," he lowered his voice so that it was drowned out by the conversation going on around us. "Not with me," he added.

"Do what?" I played dumb, ignoring the pit in my stomach.

His eyes flicked to where Jase sat. He was busy talking to one of the guys when a manicured hand slid over his shoulder. He glanced up, a sly smirk gracing his ridiculously perfect face, as Jenna Jarvis, star gymnast and head bitch of Rixon High, stared down at him with a salacious smile of her own. Without hesitation, Jase shoved his chair back slightly letting her drop onto his lap. She wrapped her arms around his neck and I almost gagged.

Suddenly, I felt Asher's arm go around the back of me. My eyes slid to his in question but in true Asher style he simply grinned.

My cell phone vibrated, and I dug it out.

Hails: Are you okay?

Me: Of course. Why wouldn't I be?

. . .

I didn't meet her heavy gaze despite feeling it burn into the side of my face.

Hails: He's just using her...

My eyes flicked to Jase and Jenna of their own volition.

Me: Doesn't matter. I knew what I was doing.

You didn't tame a guy like Jason Ford. You enjoyed whatever he was willing to give you and filed it away under 'fun while it lasted'. Jenna knew this, all the girls at school knew this, and yet, it didn't stop them trying to conquer him. To make him fall at their feet. And there had been many who had tried... and failed. But I didn't bunch myself with them because I was under no illusions when it came to Jason Ford, QB One, and Rixon's golden boy of football.

Hails: You deserve so much more xo

The *xo* made me smile. She might have been pissed at me for sleeping with her step-brother, but Hailee wouldn't stay mad for long. We were ride or die, and it would take a damn sight more than some guy to ever come between us.

Me: I love you too xo

I hit send and finally looked over at her, both of us grinning. But then something caught Hailee's eye and her face paled. I didn't need to turn around. I already knew what I'd find. But I did it anyway. To prove to myself—and maybe her—that I was in control of this situation. That Jason was just a semi-drunk lapse in judgment.

The second my eyes landed on them—Jenna plastered against him, their lips moving, tongues licking—I knew it was all a lie though. One I kept telling myself over and over, because if you kept repeating something, it had to be true, right?

My hands shook as I pushed my tray out of the way and stood up.

"Fee?" Asher's voice barely perforated the white noise in my head. Jason wasn't only kissing Jenna, he was devouring her, and I was pretty sure in about ten seconds they would be fucking in the cafeteria. Sexual energy rolled off them, hitting me like a wrecking ball.

"I- I have to go," I rushed out, trying to keep my voice even. "I forgot. I have an appointment with Miss Hampstead."

He frowned up at me; eyes narrowing, clouded with suspicion.

"I'll see you later, okay?" I forced a smile that I knew probably looked wrong.

"I'll come with you," Hailee said across the table.

"No, it's cool." I made myself meet her sympathetic gaze. "I'll see you in fourth period."

But the second I went to move I realized my mistake. To get out of the cafeteria, I'd have to walk directly by Jason and Jenna.

Crap.

Taking a deep breath, I grabbed my tray and kept my head held high. I was so proud of myself for keeping it together. Only a few more steps and I'd be clear of them and their live sex show. Until something brushed the back of my leg, and I froze. My breath caught as I willed myself to calm down. It was nothing. A gust of wind from an open window maybe, or dust particles in the air. Before I could stop myself, I looked down. Dark eyes stared back at me.

Jason.

It was Jason.

He stared at me, *through* me, as I stood there paralyzed. Jenna was still kissing him, trailing her treacherous mouth all over his skin. Skin that less than forty-eight hours ago, I'd tasted. Skin I had been kissing.

A violent shiver rolled up my spine, my stomach churning.

Move, Felicity. Just keep walking.

Jason's brow rose as he continued to stare at me, barely kissing Jenna back, but not stopping her either.

His intense gaze was cruel.

But then, I shouldn't have expected anything else.

Steeling myself, I narrowed my eyes at him, lingering for a second, and then put one foot in front of the other and kept walking. Telling myself he hadn't just ripped out my heart and stomped all over it.

2

Jason

"We need to talk," Cameron pressed his hand against my chest blocking my exit from the locker room.

"Not interested," I said coolly.

"We *are* doing this." His brow arched as he shoved me. It was only a mild push but enough for me to know he meant business.

"Fine," I shot back. "Say whatever you have to say, man, and let me get the fuck to class."

"You go to class now?" He smirked.

"Fuck you."

"Why'd you do it?" Cam let out a weary sigh, his eyes asking me a million things I didn't have the answer to.

Shrugging, I said, "Because I was drunk and she was there."

"Don't give me that bullshit. You like her."

"Like her?" I barked out. "I can't fucking stand her." Felicity Giles was exactly the kind of girl I spent my days trying to avoid. Needy. Desperate. Weird as hell.

"You really are a dick sometimes, you know that?"

"Never claimed to be anything else." I shrugged dismissively.

"I just don't get it. Vaughn was all over you. You could have taken her back to the hotel..." He let the words hang between us. We'd gone to New York for Hailee's birthday last weekend. Asher's cousin Vaughn had showed us around with her brother. She was hot. Slim with curves in all the right places, and Cam was right, she was up for it. Whispered it in my ear more than once during the night. But I hadn't gone there. Instead, I'd drank more than I should have, gone back to the hotel and found myself outside Felicity's room in the middle of the night.

"Look, it was just sex. Drunken sex. I was horny, and she was there." She might not have been my type, all geeky with no filter, but there was no denying Felicity was gorgeous. Long dark hair, narrow waist, and legs that seemed to go on for miles, even if she did stand a good few inches shorter than me. And her eyes, fuck. Two pools of sea-green that had worked some hypnotic voodoo shit on me.

Obviously.

"Just sex," my best friend repeated flatly.

"Yeah, just sex. She knows the score. It was a good time. Now it's over. So can we all just fucking move on?" I couldn't get distracted by some girl-drama, not when I had the play-offs in sight. My focus needed to be one-hundred-and-ten percent on the team. On winning State.

"So it wasn't a game?"

"Game? What the fuck are you talking about?" Irritation rippled through me.

"You didn't know?"

"Seriously, Chase, spit it out already."

Cameron was staring at me like I'd lost my fucking mind. And maybe I had. If I'd had known it would cause this much trouble, I never would have looked twice at Felicity. But then, my step-sister wasn't supposed to walk in on us.

He didn't reply, still gawking at me, so I added, "Look, I know she's Hailee's best friend, but she knows the deal. I didn't promise anything, and she didn't—"

"Will you just shut up a second," he ground out and it was my turn to gawk.

A beat passed. Another. The air charged around us.

And then he delivered the last words I ever expected to hear.

"She was a virgin."

"A virgin?" I choked out. "Is that supposed to be a joke?"

Felicity wasn't a virgin. Sure, she'd been tight, but I just figured she wasn't as experienced as Jenna or the other gymnasts and cheerleaders who rode dick like it was an Olympic sport. But she hadn't said a word when I'd gone faster. Harder. I always liked to be in control and that spilled over to sex. I never made a girl do anything she didn't want to, but I wasn't gentle either. I liked to fuck. And then I liked to get the fuck out of there. I'd tried the whole relationship thing once before and it had blown up in my face, and I wasn't *ever* looking to go there again.

I didn't do sleepovers and except for a handful of girls, I didn't do repeat performances. Sex was an outlet. Nothing more, nothing less. And like football, I excelled at it.

So how the fuck hadn't I realized Felicity was a virgin?

"You really didn't know?" Cam asked.

"Do you think I would have fucked her if I did?" He winced at my harsh tone. "She was practically begging for it."

I think. It was all a little hazy. But she'd wanted it as much as me.

"Nice, real nice." He deadpanned.

"Are we done? Because you're starting to piss me the hell off."

"Yeah, we're done." He let out an exasperated breath. "Just stay away from her, Jase. She's Hailee's best friend and things are already strained enough." He didn't say the rest; he didn't have to.

Things between us *were* strained. But then what had he expected when I found out about him and Hailee?

Growing up, she had been the bane of my fucking life. I'd hated her. Hated everything about her. But a lot had changed since senior year started. I guess that was a trending theme with it being the final year of high school.

Me and Hailee weren't exactly friends now, but for the sake of Cameron, we'd called a shaky truce.

"Is that all?" Anger laced my words. I was so fucking over all this bullshit.

"I know it's hard seeing me with her—"

"Save me the 'I'm sorry I chose your step-sister' speech."

"Jase, come on..." His hand curled around my arm. "It doesn't change anything. You're still my best friend. I've got your back. Always."

But it did change things.

It changed everything.

It had always been the two of us against the world. Now it wasn't.

And I didn't know what the fuck to do with that.

———

I pushed off the wall the second Felicity appeared. Mondays she stayed behind after school for book club.

Fucking book club. It sounded like something my grandma would have enjoyed if she were alive.

"Jason?" Her mouth fell open when she spotted me, those big sea-green eyes widening to saucers. "What are you—"

"Let's go, Giles," I said, trying to keep it as impersonal as possible. My dick had other ideas though, traitorous motherfucker, stirring to life the second my hand clasped around her tiny wrist. Remembering how it had felt to pin them above her head while I slid inside her, making her cry out my name.

"Go? Go where?" She huffed indignantly. "I'm not going anywhere with you."

"You think you have a choice?" I dragged her around the side of the building toward the gym. It was quiet, just like I knew it would be.

"Jason," she hissed, trying to yank free of my grip. But I kept walking, refusing to do this out in the open where anyone could walk by and see us.

Shouldering the door to the gym, I pulled her down the hall toward the locker room. The second we were inside, and the door closed, I was on her. Crowding her against the wall, I placed my hands either side of her head and glared at her. "A virgin? You didn't think to fucking mention that before we—"

Her scowl deepened, a low growl rumbling in her throat. It would have been impressive if she wasn't so tiny and vulnerable compared to me as I loomed over her. "It wasn't like you asked," she seethed.

"Because I didn't think—"

"Oh that's right." Her brow rose. "You're used to fucking skanks."

Jesus, this girl.

"Watch it, Giles."

"Or what, Ford?" she threw back without hesitation.

"Why didn't you tell me?" My voice softened, surprising me. It surprised Felicity too, if the hitch of her breath was anything to go by.

"It's not a big deal." She gave a lackluster shrug. "I wanted to get it over with, and you were available."

"Available?" I balked. She couldn't actually be serious. "You make it sound so—"

"What are you doing, Jason?"

What was I doing?

"Nothing, I just... shit, Felicity, you should have told me."

Sardonic laughter spilled from her lips. "What, so you could make it romantic? Buy me flowers and tell me how pretty I looked before dirtying me up. Please. This isn't a fairy tale and you're certainly no prince. It was just sex, Jason." Something flashed in her eyes, but she quickly schooled her expression.

It was too late though. I'd seen that look before. Right before I glided inside her.

Fuck.

Fuck. Fuck. Fuck.

Memories washed over me. Her damp skin, the little moans she made as I moved above her. Inside her. The way she'd clung to me, meeting me thrust for thrust.

"You're sure you were a—"

"Are you kidding me right now?" Her eyes widened.

"But you didn't..." The words got stuck in my throat.

"What, bleed? I did, you were just too wasted to notice." Shame colored her cheeks as she lowered her gaze.

I had been drunk, but I hadn't been that drunk. *Had I?* It had been dark and messy. A tangle of heated kisses and desperate touches. And then Hailee had burst into the room killing the moment and I'd pretty much hightailed it out of there, not bothering to check if she was okay.

"Can I go now?" she added, barely looking at me.

"I... what..." I choked out unsure why I felt like shit all of a sudden. So she was a virgin. It wasn't like I initiated it. She was as hot for me as I was for her.

Was I really hot for her?

I'd told Cameron it was just sex, convenient. But I couldn't deny I didn't like hearing her describe what had really gone down.

A girl's first time was supposed to be... more or something, wasn't it?

Hearts and flowers and mood lighting and all that shit. I didn't know because I didn't make a habit of fucking virgins.

"Why?" The word flew out of my mouth before I could stop it.

"Why?" Felicity frowned. "Why, what?"

"Why me?"

"Oh don't flatter yourself, Jason." She tapped my chest, smiling wryly. "I have a list and you were a means to an end."

A means to an... what the actual fuck?

"Now if you're done, I have places to be." She ducked under my arm and came up on the other side, but my hand shot out, grabbing her arm.

"What game are you playing, Giles?"

"Game?" Surprise flashed in her eyes, her earlier confidence slipping away. "You think this is a game?"

"You're telling me it isn't?"

The air electrified around us, crackling with sexual tension. My dick felt it. Hell, my entire body felt it. And it wanted more.

More Felicity.

More of her smart mouth and witty retorts. Her slender hips and pouty lips.

I needed to get a fucking grip. Because I had enough to worry about without adding a girl to the mix. Especially my step-sister's best friend.

"Go to hell, Jason." She stormed off, her anger almost palpable as she disappeared into the hall.

Long after she'd gone, I was still standing there. Processing our interaction. My body's strange response to her. She was pissed, that much was obvious—her attitude a front for her true feelings. Her closing line had been telling enough. She wanted me to stay the fuck away.

So why did all I hear was *game on*?

———

"Jason, can you come in here please?"

With a groan, I stalked down the hall and into the kitchen where I found my dad at the kitchen table, pouring over a stack of papers. "Yeah?"

"We'd like for you to join us for dinner today."

"I'm good, but thanks." No way did I want to sit around playing happy families with my old man, his new wife, and Hailee.

"Son," Dad let out a heavy sigh. "We need to move past this."

"I'm over it. I just don't want to pretend I actually give a shit."

"Jason," he snapped, eyes sliding to Denise. "I know you're hurting, but this is not the way."

Me and my old man were most definitely not father and son goals. To the rest of Rixon, Dad liked to exude togetherness. A team. The local football hero and the son set to follow in his path. But I knew the truth. I knew what Kent Ford was really about. There was a time when I'd worshipped the ground he'd walked on. But that was *before*. When he and my mom were in love. When our family was enough.

"I'll be in my room," I said, swiping a banana from the fruit bowl and retreating into the hall. Almost colliding with Hailee as she flew off the stairs.

"Sorry," she said. "I didn't see you."

"Yeah, okay," I grumbled. It wasn't like you could really miss me. Six one. Broad. Wearing my blue and white football jersey. "In a hurry?"

Hailee's brows pinched. "You want to talk?"

"Forget it." I waved her off.

27

"Jeez, I'm sorry. I just didn't expect... what you were saying?" Her expression softened, and I found myself humoring her.

"I said are you in a hurry?"

"Felicity's picking me up. We're going to The Alley."

Of course they were. I didn't get the appeal. It was a dive place on the Rixon/Rixon East border. Too many East kids came around there for my liking.

"You think it's a good idea to go there alone?"

"I won't be alone. I'll be with Flick. But it's nice to know you care." A hint of amusement played on Hailee's lips.

Before I could correct her, Felicity's horn blared outside. I knew because I'd been listening to the annoying-as-fuck sound for almost two years since she passed driver's ed.

"Right then, I'll guess I'll see ya." Hailee moved toward the door, but I called after her. "Yeah?" She glanced back.

"I didn't know."

"Know?" Her brows knitted.

I dragged a hand down my face wondering why the fuck I'd said anything to begin with. But it was out there now, hanging between us. "Yeah, about Felicity being a... you know," I explained.

My step-sister inclined her head, studying me for a second and then said, "Okay."

Okay?

What the fuck was that supposed to mean?

"I'm glad we cleared that up."

A hint of a smile lifted the corner of her mouth but then her expression turned serious. "I know we have to tolerate each other for Cameron's sake, but stay away from Felicity, Jason."

"I—" The words got stuck, but it was too late anyway. Hailee had already slipped outside and disappeared, leaving me standing there, wondering what the fuck just happened.

3

Felicity

"You're distracted," Hailee said over her sundae. "It's him, isn't it? Jason." There was a coolness to her voice that squeezed my heart.

"It's not..." I let out a heavy sigh, meeting her gaze. "I thought I'd feel good or relieved or something but now I just feel..."

I didn't know what I felt.

The list was supposed to help me push my boundaries, to step out the confines of my perfectly average life and take more risks. It wasn't like I'd planned to seduce Jason. To play his stupid game of cat and mouse. He was just there. Like a slow building wave that before I realized what had happened, crashed over me and swept me off my feet.

"Oh, Flick." Hailee reached over the table and grabbed my hand. "I could kill him for doing—"

"It wasn't his fault. I need you to know that. I—"

"You like him, don't you?"

"I can't really explain it but something's different this year." I'd never looked twice at Jason and his friends before. Neither had Hailee though, and look how that turned out. Now she was madly in love with Cameron and they were planning to go off to college together and have cute football playing babies.

"Did you think if you slept with him, he'd suddenly change? Because—"

"What? No. *No!*" I shook my head. "I know Jason isn't boyfriend material. Trust me, I know. But there's something... he makes me feel..."

Just then, the door opened and a swarm of people entered, all wearing red and white jerseys.

"Crap," Hailee grumbled as we watched the Rixon East football players stroll up to the diner counter.

"Don't they know this is Switzerland?" I whispered.

Tate, the owner of The Alley, refused to let the rivalry between Rixon High and the high school across the river, Rixon East, affect his business. Anyone was welcome here so long as they played nice. That meant no football jerseys, colors, or smack talk. It's why both football teams usually avoided the place like the plague.

"Apparently the rules just changed." Hailee retreated into herself, and I couldn't blame her. Lewis Thatcher, captain and QB for the Rixon East Eagles, had come after her once he discovered she was Jason's step-sister. It had been a shitshow, but since Rival's Week was done, we figured—*hoped*—the stupid pranks were over.

"Oh shit." I'd clearly spoken too soon as Lewis Thatcher entered The Alley, a smirk on his face as everyone sat up a little straighter. Like Jason, he was worshipped by his classmates and townspeople. But he wasn't in Rixon East now and technically, this was Rixon territory.

So what the hell was he doing here?

"Maybe we should go," I said to Hailee who was still

gawking at them. "Hails?" I kicked her leg gently under the table and her head whipped around to me.

"Sorry, what?"

"I said maybe we should go."

"And let him win? No way." Defiance sparked in her eyes. "I doubt they even recognize—"

"Ladies," a deep voice said, and we both glanced up to find Thatcher and another guy staring down at us. "Hailee and, I'm sorry, I don't think I got your name?"

"You didn't," I sassed. "Because I didn't give it to you."

The whole diner had fallen quiet, everyone straining to hear our conversation. Hailee flashed me a look that said, 'don't make it worse', but no way was I just going to sit here while he taunted her.

"You go can now." I dismissed them with my hand and focused on Hailee again. Silently praying they left. But they didn't.

"I like this one," Thatcher's friend said. "I wonder what else her mouth can do—"

"You need to leave," Hailee ground out, her hands curled around the edge of the table, turning her knuckles white.

"Funny," Thatcher leaned down into her space, his lip twisted with amusement, "Because it sounds like a warning, and yet, I don't see anyone here coming to your rescue. Do you, Gallen?"

"Don't see no one, Cap." Thatcher's dog folded his arms over his chest, glaring at me.

My eyes surveyed the diner, searching for someone—anyone—who might help us. But the handful of kids I recognized from school all dropped their gazes the second I looked at them.

Cowards.

The rest of the kids watched with a mix of interest and sympathy, and I figured they were East kids. Used to Thatcher's games.

"What do you want?" Hailee sounded disinterested, but I caught the inflection in her voice.

"Want?" Thatcher grinned. "I want lots of things, baby." He plucked a strand of her hair and brought it to his nose, inhaling deeply.

Screw this. I dipped my hand into my purse and managed to dig out my cell phone without Lewis or his dog noticing. Quickly locating Cameron's number, I fired off a text and then slid it back into my purse.

"Rumor has it you're fucking Chase now?"

Hailee pressed her lips together refusing to answer.

"Get off her, you disgusting pig," I yelled, but panic filled Hailee's eyes as she shook her head subtly.

"Want me to shut her up, Cap?" The dog said. "Because I'd love nothing more than to watch her choke on my—"

"I'd like to see you try." The words spilled out before I could stop them. Hunger glittered in the dog's predatory gaze as his hooded eyes drifted down my body.

"Pig," I muttered, angling myself away from him.

"I want you to give your boyfriend a message for me—"

"Why don't you give it him yourself?"

Relief slammed into me at the sight of Cameron and Asher standing in the door. Thatcher immediately straightened, but he didn't leave Hailee's side.

"Are you okay?" I mouthed at her, and she nodded, unshed tears pooling in the corner of her eyes.

"Fee, baby, why don't you come on over here?" Asher crooked his finger at me, and I rose, ignoring the low growl coming from Thatcher's friend. When I reached him, Asher hooked me into his side and whispered, "You did the right thing."

Although with the anger rolling off Cameron, I wasn't sure. I didn't want to incite a fight, but I didn't want Lewis to upset Hailee any more than he already had.

"She yours, Bennet?" the dog asked Asher with a snarl. "Because if she's not, I wouldn't mind taking her for a ride; see if what they say about Raider chicks is true." His laughter filled the air and a few of his teammates snorted.

My stomach washed with disgust but Asher's fingers dug into me, grounding me. "What are we going to do here, Cam?" he said. "There's only two of us and eight of them."

"I'll handle it." Cameron inched forward, the air around him charged and dangerous.

"Hailee, come here." He gave her a reassuring nod, and slowly Hailee rose from the chair. But Thatcher's hand clamped down on her shoulder.

"Not so fast, baby, we're just getting—"

"Get your hands off her."

"Or what, Chase? You're a lover not a fighter and I don't see Ford anywhere, do you?"

Anticipation crackled in the air, the whole diner watching on with fascination. A few cameras were aimed in the direction of the stand-off between Cameron and Lewis Thatcher and I knew it wouldn't be long before it was all over social media.

"You don't want to do this, man." Cameron implored, holding his hands up. "It's a public place, people are filming."

Hesitation flashed over Thatcher's face, enough for Cameron to grab Hailee's hand and yank her toward him. "Go." He flicked his head toward us, and she hurried to Asher's side.

"Maybe we should call Jason," she said.

"That is the last thing we want to do right now. Your boy can handle it."

"What's going on here?" Tate appeared looking flustered. Planting his hands on his hips, he glowered at Thatcher. "You know the rules, Son. I won't have you coming in here disrespecting—"

"Easy, old man." He held up his hands, backing away slowly "We were just getting a bite and then leaving."

Leaving my ass.

If Tate hadn't showed up right when he had, we all knew things could have ended very differently. But Lewis Thatcher tipped his head toward the door and like good little minions, his teammates filed out of the diner, Tate following them out for good measure.

"Tell Ford we'll see him soon." Thatcher blew Cameron a kiss. "Nice seeing you again, Hailee."

Asher released me and threw himself into Cameron's path. "Don't do anything stupid, bro." He pressed his hand against Cameron's chest.

"I'm cool," he said, wrapping his arm around Hailee. "Let's go sit down."

"You mean let's wait until it's safe to leave?" I said

unable to keep the sarcasm out of my voice. "What the hell was that?"

Asher and Cameron led us over to one of the booths at the back so we had a little more privacy. Hailee scooted in next to Cameron and Asher pulled me in next to him.

"He's gunning for blood." Asher scrubbed his face.

"Well, he ain't going to be gunning for blood in my place again." Tate appeared, his brows bunched together. "Cameron, good to see you, Son."

"Hey, Tate. I'm sorry about—"

"Now now, there's no need to apologize; but I won't have your little rivalry spilling into my business, you hear me?"

Cameron nodded, his jaw set.

"We had no idea they would show up here," Hailee added, the color finally returning to her cheeks.

"Yeah, well, the little shits planned it. A couple of them caused a distraction out back, or I would have been here sooner. You're more than welcome around here anytime, you know that. But not if—"

"We got it," Cameron said. "It won't happen again."

But it was promise we all knew he couldn't keep. Lewis Thatcher did what he wanted. No one could stop him from coming around here, except the police. And like the Raiders, the Rixon East Eagles were virtually untouchable.

Tate didn't look convinced, but he skulked away, mumbling something about 'football madness'. Few people in Rixon were anti-football. In fact, in my whole life I'd only ever known three people who weren't obsessed with the game: Hailee, Tate, and my mom. It was just a part of life here.

"Fuck," Asher breathed out.

"I second that," I said, dropping my head back against the booth.

"You okay?" Cameron asked Hailee, tucking her closer into his side. I envied them. Their closeness, their love. The way he looked at her like she was everything he needed, and he'd do whatever it took to keep her. I wanted that.

God, did I want it.

So why the hell did you have sex with Jason?

I ignored my inner critic, focusing on my best friend. "Maybe we should tell someone?"

"Tell who? Miss Hampstead? My mom? The principal?" She shook her head. "I can handle Lewis Thatcher."

"You shouldn't have to fucking handle him." Cameron slammed his hand down on the table, making me and Hailee flinch. "Jason should never have..."

"What did he do that was so bad?" I asked.

Jason and Lewis Thatcher's rivalry had grown with them from PeeWee through junior football camp. We'd all heard the stories of two of the best quarterbacks ever to come out of our district. The pranks and fights. But something had changed last year. The rivalry turned bitter. But no one knew the details, not even Hailee who lived with him.

"Nothing you need to worry your pretty little head over." Asher grinned.

"You think I'm pretty? How sweet." I shot back, my words dripping sarcasm. His expression fell and for a second I could have sworn he looked hurt, but then his smirk was plastered back in place as if it had never happened.

"You know Jase is going to want payba—"

"Not here," Cameron said quietly, and something passed between them. Something they didn't want me and Hailee knowing.

Dumb boys. I rolled my eyes.

"I don't want you or Jason going after Thatcher." Hailee grabbed his jaw, forcing him to look at her.

"We're not, I promise."

"Don't lie to me, Cameron. I expect it off Jason, but not you."

"What do you expect me to do? What he did to you—"

"Is done. Nothing you or Jason do is going to fix that. Let it go. I have."

Cameron dipped his head, capturing her lips in a slow, bruising kiss. Asher cleared his throat, shifting uncomfortably. "Seriously, here?" he drawled, shooting me a bemused look.

"Sorry." Hailee's eyes slid to ours as she tried to break free from the kiss. But Cameron was stronger, planting big wet sloppy kisses all over her face.

"Aaaaand that's me, gone. Come on, Fee, baby, you can kick my ass at air hockey."

With a groan, I followed him out of the booth. Asher was the joker of the bunch: always smiling, always cracking a joke. With sandy blond hair, sparkling blue eyes, and a roguish smile, he was the epitome of the All-American boy next door. And somehow, I'd earned a spot in his life. Cameron constantly teased me about getting with Asher and sometimes, I did wonder what it would be like if I went there. I mean, he seemed interested, always teasing and flirting with me. But sadly, he wasn't the guy who turned my head and made my heart beat that little bit faster. Deep down, Asher was good. His heart was pure.

Which sucked for me... because apparently I preferred bad boys with dark hearts.

4

Jason

"WHAT THE FUCK HAPPENED?" I demanded the second Cam and Asher arrived at our regular spot in Bell's, a local bar run by an ex-Raider and one of our biggest fans. My eyes flicked to Hailee who was quiet and a little pale at his side. I barely even acknowledged Felicity. I couldn't risk her pulling that hypnotic voodoo crap on me, not here.

"Well?" I arched my brow, growing impatient.

"It was Thatcher. He showed up at The Alley."

"He was bothering you?" Meeting my step-sister's gaze, my eyes bore into hers, and she gave me a small nod.

"Fuck." I raked a hand through my hair, trying to rein in the anger I felt coursing through my veins. Thatcher was supposed to be my problem. Mine and the team's. He was never supposed to go after Hailee. But that shit was on me and I'd deal with it.

One way or another, Thatcher would get what was coming to him. Even if I had to bide my time until the season was done.

My fist curled against my thigh, anger radiating deep inside me. Fucking Lewis Thatcher.

"I'll get the drinks in," Asher said cutting the thick silence. Everyone seemed to inhale a breath as they were collectively waiting for me to get my shit together. I met Cameron's heavy stare. Concern shone in his eyes as he silently warned me not to do anything reckless.

But this was me we were talking about.

And when it came to Lewis Thatcher, the temptation to go across the river and cause a little chaos was usually too hard to resist.

"I'm good," I said, my eyes flicking past him to Hailee and then Felicity. Her eyes snapped to mine, narrowing slightly.

"I'll go help Ash." I walked away, barely able to stand the knot in my stomach. "Hey." Leaning on the bar next to Asher, I gave him a tight smile.

"Hey, you okay, man?"

I grunted some inaudible reply.

"This shit with Thatcher is getting hairy," Ash went on, "You should have seen him with his hands on Hailee. I thought Cam was going—"

"He touched her?" My jaw clenched.

"He was just trying to get a rise out of Cam. I managed to get Fee out of there before one of his guys..." he trailed off, watching me intently.

I knew what he was doing and I didn't like it.

"Anyway," he said when I didn't take the bait. "Cameron held it together. I'm not sure we'll be able to show our faces around there anytime soon though. Tate, the owner, wasn't too impressed."

"You know I haven't stepped foot in that place for almost two years, right?"

Asher shrugged. "I'd forgotten how cool it was."

"Cool, really?" I fought a smirk. "You're fucking weird sometimes."

"Fuck you, man." He shouldered me. "You have a plan, right? To get Thatcher back for pulling that shit with Hailee? I know she told Cameron not to do anything, but he can't just get away with it."

"And he won't," I ground out.

"Well you know I've got your back." He slung his arm over my shoulder just as Jerry brought our beers over.

"You two ain't cooking up no trouble, are you?" One of his bushy brows rose.

"Nothing you need to worry about J." I winked and the old man laughed.

"Seen that look one too many times. Just remember you got a load riding on the next couple of games. Don't go screwing up what could be a perfect season." His eyes slid to mine.

As if I'd ever let that happen. We were going all the way this year. Anything less was simply not an option. We'd lost out to Rixon East last year and it had fucking stung. But this year, State was ours. We were five for five. Another two wins and our ticket to the play-offs was in the bag.

We gathered up our drinks—beers for me and the guys, and sodas for the girls—and headed back to our table. Mackey and a couple of the other guys had joined us, and he'd wasted no time in turning his charm on Felicity.

"So, Flick. Is it okay if I call you Flick?" he asked around a suggestive smirk.

I slid into the booth, taking a long pull on my beer.

"You can call her Felicity, jackass," Asher piped up, smacking him upside the head.

42

"But I thought..." Mackey looked to her for help, but a slow smile spread over her face, and I braced myself for whatever shit was about to come out of her mouth.

"Asher is right," she purred, placing a hand on his arm. "It's only really a nickname my close friends use. Felicity is fine."

"Close friends?" The rookie's eyes lit up. "Baby, just say the word and I can make that happen."

The girls smothered their laughter while Asher hit him upside the head again. "Fuck, man, what was that for?"

"You need to work on your game, bro."

"Khloe didn't seem to mind last night when she was sucking my—"

A chorus of 'dude' and 'Mackey' rang out around us.

"Oh, it's like that now. Just because Hailee and Fli... *Felicity*," he shot her an apologetic look, "are here, we have to tone it down."

"That's right, dipshit," Asher replied. "Because we respect women."

"Dude, didn't you hear Jase telling everyone about the chick he banged over the weekend?"

Fuck.

My head snapped up. "Shut the fuck up, Mackey. It was just locker room talk."

"Locker room talk my ass. You said—"

"No fucking buts." I slammed my hand against the table, the crack reverberating through me. I chanced a look at Felicity, hoping she hadn't heard him. But from the way the blood had drained from her face, I knew she had.

Stupid fucking rookie.

"Excuse me," she nudged Asher, "I need to use the bathroom."

"I think I'll come with." Hailee followed her out and the two of them hurried off, but not before my step-sister glowered at me.

"What the fuck was that about?" Asher frowned at me.

"Maybe she got her period."

We all gawked at Mackey. "Or maybe," Asher drawled, "They need to pee."

"Nah, chicks go to the bathroom in packs when they get their period; it's called menstrual synchronicity or something."

"I'm pretty sure that has everything to do with chicks getting their periods together, not chicks peeing together."

"All sounds the same to me." He shrugged and someone balled up a napkin and threw it at him.

"Did something happen with you two?" Asher lowered his voice enough that no one else heard him.

"Who?" I played dumb.

"Jase, come on. She looked ready to puke all over the table."

"I have no idea what you're talking about."

"Of course you don't." He grimaced, turning away from me and joining in the rest of the conversation.

I don't know what they were all getting so hung up over. So me and Felicity had sex. It wasn't my fault she was a virgin and didn't tell me. Or that Hailee had walked in on us. If anything, it was a good thing... we'd fucked whatever this weird hate-lust vibe we had going on right out of us. *Except, you didn't finish **and** you stole her fucking virginity.*

Stifling a groan, I mumbled, "Be right back." Slipping

out of the booth, I ignored the questioning stares. I don't know when I'd started caring about things so goddamn much, but I needed to clear the air. I couldn't afford any distractions this semester, and if my friends were going to keep bringing Felicity up, then she was just that. A distraction.

One I needed to nip in the bud sooner rather than later.

Determined, I headed toward the back of the bar where the hall leading to the restrooms was. Hailee and Felicity were just coming out of the women's bathroom when I entered. My step-sister immediately spotted me, her eyes on high alert.

"Hey," I said, raking a hand through my hair. "Can I get a minute?" My eyes found Felicity over Hailee's shoulder.

"I don't think that's a good—"

"Hailee," Felicity laid a hand on her shoulder. "It's fine. Go, we'll be right there."

My step-sister shouldered past me, pausing only to meet my eyes. She didn't speak. She didn't need to; her message glittering right there.

Don't touch.

Don't hurt her.

I'm warning you.

Jamming my hands in my pocket, I moved toward Felicity. "Come on." I slipped around her and down the hall. I knew this place well enough to know every nook and cranny. Shouldering the last door, I pushed it open and waited for Felicity to go inside. Her brow rose in question and I said, "Just to talk, I promise."

She gave me a tight nod.

The second I stepped into the storeroom and closed the

door, the air seemed to disappear. Felicity watched me, her eyes clouded with hesitation.

"What the fuck was that back there?"

She jerked away as if I'd physically slapped her. "Don't act dumb, Flick. I saw the way you acted when Mackey was running his mouth."

"Yeah, well, I didn't plan on becoming *locker room talk*," she shot back.

"Is that what you think? That I was talking about you?" I stepped closer. "That was a mistake. *You* were a mistake. One I don't plan on making again."

Felicity's breath hitched, pain flashing in her eyes. "Fuck you," she seethed.

"Baby," I reached out, pulling a strand of hair. "We already did that."

"I hate you." Her voice trembled.

Good. She needed to hate me. I didn't need her getting the wrong idea about us.

About me.

For as much as I hated to admit it, Hailee was right. I needed to stay away from Felicity. She was too naïve, too fucking pure. Until New York, until *me*, she'd been a virgin for fuck's sake.

I stepped forward again, putting us almost chest to chest. I hadn't planned on getting this close, but there was no denying she pulled me in. Almost made me want to finish what we started in New York. My eyes dropped to her lips; soft pouty lips I knew the taste of. Her tongue darted out as she watched me watching her.

"Jason, what are—"

"Shut the fuck up," I ground out. Her chest was

heaving, matching the way she kept sucking in tiny harsh breaths. She reminded me of a doe. Innocent and vulnerable. Waiting to be picked off by the big bad wolf.

Before I knew it, I'd slid my hand to her neck, stroking my thumb along her damp skin. She was sweating. I made her sweat. It was heady, knowing the way I affected her. Knowing that if I dipped my fingers into her panties I'd probably find her wet for me. Even though she hated me, even though she didn't want this, her body did. Something we apparently had in common.

Her body shuddered, heat radiating off her.

Perhaps Felicity Giles wasn't such a good girl after all.

The idea made my dick twitch, straining against my jeans.

"You need to leave." Her body shook now, her eyes saying a million things she would never tell me.

"And why exactly would that be?" I leaned in, my lips ghosting over her jaw up to the corner of her mouth. She inhaled sharply.

"Jason, please, don't do this..."

"You want me."

"No." It came out a shaky breath.

"Don't lie to me, babe. I can feel the heat from your body, the way you're trembling at my touch. And I bet if I do this," I let my other hand drift down her stomach, down and down, until I grazed the apex of her thighs.

A soft moan slipped from Felicity's lips and I chuckled. "Bingo."

"Why?" she choked out, swallowing hard.

"Why?" I eased back to look at her. Pupils blown, skin flushed, her arousal swirled around us. "Because I can." My mouth hovered over hers, waiting. Anticipating what she might do.

Her eyes fluttered closed, her breathing ragged. I was barely touching her, and yet, she was so responsive. So easy to work up. Felicity Giles was nothing but surprise after surprise.

"Why me?" I asked against her lips.

"W- what?"

"Why did you pick me? I don't believe that bullshit about being a means to an end. Not when you could have your pick of guys who would have treated you—"

She snorted at that. "No one at school would dare ask me out."

What the actual fuck?

I blinked, hardly able to believe what I was hearing. Sure, Felicity wasn't classically hot; usually found walking the school hall looking more of a hot mess than a girl I wanted to fuck. But when you looked past the overalls and floral print shirts and hippy style she wore most days, she was beautiful.

"You really don't know?" she whispered.

My expression must have said it all, because Felicity let out a heavy sigh. "You," she said. "It's you. You told everyone Hailee was off-limits in ninth grade, and I'm her best friend. If anyone tries to get close to me, they're going to get close to—"

"Hailee."

"Hailee." Her lips pursed as she gave me a small nod. "Apparently, I'm not worth the risk."

She didn't date... because of me.

I guess I'd never really given it much thought before.

She was Hailee's best friend; someone I was used to seeing around. Someone I barely tolerated. But now she was... *fuck!* I didn't want to feel guilty. But the unfamiliar emotion snaked through me.

A beat passed. And another.

"Jason, I should—"

"Wait, just wait a minute." I needed to think, and it was impossible with her standing there, so close, yet, so far away. My body hyperaware of hers.

"Are you okay?" Her voice was so small, so fucking quiet. I hated it, but I didn't know why.

"Okay, this has been... weird, but I'm going." She began peeling my fingers off her neck. I hadn't even realized I was still holding her like that because I couldn't think straight.

Felicity had almost made it to the door when I finally found my voice again. "Stop." I said, spinning around to meet her confused gaze.

"Jason, I—"

I was on her in a second, pressing her against the door, fixing my mouth over hers. Felicity slammed her hands against my jersey, pushing me away, but I was too strong and eventually she gave up, twisting her hand into the material and yanking me closer.

Demanding more.

Flattening my body against hers, I punched my hips forward. "Oh God," she moaned, her fingers scraping the back of my neck as we devoured each other. Tongues tangling and teeth clashing.

"Whoa." I jerked back, blinking rapidly, trying to clear my mind.

What the fuck was I doing?

"That was—"

"A mistake," Felicity said with a tinge of sadness.

"Yeah, I mean, I wasn't..." I backed up, putting some much-needed space between us.

"I get it." She closed down, wrapping her arms around her waist, barely meeting my eye.

"Felicity, I—"

"Let's *not* do this. I had zero expectations when we..." Her expression cooled like the air around us. "You don't owe me anything and I sure as hell don't owe you anything, so let's just pretend it never happened, okay? I'll go back to being your step-sister's best friend, the person you didn't realize existed."

Pretend it never happened.

"Fine. Sounds good to me," I said with an easy shrug.

"Great."

"Fine." The word echoed in my head. I was fine with that. I'd only come to talk to her to clear the air and avoid any more drama with the guys. Pretending it never happened was the perfect fucking solution.

After all she was right, she'd never been on my radar until recently; no one to me.

Better that's what she went back to. Wasn't it?

5

Felicity

"Happy game day." I flashed Hailee a wide smile, but she frowned.

"You're... happy."

"Is that a crime?"

"No, of course not, I just thought..."

"That I'd spend the week moping after Jason?" Laughter spilled out of me, but it was strained. "Like I already told you yesterday and the day before that, it was a mistake. A blip. Jason, who?"

Hailee's eyes scrutinized me. Sharp and assessing and filled with doubt.

"If it makes you feel better," I went on, filling the awkward silence, "I added another item to my list."

"You did?" Her brows went up as the school came into view.

"I did. Number eleven: Do not, under any circumstances, fraternize with the football team."

"Asher's on the football team." I felt her heavy gaze on me.

"Asher is a friend."

"Is that what we're calling it. He likes you, you know?"

"He doesn't like me. He likes the idea of me."

"We could double date." She sounded happy at the prospect; too happy.

"Hails," I glanced at her, "Don't get any ideas about me and Asher, okay?"

"Who, me?" She smiled deviously. "I have no idea what you're talking about."

"Hails, I mean it, Asher is..."

"Cute. Athletic. And totally into you."

"He isn't..." The protest died on my tongue. There were times when I did notice Asher looking at me with lust in his baby blues. But he was a guy and I was a girl. It was simple biology. Asher Bennet was a player through and through. The rumors I'd heard about his sexcapades were impressive to say the least. And he very much had a type. Much like the entire team.

And I was *not* it.

"I need to stop by the studio first thing. Coach Hasson and Mr. Jalin want to see how things are 'progressing'." She air quoted the words.

"Ah, yes, the Seniors Night portraits. And how are those coming along?" Hailee was secretive about her art, so the fact Coach Hasson had asked her to paint the annual senior football players commemorative portraits was no small thing.

In fact, it was pretty epic.

"Can I come with?"

"Hmm, I don't know, Flick. It's supposed to be a big surprise at the Seniors Night dinner."

"Please." I flashed her my best puppy-dog eyes. "The dinner is still three weeks away and I really want to see them."

"They still need a lot of work."

"Hails, they're going to be great. Mr. Jalin and Coach Hasson wouldn't have asked you if they didn't believe you could do it."

She gave me a weak smile, one that told me she wasn't as convinced as I was. "Fine. But you have to forget I ever showed you. Because Cameron has been hounding me to see his portrait and I told him no."

"Ahh, you love me more than you love him."

"Flick, come on. I love you both. Equally." Her lip quirked up.

Pulling into an empty parking spot, I cut the engine and twisted around to look at my best friend. "I'm sorry," I said, my voice nothing but genuine. "I'm sorry I almost screwed things up with you because of Jason. And I'm really sorry you had to see... well, *that*."

A violent shudder ripped through me at the memory of Hailee walking in on me and Jason. The confusion and hurt in her eyes.

The disappointment.

Her expression softened as she reached for my hand, squeezing it gently. "I'm sorry I freaked out. It's just we've hated him for so long and you're my best friend and I don't ever want to see you get hurt."

"You don't need to worry about me, Hails." My chest tightened. "I'm a big girl. Not even the likes of Jason can hurt me." But the second I said the words I knew it was a lie.

Because Jason had already hurt me. And I knew, given half the chance, he would completely destroy me.

But that wasn't going to happen, because whatever was

between us, the weird hate-lust attraction we had going, was over.

So over.

Jason, who?

———

"Holy shit, Hails. That is..." I had no words to describe the work of art my eyes were currently soaking in. It was Cameron; a painting of him poised and ready to catch the ball. Even through his helmet you could see his fierce determination, the way his eyes were homed in on their target. Nothing but him and the ball, off-page, hurtling toward him.

"I've never seen anything like it." I reached out to touch it, but she swatted my hand away. "Crap, sorry," I said, leaning closer to get a better look. "It's so realistic. Like I'm watching him move for the ball. Even his shirt seems to be moving."

"That's what I wanted to capture; the urgency of the game, the adrenaline and power."

I glanced up at her, fighting a smirk. "Steady there, you're starting to sound like a true fan."

She blushed. "I guess he's rubbing off on me."

"Admit it, you love it." Pre-Cameron, I'd had to drag Hailee to her first game and she'd spent the whole time complaining. But now, my girl was on the way to becoming the Raiders number one fan. And I couldn't blame her. If I got to watch Cameron play, knowing he was mine, I'd be converted too.

"So can I see another?" I asked, eyeing the other

canvasses, the paintings they contained all hidden with sheets.

"You really think it's good enough?"

"Babe, it's amazing. You're so talented. I wish I had your kind of natural ability... at anything."

"Flick, come on, you're good at stuff."

I snorted. "Hardly. Name one thing I'm good at?" Hailee tapped her lips, pondering it for too long. "See," I added, "Nothing."

"You like reading."

"So does half the population." I rolled my eyes.

"And you've been really good at stepping out of your comfort zone lately."

"I don't think they have a society for that at college, Hails."

"You like lists."

True. I did. Lists kept me organized; reminded me of things I needed to do. Lists for the grocery store. Lists of the celebrities I crushed on. Not to mention my senior year bucket list.

Lists made me happy.

"You're right. I am an excellent maker of the lists. It's an undervalued talent for sure."

"Oh come on." She nudged my shoulder. "You know what I mean. Just because you're not really good at one thing doesn't mean you're not good at lots of little things."

"Yeah, you're right." My smile was forced, the knot in my stomach tightening.

It wasn't that I was jealous of Hailee, I wasn't. She was gifted and I was excited for the Seniors Night unveiling. For her. But it only heightened my self-awareness of how lacking I was. It was senior year. The year of college applications and chasing future dreams. A future my parents had all planned out for me since the womb. They wanted me to follow family tradition; attend UPenn, get my business degree and work some white-collar job in the city.

Before senior year, I would have happily gone along with their plans. Because it was better than the alternative —*no* plan. But I was restless. A little voice whispering in my ear that if I went to UPenn and studied business and graduated ready to enter the big old world of white-collar employment, I'd regret it. It had been quiet before, easy to ignore, but now it was growing louder, a constant noise making itself heard.

That's how my senior year bucket list had first spawned. If I was going to pursue my parents' dream for me; instead of riding the bumpy road of uncertainty, I wanted to go out with a bang. Make senior year the best it could be.

1. *Take up a new hobby*
2. *Cut class*
3. *Attend a pep rally*
4. *Skinny dip down at the lake*
5. *Fall asleep under the stars*
6. *Go to a party at Asher Bennet's house*
7. *Drink (actual liquor) at Bell's*
8. *Go to Winter Formal... with a date (not a girlfriend)*
9. *Hook up with a random guy*
10. *Fall in crazy messy love*

I mentally recalled each item, checking the ones off I'd already completed. I'd joined book club, attended a pep rally, and partied at Asher's house. Thanks to Asher, I'd also got mildly drunk at Bell's. Number nine was a given, but I was considering giving myself a do over where that was concerned, because Jason was neither a random guy nor could our moment of madness be described as a 'hook up'.

"Hey," Hailee's voice perforated my thoughts. "Are you okay?"

"Huh, what?" I blinked at my best friend.

"You zoned out for a minute there."

"I'm fine."

"I didn't mean to hurt your feelings—"

"You didn't." My lips pressed into a thin smile. "Now what's a girl got to do to see the rest of them?" I inclined my head over to the other concealed portraits.

"Flick," Hailee groaned.

"Hails, come on... this is me." I turned on the puppy dog eyes and pout again, knowing she wouldn't be able to resist. But nothing could have prepared me for the next portrait, as Hailee pulled off the cover.

"Holy crap." The words fell off my lips in a *whoosh* of breath. It was Jason, staring right at me, his dark intense eyes fixed on my face, arm hiked ready to release the ball. I moved closer, awed by the detail. The muscles in his arm bulging, strong and powerful.

"I think it's my favorite so far," Hailee said. "Which is weird considering I still can't stand him. But he embodies the game. I think it's his eyes, the sheer determination in them. Like he *is* the game. I never really understood his obsession, but watching him train, seeing him out there on the field, I get it. He doesn't just like football, he—"

"Needs it." I couldn't take my eyes off him. I'd seen Jason play a few times now and it was always a sight to behold. But that was from the bleachers. This was intimate.

As if I was right there on the field with him, watching him command the play, his team. A shiver ran up my spine and I sucked in a shaky breath.

"It's great, Hails. Really good." I tried to school my expression, but Hailee narrowed her eyes. Trying to deflect, I asked, "Who do you have left?"

"Jones, Merrick, and Killian. I'm almost done with the rest."

"I can't wait to see them all together. Coach Hasson is going to be blown away." My eyes flicked back to Jason's portrait, but I forced myself to look at Hailee. I needed to push him to the recesses of my mind; a memory I would only allow myself to recall when I was alone with a gallon of ice-cream in reach.

"I just hope the guys like them," she said quietly.

"They will," I reassured her. They couldn't not. But as she covered Jason back up, I saw the way her eyes lingered on her step-brother. The wariness in her gaze. Things had always been strained between them and although Hailee would never admit it, I knew she wanted things to be easier. For Jason to respect her. Especially now that she was with Cameron.

"He'll love it, Hails."

"I don't know—"

"Yes you do." My lips curved in a small smile. "It's okay to want his approval. He's your brother."

"*Step*-brother."

"Does it really matter? It's senior year. Soon we'll all be going off in separate directions. But you and Jason will always find your way back to one another, because like it or not, you're family. So yeah, it's okay to want him to like it, and it's okay if you want to try to smooth things over with him."

"You're a good friend, Felicity Giles." Hailee wrapped her arms around me, hugging me tight. "And I promise to do everything in my power to make your senior year as awesome as it can possibly be."

"Ride or die," I said.

Hailee pulled away, grinning at me. "Ride or die."

6

Jason

"Yo, QB, CHECK IT OUT." Grady flipped me his cell phone. I caught it, my eyes narrowing on the tweet.

@ThatcherQB1: *Raiders better watch out, the Tigers are on the prowl #Tigersgohunting #Raiderscansuckit*

"Doesn't Thatcher's cousin play for the Tigers?" he asked me as I handed back his cell.

Shrugging, I grunted. "Fuck if I care. He's just bitter we put their asses in the ground Rival's Week." We'd played them a couple weeks back. It had been a dog fight, both teams refusing to roll over. But, in the end, we got the win, and Thatcher had gone back to Rixon East with his tail between his legs.

"Should we be worried?" Cam leaned in, whispering in my ear.

"Do I look worried?" Thatcher was clutching at straws. He couldn't touch me on the field, and he knew it.

"Hey." Cam's hand pressed against my chest as I went to move. "You sure you're good?"

"Millington are going down and I'm going to enjoy

every fucking second." I grinned, but Cameron didn't share my enthusiasm. In fact, he looked miserable as hell.

"He can't touch me out there." My expression grew serious. "You don't need to look so—"

"Grady," Coach boomed, startling us. "That better not be a cell phone I can see on game night. Lock it away, Son. Now."

"Sorry, Coach," Grady grumbled, flipping me off when I smirked at him.

"Gather in, ladies," Coach Hasson's voice echoed around the locker room. We all moved in, dropping into formation around him. I kneeled, helmet tucked onto my knee, adrenaline pumping through my veins.

"Game six," he said. "Win tonight and we're only one more game away from securing our place in the play-offs. We're the team to chase, the team to beat. But that doesn't mean we can get cocky, you hear me?"

"Yes, Sir," rang out, vibrating through me.

"Millington have a strong defense and a quick offense. Don't underestimate them. I want eyes open, give Chase a clear path, and for the love of God, keep your eye on your QB."

Our defense grunted another, "Yes, Sir."

"Chase," Coach said to the guy standing at my side. "You good?"

"Yes, Coach."

"Glad to hear it, Son. Anything changes and you let me know, okay?"

Cam nodded, his eyes sliding to mine. So much passed between us my chest constricted. He'd missed our last game due to his mom being in the hospital, but he was back now

61

and he was hungry for it. I saw it in his eyes, knew I was reflecting the same back at him. We were so close. So fucking close I could almost taste it. Last year, we'd lost out to a shot at the championship but this year it was ours. Do or die, I was getting my championship ring before I graduated.

"Anything you want to add QB?" Coach asked me, his eyes conveying every conversation we'd had during practice this week.

Keep your cool.

We're almost there.

Lead them to victory, Son.

Letting my eyes run over every one of my teammates faces, I said, "We do what we do every week, go out there and play like we want it. Like we deserve it. We're Raiders. And what are we going to do?"

"WIN," the roar of my teammates, my brothers, slammed into me, fueling the fire already raging in my chest.

"That's what I like to hear. Asher, Son, care to do the honors?"

"Sure thing, Coach." Asher jumped to his feet, bouncing around like fucking Tigger on steroids. "Who are we?" he cried.

"Raiders," our voices carried over the rumble of the crowd outside.

"I said who are we?"

"RAIDERS."

"And what are we?"

"Family."

"And what are we gonna do?" Asher grinned at me, cocky motherfucker.

"Win."

"I said what are we gonna do?"

"WIN!"

"Damn right we are," Coach punched the air with his clipboard and yelled, "Now get out there and show me what you're made of."

As we spilled from the locker room into the stadium tunnel, we sounded like a stampede, an army rushing into war. Flames licked my insides; hunger for the win coursing through my veins. I pulled on my helmet as we jogged onto the field, crashing through the cheerleader's banner like a powerful wave. The crowd was on their feet, cheering and yelling our names. The sheer force of their collective voices slamming into me. *Whatever it takes* by Imagine Dragons rose above the noise, igniting the whole place into a frenzy. This is what I lived for. On this sacred place, under the bright Friday night lights, I was the best. Worshipped like a god and revered like a star. I was an above average student, knew my way around an algebra textbook, knew my Shakespeare from my Miller, but out here... out here I was home.

I took a second, inhaling deeply, relishing the smell of freshly cut grass, letting my eyes run over the four-thousand-strong crowd. Four years, I'd played football here. Four years, I'd celebrated wins and defeats, although not many. Four years of blood, sweat, and tears. I was ready, *so ready*, for the next step in my football career. The NCAA. One step closer to the ultimate dream: The NFL. But I knew there was something about this time, senior year at high school. I'd grown from a boy into a man on this field and I would never forget my time playing under Coach Hasson, with guys I considered my brothers.

"Yo, QB, you good?" Asher yelled, and my head whipped over to him. I gave him a nod, jogging over to the rest of the guys. Anticipation rippled around us, the air crackling with excitement. It was addictive; better than any synthetic high.

"Hey, Jase." Grady flicked his head over to where Millington were huddled. "Looks like you've got a new fan club."

One of their players was glaring over at me. I stood taller, tipping my chin slightly, sending him a silent 'fuck you'. He narrowed his eyes, pointing his finger at me before dragging it across his throat.

"Yo, Coach?" I asked one of our assistant coaches. "Number twenty-three. What position is he playing?"

"Linebacker," he said warily. "Should I be concerned?"

"Nah, Coach. Just wondered."

He gave me a pointed look. "No bullshit out there, okay?"

"Did I hear someone say bullshit?" Coach Hasson called us in. "Listen up. Millington came here to win. If they don't, they can kiss a shot at the play-offs goodbye. So that means they'll be gunning for blood. Your blood. You hear me?" We nodded. "They're desperate and desperate men will do anything to get the win. Keep your cool and don't get dragged into their games. That goes for you too, QB."

"Yes, Sir." My eyes flicked over to Millington. Like us, they were now huddled around their coach, who was no doubt telling them to use every trick in the book to get the win they so desperately needed to keep their play-off dream alive.

The referee interrupted Coach's pep talk to inform us we needed to call the toss. I jogged out into the middle of the field with Cam and Asher flanking my side where we met the Millington players head on.

"Since they're the visiting team, the toss goes to Millington. What'll it be, Captain?"

"Heads," their captain said, as we all crowded in to watch the referee toss the coin into the air.

Tails. Eat shit. I grinned at him and then at number twenty-three who had come out to support his captain.

"It's your call, Raiders."

"We'll kick-off." I wasn't giving these fuckers even an ounce of breathing room.

"Sounds good. I expect a clean game. Captains, keep your players in check, and let's play us some football."

Asher and Cameron began to jog back to our team, but I couldn't resist glancing over my shoulder. Number twenty-three was jogging backward, his eyes fixed right on me, and even through his helmet, I didn't miss the words he mouthed.

Thatcher sends his love.

———

"Run, run," the whole crowd seemed to echo my words as Cameron took off with the ball, ducking and dodging the sea of orange and black players racing toward him.

"Motherfucker," I roared as he got tackled by a huge

defensive end, his body slamming against the ground with a resounding *thud*. Right outside the end zone as well.

"They're all over us," Grady jogged over to me as we walked off field.

He wasn't wrong but I didn't want to admit it. Millington had brought their A-game and if we didn't turn it around soon our 21-18 lead was going to disappear down the drain.

I clapped him on his shoulder before cutting a path toward Merrick, one of our best defensive players. "Make them pay," I said, pulling his helmet to mine. "I refuse to lose to this bunch of pussies. You feel me?"

"I feel you, QB." His eyes sparked with hunger.

"Go get 'em."

Watching as our defense lined up at the scrimmage, Coach Hasson came up to me. "What the hell is happening out there? They got you spooked or something?"

I couldn't tell him that Thatcher's cousin, number twenty-three, was making it virtually impossible for me. He'd talked shit most of the game, pushing me, taunting me, trying to get me to take the bait. I hadn't... *yet*, because I knew Coach would rip me a new one. But I wasn't sure how much more of it I could take.

"Defense will take care of it," I grunted, watching as the Millington's QB called the play. He was cocky; a real showman, preferring to keep the ball and run than use his players and pass.

Sure enough, he faked the pass, rolled around to the left and took off downfield... right into the awaiting arms of our cornerback. Their bodies fell hard, the referee rushing over to the huddle already forming around them. But it was our player with the ball.

"Thank fuck." Clapping my hands, I yanked on my helmet, ready to get back out there.

"This is the one," Coach yelled, and my eyes flicked to the clock. There was time for one more play; two if we were lucky. We had to score; anything less and we risked giving Millington the chance to flip the game.

Giving Coach a nod, I jogged over to my teammates. "This is it. The play that ends these motherfuckers. Fourteen," my eyes found Cam across the huddle. "You get to sit this one out. We're going to run Blue Right Fourteen Reverse."

"But, Jase…" someone started, but I held up my hand.

"We go with the play, got it?"

"Got it."

It was a risk—not using Cameron—but you didn't make miracles happen by playing it safe, and we needed to hit Millington where they least expected it.

"Raiders on three." I shoved my fist into the center of the huddle, waiting for the other ten fists to follow. "One, two, three."

Our battle cry rang out around us, the crowd's roar igniting a firestorm inside me. They believed in us, in *me*, cheering us on until the bitter end. And we were about to give them the victory they deserved.

That *we* deserved.

Millington stepped up to the scrimmage, eyes hard, jaws set. They were the predators now, and we were the prey. But first they'd have to catch us.

"Blue Fourteen, Blue Fourteen, hut." The ball snapped

to me and I caught it with nothing more than muscle memory. Dropping back, I extended my arm ready to hand-off the ball to my running back. He barreled past me and took off, as I darted right, ball cradled in my arm, head down. The fake play had given me the time I needed to gain yards, but it didn't take long for the Tigers' defense to realize I had the ball. They barreled toward me like a runaway train. I pushed harder, my muscles pinging with exertion, the air *whooshing* around my helmet as I kept running.

"Go, GO! The entire stadium seemed to yell, propelling me forward. Giving me the strength I needed to make one final push.

Someone reached for me and I leaped to the side, the *thud* of their body hitting the ground behind me reverberating in my ears.

Fifteen yards... ten... five. I was so close. So fucking close I could already hear the echo of 'touchdown' ringing in my ears. But a Millington player appeared out of nowhere slamming straight into me, the ball fumbling out of my hands. "Fuck," I grunted, the ground beneath me breaking my fall.

"That one's for Thatcher." Twenty-three came down hard on me. His elbow—or was it a fist—clipping my ribs with purpose. Once. Twice... Pain splintered through my side.

"Get the fuck off me," I sneered, pushing him off. He rolled away, clambering to his feet. The second I was upright, I got up in his face, barely aware of the game still going on around us. "What the hell was that?"

Dead Man Walking had the balls to smirk.

"Oh, you think this is funny. You piece of shit." I lunged for him just as the announcer called, "Touuuuuuchdown."

"FORD, GET THE HELL OVER HERE NOW," Coach Hasson barked just as my hand twisted into twenty-three's jersey.

"Better run, bitch b—"

Yanking him forward, I smashed my helmet against his. "Tell Thatcher if he wants me, to come get me. He knows where to find me." Anger radiated through me and when a hand landed on my shoulder, my head whipped around so quickly I got whiplash.

"Let him go, man," Cam said coolly. "He isn't worth it."

"How's your girl, Chase?" Twenty-three wore a shit-eating smirk. "When you're done with her, let me know. I wouldn't mind taking her for a—"

Cameron barreled me out of the way and tackled him, the two of them crashing to the ground. Suddenly we were swarmed by a sea of orange and black, blue and white, players pushing and shoving while Cameron wailed on twenty-three. His helmet was off now, Cam's too.

"Raiders, get the hell over to the sideline, NOW!" Coach grabbed my shoulder. "Rein your players in, Captain." His voice was icy cold. Enough that it snapped me out of the red mist, and I started pushing my teammates away.

"Go, get over there." I flicked my head to the sideline where the remainder of our team was gathered.

"Let's go, Chase." Coach and one of Millington's coaches pulled Cam off Thatcher's cousin; Coach Hasson handling my best friend while their coach helped his player to his feet.

"Coach, it wasn't—" I started, but he levelled me with a glare that said, 'shut the hell up'.

"We'll deal with this once we're in the locker room. Get in there and wait for me, you hear me?" Disappointment dripped from his words, sitting heavy on my chest.

I slung an arm around Cam's shoulder, but he shrugged me off, storming away. "Motherfucker." I threw my helmet down and kicked it, sending it flying into the water table.

"Ford!" one of the coaches yelled, but I didn't stop. I didn't even look back as I followed the rest of our team into the tunnel. We'd gotten the victory. But it had ended in a shitshow.

All because of Lewis fucking Thatcher.

7

Felicity

Coach Hasson's voice echoed through the doors. He wasn't just pissed about what had just happened, he was furious.

"Maybe we should go?" I winced, as his tirade continued, eyeing Hailee as she paced outside the team's locker room like a caged animal. We weren't supposed to be back here but being the star quarterback's step-sister and star wide receiver's girlfriend swayed the security guy's decision to let us wait.

"You can go if you want to," she said, one arm wrapped around her waist, the other bent so that she could chew her thumb, "but I'm not leaving until I know Cameron's okay."

"Okay." I went to her. "We'll stay."

"I still can't believe he did that." Silence settled over us, but it didn't last long when a couple of minutes later, the door swung open and the team started filing out.

Joel Mackey noticed us first. "You better get in there, Hailee." He grimaced. "Your boy is in a bad way."

The blood drained from her face as she looked to me. "Can you... I mean..."

"Hailee," Jason's voice cut the air like a knife.

She rushed over to him. "Is he okay? What did Coach

say? Is he hurt?" The questions spewed out of her and Jason looked completely out of his depth.

Dragging a hand down his face, he took a deep breath. "Cam needs you," was all he said, flicking his head to the door. "You should go be with him."

Her glassy gaze settled on me and I smiled. "Go, I'll be fine."

"Fear not, Hails." Asher appeared, making a beeline for me. "We'll make sure she gets home okay."

"You're sure?"

"Go, he needs you."

She gave me an appreciative smile before turning it on Jason. "Thank you," she mouthed before disappearing inside.

"Will Coach—"

"She doesn't need to worry about Coach," Jason said as he shouldered past Asher and disappeared down the tunnel.

"Come on." Asher slung his bag over his shoulder and motioned his head in the direction of his teammate, sending water droplets spraying everywhere.

"Asher," I moaned, following after Jason. "Now I'm all wet."

"And I haven't even touched you yet."

I glanced over at him, eyes wide and cheeks flushed.

"Relax, Fee, baby, I'm joking."

"Oh, okay." Embarrassment flamed my cheeks as we hurried after Jason.

Outside, most of the crowd had already dispersed. A few of the guys hung around to take pictures and sign jerseys and balls and other game paraphernalia, but Jason didn't stop for the die-hard fans. He didn't even acknowledge them.

"Go on ahead," Asher said, "I'll be right there." He stopped to take a photo with a couple of kids who had their faces painted with the Raiders logo.

When I reached Jason the words, "Where's Asher's Jeep?" fell from my lips.

"I drove."

"Oh," I said, eyeing his car.

Jason kicked the gravel, sending a plume of dust into the air. Everything about him screamed 'stay away'. A murderous expression. Waves of anger rippling off him. The way his jaw clenched so tight it looked painful.

He was a nuclear bomb just waiting to detonate.

And suddenly, I didn't want to ride anywhere with them. Even if Hailee had driven us here and was now attending to Cameron's *needs*.

"Change of plan." Asher sauntered up to us, his lip in a grim line. "My parents are on their... aaaaand here they are." Headlights illuminated the three of us, and I glanced over to where his gaze was fixed.

"They want to take me to dinner."

"They do?" My expression must have given me away because Asher chuckled.

"Don't look so worried, Jase can take you home. Can't you, QB?"

The guy in question grunted something inaudible.

"I can walk," I rushed out, wanting nothing more than the ground to open up and swallow me whole. "It's not far."

"Fee, baby, just get in the damn car." The words were

for me, but Asher was looking at Jason, a silent message passing between them.

"You should come to Bell's later," he finally turned his attention on me. "Drinks are on me."

"I don't know," I said quietly. "Maybe, if Hailee—"

"Think about it." He winked and gave Jase a two finger salute before heading toward his parents' car.

Silence lingered, swirling with Jason's anger.

"I'll walk, you don't—"

"Get in the car," he ground out.

"Excuse me?" Indignation burned through me as I lifted a brow at him.

"I said get in the fucking car." He stomped around to the driver's side and almost tore the door off its hinges before throwing himself inside and slamming it shut.

I needed to leave. To put as much distance as possible between me and the brooding angry guy in the car. But there was something about his anger, the way he'd held back throughout the entire game. I'd watched him, even when I'd tried not to. Twenty-three had been all over him. But Jason hadn't taken the bait. Even when they were both up in each other's faces, he had maintained control. But something had changed when Cameron tried to intervene. And the only thing that tied Jason and Cameron together, except football, was Hailee.

The window rolled down, startling me. "Last time, Giles," his voice hit me straight in the stomach, "Get in the goddamn car."

————

Jason didn't take me home. He didn't even take me to his house, not that I'd expected him to ever do that. I didn't. But I also didn't expect him to take the road out of town and pull over by the lake. The sandy lot was quiet, nothing but the gentle rustle of leaves and my heart beating violently in my chest.

"So..." I said, trying to lighten the mood. "Nice view." Risking a peek over at Jason, I was surprised to see the corner of his mouth lift.

"Want to talk about it?"

"No, I really don't."

"What did twenty-three say to Cameron?"

"You noticed that, huh?"

"I..." My lips pressed together, not wanting to admit I'd noticed everything.

Brushing over my slip, he added, "You don't want to know."

"Try me."

Twisting his body slightly, Jason pinned me to his leather seat with those dark intense eyes of his. "It wasn't supposed to happen like this." His voice was cold. "She wasn't supposed to—"

"You think this is Hailee's fault?" Incredulity filled my voice. "You spent the last six years treating her—"

"I know." Jason's fingers jammed in his hair, tugging in frustration. "You think I don't know that? Hailee was nothing to me, *nothing*, and now... now she's in the middle of this thing with Thatcher and I don't know what the fuck I'm supposed to do. I don't know how to..." He stopped himself, pain glittering in his eyes.

"Care?" I whispered. "You don't know how to care?"

"I'm not the good guy here, Felicity. I want to win State, graduate high school, and get the fuck out of this town and go to college. That's it. That's my lot. And Thatcher is fucking everything up." The sound of his fist colliding with the steering wheel reverberated through the car. There was barely any air before but now I could hardly breathe; Jason's anger tangible.

"I just need for it to stop. Just stop for a fucking second." Head tipped back, he screwed his eyes shut, sucking in ragged breath after ragged breath.

"I'm here, if you want to talk." The words shattered the silence.

"You wouldn't understand."

"Because I'm not popular? Because I don't know what it's like to be put on a pedestal by the entire town? You're right," I gave a little sigh, "I don't know what it's like. But that doesn't mean I don't understand what pressure feels like."

Jason's eyes slid to mine, filled with a rare glimmer of vulnerability I knew not many people, if any, got to see. "Sometimes it feels like I can't breathe without the whole town watching." Surprise flashed across his face, as if he couldn't believe he'd said the words.

I waited, hoping he'd give me more. Hoping he'd let me in. But his stone mask was already back in place.

Jason was tortured. Over Hailee. Over his dad and her mom having an affair. His mom leaving. Carrying the weight of the team. The rivalry with Rixon East. It all sat squarely on his shoulders. And although I didn't want to understand him, to try to figure out what went on inside of the head of Rixon's prodigal son of football, part of me got it.

Because although it wasn't the same, although I didn't have the pressure of an entire town rooting for me and my future; I had my parents' pressure. And sometimes that alone was almost too much to bear.

"Sometimes, when it all gets too much, I make a list." The words were out before I could stop them.

"A *list*?" Jason snorted.

"Yeah, it helps me process things."

"And these lists," his voice was drenched in sarcasm, "What do you put on them?"

"Anything really. Sometimes I use them to help me organize my life: to do lists, grocery store lists, homework lists—"

"You have a list for homework." His brow went up and then he smirked. "Of course you do. What else?"

"Celebrities I'd like to date, books I want to read, that kind of thing."

"And your senior year bucket list?"

"How did you...? Asher," I groaned. "Asher told you." I felt my cheeks burn.

"Don't worry. He didn't tell me what's *on* the list."

Because he didn't know. He and Cameron had overheard me talking to Hailee about it once. But I refused to share the details, because, holy crap, that would be embarrassing.

About as embarrassing as Jason asking me about it.

"Good. That's good."

"Why do you look so worried, Giles?" He leaned closer slightly, taking the air with him. "I'm not on the list, am I?"

Oh no.

He was doing it again. Looking at me like he wanted something.

Something I knew I shouldn't give him.

"We should probably head back," I said trying to keep my voice even. "It's getting late and you're meeting Asher at—"

"Giles," he said, sliding his hand along my collarbone and up my neck. His thumb stroking my pulse point. "Stop talking."

"But I—" The pad of his thumb moved against my lips, dragging downward and making my bottom lip *pop*. My tummy clenched; his touch like fire, burning me inside out. I didn't want to feel like this, to respond like this, but I couldn't help it. Where Jason Ford was concerned, my body had a mind all of its own.

"Don't you ever just want it to stop?" he whispered so quietly I almost didn't hear him.

"S- stop?"

"Yeah, the constant noise and pressure and... *everything.*"

More than you know, I wanted to say; but I couldn't speak because his lips were right by mine.

"Ja—"

He kissed me. Just a gentle brush of his mouth over the corner of mine. It might as well have been a hot desperate kiss for the way my body reacted.

My breathing was labored but nowhere near as ragged as Jason's.

"Last chance to tell me to stop, Giles," he rasped, his eyes boring into mine.

Stop, the word formed on my tongue, but melted into

nothing before I could say it. Because no matter how much I knew this was a bad idea… no matter how much I'd regret it later… no one had ever made me feel the way Jason did. So alive. So desired.

"I don't want you to stop," I breathed. The carnal growl that vibrated in Jason's chest turned my blood to molten lava. He wanted this.

Wanted *me*.

And in that moment, I didn't care if he'd regret it, or never look at me again. Right here, right now, I needed him to touch me. I needed him to make me *feel*.

He didn't devour me the way he had before. This time his kiss was slow, deliberate. He took his time acquainting himself with the shape of my lips, licking and nibbling. I slid my hand up and over his shoulder, feeling his hard muscle ripple beneath my touch.

"Get over here, Giles." His hand found my thigh and he helped me climb over the center console and onto his lap, straddling him.

"Fuck," he grunted, pain etched on his face.

"You're hurt."

"It's nothing." Jason dragged me closer.

It was close. Too close. Intimate and intense, the low body of his vintage car not built for heavy make out sessions.

There was a split second, as I settled over him, that our eyes connected. Eyes hooded, burning with lust, Jason looked deadly; but there was something else, something underneath the dark mask he wore. It was gone in an instant, his mouth quickly finding mine again as he ground into me, showing me just how much I turned him on.

And dear God, if that didn't go straight to my head.

I understood it now. Why girls chased bad boys, hoping to be the one to tame their wild ways. For this, right here, the ounce of power my body had over him. The way my kisses made him grow harder, made him hungry for more.

I wasn't foolish enough to believe it meant anything—I knew it didn't. But how could I not feel all warm and gooey inside knowing that out of all the girls he could have been here with, he was with me.

He'd *chosen* me.

Don't run away with yourself, Flick. He didn't choose you. You were there. Convenient. Like a grab-and-go snack. I shut the intrusive thoughts out. There would be time to analyze and regret later.

"You have too many fucking clothes on," his voice was rough against my skin, as he worked my Raiders sweater up and over my head. The thin tank underneath molded to my curves and Jason's eyes homed straight in on the swell of my breasts. "Gorgeous," the word formed on his lips.

I slipped my hand between us, desperate to feel his skin, to explore his body, sculpted to perfection from hours and hours of physical conditioning. But he snagged my wrist, smirking at me. It was almost dark now, the canvas of stars twinkling down on us like distant spectators; only the silvery hue of the moon illuminating our profiles. If it was possible, it made him look even more devastating.

"Ja—"

"Ssh." He silenced me with a finger pressed against my lips again, while his other hand slid down my chest, trailing a path between the valley of my breasts, and down my stomach. I sucked in a harsh breath when he grazed the waistband of my leggings but it didn't deter Jason. He continued his exploration of my body, touching and kneading, smoothing his fingers over my skin. But when he dipped his hand inside my leggings, I could barely contain the moan building in my throat.

"So fucking wet," he said gruffly, not giving me chance to catch my breath or process what was happening, as he pressed a finger inside me.

"Oh God," I moaned, rocking against his hand, needing more.

Needing so much more.

My head dropped back, exposing my neck and collarbone to him. Answering my silent plea, Jason dipped his head kissing the hollow of my throat, sucking gently. Driving me wild.

"Jase," I panted, the intrusion of a second finger making me wince. But only for a second, as pleasure flowed through me like a gentle wave.

I was lost in the intense sensations. The warm current flowing between us, *through* us. The intimate position. The feel of his hot mouth around my breast as he worked his fingers inside me, circling his thumb over my clit.

"I'm so close," I whispered, barely able to recognize my own voice. My legs began to shake as Jason went deeper, harder. I'd never let anyone touch me like this before. Not the way Jason did. As if it wasn't about my pleasure at all, but his. As if my body was his to play however he wanted.

It occurred to me, in that moment, maybe it was.

I dropped my head to look at him. Sure enough, he was watching me with eyes so dark they looked black. A lazy smirk was plastered on his face as he increased the tempo.

"You like my fingers inside you?" he asked as if I could possibly respond with anything other than a small nod.

"Oh God, Jason..." I couldn't breathe, my orgasm slamming into me like a tsunami.

"Come for me, Felicity," he rasped, still watching me. "Come all over my fingers."

His dirty words sent me over the edge, as my body clamped down. I took a shuddering breath, trying to swallow down the urge to call his name over and over.

I collapsed into him, sliding my hands around his neck. But Jason pushed me back, his eyes narrowed and clouded as he slowly brought his fingers to his mouth and sucked them clean.

My tummy clenched.

Christ, he was beautiful. A dark and dangerous angel.

"What?" I asked as he continued watching me, but his cell vibrated, cutting through the thick silence that had descended over us. Jason leaned around me and grabbed it.

"Is there a problem?" I asked when I noticed he'd gone tense beneath me.

"We should go. Everyone's meeting at Bell's." His voice was cold, detached, and I knew whatever had just happened between us was over.

I tried to temper the dejection squeezing my heart as I clambered off him and sat back in the passenger seat. He handed me my sweater without a word, fired up the engine and backed out of the sandy lot.

It wasn't until ten minutes later, when I climbed out of his car trying to reconcile what had just happened, I realized he hadn't let me touch him. Before he got the text, before the temperature had cooled a gazillion degrees between us, Jason had gotten me half-naked and played my body the way he played the game: sure and confident and one hundred percent in control.

But he hadn't let me touch him back.

If we hadn't been interrupted would he have?

Something told me it was better not to ask... because I probably wouldn't like the answer.

Jason

BELL'S WAS CRAMMED, everyone showing up to celebrate with the team. We usually partied at Asher's, but since his parents were in town, we'd come to the bar instead.

"Hey," he said, waving me over. "Where's Fee?"

"Fuck if I know."

"You didn't offer to bring her?"

"No I didn't offer to bring her. What am I, her damn babysitter?"

Asher eyed me carefully. "What's up? You seem pissy?"

My brow arched. "Thatcher sending his cousin to do his dirty work not enough reason to be pissed?"

"Yeah, I just thought... it doesn't matter."

He wanted to ask about Felicity; it was right there in his eyes. But she was the last thing I wanted to talk about—especially with him.

I'd fucked up again earlier. I should never have driven her out to the lake and kissed her. *Or put your hands on her.*

She just made it all so damn easy. Nothing like Jenna or the other girls I was used to being around. Felicity was just content being there; talking and listening. And some of the shit that came out of her mouth... well, it was gold dust, and strangely, I found myself craving whatever weird assed sentence was going to come out of her pouty mouth next. But nothing was as intriguing as the way she let me handle her body. She handed me complete control, as if she trusted me with every fiber of her being. Which ironic considering I was the last person on Earth she should trust.

Despite her serious lapse in judgement where I was concerned, Felicity was a smart girl who gave as good as she got. But when I put my hands on her skin, my mouth on hers, something changed. It was addictive.

She was addictive.

But she was also off-limits for so many fucking reasons I should probably make a list.

Yeah, she'd love that.

I fought a smile.

"What's got you grinning like the Cheshire Cat?" Asher nudged me, taking a long pull on his beer.

"Nothing, just thinking." His frowned deepened as if I was a puzzle he was trying to solve.

"How's the ribs?"

"I'll live." I shrugged, chugging down my beer. Thatcher's cousin had gotten in a couple of hard digs, and I had a nice bruise forming, but it wasn't enough to do any real damage.

Just then, the door swung open and Cameron and Hailee walked in, Felicity trailing in behind them, looking like a deer caught in the headlights.

Fuck.

I hadn't anticipated seeing her again tonight.

"There he is," Grady called. "Get over here, Rocky Balboa, drinks are on the house."

The whole place cheered causing Cam to duck his head.

Pussy.

He never did eat up the limelight like the rest of us, and now he was with Hailee, he was even more inclined to linger in the background. I'd always given him shit for it. Back when we were kids and people began to take notice, I couldn't understand why he rarely lapped up the attention. But now I wondered if Cam was onto something. If maybe he knew all along that if you stayed in the limelight for too long, it would eventually burn your soul until there was nothing left but ash.

Cameron was sporting a nice shiner underneath his left eye. I had to give him props, I didn't know he had it in him. Because what they said was true: girls really did make you crazy. And my best friend was two screws loose over my step-sister.

"Fee, baby, you came."

"I... Hailee insisted." She kept her eyes on Asher, refusing to look at me.

It shouldn't have bothered me so much, but it did.

"Well, let's get you ladies a drink." He leaped up and slung his arm round her shoulders. I followed him up.

"I'll be at the pool table."

Hailee caught my eye, but I simply tipped my chin and kept on walking.

———

"Hey, Jase, good game tonight." A petite blond sidled up to me, running her hands suggestively up my chest.

"Hey..."

"Marissa," she purred, her eyes full of intention. "I'm on the swim team.

"You must love getting wet then," one of the guys hollered. I glowered at him, dragging my eyes back to Marissa, expecting to see her mild disgust at his words. But in true jersey chaser fashion she batted her eyes, fingering the collar on my Henley.

"Oh, I love getting wet." The words teased off her tongue slowly. "I don't suppose you could help me out with that, could you?"

Marissa was hot. Tight body accentuated by the mini skirt and one size too small Raiders tank she wore. Bringing my thumb to my lip, I let my eyes drift down her curves. She was exactly my type. Slim. Athletic. And down for whatever. But something was missing. That something was currently giggling at Asher like he hung the fucking moon.

"Jason." Marissa's hand grazed my semi-interested dick, commanding my attention. "I said do you want to get out of here?"

"Maybe later. It's still early."

Rejection flashed in her eyes, but then her seductive smile slid back in place. "You know where to find me." She flicked her head toward a group of girls.

"Yeah." I grabbed my bottle of Bud and took a long pull.

"Jason Ford passing up fresh pussy?" Grady came up beside me. "Hell must have frozen over."

"I'm not sure she could handle me." I smirked.

"Oh shit, you're bad, Cap. So fucking bad. But if you're not gonna indulge, mind if I—"

"Be my guest, man."

He slapped me on the back as he passed, making a beeline for Marissa and her carbon-copy swim team friends. He was quickly joined by Mackey and a couple of other rookies. They were worse than dogs in heat. Thank fuck I didn't have to work for it. Being QB One meant something in Rixon; but being Jason Ford—son of local football hero Kent Ford—*and* QB One meant everything. Guys wanted to be me and girls wanted to screw me. Everyone wanted their fill. And until recently, I'd soaked it up. But when everyone wanted a piece of you, the chance to say they knew you... partied with you... fucked you... or even fought with you, there wasn't much left to go around. It was a catch twenty-two, a rock and really fucking hard place. Because I loved the game, loved it more than anything in the world. Cut me open and I was pretty sure I'd bleed football. But it came at a price. One everyone thought they would happily pay until it's *your* life. Until you don't know who you can trust or who wants to use you as a steppingstone to their five minutes of small-town fame.

It's why I'd hated Hailee so much when she'd first moved here. She was so judgmental, sweeping in with her holier-than-thou attitude, assuming she knew what I was like.

Who I was.

So I liked sex, but didn't want to date or get tied down to one girl? The last thing I wanted was to put down roots here. Rixon was merely a steppingstone to bigger and better things. And I had one plan: to achieve what my old man couldn't and get drafted to the NFL. An injury had ended his career in senior year of college. His dream might have gone up in smoke but his legacy lived on.

Me.

And I was going all the way.

No matter the cost.

"Something on your mind?" Cameron pulled up a stool next to the high table beside me.

"Nah, just watching Grady make an ass of himself."

"You know, you can come sit with us."

"I know."

"What I'm trying to figure out is if you won't come over because of Hailee or Felicity or both of them?"

"Look, Chase, I'm happy for you, I am. Does it freak me out you're boning my step-sister? Hell yes." I shuddered. "But I get it. You need her, she needs you, yada yada yada."

"You say it like it's a bad thing."

My eyes levelled him. "You gave up Penn for her." Cameron had always been coming to Penn with me. We were going to dominate the Quakers and kick some Ivy League ass. But then his mom got sick and he and Hailee... well, things changed. He changed.

Cam let out a heavy sigh, raking a hand through his hair. "I thought we were over this? I get football is important to you, but there's more to life—"

"Is this the part where you tell me that one day I'll meet *the one* and realize I want to settle down, get married, and pop out a couple of kids? Because if it is, you're wasting your breath."

"I know Aimee hurt—"

"You think this has fuck all to do with Aimee? She was nothing but a conniving piece of shit like her brother."

"Jase, come on, this is me. You don't need to put—"

"Aimee was a mistake." A huge fucking mistake that came back around to bite me in the ass. If I'd have known she was Thatcher's sister from the get go, I never would have looked at her, let alone touched her.

"It's okay to admit you felt something..." Cameron trailed off when I glared at him. Hard. He didn't get it. I didn't want to feel. I didn't want to care about anyone other than myself and my future. Caring made you vulnerable. It opened you up to a whole world of hurt I had no interest in feeling. Besides, when I cradled the leather ball in my hands, I had everything I needed.

"Okay, I won't say another word. But you should still come sit with us. I know it'd mean a lot to Hailee." Cam stalked back to their booth, and I let my eyes drift over to them. Hailee was gazing up at him with stars in her eyes and Asher was busy entertaining Felicity with nothing but a beer mat and his nose. It would have been easy to go sit with them, to pretend I was okay with how much everything was changing. But then, Asher leaned forward, brushing a wisp of hair from Felicity's face and my hand tightened around the bottle. He was touching her and she was loving every second.

Fuck that.

And fuck them.

"Jerry," I called as I approached the bar. "I'm gonna need something stronger."

"Come on, Jase, you know I can't—"

"I like you, J, but it's either serve me the damn liquor or I'll go get it elsewhere."

He let out a resigned sigh and shook his head. "You remind me of him, you know. Back in the day."

"Spare me the 'you're just like your old man' crap." I nursed my empty bottle, waiting for Jerry to pour my new drink.

"Even sound like him too," his chest rumbled with laughter. "I'm cutting you off after two."

"Three." I rose a brow.

"Fine, three and you're done." He pushed a glass of whiskey toward me. It wasn't exactly the drink of champions, but I'd acquired the taste when me and the guys used to raid my dad's liquor cabinet back when we were kids.

Just like my old man, the words made me shudder. He was everything I was trying not to be. The prime example of someone letting it all go to their head. It didn't matter that Dad had me and Mom at home. Some skirt only had to bat her eyes in his direction and he'd be foaming at the mouth. My mom, now there was an example of a strong woman. She'd stuck by Dad through it all: the depression, the melancholy, the endless string of faceless women. But everyone had a breaking point, and Dad had found hers. Mom finally walked away and I had to choose—a new life, new school, and new team, or Rixon. A decision I would never forgive him for.

A decision my mom had never forgiven me for.

"There you are." A familiar hand slid over my shoulder.

"Jenna," my voice was clipped but it didn't deter her from sliding into the stool beside me.

"Drinking all alone?"

"Just catching my breath. You know how it is after a game."

"I know how it can be." She walked her fingers over my arm. "You look tense."

Tense was the fucking understatement of the year.

"I can help with that."

My eyes slid to hers in question. Of course I knew where this was going, the only way it ever went between us. But my dick wasn't in it, not tonight.

Unperturbed, Jenna leaned in, brushing her lips against the shell of my ear. "Meet me in the storeroom in five."

"Oh yeah, you going to make it worth my while?"

She pulled back, running her tongue across her bottom lip, a slow seductive sweep. "I think we both know that when we're done, you're gonna be feeling a whole lot better." She stood up, making a show of flicking her long blonde hair off her shoulder and letting me get a front row seat to her impressive rack.

"Five minutes." She mouthed before sauntering away, heading straight for the back of the bar.

"That one has trouble written all over her."

"Maybe I like trouble, old man."

"I knew another guy who said exactly the same thing once." Jerry gave me a knowing look, whipped the towel off his shoulder and began wiping the counter.

I hadn't wanted Marissa. She was new. All shiny and eager. Probably hoping she could impress me enough to want to stick around. But Jenna knew the score. She knew it was nothing more than sex between us. A way to burn off some steam and relax.

And given how tense I was, I knew I'd be a fool to resist

what she was offering. Decision made, I downed the rest of my whiskey and made my way to the back. But before I disappeared down the hall, I glanced back, searching for my friends. For Felicity. She was still laughing at Asher, her eyes alight and lips curved. She looked happy. My chest tightened, Jerry's words rattling around my head. He was wrong. I wasn't my father.

I would *never* let myself become my father.

But I was no saint either.

9

Felicity

"ARE you sure he won't come back here?" I asked Hailee for the millionth time since we left Bell's.

"He rarely comes home Friday night, either crashing at Asher's or..." she trailed off, giving me a sympathetic smile.

Jason had barely looked twice at me at Bell's, and every time he did, it was with a scowl painted on his face. As if that wasn't enough, I'd watched him follow Jenna Jarvis into the back and return a while later with a lazy smirk and fresh wrinkles in his Henley.

"It is what it is." My lips pursed.

She shook away her grim expression. "Anyway, we didn't come back here to mope over stupid boys; it's girls' night. Are we going with Scott Eastwood in The Longest Ride or shall we go old school with a bit of R Patz in Breaking Dawn?"

Smothering a giggle, I shot her an incredulous look. "I still can't believe, you, Hailee Raine, are a closet Twihard."

"What?" She shrugged with no sign of remorse. "He's hot."

"If you say so. I'm more of Tim Riggins kinda gal. You can keep your sparkly vampires; I'll take Friday Night Lights any day of the week."

"Maybe that's your problem," she quipped, setting up the film.

"Says the girl dating her very own football star." I rolled onto my stomach and grabbed another handful of popcorn.

"I'm dating Cameron, the person. Who just so happens to play football."

"Yeah, yeah, keep telling yourself that." I grabbed a pillow and threw it at her. Hailee caught it and settled down on her bed, hitting the light switch and plunging the room into darkness.

"This is nice," she said through a yawn. "You, me, just like old times."

"Uh-hmm." I wondered if she'd still be saying that if she knew what I'd been doing with her step-brother less than a few hours ago.

Dear God, what had I done? Letting him touch me like that. But it was like I became someone else around him; someone who thrived on his cruel words and cocky charm.

It was unlike me. But maybe that was the problem. Maybe I liked the fact I felt different around Jason. Powerful and sexy. Instead of the wallflower I'd been for most of my life.

Hailee was immersed in the film, *oohing* and *ahhing* to all her favorite parts, until my eyes grew heavy and the moving images started to blur.

I woke with a start. "Hailee?" I whispered, but she was out cold, her muffled breaths steady and shallow. The glare from the television illuminated the room, guiding my path as I climbed to my feet, stretching out the kinks in my neck. The digital clock on her nightstand read one in the morning. We must have been sleeping awhile.

Deciding to pee before I tried to get comfy again, I ducked into Hailee's bathroom. Not bothering to turn on the light, I left the bedroom door ajar instead. Once I was done, I washed my hands, catching my reflection in the small wall mirror. I looked the same. Same green eyes, same brown hair, and beauty spot on my upper left cheek. But I felt different. Something inside me was changing.

I was changing.

And I didn't know how to make it stop, whether I even wanted to.

"You gonna stand there all day or are you done?" The low growl catapulted my heart into my throat.

"Jason, what the—" He closed the distance, brushing past me to pull the door separating Hailee's side of the bathroom and her bedroom closed. "Let me out." My eyes narrowed as I took in his disheveled appearance; the bitter scent of whisky lingering on his breath.

"Why the fuck are you here?" he ground out, rubbing his jaw. There was a slight slur to his words and I realized he was drunk.

Crap.

I could deal with sober Jason, but drunk Jason... drunk Jason was what had landed me in this situation in the first place.

"I'm with Hailee. She invited me. It's girls' night," I said as if it mattered. Of course it didn't freaking matter.

Edging backward, my hands searched desperately for the door handle.

"You're everywhere, like a recurring nightmare." His words hit me straight in the heart.

"You came in here first—"

"It's my fucking bathroom." Anger blazed in his eyes as he stalked toward me, so close if he reached for me, I'd be right there.

"It's Hailee's—"

"I don't give a fuck. You shouldn't be here." He dragged a hand through his hair, pulling at the ends in frustration.

"So let me go," I whisper-hissed, done with his bullshit. I didn't ask for this. I didn't ask for any of this. Okay, so maybe I had a hand in blurring the lines between us, but he'd made it perfectly clear where we stood, and it wasn't like I was begging him to give me a chance.

"Is that what you really want?" His hand came for me, splaying against the side of my neck, his thumb tracing up and down.

"Yes," I said shakily.

"You sure?" Jason leaned in, his breath hot on my skin, his lips dangerously near the soft spot right beneath my ear. "Because I'm not so sure. I think you like this, like what I do to you." He inhaled deeply, inhaled *me*, and my legs almost gave way.

"Jason, stop." I fisted my hands at my sides, knowing if I touched him it wouldn't end well.

"Stop?" There was a wicked glint in his eye as he lifted his face to me. "You think *you* get to say when *this* stops?"

"I'm not going to play this game with you, not anymore."

He was drunk, his words crueler than ever, his touch harsher.

"Game? You think this is a game? This isn't a game; it's bloodsport, baby. And you... you couldn't have made it any easier if you'd tried."

Tearing myself from his hold, I stepped back, my body hitting the wall. "Get out," I said, coldly. "Now."

He blinked, confusion clouding his glassy eyes. "Feli—"

"Get. Out. Before I do something we'll both regret."

His heavy gaze lingered on me for a second before he staggered out of the bathroom, and I slumped against the wall, releasing the breath caught in my throat. Wondering how the hell I was ever going to survive Jason Ford.

———

Everything went back to normal after that. Whatever had happened between me and Jason in his car, was filed under 'epic screw ups', and I spent the weekend trying my best to forget our middle-of-the-night moment in the Ford-Raine bathroom. Of course, I didn't breathe a word of it to Hailee.

It had hurt, a sharp pain splintering my chest, that he could go so quickly from kissing me, touching me, to being with Jenna. But it was just another reminder I needed to push all thoughts of Jason Ford out of my head.

At least, that was the plan.

"Felicity?"

"Huh?"

"Are you okay, sweetheart?" Mom frowned. "I was calling you and you were completely zoned out."

"Late night studying," I said around a fake yawn. "You know how it is."

"I know it's senior year, baby, but I don't want you making yourself ill. A good night's sleep—"

"Makes for a healthy mind. Got it, Mom."

"You know your grandma, God bless her soul, used to drill that into me every day."

"I know, Mom." *Just the way you drill it into me.*

"Senior year." She slid a plate of pancakes toward me before helping herself to another mug of coffee. Apparently, once you were an adult, a healthy mind ran on a good night's sleep and two coffees before eight. "It only seems like yesterday you were born."

Silently groaning, I ate my breakfast while Mom took a trip down memory lane. By the time I was done, she was a little teary-eyed. "We're so proud of you, Felicity, and to think you're following in our footsteps."

"Sure thing, Mom." I regurgitated the same response whenever she brought up college.

"Although," she went on, "I'm not sure how your father is going to cope. He barely slept when you were in New York."

"It was one night," I reminded her.

"I know, I know. But New York is just so..."

I filled the silence with adjectives. *Big. Amazing. Inspiring. Alive.* I should have known she would say, "Overwhelming."

"I don't know, I kind of liked it." And it had absolutely nothing to do with giving a certain brooding Raider my v-card.

"Really?" Her nose scrunched up. "I found it to be so gaudy. Anyway, your father and I agreed, no more road trips until after graduation, young lady. I'm not sure his heart could take it, and you know Doctor Garrick said he needs to watch his blood pressure."

"Mom, I don't think my one-night stopover set off Dad's

blood pressure, I think his endless late nights at the office did." He was rarely ever home and if he was, he brought his work with him.

"He just wants to provide for us, baby, for you. A strong work ethic is so important these days."

"I know," I murmured the words, suddenly feeling guilty. Dad did work hard for his family.

"One day you'll understand." Her eyes held nothing but warmth, as if she was doing me a favor. Protecting me. Keeping me safe from the monsters of the world. But what she failed to realize was, she was stifling me.

I was stifled.

But I couldn't tell her that.

Not unless I wanted to break her heart.

So I pressed my lips together and smiled, hoping she couldn't see I was already tainted by a monster.

A monster who wore a blue and white jersey and ate girls like me for breakfast.

———

"Miss Giles," the gruff voice startled me. "Just the girl I hoped to find."

My brows pinched as I gawked at Principal Finnigan, trying to rack my brain for any recent indiscretions he might be here to reprimand me for.

When the silence went on for a second longer than normal, I finally found my voice and said, "I'm sorry, did you want me, Sir?"

"Indeed." He smiled faintly. "This is Mya Hernandez, a

transfer student from Philadelphia. I was hoping you could buddy up with her and help her settle in."

"Me?" I blinked, certain I'd misheard. "You want *me* to buddy up with her?"

"Well, I don't know of any other students called Felicity Giles, do you?"

"No, Sir."

"Well, then," he said, "I'll leave you girls to get acquainted. Mya already has her class schedule. If you have any issues, please see Miss Hampstead."

He smoothed down his blazer and took off down the hall, leaving me and the new girl staring awkwardly at one another.

"Listen, it's cool," she said with a hint of a Latina accent. "I don't need you to babysit me. Just point me in the direction of," she scanned the paper in her hand, "AP History, and I'll tell Miss Hampstead you were more than helpful."

"Mya, right?" I asked, ignoring her brush off. "I'm Felicity. It's nice to meet you."

"Yeah, whatever." She hitched her bag up her shoulders and glanced around.

"I love your hair, is it—"

"Natural?" Mya rolled her eyes.

"Sorry, I didn't mean—"

"No, I'm sorry." Her hard expression softened. "That was rude of me. It's just hard, you know, transferring partway through the semester of senior year."

"You're from Philadelphia?"

"Badlands," her voice lowered significantly.

"Isn't that like..." The words lodged in my throat.

"The ghetto?" Her brow went up as she gave a strangled laugh.

"That's not..." My cheeks flamed. "I didn't..."

"Badlands is not The Hamptons, that's for sure, but it was still home, you know?"

"You've been?" I changed tack. "To the Hamptons, I mean? I always wanted to go, but my mom and dad prefer culture to the beach." Quiet culture: museums and galleries and historical buildings.

"I went once. Didn't think it was all that. That whole scene isn't really my thing." Mya snorted, pushing her spiral curls from her face. She was beautiful: all bronze skin and a slim but curvy frame. She reminded me of Amandla Stenberg.

I smiled to myself. Girls at Rixon fit into two categories: Plastic Barbie jersey chasers and the rest of us. One look at Mya and I knew she was like me and Hailee. Well, pre-Cameron and a certain star quarterback that would remain nameless.

"What?" Mya frowned at me as I studied her.

Slipping my arm through hers, I leaned in close. "Are you a football fan, Mya Hernandez?"

"I prefer basketball."

My smile grew.

"Why are you looking at me like that?" She frowned.

"Oh nothing, but I think you and I are going to be great friends," I declared, dragging her down the hall. "Welcome to Rixon High."

———

"So this is the cafeteria," I announced as Mya trailed behind me. She had insisted on doing her own thing at lunch, and I had insisted she come with me to meet Hailee. Apparently, my persistence outweighed hers.

"Aaand it looks just like my old cafeteria except without the drug dealing and fights."

My head whipped around and I knew my mouth was hanging open like a fish.

"Joke," Maya said. "I'm joking. Well about the drug dealing, mostly."

"It was that bad?" I asked as we joined the line.

"Fallowfield High was a jungle. I'm lucky I escaped."

"How did you?"

"Long story," was all she said before turning her attention to the lunch items. "Same shit food though."

"Oh, I don't know. The tacos are usually good and Friday is spaghetti day."

"Hmm, sounds delicious," she replied drolly.

"Just wait, you'll see."

"And who might this be?" Asher had impeccable timing. I'd hoped to get Mya situated before introducing her to anyone else. But from the way his gaze drifted down her body and back up, I knew Asher would need no introductions.

"Asher Bennet." He held out his hand. "You must be the new girl."

"This is Mya," I said when she pursed her lips in defiance, staring at his hand like he had an infectious disease.

I was growing to like this girl more by the second.

Asher quickly recovered, running his fingers through his messy blond hair. "You like football, Mya?"

"It's not usually my scene, no."

"We'll have to change that then because you just landed yourself in Rixon."

"Am I supposed to know what that means?"

"You'll see." He winked at her before turning his attention to me. "Looking good, Fee, baby." Then he strolled away as if it was nothing.

"Why is everyone staring at us?" Mya asked.

"Because you just caught the eye of a Raider." My stomach knotted at the words, which was weird because if Asher turned his attention to the new girl, at least it meant he wouldn't be looking at me anymore.

Didn't it?

"*So* not interested." Mya loaded her tray with lunch items.

"Boyfriend?" I raised a brow.

"*Ex*-boyfriend. And I'm not looking to replace him anytime soon."

"Ah, I see. Bad break up?" We moved along the line.

"The worst." Pain flashed in her eyes, but it was gone in an instant. Mya was hardened. Aloof. She reminded me a lot of Hailee pre-Cameron.

We paid for our lunch and weaved through the masses to our table. Hailee was already there. She looked up and smiled. "You must be Mya. Welcome to Rixon High. I see Flick already got her claws in you." My best friend fought a grin.

"She's persistent, I'll give her that."

"Hey," I protested. "I am sitting right here."

"We know," they both said in unison and I gawked at them.

"I'm beginning to think this was a bad idea. Now there are two of you."

"Strength in numbers, am I right?" Mya held out a fist toward Hailee who stared at her. When she awkwardly bumped it against Mya's knuckles, it was my turn to snicker.

"Rixon is small town; there isn't a lot of diversity around these parts."

"I can see that." Mya let her eyes wander around the cafeteria. While I hadn't blinked twice at her style—the holey boy jeans, shirt tied around her waist, khaki tank top, and military style boots—others were looking.

"So break it down for me."

"Football team." I motioned over to where Asher and the rest of the team sat. He gave us a two fingered salute and Mya snorted.

"Is he always so..."

"Annoying?" I asked. "Pretty much. We hated on the team until this year but since Hailee is dating—"

"Hold up," Mya jerked back. "You're dating him?"

"Whoa, no. I'm with Cameron. See the one with the dark short hair, cherry blossom tattoo?"

"Nice, very nice. But still a football player? Damn, girl."

"Tell me about it." Hailee smiled shyly. "It was never the plan but..."

"You can't help who you fall for." Mya finished as if she knew all about complicated relationships. "Got it."

"Football is a huge deal here," I went on. "The Raiders have a real shot at State so expect things to get a little crazy around here over the next few weeks."

Mya grimaced. "Is there anything to do for fun in Rixon that doesn't involve football?"

"There's Ice T's, the ice cream parlor; and The Alley."

"Let me guess, bowling?"

I nodded. "It has a diner and arcade too. It's probably one of the only places untouched by football around here." Well, it had been until recently, but I didn't tell Mya that. I didn't want to scare her off for good.

"So we've got ice cream and bowling. Anything else?" She smirked.

"Hmm, in the summer we go down to the lake and swim, that's pretty cool."

"You're really living your best life here, huh?"

"Like I said, small town." Hailee smiled, forking some pasta into her mouth.

Mya's gaze flicked back over to the football tables. "Guess I'd better readjust my expectations then." There was something in her eyes, a sadness edged with lust. Mya talked a good game about hating football, just like the rest of us who tried to remain unaffected. But the truth was, when you lived in a place like Rixon, football infiltrated your life even if you didn't want it to.

When her eyes landed on mine again and she said, "Should I even ask if you have a basketball team?" I realized maybe I'd misjudged her after all.

10

Jason

"DID YOU SEE THE NEW GIRL?" Grady asked me as I got ready for practice.

I shrugged, pulling on my shoulder pads.

"I saw Bennet introducing himself." Mackey winked over at him. "You thinking of slumming it?"

"Not cool, bro," Asher's jaw clenched. "Not cool."

"What? I'm just saying she looks *Straight Outta Compton*." He rapped the words.

"Mackey, do us all a favor and shut the fuck up, yeah?"

"Sorry, Cap, I was only messing around."

"Fucking idiot," Asher grumbled, shouldering him and heading out of the locker room.

"I think Bennet's got a crush on the new girl," Grady said, and snorts of laughter rang out around the room.

"Maybe you should all quit gossiping and focus on the game we have coming up?" I shot each one of them a harsh look before going after Asher.

I didn't give a fuck about some new girl, but I'd seen her sitting with Hailee and Felicity at lunch. Of course my stepsister and her best friend would take in the stray.

Rolling my eyes, I made my way over to Asher and Cameron. "Hey, you okay?"

"Who, me?" His brows waggled. "I'm good." Trust Asher to brush it under the rug.

"Who is she anyway?" I asked.

"I heard she transferred from Philly. Mia or Mya or something," Cameron offered. "The principal asked Felicity to help her settle in."

"Sounds about right."

"Okay, ladies, bring it in," Coach Hasson yelled. Once we were listening, he said, "Game seven and it's going to be a tough one. Fenn Hill are the team to beat this season. Their offense have been unstoppable, not to mention, they have eleven division one picks. And we're playing at their place. I'm not going to sugarcoat it; you're going to need to bring everything you have to get the win. And we need that win."

Because this win was our ticket to the play-offs.

"We've got this, Coach," I said with confidence. The Falcons were good, but we were better.

"I'm glad you think so, Son, because after Friday's game, you need to prove yourselves. I'm not going to rehash what happened because we drew a line under it Friday." Yeah, after he'd chewed us out like we were kids caught with our hands in the cookie jar, before issuing Cameron a warning. "But you'd better hope to God you don't pull that shit again. I don't care if their players are talking smack about your dead grandmothers out there. Let. It. Go. Do I make myself clear?"

"Yes, Sir."

"Good." His eyes landed on me. "Warm them up, QB."

"Let's go," I roared, leaping to my feet. After Friday's

game, I was itching to get back on the field; to prove to everyone—and myself—that we were the best.

But then I spotted two familiar faces in the bleachers. Jogging beside Cameron, I grumbled, "What are they doing here?"

"Hailee needs to work on her last couple of raw sketches for the Seniors Night thing."

Pressing my lips together, I swallowed the reply on my tongue. Hailee I could deal with, but Felicity?

"I didn't sign up for this shit."

"Don't be a dick," Cam levelled with me with a hard look. "You know how important this project is to Hailee. Besides, she's been out here almost every practice and you haven't..." Realization sparked in his eyes. "But you're not talking about Hailee are you?"

"I have no idea what you're talking about."

A slow smirk tugged at his mouth. "Sure you don't." Cameron clapped me on the back before joining the rest of the guys in formation for warm-ups. "I'm going to enjoy watching you fall", he called, and I stared blankly at him.

Because what the actual fuck?

———

Practice was brutal. Coach made us run drills until my muscles burned and my bones ached. He was concerned about the game against Fenn Hill. It was right there in the way he pushed us harder. Demanded more. Insisted we give everything we had to give and then some. By the time we made it back to the locker room, I was ready to fall into bed and sleep for a week. Not that it was ever an option.

"Yo, QB, Thatcher is running his mouth again."

My spine straightened as Grady came over, handing me his cell.

*@**ThatcherQB1**: Better run, better hide, the Falcons are on the hunt #Falconsforthewin #Raiderscansuckit*

"He's really not giving this thing up, is he?"

"He's all talk." I flipped Grady's cell back to him.

"And if he isn't all talk?" Cameron dropped down on the bench next to me.

"I can handle Thatcher."

"Like you handled him when he was at The Alley putting his hands on Hailee?"

"That's not fair and you know it."

"You're right." He let out a strained breath. "I'm sorry. I just can't stand the idea that he was anywhere near her."

"It won't happen again," I said, even though I knew it was a promise I couldn't keep.

"You don't really think he'll show Friday, do you? Maybe we should talk to Coa—"

"Have you lost your fucking mind? The last thing we need to do is take this to Coach. If Finnigan finds out about this, it won't end well for any of us. He's already watching my every move." Determined to 'clean up' the reputation of the football team, the new principal had made it his priority to make sure his football team behaved. Except, it wasn't his team, not really. A fact he hated. But Coach Hasson and the school board could only protect us so much.

The need to get Thatcher back burned through me. But

I had to be smart about getting payback. Because the team had worked too damn hard to risk everything.

I'd worked too damn hard.

"Thatcher will get what's coming to him," I said quietly, feeling vengeance boil my blood.

"That's what worries me." Cameron gave me a pointed look before standing up and grabbing his bag. "I'll see you tomorrow," he said before walking away.

There was a day when we did everything together. But now he had Hailee and everything was different.

And fuck me, if it didn't suck.

I grabbed my shit and headed out. I didn't expect to run into Asher and Felicity in the parking lot, laughing and joking like old friends.

"We're thinking of heading to Bell's, you want to come?" Ash said with an easy smile, as if she was part of our group now. I frowned, my eyes sliding to hers in question. She lowered her face, heat creeping into her cheeks.

"What, are you two now like fuck buddies or something?" Felicity blanched while Asher's eyes shuttered as he let out a heavy sigh.

"Jase, come on, it isn't like that—"

"Whatever. It's none of my business. You do you, but I think I'll pass."

"Maybe I should go," her soft voice drifted over me like a warm current. I was being a dick, but she was everywhere I fucking turned.

"You don't need to go. I said we'll hang out and we will." Asher narrowed his eyes on me, daring me to argue. Then it hit me, that maybe this was all part of some game. His way of trying to get me to admit I liked her.

I didn't.

She just got under my skin. That was all.

But as I skulked away from them, I wasn't so sure anymore.

———

"Let's go, ladies, onto the buses." It was Friday evening and the entire team and cheer squad were crammed onto four buses that would take us to Fenn Hill. Our fans following in their cars behind us.

It was a sight to behold; half the town making the forty-minute ride to come out and support the Raiders. But everyone wanted to see us win; to move one step closer to State. And it helped; having a big presence in the crowd at away games. Their constant roar like fuel to the fire.

Our fire.

I watched from the window as Cameron said goodbye to Hailee. Felicity and the new girl lingered on the periphery, pretending not to watch. All week I'd avoided her; and all week my mood had deteriorated.

Fucking girls.

Let them in and chances were they would screw everything up, but keep them at arm's length... and chances were they would screw everything up. It was a no-win situation.

I'd rationalized that my strange fascination with the girl who made lists and attended book club and owned some downright fucking ugly shirts was nothing more than the fact she'd been a virgin and I hadn't rocked her world because Hailee walked in on us.

The plan had been to fuck her out of my system with Jenna, but I was starting to wonder if I just needed to fuck *her* again. I shook the stupid idea out of my head. Going there with Felicity again was a one-way street to a headache I didn't want or need.

With everyone finally on board, Coach Hasson stood at the front, staring out at us the way he did whenever we had a big game ahead of us—which was every game we ever played.

"Listen up, ladies," he boomed. "I want your best behavior tonight. We're playing away from home which means you're not only representing your team, you're representing the school, and the town. I expect nothing but professionalism, understood?"

A grumble of 'Yes, Sir' echoed around me as Coach's hard stare bore into me. He was still pissed about the game against Millington and he had every right to be. But he wasn't the one out there, on the field. Sometimes decisions were taken out of our hands; sometimes the decision was made so quickly you didn't have time to weigh up the consequences. You were all up in some fucker's face before you could stop yourself.

"Hey, you okay?" Cameron nudged my shoulder.

I gave him a tight nod. I was more than ready for the game. Eager to get out there and kick some Falcon ass. It was everything else that was sitting heavy on my chest. As if I needed any extra pressure, Grady leaned over the top of my seat and shoved his cell in front of me. "Did you see this?"

"Grady," Cam warned, but it was too late. My eyes ran over the tweet, jaw clenching at Thatcher's taunt.

*@**ThatcherQB1**: What's that I hear? The Raiders crying like little b%&$es #Falconstakenoprisoners #Raidersbetterhide*

"He's just trying to get in your head." Cameron said, snatching the cell out my hand and shoving it back at Grady, mumbling something to him about 'stopping that shit'.

"Yeah, well it's working," I said coolly.

"You can't let him in, man. He knows the Eagles are out of the play-offs and now he's trying to sabotage our shot."

I concentrated on my fist as it pressed against my thigh, uncurling and curling it. Squeezing until the blood drained from my hand. Thatcher was under my skin, like an annoying itch you couldn't quite get rid of no matter how hard you scratched.

Asher's face appeared between the gap in the two seats in front of us. "Maybe we should just go over the river and give him what he wants?" Mischief lit up his face. Asher might have been the joker of the bunch, but he was always down for a rumble.

"Seriously, you think that's going to solve anything?" Cameron let out a frustrated breath.

"Better than sitting around waiting for him to come at us." Asher turned back around.

"Don't listen to him," my best friend's tone was serious. "Thatcher will get bored eventually."

But for as much as I wanted to believe him, I couldn't. Thatcher would keep coming, keep pushing my buttons, until eventually I snapped.

Because we were more alike than I gave him credit for.

I'd hurt his sister... and now he was determined to hurt me. I'd been arrogant enough to think I was untouchable. Believed Thatcher couldn't hurt me because the list of people I gave a shit about was next to none.

But I cared.

Deep down, I fucking cared. And I hated it.

Because caring made me vulnerable.

It made me weak.

Something I couldn't afford to be.

11

Felicity

"Remind me why I agreed to come to this thing again?" Mya grumbled as I dragged her and Hailee to the concession stand for pre-game refreshments.

Fenn Hill had a much smaller stadium than our school, but it didn't stop the crowds swarming. Our blue and white painted faces and shirts and ball caps barely made a dent in the sea of yellow and green.

"It's fun," I yelled over the noise.

"Fun?" Mya arched a brow, glancing at Hailee who threw up her hands.

"Don't look at me. I'm only here for Cameron."

"I'm confused," our new girlfriend said. "I thought you hated the football team and the whole 'institution of the game'?" She air quoted Hailee's words from earlier this week.

"Oh, we do," I explained. "But we're also embracing it this year."

"Right." Mya frowned. "So which one do you want?"

"Want?" I spluttered, almost choking on her insinuation.

"Well, yeah. I mean it makes sense why she's here." Mya pointed at Hailee. "But what I can't figure out is why you're here if you're not crushing on one of—"

"There is no crushing," I rushed out, a little too quickly. "I so happen to enjoy the odd game of football. Even if the whole institution is whack."

"So you're in denial." Her brow went higher.

"I'm not..." The argument dried on the tip of my tongue. "I just want to support Cameron and the guys."

"*The guys?* You mean Asher and Jason—"

"Well, well, if it isn't Chase's girl and the sassy one." Thatcher's friend, the one he'd called Gallen appeared, his predatory gaze fixed right on me. "Looking good, baby."

"What the hell are you doing here?" I blurted out.

"I came to see the game, what else would I—"

"Is Thatcher here?" Hailee was as white as a sheet.

"You didn't think I was going to let Gallen here have all the fun, did you?" Thatcher rounded his friend and narrowed his eyes on Mya. "Who's the new girl?"

"No one to you," she retorted, folding her arms over her chest.

"I didn't know Ford had taken to slumming it."

"You can't say that," I shrieked, stepping in front of Mya, shielding her from Thatcher's superior smirk. "You don't even know her."

"I have eyes, sweetheart."

People were watching now. Even the hot dog guy was gawking at us instead of doing his damn job.

"Just go," I lowered my voice, my eyes pleading. "You're making a scene."

Thatcher edged closer, taking the air with him, until my breath caught in my throat. "You've got balls; you know that, sweet thing? I was planning on playing with Chase's girl a little more, but perhaps I'll play with you instead." His hand snaked out and brushed the side of my neck, eliciting a violent shudder inside me.

"Get your fucking hands off her." Mya stepped up beside me, anger rolling off her. "Before I scream."

Thatcher's head whipped over to her and a twisted smirk graced his deadly expression. "Screaming only makes me hotter, baby."

Smacking his hand away, I stepped back, pulling Mya with me. Gallen smirked, making no disguise of the fact he was blatantly eye-fucking me.

Bile rushed up my throat. These guys were pigs. Worse than anything I'd ever witnessed from Jason and the team, and that was saying something. They didn't look like guys who wanted to have a little fun with us. They looked like guys who wanted to humiliate us.

To hurt us.

"Come on," Hailee said, her voice quiet. "We should go."

I pulled Mya away, trying to ignore the two sets of eyes biting into my skin. "Do I even want to know?" she asked as we abandoned hot dogs and melted into the sea of people.

"Oh, that was Lewis Thatcher, the quarterback and alpha-jerk of the Raiders rivals, The Rixon East Eagles."

"I'm sorry I asked." She half-laughed. "So when you said Rixon takes football very seriously, you really meant—"

"As serious as a heart attack." My lips curved in a tentative smile. "It can get kind of crazy. There is *no* love lost between Jason and Thatcher."

"And here I thought moving to some small town in the ass crack of nowhere was going to be boring."

"Hey," I protested. "Rixon isn't in the ass crack of nowhere."

"It isn't the city either. But I'm glad Principal Finnigan stuck us together." Her expression softened, something I suspected not many people got to see.

"Me too. Come on." Linking arms with her and Hailee, I pushed all thoughts of Thatcher out of my head.

We had a game to win.

———

"Holy crap, this is invigorating." Mya grinned beside me as we watched our offence celebrate a touchdown. Their sixth of the game.

"What did I tell you? Hate the players, don't hate the game." Flashing her a wink, I chuckled, bouncing on the balls of my feet, waving my hands in the air like a crazy person.

Hailee was quieter, her eyes zeroed in on Cameron as he fist-bumped his teammates before jogging off field.

It was the fourth quarter and we hadn't seen Thatcher and his friend again. But we'd watched the Raiders kick the Falcons ass all over the field. Our fans, although four times smaller than the home fans, were louder, hungrier, and the buzz in the air was electric.

"Almost there," I squeaked, grabbing Hailee's hand and squeezing.

I knew how important it was for her to be here for Cameron after everything they had been through.

The final whistle went and our tiny section of the bleachers erupted. Even Mya was on her feet, hooting and hollering as the high of the win settled deep in our bones.

It was weird. Throughout high school I'd never been part of anything. I wasn't in band or on the cheer squad. I didn't get invited to parties or to join the debate team or compete for an athletics club. I had Hailee and our simple lives—hanging out at The Alley, gate-crashing the odd party, eating our body weight in ice cream at Ice T's—and it was enough.

Until I wanted more.

Until I wanted to soak up every experience I could in senior year and experience all the things I'd never gotten to because we'd been outcast by our peers all because of Jason and his stupid grudge against Hailee. But here, cheering on the team, I felt like I belonged.

As soon as the players disappeared off field, we all filed out of the bleachers and into the parking lot where the team buses were waiting. The second Jason appeared, leading the team out of the Falcons' building, a huge round of cheers greeted our heroes. The guys split off, searching for their friends and families among the gathered crowd. Cameron and Asher made a beeline for the three of us, while Jase chatted to Coach Hasson and his father. I pretended to listen to Asher as he recounted every play and pass, every tackle and sack. Really, I was watching Jason. His tight expression as his father gripped his shoulder as he talked animatedly with the coach.

"Fee, baby, what's got your..." Asher craned his neck around, the sparkle in his eye dimming. "Oh."

"Sorry," I gave him my best smile. "You were saying?"

"Well, I was about to invite the three of you to the party at my house tomorrow..." I hated the dejection in his voice but there was no use in trying to fix it. He'd seen me looking at Jason, and I knew he knew how I felt.

Even if I'd never told him.

"You like to party, Mya?" Asher slung his arm around her shoulder, and I swear a small growl formed low in her throat. "Message received." He edged away, shooting her a lazy grin. "But seriously, you should come tomorrow. My place is the only place to party. Hailee will be there, right, Hails?"

"I guess." She shrugged, glancing up at Cam who was too busy staring at her with such emotion I was pretty sure he hadn't heard a single word Asher had just said.

"I'll go if Felicity goes."

My head snapped over to Mya and she lifted a brow, some indecipherable expression on her face.

"What do you say, Fee, baby? Party at mine tomorrow?"

A few weeks back, my immediate answer would have been yes. It was on my list, a rite of passage for kids of Rixon High. But that was before sex with Jason; before the heated looks and stolen kisses. Before Asher's puppy-dog eyes followed me everywhere.

God, everything seemed so complicated now.

"Will there be dancing?"

"There is always dancing." His brows waggled suggestively.

"I'm not talking about *that* kind of dancing, Asher." I'd heard the stories.

"There can be any kind of dancing you want."

He was flirting. Nothing he hadn't done a hundred

times before, but every time he did it, I felt more and more confused.

"Fine, we can go." My eyes slid to Mya who gave me a curt nod. She was hard to read. But I didn't miss the way her eyes lingered in Asher's direction.

She liked him.

He liked me. At least, I think he did.

And I liked Jason.

If this didn't have disaster written all over it, I don't know what did.

"Yo, QB," Asher beckoned Jase over. He strolled toward us, his eyes cool. "We heading to Bell's later?"

"Not tonight, my dad wants to… celebrate. But I'll be at yours tomorrow." His gaze found mine, narrowing. I could feel it running over my skin, burning. He looked wired. The adrenaline of the game, no doubt.

"You good, Jase? You look a little—"

Jason broke our connection to glare at Asher. "I'm good," he growled. "Coach wants us on the buses stat."

"Guess this is goodbye, ladies. Until tomorrow?"

Jason paused, glancing back at us. "You invited them?"

"Well, yeah, I didn't—"

"Whatever." He stomped off, and I let out a shaky breath.

"What crawled up his ass?" Asher asked Cam.

"I think it's just the pressure of everything."

Or the fact he was a moody asshole.

Coach Hasson and his assistants began rounding up the team to get on the buses, while a few fans lingered to wave them off. We hung back too because we were *those* girls now.

Strangely, I didn't mind.

"Do you think we should have told them?" I asked Hailee as she made moon eyes at Cam.

"And worry them for nothing? No." She folded her arms around her waist and I saw the flicker of doubt in her eyes. Hailee didn't like keeping secrets, least of all from Cameron. But we'd decided not to tell them about Thatcher being here to avoid any more trouble.

"Come on, we should go," Hailee started toward my car but paused when Thatcher appeared. He leaned casually against the hood, throwing a wolfish grin in our direction. I glanced back, hoping the team buses were still there, but they were already disappearing down the road.

Crap.

"Hmm, Hailee, what do we do?"

"Just play it cool," she said. "He won't do anything. He just wants to use us to get to the guys."

Which is exactly what I was worried about.

"He really doesn't know when to quit it, does he?" Mya asked as we inched closer.

"Ladies," he drawled just as his friend and another guy stepped out of the shadows.

There were still a few people in the parking lot, but they were all heading back to their cars, paying the three of us no attention.

"Should we shout for—"

"No," Hailee said, rolling her shoulders back. She was used to Jason's games; his cruel pranks. But this felt different. It *was* different. Hailee was no one to Thatcher, but she was someone to Jason and Cameron, and he knew it.

"What do you want, Lewis?" she said as we reached them.

"I want a lot of things." He let his eyes run down the length of her body.

"Yeah, well, so do I, but we can't always get what we want. You should probably leave."

"Or what?" He pushed off the hood. "I saw the buses leave. Your brother and boyfriend are on their way back to Rixon and you're here, all alone."

"She's not alone." Mya stepped forward.

"Yeah, she has us," I added, digging my hand in my pocket, my fingers grazing the corner of my cell.

"Ooh, I'm scared." The three of them burst into laughter. Until Gallen's eyes homed in on me... and my hand.

"What you got there, cutie?" He approached me and I backed away, my heart galloping in my chest.

"N- nothing," I cried, staggering back until my back hit the side of a truck. But Gallen didn't stop. He kept coming until he'd caged me in, his hands pressed flat either side of my head.

"You aren't trying to call for reinforcements, are you?"

"Fuck you," I seethed, my defenses working overtime.

His eyes flared, "Oh baby, I'd love nothing more than to fuck you." He trailed a finger down my neck and between the valley of my breasts. My chest heaved with a shaky breath as I turned my head away from him. But he grabbed my face roughly, pulling me back to him.

"Just one taste," he groaned, grinding his hips into me, as his tongue snaked out across my lips.

"What the hell is wrong with you?"

He grunted with pain, the unwelcome pressure of his body against mine disappearing as he stumbled away. "What the fuck?"

Mya advanced on him, her fist clenched.

"Fuck's sake," Thatcher grumbled. "If you want something done..." he trailed off, leaving Hailee to come up to me. "You," He jabbed his finger at Mya, "Keep your fists to yourself." He gave the other guy a nod and he grabbed Mya's hands pulling them behind her back.

"You can't do this," she thrashed against his body. But her fight only made the guy smirk.

"Now where were we?" Thatcher's eyes darkened. "What I'm trying to figure out is are you Bennet's girl or Ford's?"

"W- what? I'm not..."

Thatcher lowered his face to mine; so close I could feel his warm breath dancing over my skin. My stomach churned.

"Bennet wants you. I've seen it. The way he watches you, touches you. And Ford doesn't like it. I saw him tense just now."

He'd been watching us? Waiting for them to leave?

Oh God.

"I'm no one. I'm Hailee's friend, that's all."

"So you haven't given it up to Bennet or Ford? Maybe both of them?" His brow rose. "Maybe under this little miss innocent act you have going, you're nothing more than a dirty little slut."

I pressed my lips together, trying to swallow some of the fear and panic rushing through me. Not to mention the truth.

Thatcher narrowed his eyes, assessing me. "You're lying," he said. "You're someone all right and my money is on—"

"Shit, Cap," Gallen said, not so cocksure now. "Security. We need to go..."

"Yeah, okay." Thatcher stepped back, running a hand down his face, his eyes still fixed on me. "Until next time." He grinned.

Silence stretched out before us, the air turning icy cold. Then he said, "Oh, and tell Ford I'm coming for him."

12

Jason

"WHO THE FUCK are all these people?" I grumbled. I'd gotten to Asher's house an hour ago and grabbed a six-pack before taking my usual chair out back, but there were people everywhere.

"It's a party. We're celebrating, remember?"

Of course I fucking remembered. We were in the play-offs. But after a disastrous dinner post-game, with my father and Denise, I wasn't exactly in a people kind of mood.

"Did you invite the whole fucking school?"

Asher grinned. "Only the bright and beautiful. Who's beautiful?" he yelled and everyone went nuts, screaming and cheering. *Always the showman.* I rolled my eyes.

"Where's Chase?" I asked.

"Inside with Hailee, but I'd steer clear of them if I were you, seems like there might be trouble in paradise." Asher took a long pull on his beer.

I was already out of my chair though, stalking toward the house. The last thing we needed was our star wide receiver to lose his cool over some shit with my step-sister. The team needed Cam in the play-offs.

I needed him.

"Your funeral, man," he yelled.

Inside wasn't much better; bodies packed into every corner of the Bennet's huge house. They were rich—filthy rich compared to the rest of us—and they didn't mind Asher using the place for party central given they were out of town a lot. I couldn't figure which was worse: having parents who cared but were never around, or having a dad you didn't see eye-to-eye with who refused to stay out of your business. It seemed like parents were a pain in the ass whichever way you looked at it.

I searched the ground floor for Cam and Hailee before moving upstairs. Cam hadn't always had it easy growing up, and since the Bennet's had enough guest rooms to open a motel, they had given him his own room. He didn't use it much anymore, but I knew if they were anywhere, that's where they would be.

Raised voices made me pause when I reached his door.

"Tell him, Cameron."

"And then what? What do you think telling him will do except incite war?"

I crept closer, straining to hear, the hairs along the back of my neck standing to attention.

"So what do we do? Wait until Thatcher really hurts one of—"

I burst into the room, my eyes narrowed to slits. "Tell me what?"

"Jase, man, we didn't know—"

"Tell. Me. What?" I focused on Hailee since she was the only one who thought telling me whatever the fuck had happened was a good idea.

"Thatcher was at the game last night."

"What the hell did you just say?" I saw red, my fists clenched, liquid fury coursing through my veins.

"We saw him before the game and again after..." Hailee's eyes slid to Cameron who was deadly still.

"And why the fuck am I only just finding out about this?"

"Hailee only just told me. I swear, man."

"It's true," she added. "I didn't know what to do and Flick—"

"What does she have to do with all this?" Hearing her name set off my pulse, my heart jack-hammering in my chest.

"Thatcher's friend..." She hesitated, my mood darkening by the second. "He..."

"Hailee, spit it out or so help me—"

"Jase, man, you need to calm down," Cam offered, but I levelled him with a cold look.

"They really scared her, Jason. He had her pinned to the wall and he tried to—"

I couldn't hear anything over the roar of blood pounding between my ears.

"You okay, man, you look a little white?"

"H- he *touched* her?" The words almost choked me.

"Not like that, but he grabbed her and said some things. And his friend held Mya back after she punched him."

"She did what?" I rubbed my temples, this was getting worse by the second.

Hailee nodded. "She hit him and he left Flick alone but then Thatcher—"

My fist slammed into the wall beside me, the crack of bone against drywall reverberating through me. But I barely felt any pain, too consumed with the idea of Thatcher anywhere near Felicity.

"He knows she's someone, Jason." Hailee let the words hang between us, the insinuation like a slap in the face.

"Where is she now?" I asked, barely able to see straight.

"At home. She didn't want to come. I think it's affected her more than she wants to let on. She's been holed up at her house all day."

"And you? You're okay?"

If Hailee was surprised at my concern, she didn't show it. "I'm okay," she said, reaching for Cameron's hand. "I know this gives you reason to go after Thatcher, but it's what he wants. You're in the play-offs now. If you put one step wrong off the field, Principal Finnigan could pull you for the rest of the season."

Didn't I know it.

"You don't need to worry about me," I said, "I'll be fine. You two going to be okay if I go?" I lifted a brow at Cameron who gave me a tight nod.

"He isn't worth it," he reminded me. "Don't play into his hands."

"I don't plan on it." But Thatcher would get his, one way or another he would pay for all this.

But right now, I had bigger things to worry about.

———

Felicity's house was steeped in darkness when I pulled up outside. Cameron and Hailee had tried to warn me about coming here, but as soon as her name left my step-sister's lips, all rational thought went out of the window.

I had to know she was okay.

Maybe it was guilt over the fact she wouldn't be in this mess if it wasn't for me, or maybe it was because she meant more to me than I cared to admit. Whatever it was, I wasn't leaving until I saw her with my own two eyes.

So why had I been sitting here for the last ten minutes unable to get out of the damn car?

"Fuck it," I mumbled, shouldering the door and climbing out. I'd never called on a girl before; never stood on the doorstep and waited for them to appear. It wasn't my style. Wasn't something I ever imagined myself doing... yet, here I was.

But the second I hit the Giles' porch, I froze. It was late on a Saturday night. What if her parents were home? What if her old man answered the door and saw me standing here? He'd recognize me; everyone in town did. Then there would be questions, assumptions... Fuck.

There was no car in the driveway unless you counted Felicity's ugly sunflower yellow Beetle.

Retrieving my cell, I sent a quick text to Hailee.

Me: Are her parents home?

Haile: How the hell should I know? Is their car there?

Me: I don't think so.

. . .

Hailee: You should be good then. I hope you know what the hell you're doing.

I ignored that, not wanting to admit I didn't have the first clue what I was doing.

Knocking gently, I waited. And waited.

And waited some fucking more.

There was every chance she was asleep. But it wasn't good enough. I needed to see her, to hear her side of what happened.

I needed to know she was fucking okay.

Me: I need her number.

Hailee: No way.

Me: Please. I wouldn't ask if it wasn't important.

Hailee: If I do this, and I haven't decided I will yet, you have to promise me not to hurt her. Ever.

. . .

Shit. How could she expect me to agree to that?

Hailee: So…. what'll it be?

Me: I promise to only ever do what I think's best for her…

Hailee: Jason, that isn't the same thing.

Me: It's all I have right now. What's it going to be, little sis? Am I getting her number or am I breaking and entering your best friend's house?

Hailee: JASON!!! Don't you dare…

Me: I'm joking.

For the most part. Because I wasn't leaving without seeing Felicity. Another text came through with a cell phone number. I added it to my contacts and opened a new message chat.

. . .

Me: Open your door.

Felicity: Who is this?

Me: Come find out...

A couple of minutes passed, and I was beginning to think she'd barricaded herself inside while she waited for the authorities to arrive. But then the curtain twitched and a couple seconds later, the door creaked open. "Jason?" Felicity yelped. "What are you—"

"Don't I get an invitation inside?" I forced my eyes to stay on her face and not her bare legs.

"Why would I invite you inside?" She glared at me. "And what are you doing at my house anyway? It's late. I was asleep."

"Just open the damn door, Felicity," I breathed out. "Hailee told me what happened last night with Thatcher."

"So you came over here to do what exactly?" Her lips pursed, taunting me. Her eyes daring me to admit it.

"You're really going to make me say it?"

Silence stretched out before us while Felicity waited for me to make my choice.

"Fine, woman. I came because the second I heard he had his hands on you, I wanted to kill something." Preferably him.

Bitter laughter spilled out of her soft lips. "So you're jealous? That's it?" Her brow shot up in challenge.

"Jealous of Thatcher?" I seethed. "I'm not fucking jealous."

"No? Because from where I'm standing, it looks like you are. Didn't you like hearing Thatcher and his friend had their hands on my body? They were so close to me, I could feel the warmth of their breath against my skin." My body began to tremble with rage as she kept talking. Kept describing what Thatcher and his guy had done to her.

"Felicity..."

"What, Jason?" she said, sharply. "Does it hurt to hear they wanted me? That they wanted to *hurt* me? Because I think he would have. I think he would have taken me right there—"

"Stop, okay," My chest heaved, and I rubbed my breastbone trying to ease the tightness. "Just stop."

"Why? Why should I?" Unshed tears collected in the corners of her eyes and I suddenly realized she wasn't baiting as much as unleashing her own anger at the situation.

"Let me in, Giles," I said, sliding my foot into the gap.

"No." A single tear escaped, rolling down Felicity's cheek. "You need to leave. Just go, Jason."

"Come on, babe. Let me in."

"You don't care about me," she whispered.

"I care," I admitted. "I wouldn't be standing here if I didn't."

Her eyes flew to mine, searching. Looking for answers I didn't have. It was a battle of wills and I didn't know who would break first.

"Fine," she eventually relented, "but you can't stay. My parents are—"

"Who said anything about staying?" I smirked as I stepped inside earning me one of her trademark eye rolls.

The door clicked shut behind us and I flinched, the sound like a gunshot to the chest.

What the fuck was I doing? She was okay, I could see that. Maybe a little shook up and angry, but she'd sassed at me the way she usually did. The fight sparking in her sea-green eyes.

"Nice place," I said, filling the awkward silence.

"It's not much different to your house." She smiled faintly, leading me down the hall I knew would open out to the kitchen.

"You didn't come to the party?"

"I didn't feel much like socializing." Her shoulders lifted in a small shrug as she went to turn away from me.

"Hey." I grabbed her arm and pulled gently, backing her up against the counter. Her breath hitched, her eyes alight with so much emotion I felt winded. How could one girl— one quirky, no-filter, pain-in-the-ass girl—affect me so much with a single look?

"You okay?"

"I..." Felicity slid her hands up my chest, her touch like wildfire, blazing a trail of heat. "I think so."

"Thatcher just wanted to scare you."

"Yeah, well, it worked."

My chest squeezed again. Too many people were being dragged into this thing between me and Thatcher. First Hailee, then Cam, and now Felicity. If I wasn't careful, soon there would be too many moving pieces for me to keep tabs on.

"What did you do that was so bad?" Her voice was quiet even in the silence.

Shit. She could have asked me any other question and I probably would have answered... but this was the one thing I never wanted her to know about me.

But instead of clamming up and distracting her with kisses and touches, I found myself saying, "There was this girl."

Felicity tensed, her eyes full of bewilderment. "A girl? Like Jenna?"

"No, not like Jenna." I grimaced. "Jenna is no one."

Felicity arched a brow at that.

"She's just someone to pass the time. A willing body." Jesus, it sounded so fucking awful out loud.

"Ew, gross," she mumbled, dropping her eyes.

"Hey," I slid my fingers underneath her jaw and tilted her face up, "you asked."

"I know, I just... ugh, I hate her."

"You sound a little jealous, Giles." The idea had me feeling a little smug.

"It's not exactly on my list to watch the guy I'm..." She stopped herself and I found myself wanting to pull the words out of her but I wouldn't. "It hurt seeing the two of you together is all."

"Together, me and Jenna weren't..."

Fuck.

Bell's.

"That wasn't what it looked like."

"You mean you didn't take her back to the storeroom

and fuck her?" Her eyes darted away. "Could have fooled me."

My spine stiffened; the urge to argue with her strong. Felicity was only half-right; I hadn't fucked Jenna that night, but she had given me head.

Shame was a feeling I was unfamiliar with, but it didn't dull the impact.

"I didn't fuck her," I said, as if it mattered.

"Whatever, Jason." She looked at me again. "This, us, it's all a game. And like I said the other night in your bathroom, I'm not sure I want to play anymore."

The bathroom. Shit. That had been a mistake. I was drunk and angry and she was right there, my own personal punching bag.

Rather than acknowledge that clusterfuck, I inched closer, erasing the sliver of space between us. "You sure about that?"

Felicity's lips parted on a soft intake of breath. "What are you doing, Jason?" Her voice trembled.

"I thought it was obvious. I'm here because I couldn't stand the idea of Thatcher hurting you."

"Because you're jealous." It didn't come out sassy this time.

"I'm not..." Rubbing the back of my neck, I mulled over what to say next. When really all I wanted to do was kiss her. After all, didn't they say actions spoke louder than words?

"You're so fucking beautiful." My lips hovered dangerously close to hers. It would have been so easy to crash my mouth down on hers. But I wanted to savor her, to taste every inch of her skin.

I wanted to lose myself in her, and that disarmed me.

"Your eyes are so dark," she said. "It's like they're black."

"They say the eyes are the window to the soul. So what does that say about me?"

"I think it says you're deadly." Felicity leaned into me, our noses brushing, lips almost touching.

"Deadly, huh?"

We moved closer still.

"And dangerous..."

"Definitely dangerous," I echoed, tasting her. Once. Twice.

"Don't prove me wrong, Jason," her words slammed into me but I didn't have time to process them, because her mouth sealed over mine and I knew the game had just changed.

And I wasn't sure of the rules anymore.

13

Felicity

JASON WAS IN MY HOUSE.

It shouldn't have been the only thought consuming my mind as his lips trailed over my skin, nipping and sucking, but it was.

Jason was here.

Because he was worried.

About me.

I didn't know what to do with that.

I wanted to store it for future reference; to lock it away for the next time I needed to remind myself he wasn't just a conceited asshole. But I knew it was a dangerous thing—to let myself believe this meant anything more than right here, in this moment. Jason belonged to Rixon. He had the hearts of almost every single person in our small town. There wasn't room for mine too. Yet, I found myself falling down the rabbit hole anyway.

Somehow, we managed to make it upstairs to my room without breaking contact. Our clothes scattered in a haphazard trail from my door to my bed which looked better than ever with a half-naked Jason Ford sprawled over it.

"Come here." He crooked a finger at me, pushing up on

140

his elbows to watch me. When I reached the bed, he shuffled to the edge, planting his feet on the floor. "You always sleep in a Raiders t-shirt?" He fingered the oversized blue and white shirt, pulling me until I stood between his legs.

"I'll take the fifth," I said around a coy smile.

"You will, huh?" His hands painted a torturous path up and down my legs, every time inching higher until his fingers were brushing the apex of my thighs. "I like you in Raider colors." His eyes glittered with lust, but I tried hard not to read between the lines.

Don't get sucked in.

Don't fall for his bedroom talk.

Don't let this become more than it is.

"But I think I prefer you like this." He pushed the shirt up my hips, all the way over my body until it was bunched around my shoulders. I pulled it off the rest of the way, baring myself to him.

"Perfect," his voice was strained and I loved it. Loved that I affected him so much because God only knew, he made me melt.

The old me, the me before senior year, wanted to ask a million questions.

What did this mean?

Did he want me or just hot anger-fueled sex?

Did he feel even an ounce of what I felt for him?

But the new me, the girl with a senior year bucket list, stuffed down all the doubt and willingly walked into the lion's den. Because deep down, maybe I did want my chance to tame the beast.

Jason smoothed one of his hands up my stomach

causing me to shiver. "You like that?" He asked huskily, staring up at me with a lazy smirk. "What about this?" His fingers closed around one of my nipples, pinching, and a bolt of pleasure shot through me.

"Oh God." I tried to swallow the moan building, but his touch was like kryptonite.

His other hand joined the party, rolling and plucking until my knees began to buckle.

"Jason, stop, I can't..."

"Too much?"

I nodded, my body melting against him. Before I could catch my breath, he'd pulled me onto the bed and rolled me beneath him. "Do you have any idea how much it turns me on knowing no one has been here?" He slid his hand between us, cupping me. "Except me."

Jason pressed a finger against me, rubbing me through my damp panties. I wanted him to pull them to the side and touch me, *really* touch me, but he seemed content in taking his time. Teasing me. Driving me wild.

He rocked back, standing at the foot of the bed. His tight-fitting boxers left very little to the imagination and I almost came right there when he grasped himself, squeezing roughly.

"Jason..."

"What do you want, babe?"

Everything, I wanted to say. But instead, I squeaked, "You."

Eyes dark and hooded, he climbed back over me, kissing me deep and hard. Our tongues danced a fast-paced rhythm, tangling and swirling together until I wasn't sure where I ended and he began.

His hard length rocked against me, making me wetter, needier. My sexual experiences left little to be desired compared to this. Jason was barely even touching me and I felt him everywhere; my synapses firing off in all directions, heat swimming in my veins.

My hand glided down his hard abs, cut to perfection from hours and hours of physical conditioning. But when I grazed his dick, Jason snagged my wrist, pinning it to the mattress at the side of my head.

"Patience," he said against my lips before diving back into the kiss. His tongue stroked every inch of my mouth before he moved to my jaw, drifting down the slope of my neck and along my collarbone. I writhed against him, desperate for him to end the sweet torture. But something told me he was only just getting started.

The thought both exhilarated and terrified me.

On a normal day, Jason was a lot to handle. Too much. But like this—half-naked, his skin pressed up against my skin, his mouth latched onto my neck, his hands curled into the flesh on my hip—he was lethal.

Jason broke the kiss again but only to move down my body. He dipped his tongue into my navel, swirling it around. Something so insignificant wasn't supposed to feel so erotic, but it did. My toes curled, my body aching to be closer to him.

"These need to go," he whispered against the inside of my thigh, dragging my panties down my legs. I was naked now, fully exposed to the guy I knew would never give me everything I needed.

Everything I wanted.

But I couldn't find it in myself to care, not with his

mouth hovering over my most intimate place. "Has anyone ever kissed you here?" he asked huskily.

"N- no," I panted.

He grinned wickedly before diving for me. His mouth and tongue hot and heavy as he licked and stroked. Jason pressed a finger inside me, then another. I moaned, his name falling from my lips like a prayer.

"You taste so fucking good." His other hand trailed back up my body, resting between my breasts, pinning me to the bed as he dived back in, eating me with an intensity that had me moaning and bucking off the mattress.

But Jason was a tease. Pulling away every time I almost fell off the edge. Taunting my warm skin with tiny kisses along my inner thighs, rewarding my cries with a deeper press of his fingers. My hands fisted his hair, desperately trying to move his head to where I needed him most, but he was strong.

And I was a breathless wrung out mess.

"Jason, please..."

Finally, he relented, attacking me with his mouth, his tongue licking and flicking my clit with fervor. My body began to tremble, the force of my orgasm tearing through me before I had time to prepare myself.

Jason climbed back up my body, licking his fingers clean before tracing them over my lips. "See how good you taste." I sucked one into my mouth, high on the lust burning in his eyes, the carnal growl rumbling in his chest as I tasted myself on his finger.

"I think I'm dead," I breathed out, barely able to form words.

"They don't call me God for nothing." He smirked before kissing me, long and deep and painfully slow.

"I want to feel you," I yawned, my hand drifting down his cut abs.

"Later," he insisted, rolling off me and tucking me into his body, my back to his solid chest.

"Are we spooning?" I asked, confused he wanted to cuddle rather than have sex.

"You're exhausted," was all he said as the weight of what had just happened settled over us. After a couple minutes of silence, I asked, "Jase, what are we doing?"

He stiffened behind me and I half-expected him to get up, yank on his clothes, and make a run for it. But he didn't. His lips pressed tiny kisses along my shoulder, stirring a fresh wave of desire in my tummy.

"That feels so good," I whispered, tilting my head to one side.

"*You* feel good."

Three little words that took root in my chest and exploded into hopes and dreams and things I knew better than to want with him.

Oh God. What had I done letting him into my house?

Into my heart?

I closed my eyes, trying to rein in the panic swimming in my veins. My mom had always told me to wait, to give myself to the right guy. The guy who would protect my heart, keep it safe, and treat it with respect.

And here I was, in bed, selling my soul to the devil. Because even though I wanted more, even though I wanted him to say this was the start of something, I knew better.

Jason Ford was a beautiful disaster waiting to happen.

And I was right in the eye of the storm.

———

My eyes fluttered open, and I stretched, my muscles still drenched in pleasure.

"Jason?" I smiled around his name. "Did I fall to—"

Crap.

I bolted upright, the stream of light like a bucket of icy water. It was morning, which meant—

"Felicity, baby, are you awake?" Mom's voice filtered through the door.

"Jason?" I whisper-hissed, my eyes darting around the room, hoping I might find him hidden in the closet.

He wasn't of course.

There was no sign of him. No puddle of his clothes on my floor and the slightly indented sheets beside me were already cold.

Jason had left, and it had been awhile.

"Flick, sweetheart, are you awake?" A knock sounded on the door, before it clicked open and Mom's head appeared.

"Hi, Mom." I gave her a weak smile, pulling the sheet up around my body. "How was date night?"

"Oh, you know your father, it was all very nice." Code for they went to their favorite restaurant, ate their favorite meals, and then moved on for dancing at their favorite bar.

"One of these days, you should surprise him." The words spilled out.

"Surprise him?" Her brows pinched. "I'm not sure your

father would appreciate that. You know he doesn't cope well with change."

"It was just an idea." I ducked my head, feeling silly suddenly. I never commented on my parents' relationship. They were happy, content in their life together. So what if they liked routine?

"Are you okay?" Mom asked. "You look a little... I don't know... sad."

"I'm fine, Mom, just tired." I yawned for effect.

"Are you seeing Hailee today? We miss her."

I miss her too. I swallowed the words. We hung out all the time still, ate lunch together at school every day, and did all the things we did pre-Cameron, but she had someone now.

Someone who wasn't me.

"I'm not sure. I think she said something about hanging out with Cameron and Xander." Cameron's baby brother was the cutest and he'd taken a real shine to my best friend. But then, who wouldn't?

"You could go with them? Just because she has a boyfriend now, doesn't mean—"

"Mom," I sighed. "It isn't like that. I'm happy for her. She deserves this."

"Oh, sweetheart, I didn't mean... Of course you should be happy for her. I just meant, I remember what it's like to lose your best friend to a guy." She gave me a warm smile. "Your day will come, Felicity. High school can be a confusing time. But soon you'll be in college and I'm sure you'll meet a nice, intelligent young man who will sweep you off your feet."

"Like Dad swept you off your feet?"

Her eyes lit up. "Exactly. Guys in high school have a lot of growing up to do. Why date a boy when you can wait a few months and date a man; am I right?" She winked playfully.

"Oh God," I grumbled, throwing a pillow at her. "Get out of here. It's too early for this."

"Okay." Her soft laughter washed over me. "But if you hurry, I'm making bacon and eggs."

"Sure thing, Mom."

She left and I sank back down against the pillows, trying to ignore how much her words affected me.

Grabbing my cell off the nightstand, I closed my eyes and took a deep breath. Maybe this was the start of my fairy tale? Maybe this time I would get my prince?

But when I finally looked at the screen, there was nothing.

Maybe Jason didn't want to wake you? I knew better though. Jason had bailed when things got too intense. Yet again, he hadn't let me touch him. He hadn't wanted to have sex with me. He hadn't even bothered waking me to say goodbye. Because he was keeping me at arm's length. He'd given me so much last night, but he refused to give me the one thing that I really wanted.

His heart.

14

Jason

"So what happened?" The first words out of Cameron's mouth weren't a surprise. Of course he was going to want to know what happened with Felicity. But what was I supposed to tell him when I still didn't know what the fuck had happened?

"So you did go over there?" Asher added, shooting me a sly grin. "I knew the excuse about your old man was a lie."

"We talked," I deadpanned, loading more weights onto the chest press as Cam got into position.

"Talked." His brow went up. "You expect us to believe that?"

Shrugging, I played it cool. They didn't need to know Felicity and I had shared a moment. Whatever the fuck that meant. Or that I'd held her like she was the most fucking precious thing in the world. Then as soon as she had fallen to sleep, I'd hightailed out of there without so much as a goodbye because I'd panicked. Because for the first time since Aimee, things felt quiet. There was no expectation crushing my chest; no weight of the team, of winning State, there was just me and a girl and silence.

They didn't need to know that at all.

"Believe what you want; it's the truth. She told me

exactly what happened with Thatcher and his goons and then I left."

"Right," Cameron said, leaning down on the bench. "And I'm not head over heels in love with your step-sister."

"Really?" It was my turn to raise a brow. "You're really going to throw that shit in my face?"

"It's in your face whether I throw it or not." He blew out an exasperated breath. "Hailee and I are endgame. The sooner you get on board with that, the easier things will be on all of us."

"Endgame. You think you and her are..." Fuck. I couldn't even say the word. I knew he loved her; knew she felt the same... but endgame?

From the look of complete seriousness on Cam's face though, I had underestimated just how deep his feelings ran.

"I'm following her to college, man. You think I'd be doing that unless I plan on putting a ring on it one day?"

"Fuck off," I said. "Now I know you're yanking my chain because there's no way in hell you're seriously suggesting one day you might—"

"Marry her?" A faint smile tugged at his mouth. "Serious as a heart attack."

Asher snorted and I levelled him with a hard look. "Are you hearing this?"

"Oh I'm hearing it and I can't say I'm surprised."

I groaned, spotting the bar for Cam. "But we're too young for all that shit. We've got our whole lives to settle down." It wasn't even on my radar yet.

Girls were a commodity, something to help me unwind after a tough game or a grueling training session. Besides, I didn't have time to worry about anyone else; not when I had to prove myself at Penn next year.

So why did you go over there, jackass? I ignored the little voice rattling round my head. I could be worried about Felicity getting caught in the crossfire without getting attached. It didn't mean anything, except my heart wasn't as black as everyone made it out to be. She was Hailee's best friend, and innocent in all this shit with Thatcher.

That's all it was.

"Hailee grounds me," my best friend said as if it was the simplest thing in the world. "When everything was falling to shit, and stuff with Mom was at its worst, she was there. No questions asked. Not because I wear a Raiders jersey or because she sees me as a meal ticket." He flopped back on the bench, heaving a deep breath. "I'm lucky to have her."

Yeah, until she grew bitter and began to resent his ass for the commitment and dedication required to make something of yourself in one of the country's top college football teams. High school football stars might have been treated like gods amongst men, but college was a whole other level of worship. Especially if you made waves, which I fully intended on doing. Penn hadn't asked me to commit early because they thought I'd be a valuable asset to their team—they thought I had potential to be *the* asset.

Even if I wanted someone by my side through it all— *and I didn't*—there wasn't enough to go around. I couldn't be committed one hundred percent to the game *and* committed to some girl. Being the best required sacrifice, one I was all too willing to make.

"It's not for me," I said with conviction.

"No one would put up with your brooding ass anyway." Asher grunted as he worked the free weights.

It was a joke.

He was joking.

Yet, it didn't stop the strange tug in my chest.

"Seniors Night next week. You ready, man?" he asked changing the subject.

"Figured I'd wing it." I shrugged, folding my arms over my chest.

"Coach will be pissed you haven't got some motivational speech prepared."

"Coach can suck it."

"Try saying that to his face." Asher smirked, his expression sobering with his next words. "You know it's funny, I've waited my entire life for this. State. College. But now it's almost here all I can think is I'm not ready to say goodbye."

"Nawww, you gonna miss us, Bennet?" I mocked.

"We can't all be untouchable like you, Jase. Yeah, I'll miss you guys. You're my best friends. Starting college, having to prove yourself all over again... I'm not going to lie, it freaks me the hell out."

His words sank into me. I'd never really given it much thought. Not when I'd had my eyes set on playing for the Penn Quakers for pretty much my entire life. It was in my blood; my legacy. My old man had the perfect career there until an injury ripped the dream out from under him. And when I came along, his dream became my dream. I'd been working toward taking Penn by storm for as long as I could remember. Now it was almost time. So while I loved my friends like brothers, I wasn't worried about going off to college next fall. Because I'd been counting down the days since my old man gave me my first football.

And it was almost time for my dreams to become a reality.

———

"So you and Felicity, huh?" Hailee breezed into the kitchen.

"Excuse me?" I played it cool, leaning back on the counter, draining the rest of my protein shake.

"She said you had a good *talk* Saturday night?" She gave me a suspicious look.

"We talked, yeah. I wouldn't say it was good."

"So nothing happened?"

"Why?" My brows furrowed, "did she say it did?"

"Nope."

"Well then, nothing happened."

"Jason, don't do that. Don't deflect. I told you not to—"

Pushing off the counter, I brushed past her. "You don't need to worry, *little sis*, me and Felicity are just friends."

"Friends?" She snorted. "You really expect me to believe that you and... you're up to something."

Letting out a frustrated breath, I spun around, meeting Hailee's narrowed gaze. "What the fuck do you want from me? I overlooked the fact you and Cameron—"

"Oh, for Christ's sake, we love each other, we're in love. Trust me, it would be a damn sight easier if I didn't love your best friend. But I do. And I won't apologize for that. If only you'd drop this macho don't-care-about-anyone bullshit maybe you'd understand. Or even let someone—"

"Careful, *Hails*, you're starting to sound like a romantic, and I know you know better than to think life is one big ole fairy tale and everyone gets their happily-ever-after."

"Agh," she threw up her hands, "You're so frustrating. I give up." Hailee stomped out of the room and I couldn't help but smirk. Getting under my step-sister's skin had once been one of my favorite pastimes, but now I saw it for what it was; juvenile sibling rivalry that had crossed a line.

I downed the rest of my shake and grabbed my keys.

"Jason," Denise's voice grated across my skin like nails on a chalkboard. "I was hoping to catch you before you left."

"I need to go, or I'll be—"

"This won't take a minute." She gave me a strained smile. "It's Hailee, she still won't talk to me."

"Not my problem."

"I know the two of you still don't see eye to eye, but I thought... well, I thought after everything, you might talk to her for me?"

"You want me to talk to Hailee about how you what? Ruined my family? Lied to her all this time? Stood by and did nothing while we terrorized each other? Tell me, Denise, what exactly should I talk to her about?"

Shame burned her cheeks as she spluttered, desperately trying to take control back of the conversation. I might have tolerated Hailee now because of Cameron and our shared hatred for our parent's deceit, but I didn't owe Denise anything. She represented everything I despised.

"Jason," she sniffled barely holding back the tears, "that's not fair. Me and your father never meant to hurt anyone."

"That's just it though, Denise, isn't it? No one is ever

supposed to get hurt but they always do." The words hit me square in the chest.

It was the truth. People always found a way to hurt one another. Screw each other over in the name of love... greed... jealousy.

"I can see this was a bad idea; forget I said anything." She hurried out of the kitchen, her sobs punctuating the tension.

I probably should have felt even an ounce of guilt at making my stepmom cry, but the truth of it was, adults were supposed to set the standards. To teach their kids respect and integrity. My old man might have taught me how to throw a perfect pass, but he failed miserably when it came to teaching me how to be a stand-up guy. Even after losing his shot at going pro, after meeting Mom and settling down, he couldn't give up his football-star life. He and Mom spent years pretending, years of playing their roles as doting father and mother, husband and wife. When really it was all a sham. Mom stayed with him out of obligation, while he clung onto a dream that would never be his, finding solace at the bottom of a bottle or a stranger's bed. I never wanted to treat someone the way Dad treated Mom. Someone he was supposed to care about, to love. Which is why I planned on never settling down. I'd seen enough news articles on football players and the impact of the game on their personal lives and relationships to know that it wasn't worth the headache or heartache.

It wasn't worth it.

But football, the game, *that* was worth it.

It was all I needed.

———

By the time I arrived at school, first class was already in session. Not that it mattered I was late. Teachers regularly turned a blind eye to my tardiness or absence. Instead of sneaking into AP Math, I decided to hit the gym. After my run in with Hailee and then Denise, I needed to burn off some extra steam, and practice wasn't until after school.

But even after a good work out, I was still restless. It coursed through my veins, making it hard to focus. Usually, I'd text Jenna or one of the other gymnasts or cheerleaders to see if they wanted to help me relax, but the only person I wanted to text was the one person I shouldn't.

I'd snuck out of Felicity's room yesterday morning for a reason. To avoid any awkward conversations, where she got the wrong idea, and I had to dig my way out of the hole I'd gotten myself into in the first place. But my dick seemingly didn't appreciate not getting his because before I knew it, he had me pulling out my cell phone and texting her.

Me: Where ru?

Felicity: You are alive then? I thought maybe you'd been abducted by aliens...

Me: I didn't want to get you into trouble with your parents.

. . .

Felicity: That almost sounds sweet... if it were true.

Me: It could be true.

It wasn't, but I wasn't about to tell her that.

Felicity: But we both know it isn't. What do you want, Jason? I'm in class...

I smirked at her reply. Even via text conversation I could imagine her sassing me; hand on one hip, eyes wide and simmering with indignation. Her mouth all pouty and begging for attention.

Fuck.

This had shitstorm written all over it; yet, I couldn't seem to stop myself. I was so used to girls doing whatever I asked, jumping at a chance to be with me, that Felicity's banter was refreshing. So much so, I wanted more. Craved it like an addict craved their next hit. Because while I didn't need a distraction from football, maybe a distraction from all the other bullshit around me was exactly what I needed.

. . .

Me: Meet me after class.

Felicity: I can't. I have this thing called class; you should look it up sometime.

Me: Skip. I bet it's on your list...

The three little dots indicated she was replying, but time passed and still nothing. I'd been joking about the list thing but figured I'd hit the jackpot.

Me: I'm right aren't I? It's totally on your list.

Felicity: I've cut class before.

Me: And I'm a virgin. Come on, skip class and check another thing off your list... I'll make it worth your while.

Felicity: You really shouldn't make promises you have no intention of keeping!

. . .

Me: Maybe this is one promise I want to keep?

I was pretty sure I wasn't supposed to feel so smug about luring her in, but I couldn't deny it left me feeling all kinds of awesome.

When she didn't reply, I typed another text.

Me: We can finish what we started at your house?

Felicity: When you came over and we TALKED?

Me: The only words I remember you saying are, 'Oh God' and 'More'. Come on, Giles. It's senior year. You're running out of time and you know you want to.

Please want to. I stared at my cell, willing her name to appear.

Felicity: You're going to have to work A LOT harder than this.

. . .

Shit. I hadn't expected it to get this far, not really. But now she was in, I didn't plan on backing out. One more taste. That's all I needed.

At least, that's what I kept telling myself as I sent:

Me: Challenge accepted.

15

Felicity

"Hey," Mya jogged up beside me. "What's got your attention?"

"Oh nothing." I shoved my cell in my pocket and flashed her a bright smile.

"Oh, really, the same nothing that had your attention at lunch and in government?" Her brow rose. "Come on, you can tell me. It's one of them, right? Asher or Jason."

"Ssh," I grabbed her hand, pulling her closer.

"Shit, my bad. So I'm right?" She lowered her voice conspiratorially. "It *is* one of them. You know I heard Jason left the party in a hurry Saturday." Her brows waggled.

Pressing my lips together, I kept walking, but Mya followed. "You can talk to me, you know?" she went on, "I know what it's like to want someone... *bad* for you."

My eyes darted to hers. "I don't..."

"Girl, it's written all over your face every time he enters the room."

Oh God.

The color drained from my cheeks. "Is it that obvious?"

"Seriously?" Mya's mouth lifted in a half-grin, not that anything about this was amusing. "You're fooling nobody but yourself."

161

"Crap. This wasn't supposed to happen. I wasn't supposed to..." I stuffed down the words.

"Fall for him?"

"I'm not... it isn't like that. I know it's doomed. He's Jason Ford for Christ's sake. But there is something there." Something that was proving pretty damn hard to ignore. Especially since he wasn't making it easy to forget him.

My cell vibrated again, and Mya nudged me, urging me to look at it.

Jason: Dancing naked under the rain?

"That is Jason, right? *The* Jason Ford? Because damn girl, what did you do to him?"

"It's silly really." I didn't return his text, giving Mya my full attention. "I created this list for senior year, kind of like a bucket list."

"Neat."

"You think?"

"Yeah, I mean, life is for living, right? If having a list keeps you accountable, then why not, I say." Mya slipped her arm through mine. "So what exactly is on this list, or is it a secret?"

"I don't go around publicizing it, if that's what you mean."

"It's something for you, I dig that. But Jason knows about the list?"

"Yeah, Asher let it slip."

"Asher?" Something flashed in her eyes. "What's his deal anyway?"

"What do you mean?" We reached the room where book club held their weekly meetings.

"Doesn't matter," she backtracked. "This your stop?"

"Yeah, I pushed myself to take up a new hobby this year."

Mya glanced at the temporary sign on the window and frowned. "And you chose book club? That doesn't sound very bucket list."

"Hey, it's a start."

"Yeah, but come on, you can do better than *book club*."

Her words sank into me, cracking open every insecurity I'd ever felt about myself. All my fears about becoming my parents.

Mya was right—book club was safe. It wasn't pushing any limits or breaking any chains. It was something my mom would have done when she was at school.

I shuddered.

"Oh dear God, I'm becoming my mother," I grumbled, suddenly wishing I'd have signed up to wizards and muggles or JROTC.

"You want to make memories, right?" I nodded, unsure where she was going with this. "Then you need to think big. You need to think so big that when you look back at high school in twenty years' time you can say you had zero regrets."

"Zero regrets, I like the sound of that." Even if it did terrify me.

"Ready to show me that list?"

Was I?

I doubted I'd ever be ready, but if I wanted senior year

to be epic, maybe I needed Mya's help more than I cared to admit.

———

"I'm home," I called, dropping my keys on the sideboard and making my way into the kitchen.

"Hey, sweetheart, how was your day?"

I spent the day evading this hot guy's text messages, overhauled my bucket list with my new friend from the city, and seriously considered cutting class. But not wanting to give my mom a heart attack, I went with, "It was the usual. You're home early?"

"Dentist appointment. I scheduled you for next month."

"Thanks, Mom."

She pushed a glass of juice toward me before going back to the pan of spaghetti. It was Tuesday which meant spaghetti. Tomorrow would be pot roast, and Thursday Mom liked to live on the edge with steak *and* chicken fajitas.

"Me and your father were talking yesterday and thought now is a good as time as any to start contacting businesses in the city who might be able to give you an internship next summer."

"It's only November, Mom. Isn't that a little premature?"

"Absolutely not. Making the right contacts now could be crucial for your future."

"I'll get right on that," I murmured, tapping out a tune on the counter. "Hey, Mom." I asked after a couple of minutes silence. "What's the most adventurous thing you did in high school?"

She glanced over her shoulder, brows pinched with confusion. "Adventurous thing?"

"Yeah, like sneak out after dark or make out behind the bleachers."

"Felicity Charlotte Giles, what on earth has gotten into you?" A slight pink streak appeared across her cheeks.

"It's for a school project," I lied. "For English."

"A project you say, well," she dried her hands on the towel shoved into the waistband of her pants, "Let's see, there was that one time me and your father played hooky to go down to the lake for a picnic. We'd been dating six months and he wanted to make it special. Then there was the time we made out at the back of Mr. Kavendish's classroom during Romeo and Juliet, that was particularly daring."

"Rad, Mom." I mocked, feeling my stomach sink.

"Sorry if my stories aren't cool enough for you, baby, but we were good kids. We didn't go looking for trouble and we were happy to live within the rules."

I knew the story well. My parents were high school sweethearts who went on to college, graduated, and found jobs in the city. Together. Then I'd come along, their unplanned surprise, and upset all their plans. They never made me feel anything less than loved and cherished, but sometimes I wondered if their overbearing interest in my future was their response to having a child they weren't prepared for.

"Do you ever regret only ever being with Dad?"

The lines around her eyes deepened. "The school really wants to know this stuff?"

Shrugging, I quickly fumbled for something to say. "They want us to compare senior year back in the day to senior year now, that kind of thing. They didn't really give us set questions or anything. I just thought... well, you and Dad have been together forever. That can't have always been easy."

"Were we young? Of course we were. But when you know, you know, sweetheart. And I took one look at your father and knew he was the one."

"What do you think has been your recipe for success?" Because where a lot of marriages ended in heartache, my parents had weathered the storm.

"Hmm, let's see. Communication, never going to sleep on an argument, and routine."

"Routine?" I squeaked. "Jesus, Mom, you make it sound so romantic."

"Baby, your father is about as romantic as that wooden spoon." She flicked her head to the utensil rack. "But he's always been there for me, and that's what really matters. I'd rather have a lifetime of your father than a few months of fire and passion."

I found it a little sad that she didn't think you could have both. But who was I to judge? They were happy enough and one hundred percent committed to each other and our family.

"Favorite senior year memory?"

"That one's easy." She smiled wistfully. "Prom. It was magical. Just how the movies portray it. Your father bought me a beautiful corsage and drove us to the school gym in his rusty old Buick. We coordinated our outfits and danced the night away with our friends. It was perfect."

"I bet there was a rockin' after party?"

Mom laughed softly. "There was none of that back in my day." I didn't believe that for a second which could only mean one thing: my parents weren't invited, or more likely, they refused to go.

"Felicity, is everything okay?" Mom switched direction. "You seem distracted lately and I'm not going to lie, baby, it's worrying me."

"I'm fine, Mom." *Except I can't stop thinking about a guy. A guy I know will break my heart if I give him even half a chance.*

"Don't drop the ball now, okay?" Her expression softened. "A lot of people think once college applications are done, senior year is a chance to let your hair down. But it's a chance to start thinking about the future, about the kind of person you want to become."

"Got it, Mom, hair down, future." Her words left a bitter taste in my mouth.

"You've been such a good girl, Felicity. Now Hailee has a boyfriend, I worry you might lose focus. The football team are a bad influence. Athletes get so much handed to them for free but real life isn't like that."

"Cameron is a good guy."

"I'm sure he is, baby." She gave me a dubious smile. "But you want more out of life than to end up as some trophy girlfriend, don't you?"

"Whoa, slow down." My hands went up, my eyes wide. "We're talking about Hailee and Cameron, not me."

Mom came over and brushed my bangs from my face.

"You're beautiful, Felicity. Inside and out, and boys will notice that. I only hope that when they do, you choose wisely."

"Mom, I'm a teenager. We're supposed to screw up and get it wrong occasionally." I laughed but it came out all strangled.

"We're Giles', sweetie. You know what that means." The urge to roll my eyes was strong but I remained expressionless as she said, "Planned, prepared, and punctual. That's all you need in life."

"Sure thing, Mom. I'm going to head upstairs and do my homework. Get a head start."

Her face lit up. "That's my girl. I'll shout you when dinner is ready."

With a small nod, I left Mom with her plans and headed for the sanctuary of my bedroom. Inside, I kicked off my shoes, grabbed the folded scrap of paper from my bag, and dropped down on the bed. My list was a mess. Nothing planned or prepared about it. But I couldn't deny that despite my mom's unintentional warning, Mya's additions made my pulse race.

1. ~~Take up a new hobby~~ *Explore alternate career paths*

   2. *Cut class*

   3. *Attend a pep rally - DONE*

   4. ~~Skinny dip down at the lake~~ *Get a tattoo*

   5. *Fall asleep under the stars*

   6. ~~Go to a party at Asher Bennet's house~~ *Crash a party in style*

   7. *Drink (actual liquor) at Bell's – OVERDONE*

8. Go to Winter Formal... with a date (not a girlfriend)
9. ~~Hook up with a random guy~~ First time do over
10. Fall in crazy messy love (with someone NOT JF)
11. Do not fraternize with the football team!!!

Snatching my cell off the nightstand, I found her number.

Me: So my new list...

Mya: Don't tell me you've already changed your mind?

Me: No, no, it's just my mom, she's big on being planned and prepared...

Mya: Good thing your mom isn't the one with the list then ;)

Me: Ha-ha! Am I silly? Is this whole thing stupid?

Mya: You're scared?

Me: My parents have my whole life mapped out for me. What if I do the list and realize their life isn't the one I want?

Mya: I think that's okay. Wanting to make

**our parents happy is perfectly normal, but not
at the expense of our own hopes and dreams.**

I mulled over Mya's words, but another text came
through before I could type a reply.

**Mya: Did you figure out what you're going to
do yet?**

Me: No...

**Mya: Okay, when you were little, what did you
want to be?**

Me: What does this have to do with my list?

My cell started blaring, Mya's name flashing across the
screen. "Hello?" I said.

"It might seem dumb, but just hear me out, okay?"

"Fine," I grumbled. "I've always loved animals, but my
parents never let me get a cat or dog. They were worried
about allergies and safety and all that stuff. One summer, I
found a stray dog. Scrawny undernourished little thing, but
it had the cutest face and I wanted it to be mine so bad. I
lured it into our garden shed, gave it some blankets and
food."

"What happened?"

Sadness washed over me. "Mom found out and made me take it to the local pound. I cried for a week." A tiny part of me was still bitter about it all these years later.

"Dogs, really? I had you down as more of a girl scout."

"Nope. I always wanted to be veterinary doctor."

"So start there..."

"Start where exactly?" She was making no sense.

"You're not sure you want to follow in your parents' footsteps, right? So you need to figure out your own path."

"I guess." A heavy weight settled on my chest. "I'll see you tomorrow."

She chuckled softly. "Is that your way of telling me I overstepped?

"Not at all. You've given me a lot to think about. Thank you."

"Hey, what are friends for, right? I'll see you tomorrow."

We hung up and I stared up at the ceiling, replaying the conversation.

I'd always been the good girl. Agreeable and passive, all too willing to go along with my parents hopes and dreams for me because it was what was expected. But if senior year so far had shown me anything so far, it was that some things in life required you to take a risk. They required you to let go of all your insecurities and doubts and take a leap of faith. Maybe they would work out and maybe they wouldn't, but at least you would know you tried.

I wanted that.

I wanted to take risks and throw caution to the wind.

I wanted to go after what I wanted. Have fun discovering a new path, one I carved for myself.

I wanted to fall head over heels in love despite everyone warning me it would only end in heartache.

God, did I want that.

But could I really do that with Jason, knowing it would never mean the same to him as it would for me?

My cell bleeped, another incoming text. I opened it eagerly expecting some more advice from Mya, but Jason's name stared back at me.

Jason: What are you doing right now?

After typing and deleting at least three replies, I went with the truth.

Me: Lying on my bed about to start some homework.

Jason: You're killing me, Giles. Come meet me... or better yet, I could come to you. I remember your bed... it's comfy.

I fought a grin. To my complete surprise, Jason was turning out to be very persistent.

Me: No and no. I need to get this done and my mom is home.

Jason: Mom's love me.

My chest squeezed at his playful words. Damn him for doing this to me, offering me glimpses of the guy I knew was hiding beneath his cool, indifferent exterior. Glimpses of a guy I knew would never surface permanently.

Me: I'm not sure my mom would.

Jason: She's not a fan? I'm wounded.

Me: Like you don't have enough middle-aged women fawning over you.

Jason: But I don't want them...

My heart fluttered at his words. At everything he *wasn't* saying.

Me: Goodbye, Jason. I'll see you at school tomorrow.

Jason: You know I didn't get to where I am without a fuck load of persistence and focus... When I want something, I go after it.

I didn't text back. I didn't know what to say. But proving himself true, another text came through.

Jason: We both know you're going to end up under me again, Giles. Why not save us both the heartache and give in?

Me: And for a second there, you actually had me fooled. Goodbye, Jason.

He didn't reply but it didn't matter. The damage was already done. He'd gone and pushed the right button to piss me the hell off. But he'd also made a huge dent in my armor, and I knew if he kept it up, I wouldn't be able to resist for much longer.

Even more alarming, I really didn't want to.

16

Jason

Smirking to myself, I hit send on my latest text to Felicity.

Me: Skinny dipping in the lake?

Felicity: Are you serious? Do you know what kind of things lurk in there?

Me: I can think of a few…

I smiled, my eyes darting around the cafeteria to make sure nobody was paying me any attention.

Felicity: Behave!!!

Me: Come on, Giles, say yes. Let's cut class and live on the wild side…

Felicity: I have study hall.

Me: Study hall? It's senior year…

Felicity: We don't all have a free pass to do whatever the hell we want. Unlike some people...

Me: Think of your list!

Felicity: Goodbye, Jason.

Damn, she was really playing hard to get. I thought I almost had her the other day, but then right at the last minute, she'd pulled the rug out from under me. I wasn't used to working so hard for a girl. But Felicity wasn't just any girl. A fact I could finally admit to myself without breaking out in a cold sweat.

I risked peeking over at where she, Hailee, and Mya sat at their usual table. "Looking for me?" Jenna's hand slid over my eyes, her lips grazing my cheek. I peeled her fingers away and glanced up at her.

"What the fuck was that?"

She reeled back, indignation flaring in her eyes. "What, I can't say hello now?" Flicking her silky blonde hair over one shoulder, she sat down next to me.

"That wasn't hello; that was you marking your territory."

"Don't be such a drama queen. It was one little kiss; we've done much more than that in public before."

My spine snapped straight, the knot in my stomach tightening as I glanced over at Felicity. She was busy talking to Hailee, not paying me any attention. But if she looked over here...

Why does it matter? It's not like you're hers or anything.

"Jason?" Jenna's hand grasped my knee. "I said where did you get to Saturday at the party? I looked for you."

Forcing myself to look at her and not at Felicity, I said, "I had shit to take care of."

Her expression hardened. "Shit to take care of? That's all I'm getting?" She was drawing attention now; my teammates pretending not to listen as they ate their lunch and talked among themselves.

"Careful," I ground out. "You're starting to sound like a girlfriend and we both know I don't do girlfriends."

Her hands slid up my chest as she leaned in, giving me a perfect view of her rack. "You keep saying that, and yet, you keep coming around for seconds and thirds and fourths..." She licked her lips in what I assumed was an attempt at seduction. But all it did was make me bristle.

"I come around because you're good for it. Nothing more, nothing less." I pulled Jenna's hands free of my chest and shoved them back at her.

Someone snorted. Everyone watching to see what I would do next. Everyone including Felicity. Her gaze burned into me, forcing me to look at her. There was so much in her eyes, I didn't know which emotion to pluck out first.

But Jenna shrieked, "You're such a self-absorbed asshole, Jason. One of these days you'll come around and I'll tell you no." She sounded genuinely hurt as she fled from our table.

"There goes gym pussy for the foreseeable," someone groaned. But I didn't give a fuck. I only had eyes for the girl glaring at me like I'd just called her out in front of the entire cafeteria.

My cell vibrated and I pulled it out.

Felicity: What the hell was that?

Me: I have no idea what you're talking about...

My eyes lifted to hers again as I fought a grin.

Felicity: Jenna seemed upset.

Me: Don't know. Don't care.

Felicity: What do you care about, Jason?

You. I care what you think. But I couldn't type the words. Not here, not now.

Maybe not ever.

"Someone interesting?" Asher called across the table.

"Nah, just my old man."

"Right." He saw right through my ruse. "I'll catch you later."

I watched through narrowed eyes as he rose from his chair and made his way over to Felicity and the girls. Without asking for permission, he dropped into the seat beside her and slung his arm over her shoulder. Challenge danced in his eyes as he glared at me across the room.

Motherfucker.

I loved Asher like a brother, but he was pushing this thing with Felicity too far.

"What's up with that?" Grady nudged my ribs. "You think he's banging her?" He flicked his head over to where Asher was holding court with Felicity.

"How the fuck should I know?" I growled.

"Whoa, dude, no need to get pissy with me. I figured if anyone knew the deal with them two, it'd be you. Although I can't see it myself. She's so fucking weird. Has stage five clinger written all over her."

"Grady?"

"Yeah, Cap?"

"Shut the fuck up."

He ducked his head, forking a mouthful of salad into his mouth. The guy had no fucking filter.

Asher caught my eye again, a smirk tugging at his lips. Without another word, I jerked away from the table and stood up. "I'm out," I said.

"See you at practice?" Grady asked, and I nodded.

As I stalked out of the cafeteria, I sent Felicity another message.

Me: Do you want him?

Felicity: Excuse me?

Me: Don't play dumb, Giles. Do. You. Want. Him?

Felicity: Careful, Jason. You sound awfully

jealous for someone who doesn't care...

My jaw clenched, anger radiating through me. She knew exactly which strings to pluck to get a reaction. But jealous?

I didn't get jealous.

I was Jason fucking Ford.

But as I moved down the hall, kids diving out of the way to make room for me, all I could picture was Felicity smiling up at Asher, his arm hung over her shoulder. And I wanted to kill something.

———

"Run it again," Coach yelled from the sideline. There wasn't a muscle in my body that didn't ache, but I welcomed the burn. The burn numbed everything else. Tamped down all the unfamiliar emotions that had taken root in my chest, snaking through me like slow acting poison.

"If I didn't know better," Asher taunted from the scrimmage line. "I'd say you had a bad case of blue balls."

"Fuck off, Bennet," I snapped, getting ready to call the play.

"I'm just saying, you don't seem yourself."

"Ash," Cam warned from his wide position.

"Chill, he knows I'm only yanking his chain." He flashed me a smug grin.

I called the play and barked, "Hut," as I received the ball and dropped back to make the pass to Cam.

"Nice," Coach boomed. "Keep playing like this and we

won't have anything to worry about Friday. Everyone hit the showers, I'll see you tomorrow."

Yanking off my helmet, I tucked it under my arm and started toward the locker room.

"Hey," Ash jogged up beside me, "Serious talk. You okay? I was only—"

"What the fuck are you doing?"

"I'm not doing anything."

"Don't give me that bull." My eyes slid to his, narrowing. "You're pushing me. Why?"

"I'm not..." He pressed his lips together, mulling over his reply. "Fine. I don't get it, okay? You like her. I know you do. And for some bizarre reason, she likes you too."

"And?"

"You're too fucking stubborn to do anything about it."

"Maybe I don't want to do anything about it." The lie soured on my tongue. I wanted to do something about it all right, but I knew I shouldn't.

The rest of the guys gave us a wide berth as we slowed down.

"Come on, Jase, this is me. I know you better than that and I know no girl has ever got under your skin the way she has. Tell me I'm wrong?" His brow rose.

It was my turn to smother my reply.

"Didn't think so." He flashed me a knowing grin.

"You like her," I said.

"It doesn't matter." Asher shrugged in that easy laidback way of his, but I saw the tightness around his eyes.

He *did* like her.

Probably a whole lot more than he'd ever admit.

"So what's the plan? Try and talk me into giving her a

shot and then you hang back in the wings waiting for me to screw it up and swoop in and fix her broken heart?"

It was a joke. An attempt to wipe the smug smile off his face. But it backfired because the second the words left my mouth, I realized it was probably true. I would screw it up and he would be there, waiting to wipe away her tears.

"Admit that you like her, and I'll back off," he said. "I know it kills you seeing me flirt with her."

"You've lost your fucking mind." I barged past him and kept walking. Asher didn't know the first thing about what I felt.

Dammit, I didn't even know.

"Jase, man, when are you going to stop and pull your head out of your ass?"

Stopping, I glanced back, eyes narrowed to slits.

"She won't wait forever." He just wouldn't stop pushing. "And yeah, maybe I will be around to help her forget all about you. Then what? You just gonna sit by and watch me move in on your girl?"

My girl?

It shouldn't have sounded so damn good.

"You'd choose her over me?" I deflected his slip of the tongue.

"What are we, five?" He ran a hand down his face. "All I'm saying is, you'd better figure out what you want because I'm sure there are plenty of other guys just waiting to take your place."

"Is that a threat, Bennet?" I stood taller, irritation rippling up my spine.

"You're a dick, you know that?"

"Never claimed to be anything else."

"Just don't destroy her, man. She's strong but she's not that strong." He moved around me, not sparing me a backward glance, while I was left standing there wondering when life got so complicated.

The answer as clear as day.

Felicity fucking Giles.

———

I was done waiting.

The plan was simple—lure Felicity into meeting me and fuck her clean out of my head. Because Asher was right, she was under my skin. Burying herself deeper and deeper. She'd been the one to tell me she wouldn't play my games, yet it felt like she was running circles around me. And for as much as I wanted her, wanted to taste her lips again, to soak up the quiet that existed whenever she was around; deep down, I knew this thing between us could never work.

Me: Tonight. You, me, and every item on your list you haven't completed.

Felicity: I never had you down as a dog lover...

Me: WTF?

Felicity: Nothing, forget I said anything.

Me: You're so fucking strange.

Felicity: So you like to keep reminding me.

Shit. Not the best way to score brownie points. Considering my reply, I went with the truth, for once.

Me: What if I told you, I like your brand of strange?

Felicity: Hold the phone. Did Jason Ford just admit he likes something?

Me: Easy there, Giles. I said I like your strangeness... I'm not sure it's a reason to be flattered.

Felicity: You like me.

Yes.
Yes, I do.
But I couldn't tell her that. So instead, I went with something typical jock-asshole.

Me: I'd like you bouncing on my dick more.

Felicity: Okay.

My eyes almost bugged out of their sockets.

Me: Okay, you want to bounce on my dick?

Because I've got to say, Giles, I'm a little surprised…

Felicity: Very funny! Okay, I'll meet you…

My pulse ratcheted.

Me: Yeah? After school? Or now?

Felicity: Cutting class is on my list.

I smirked triumphantly. I fucking knew it.

Me: Meet me after second period, round by the locker room.

Felicity: You've really given this some thought.

Me: I think about a lot of things.

Her. Naked. Underneath me.

Felicity: Goodbye, Jason. I'll see you soon.

17

Felicity

I'D LOST my freaking mind.

It was the only explanation as I hid out in the girls' bathroom until the hall had emptied. When a good five minutes after the start of third period had passed, I slipped out of the bathroom, ducked down the hall and straight out of one of the side entrances. My heart pounded in my chest as I crossed the lawn and went around the back of the building. But it was nothing compared to how it galloped away when I spotted Jase's Dodge Charger, the engine humming just like the gentle hum beneath my skin.

He looked completely at ease as I opened the door and slid inside. "I didn't know if you would come."

"Just drive," I clipped out, my eyes wide as they darted around looking for any sign that I'd been caught.

"Don't look so worried," he said smoothly. "No one will even know you're gone."

I threw him an 'are you for real' look and he chuckled darkly.

"It's easy for you to say," I said. "You're allowed to do whatever you want and no one bats an eye."

"Oh, I wouldn't be so sure of that."

His eyes swept over me, making me shudder and my

tummy clench. But I tried to ignore his suggestive tone, the flare in his eyes.

Too late, you already gave him all the power agreeing to cut class.

"If you want to go back, I can—"

"Just drive," I repeated.

"As you wish." Jason smirked as he pulled off and headed out of the school gates. "You know, it might help if you breathe."

I shot him daggers and he chuckled again.

A few seconds of silence passed and then he said, "I was sorry, about Sunday morning."

"No you weren't," I replied, resigned more than angry. Jason was Jason. He hadn't promised me anything, and I hadn't asked for anything. So the fact I was in the car with him when I should have been sitting in third period English wasn't lost on me. But I couldn't seem to make rational decisions when it came to Rixon's bad boy star quarterback.

Maybe I was more like Jenna Jarvis and the gymnastics team and cheerleaders than I realized. But they didn't have a list. They didn't want to live every second of senior year as though it was their last.

I did.

At least, that was my excuse for my behavior of late.

"You're not what I expected, Giles," he murmured, his words making me sit a little straighter.

"Am I supposed to know what that means?"

I was me. Nothing more, nothing less. Until recently, Jason had made no effort to hide the fact he found me annoying. But now he looked at me differently, talked to me in a way I never expected.

It was all very confusing.

Any normal girl might have believed it meant she was special or that she was capturing the heart of the guy she liked. I knew better. I knew you didn't capture a guy like Jason, you were granted an audience; allowed to breathe, to talk, to *be* in his presence.

And for some reason, right now in this moment, he had chosen me. Given *me* the royal nod. I smothered a nervous laugh.

"What?" he asked as my eyes drilled holes into the side of his head.

"Nothing."

"I can hear you thinking from all the way over here, spit it out." The corner of his mouth lifted.

"I'm just wondering what it's like to be you. Loved by an entire town, worshipped by most of your classmates. Guys want to be you, girls want to..." The word lodged in my throat.

"You can say it, Giles, I won't tell."

"Fine, girls want to fuck you even though they know that's all they will ever get from you."

That made him shift uncomfortably in his seat.

Good.

Asshole.

"Maybe I'm worth the ride," he threw back, and I snorted.

"No one is *that* good in bed."

"Is that a challenge?" He glanced over at me, daring me with his dark intense gaze.

"Shouldn't you be watching the road?"

"I don't know, the view from here is pretty incredible." He winked before turning his attention back to the road.

I silently screamed at my emotions to batten down the hatches because whether he knew it or not—planned it or not—Jason was knocking down my defenses one by one.

He's Jason Ford. Jason freaking Ford. He doesn't date.

He doesn't do commitment.

He doesn't fall in love.

Internal pep talk over, I smoothed down my skirt and said, "So where exactly are we going?"

"It's a surprise."

"I bet that's what you say to all the girls." I winced at how desperate the words sounded. But I had a serious case of foot-in-mouth syndrome on a good day, let alone when Jason was around to flummox me with his smooth lines and easy charm.

I waited for his reply, but it never came. Instead, he pressed his lips together as if to keep his reply from escaping.

Weird.

Silence followed. Thick and heavy; the kind that didn't feel uncomfortable but wasn't entirely comfortable either. I forced myself to look out of the window, to watch the town roll by, giving myself space to breathe and prepare for whatever Jason had up his sleeve.

Eventually, we began to slow, but only because Jason had turned off the main road onto an overgrown track that meandered through the trees.

"The lake?" I asked, a thrill shooting through me. He'd brought me here before, but we'd parked in the sandy lot at the entrance. Jason showed no signs of stopping this time.

"Don't worry," he said, "we're not going swimming. Not today, anyway."

The car jerked and bounced over the uneven terrain. I hadn't been out here in years, since me and Hailee had stopped swimming at the lake a few summers ago.

"What?" Jason's gravelly voice washed over me.

"We used to love it out here."

"So why'd you stop coming?"

"You're kidding me, right? The summer after you stole Hailee's clothes and bike and she had to walk home half-naked in the blistering heat... sound familiar?"

His lips pursed.

"You were a total jerk to her."

The car came to an abrupt stop near the water's edge. "Yeah, well things change."

"Do they?" I asked, desperate to know what he was thinking, to get inside his head and uncover his deepest darkest secrets.

When he didn't answer, I whispered, "What are we doing, Jason?"

"I thought it was pretty obvious." His lip curved smugly.

"Jason..."

"What do you want from me, Giles?"

"I want to know you. Not the Jason Ford everyone else gets to see, the *real* you."

"The real me, huh?" he scoffed. "I don't think anyone wants to know the real me. All they want is the football star, the jock, the guy who can propel them to social greatness. People want the illusion, not the real thing."

"I do." The words came out small.

"And what if you don't like what you find?" His expression softened, not much, but it was there. "What if underneath the number one jersey there's nothing but darkness?"

"I don't believe that. You care, Jason, I know you do. About Hailee, about your friends..." *About me.* The words lodged in my throat. "You're not just the conceited asshole you let everyone believe you are."

"Let's get one thing straight," he said, his eyes pinning me to the spot. "I am. I'm not the reformed bad boy and I'm not looking to be changed by..." He swallowed the words and I felt myself flush with indignation.

"You think I want to change you?"

"All girls do."

"Let's get one thing clear, Jason," I shot back, my voice low and sultry, "I'm not all girls."

Heat flashed in his eyes as he leaned closer, taking the air with him. "I'll break you. You know that, right? This, whatever this is, won't end well."

Run, the little voice in my head screamed, *run far away and never look back.*

But I didn't reach for the door handle. Instead, my hand reached for him, twisting into his jersey and yanking his mouth to mine.

"You're fucking crazy," he murmured, meeting my lips halfway, attacking me with his mouth, with frantic licks of his tongue. Jason kissed like it was the final play and the whole game was on the line.

His hands wasted no time running down my body, palming my breasts through my sweater. "Off, now," he commanded as if his words were gospel. Perhaps they were, given how quickly I helped him peel it over my head. His lips twisted in a wolfish grin as he appraised my body. "Ever been fucked on the hood of a car, babe?"

We were back to that.

Not Giles.

Babe.

I didn't know which I hated more.

"Jason," it was a breathless whisper, "you know I haven't."

"That's right you haven't because I'm the only guy to ever have this." His hand glided down my stomach, finding the waistband of my leggings.

"God, I hate you," the words flew out of my mouth before I could stop them.

His head lifted, confusion pinching his expression. "Funny, because from where I'm sitting, it looks a lot like you'd do anything to bounce on my—"

"Jason! Stop."

"Stop?" His brow shot up. Before I could process what was happening, Jason pulled me onto his body, forcing my legs apart to straddle his thighs. "You want me to stop?" He rocked into me, his erection hitting my stomach.

"I... yes... no." I tried to smother the moan building.

"Which is it, Giles, because you're sending me mixed signals over here?" He continued rocking into me while his hands played lazily with my breasts.

"I can't think when you're..." Pleasure rippled through me. But it wasn't enough.

It wasn't nearly enough.

"What, babe? You need more?" Jason's hand slid up my

throat spanning my neck so that he could push me backward gently. Then he sucked the skin there.

My hands twisted harder; pulling him in, pushing him away, I was no longer sure.

"Say it," his voice echoed around us. "Tell me you want me, want this."

"I..." *Don't do it, don't give him so much power over you.*

"Say the words, babe." His thumb pressed into my center, causing me to jerk above him.

"I want you," my voice trembled, mirroring my body. "I want... this." The words left me in a sharp exhale. Victory flashed in his eyes, the air around us shifting as an understanding settled between us.

I did hate him.

I hated that he made me feel so alive, so desired.

I hated the way he knew exactly how to kiss me, touch me, to get me to fall at his feet.

But most of all I hated how I didn't hate him, not even a little bit.

"Relax," he said as if he knew I was all up in my head. "If it makes you feel any better, I hate you too." His thumb brushed my neck slowly before he chased his touch with his lips. "I hate how I can't stop thinking about you." *Kiss.* "I hate that you say the most ridiculous things." *Kiss.* "But most of all I hate that Thatcher and his goon had their hands on you. I hate..." His lips touched my skin again as my heart crashed against my ribcage.

This wasn't the plan.

He wasn't supposed to say all of this, to feed the small part of me dreaming of a different time and place. A time and place where Felicity Giles could ever end up with a guy like Jason Ford.

I waited for his words, greedy for more. But they never came, replaced with hot kisses as he dragged his tongue up and down the hollow of my throat. Disappointment flooded my chest but deep down, I wasn't surprised. Jason would never admit the truth. That there was something between us. That this was more than just sex. And for as much as it hurt, maybe it was better this way.

His hands were all over me now, his mouth the same.

"Jason," I said, gently tugging his hair. "Slow down."

He lifted his face, brow arched. I took advantage of the moment, pushing my hands against his chest to move him back. Then I fumbled around to find the recline handle and pulled.

"What the fuck?" he grunted, and I stifled a giggle. Jason needed control. He needed to hold all the power. But this time, I wanted to be in the driving seat.

I wanted to drive *him* wild.

"What game are you playing, Giles?" he asked, his hands gripping my hips as I gently rocked above him. We both groaned, and another thrill shot through me. He was at *my* mercy now.

With my newfound confidence, I hooked my hands into the waistband of my leggings and pushed them down over my hips. It was no easy feat getting them off, but I managed. If Jason noticed my clumsy striptease, he didn't comment, his hooded gaze too busy eating up every inch of my bare skin.

"Fuck, you're beautiful," he whispered.

Yeah, fuck. His words were like a poisoned arrow through my heart.

As if he noticed my hesitation, challenge glinted in his eye. He was ready to pounce, to take back the power and flip this whole thing on me. But I wasn't backing down. I wasn't just a pawn in his game.

I was the goddamn queen.

And this queen wanted her king to kneel at her feet.

Sliding my hands around my ribs, I unhooked my bra and let it slide down my arms. Jason didn't speak, he didn't have to. His eyes betrayed every thought running through his head, and even though I knew it was only temporary, I had him right where I wanted him.

"Take it off," I demanded, my eyes fixed on his jersey.

"Okay, I'll play, babe." There was a hint of amusement in his voice as he leaned forward to yank his jersey off. He was so beautiful; a perfectly sculpted Adonis. Who in this moment, was mine. Not Jenna Jarvis' or the gymnast team's. Not Rixon High's or the team's or even the town's.

Mine.

But you can't keep him, Felicity. Don't forget that. **Never** *forget that.*

My hands trailed down his abs, counting every ridge until my fingers hovered precariously close to the waistband of his sweats. Without giving myself any time to hesitate, I gently pulled, waiting for Jason to lift his butt off the chair so I could wiggle them off his hips.

Holy crap. He was rock hard.

His smooth chuckle sliced through the tension crackling around us. My eyes lifted to his. "What?" I asked.

"I'm just wondering if you're brave enough—"

I palmed him roughly, his groans filling the car. "Shit, Felicity." My name on his lips was like music to my ears.

"Condom?"

"Glove compartment."

Of course he kept a stash of condoms in his glove compartment. I rolled my eyes and his brow rose, his gaze hooded, hazy with lust.

With great skill, I managed to lean over and retrieve one. Jason surprised me by capturing my wrists and pulling me down. He kissed me hard, bruising my lips and leaving me breathless. I could almost feel his mind working overtime, hear his thoughts.

But I was too far gone to care. I needed Jason more than I'd ever needed anything before.

It was terrifying.

Exhilarating.

And completely crazy.

He watched me, pupils dilated, as I freed his dick and tore open the wrapper, rolling it over him. His breath was ragged, his muscles rippling with every sharp intake of oxygen.

One hand rested on his shoulder, I rose over him, hooked my panties to one side, and slowly sank down on him.

"Fuuuuk," Jason ground out, his hand clamping down on my hip, trying to steady me. But I wasn't about to let him take the lead. Not now, not when I finally held some of the power.

Even if it was only temporary.

18

Jason

FELICITY LOOKED LIKE AN ANGEL. Eyes clouded with pleasure, lips parted in a soft moan.

A dirty sassy angel.

My angel.

She'd caught me completely off guard when she took control. I didn't think she had it in her, but I should have known better because where Felicity Giles was concerned nothing was as it seemed.

And I fucking loved it.

"Yeah, just like that," I hummed, driving my hips up as she rocked above me.

It didn't matter we were by the lake, in the middle of the day where anyone could see us. The second my lips touched her, I knew there was only one way this ended. From the way she was riding my dick, she did too.

My hands roamed over her body, desperate to touch and explore every inch of her skin. Her soft curves, the gentle slope of her hips, her perfect tits.

I couldn't get enough of her.

"Jason..." My name slipped from her lips, caught somewhere between a sigh and moan, the needy sound a direct line to my dick.

I wanted to take to control, to grab her waist and show her exactly how I liked it, how I needed it, but she'd worked her voodoo bullshit on me again because I couldn't do anything but sit back and enjoy it.

Enjoy her.

Every roll of her hips. The way she rose above me ever so slightly, holding the tip inside her and then sinking back down slow and deep. I'd never worried about a girl owning me before because there had never been a girl who had come close. Not even Aimee held that mantle. Felicity was different though. She was everything I never knew I needed.

It was a damn shame I couldn't keep her. And I couldn't. Because while she felt fucking fantastic riding me, this, right here, was where we had to end. Before she became the wrong kind of distraction.

The kind of distraction I'd vowed never to fall for.

My chest tightened as I tried to get my head back in the game. "What is it?" she asked, barely able to catch her breath. "What's wrong?"

"Nothing," I replied coolly. "Come here." My arm looped around her waist as I sat up putting us chest to chest.

"Jason, what are you—"

"Ssh." I whispered, rocking back and forth, the intimate position so much deeper and intense. I could feel every inch of her pressed against every inch of me and it was fucking breathtaking. In that moment, it was hard to deny how perfect she was. The way her body molded to mine, like two pieces of the same puzzle.

"You weren't supposed to..." her voice was broken with pleasure.

"Do you have any idea how crazy you drive me?" The words hung between us as I slowly regained control of her body.

Her.

Felicity buried her face in my shoulder as my hand threaded into her hair and our rhythm increased stealing the breath from my lungs. *I'm going to fuck you right out of my head.*

She froze, her body rigid above me.

Shit.

I hadn't meant to say the words aloud. But now they were out there; a vast ocean between us.

"Felicity, I—"

She grabbed my lips, forcing them together as she moved faster. Harder. Chasing the fall.

Her body began to tremble, her breath choppy and labored. The familiar tingle at the base of my spine told me I was close. Ready to fall right alongside her; she just needed one final push. Dipping my head, I closed my mouth around her nipple and bit down gently. Her cries echoed around us, pleasure crashing into me like a freight train. But like any good high, the inevitable comedown sucked ass.

Felicity clambered off me, grabbing her leggings and sweater and awkwardly dressed herself.

"That's something for your list," I said through strained laughter. I sounded like a fucking idiot. As if some lame assed joke about her list changed the fact I'd accidentally slipped out I wanted to fuck her out of my head.

"We should get back to school." Her voice was cold,

sending the temperature inside the car down by a few degrees. "I don't want to miss fifth period."

"Uh, yeah." I tucked myself back into my sweatpants and pulled on my jersey. Things had gone from great to shit in two seconds flat all because of my big fucking mouth.

But this is what you wanted, right?

One more time with her. A chance to rectify how things had gone down in New York.

The ride back to school was painful. Felicity barely looked twice at me and every time I tried to fill the suffocating silence, the words died on the tip of my tongue.

It was a clusterfuck.

Exactly what I'd known would happen, but I'd gone and done it anyway. Felicity wasn't Jenna or any of the other chicks I usually went with. She was different.

I was different around her.

All too soon we rolled into the parking lot, school looming up ahead. "Felicity, I—"

"Save it, Jason. I knew what this was. I knew and I came anyway. But it's done now, right?" She didn't sound sad or pissed, just resigned. "You've fucked me out of your head so I guess we can just both move on."

"I..." *Say something. Say anything.* But nothing came out, my thoughts too incoherent to form words.

"Okay then..." Felicity grabbed the door handle and pushed. But not before turning back to me. "I guess it's true what all the girls say about you," she said, holding my conflicted gaze.

"Yeah, and what's that?" I managed to choke out.

"You're worth the ride." Her eyes didn't sparkle and her voice was devoid of any emotion. "See you around, Jason."

Then she was gone.

It fucking stung to see her walk away, but I knew it was better this way. Better she thought I was just a cold-hearted bastard who had used her in a game of push and pull. Cat and mouse. But the truth was, I wasn't so sure anymore. And although I'd never do it, for the first time in my life, I wanted to chase the girl.

Life wasn't a fairytale though. The only happy ending I needed was the one where I won State, went off to college, and made my dream of going pro a reality.

———

"Okay, ladies, gather in." Coach beckoned us over. "Two games to go before the play-offs." The guys began cheering but I barely managed a grumble.

"Okay, okay, you're excited, I get it. You've earned it. But we need to keep our heads. Tomorrow is Seniors Night, which means best behavior. There'll be the formal walk out at the game and then the presentations at the party afterward. Mrs. Hasson is cooking up something special for the occasion so I want to see you all in your best clothes. Grady," he looked at the guy across from me, "that means you too, Son. If I see you in so much as a pair of sweats or a jersey, I'll break out my old dinner jackets. Consider yourself warned."

A few of us snickered while Grady flipped me off behind his helmet.

"Any questions?"

"No, Sir."

"Good. Don't forget we have Miss Raine's unveiling too.

I want you to remember to show her some respect. She's worked tirelessly on this project and I think I speak for the whole team when I say I'm excited to see what's she's created."

My eyes went to Cam who had a goofy grin painted on his face. He was so gone over my step-sister it left a sour taste on my tongue.

"It's just nearest and dearest Friday. Right, Coach?" I don't know why I asked the question, and I instantly wanted to take it back when all eyes landed on me. Asher was smirking but Cam looked worried. I hadn't told them about earlier with Felicity, but they knew something had happened because I'd been a dick during practice, taking my frustrations out on my teammates.

"Something you want to tell us, Jase?" Coach asked with a hint of amusement.

"Nah," I kept my voice even. "Just wanted to make sure we weren't inviting the entire class."

"Rest assured it'll be intimate, Son. The team, close family... girlfriends," he scoffed at that, "and the cheer squad."

A rumble of appreciation echoed around the field.

"*Best* behavior, remember?" Coach shot us a bemused look. "Okay, get out of here. Jase, a word please."

I hung around, waiting, while my teammates headed for the showers. "What's up, Coach?"

"All set for tomorrow?"

"Sure thing." I ran a hand over my damp hair and down the back of my neck.

"I just wanted you to be aware. Principal Finnigan has asked your father to give a speech at the presentation."

My spine stiffened. "I see."

"Now, I know the two of you haven't always seen eye to eye, but he's your father Jason, and the town consider him to be—"

"A local hero." As if I needed any more of a reminder.

"It's out of my hands but I wanted to give you a heads up."

"Thanks," I grumbled.

"Piece of advice, Son. It's important to know where you came from, but you don't have to let it define you. You've earned this, Jason, and when we're crowned State champs, you can rest easy knowing *you* made it happen. Not your father or his legacy. Football might be in your blood, but you have a rare gift that's all yours, Son. Own it."

"Thanks, Coach." I barely got the words out over the lump in my throat.

He gave me a small nod. "Now get in there with the rest of them."

As I walked off field, I couldn't help but wonder what it would be like to be normal. To walk out tomorrow with my family, a girlfriend maybe. People who loved me unconditionally, not because of who I was and where I was going, but for the person behind the jersey.

The person behind Rixon's golden boy of football.

I couldn't even remember the person I was before. Before Varsity football, and state records; before being scouted by some of the best colleges in the country. Most people spent their whole lives chasing their dreams, trying to turn fantasy into reality. Yet, here I was, barely eighteen, with the whole world at my feet. My dreams were right there for the taking. It should have been the best fucking time of my life and it had been until recently. Until I started to care. But I couldn't afford to care. I couldn't afford to open myself up to distractions. To make myself vulnerable. Not now. Not when I was so close.

———

Later that evening, I found myself in the last place I wanted to be: riding with Hailee in awkward as fuck silence. She didn't mention Felicity and I didn't ask. I figured her lack of third degree meant Felicity was keeping secrets from her best friend, which suited me just fine.

"Thanks for helping me do this," she finally said as we pulled up outside the side entrance to the Arts Department.

"Yeah, well, Coach gave me no choice." I dragged a hand down my face.

"I see." Her expression hardened. "I just thought... It doesn't matter, come on." Hailee climbed out of my car and I let out a heavy sigh, thumping the wheel. It wasn't supposed to sound so bitter, but it was too late now. Reluctantly, I shouldered the door and followed Hailee into the building.

"So there are nine portraits in total," she said without looking at me. "Each one has been wrapped for transportation and Coach and Mr. Jalin already took the display equipment over to his house.

"Got it." The Arts Studio wasn't a part of school I was familiar with, but Hailee seemed completely at ease as she guided us through the network of adjoining rooms. The air was thick with the smell of paint and cleaning fluid.

"It takes some getting used to."

Silence settled between us. But it felt suffocating.

"So art, huh? Cameron says you're pretty good."

"I hope so since it would be kind of embarrassing if Coach unveils the portraits and they resemble children's artwork." Her lips curved slightly, and I found myself smiling back.

"I guess it was a dumb question."

"Not dumb," she gave me a half-smile. "I know this is weird for you, Jason. Me being a part of your life. But it would make things a lot easier if we could at least try to get along?"

"It'd really piss our parents off." I smirked. But Hailee's smile was gone. "You want to forgive her?"

"I don't want to forgive her, no, but I don't know how much longer I can freeze her out. It's senior year. I leave for college next year." Sadness edged into her expression.

"So, what? They get a free pass just because we're flying the nest?"

"Jason," Hailee pinched the bridge of her nose. "Don't you find it exhausting all the time?" When I looked at her with a blank expression, she added, "Holding onto so much hate and bitterness?"

"I don't hate everything."

She gave me a pointed look and I felt my jaw clench. "You don't know what it's like to never know someone's motives, to not know who you can trust," I said. "People think it's so easy being the hotshot football player, but do you know how old I was when scouts first started approaching me?"

"Thirteen?"

"Eleven. I was in sixth grade. While most kids were playing king of the hill and capture the flag, I was running drills and working with my dad on conditioning programs." Because there was no other path for me. I was going to fulfill his dream whether I liked it or not.

"I had no idea—"

"It doesn't matter." I shrugged dismissively, kicking the floor with my sneaker. "By the time you arrived in Rixon, I'd caught the eye of four Division One teams. Four. People started taking notice. Suddenly my life wasn't my own; it was my old man's, my football coach's, even the town's. When all I wanted was to play football."

I always loved the game, that was never the issue. But I hadn't realized back then, that one day, it would mean shouldering the expectation of an entire town.

A flicker of sympathy passed over Hailee's face.

"Shit, you don't want to hear this, we should probably—"

"Thank you," she said, "For telling me."

Why had I told her?

It was a long time ago and I wasn't a kid anymore. Being in the spotlight came with the territory, and the light would only get brighter when I went to college. To survive you had to build walls. Maybe I'd built them higher than others, but it was only because I wanted it more than most.

"It explains a lot." A smirk tugged at her mouth.

"Oh yeah?"

"All that pressure, the expectation... it explains why you're a grade-A asshole." Hailee laughed softly, her eyes twinkling. But I didn't laugh. I didn't even smile. Because she was right.

I was an asshole because I could be. People treated me like the prodigal son of football and somewhere along the way, I started acting like it. But what most people didn't realize was, it was a defense mechanism. A way to protect myself.

"I'm joking, Jason." Hailee added when I didn't reply.

"No you're not."

"Then maybe, but now? Now, you're not so bad." She grabbed the door handle to studio two and slipped inside. "What the—" Her words trailed off and I stepped up behind her to see what had rendered her speechless.

Art supplies were strewn everywhere. Red and white paint was splashed up the walls, and across the canvasses lying haphazardly around the place.

"I can't believe someone did this." Hailee's voice trembled as she swiped tears from her eyes. "It's all ruined; the Seniors Night project is ruined."

I looked at my step-sister, the person whose life I'd made a misery in the past, and felt like the worst kind of shit. For so long, I'd used Hailee as a punching bag to deal with my anger at her mother and now she was being used in the same way by someone else.

All because of me.

For a moment it was like I was looking in on us, for the first time actually looking beyond the armor I put around myself, the 'hurt people before they hurt me' principles I lived by, and I didn't like what I saw.

I stepped closer to her and I put my hand on her arm, causing her to jump slightly, as her attention shifted from the ruined canvasses. "We got this, okay? What do you want me to do to help?"

Hailee took a deep breath. "Can you help me get them back on the stands?"

I nodded.

The silence was deafening as we worked together to clean up the studio. I spotted my face amongst the chaos. Cam's too. Some of the canvasses looked worse off than others. When we stood back to survey the wreckage, Hailee let out an exasperated breath. "Tell me this isn't what I think it is," her body shook with anger. "Tell me Thatcher didn't break in and ruin my hard work because of some stupid football rivalry. Tell me, Jason." Her eyes flew to mine, pinning me to the spot, making me feel five inches tall.

"I can't," I ground out, my fists curled tightly against my thighs as I took in the devastation. Art wasn't my thing, but I knew how hard Hailee had worked on the project. How many hours it had taken her to paint each portrait.

A beat passed.

Another.

Until I could hear nothing but the roar of blood between my ears, the *thud thud thud* of my heart against my ribcage. "I'm so fucking sorry," the words sliced through the air like a hot blade through ice, as my fist smashed into the wall.

"Shit, Jason," Hailee rushed over to me, trying to get a look at my hand. But I shook her off, cradling it against my chest.

"It's fine," I said. It wasn't, but I'd had worse. It was nothing a little ice and a few shots of whisky wouldn't solve.

"You weren't supposed to see it until tonight." She sniffled, ignoring my apology.

"I never realized you were so talented." Even covered in red and white paint splatters, I could make out the intricate detail of my helmet, the way my shirt seemed to ripple as I hiked the ball. It wasn't just good.

It was fucking incredible.

"You should have seen them before..." she trailed off, sadness radiating from her.

"Can you fix them?" The one of me was the most affected but at least four seemed to have escaped the paint splatters.

"I'm not sure. I'll need to talk to Mr. Jalin."

"Hailee—"

"I know what you're going to say, Jason, and I get it. If we bring Thatcher into this, Principal Finnigan will intervene. But I have to tell Jalin. I'll think of something to protect you, but everyone's going to know something happened when we unveil them tomorrow. Maybe if we get this place tidied up and I speak to him, we can control the story."

It wasn't ideal. But it wasn't like we had a list of options.

"When did you get so devious?" I asked around a half-smirk, brushing over the fact she was prepared to lie to protect me because I didn't know what the fuck to do with that.

"I learned from the best." She shot me a knowing look.

"You know, if I didn't hate you so much, I think I could probably grow to like you."

"The feeling is entirely mutual." Hailee mirrored my

expression. "Come on, we have a lot of work to do if we want to get this place tidied up before class tomorrow."

I pulled out my cell phone.

"What are you doing?" Hailee sounded wary.

"Calling in reinforcements."

19

Felicity

"Want to talk about it?" Mya asked me.

"Nope. I want to get wasted, flirt with cute guys, and then eat my body weight in ice cream. Maybe not in that order." I took a long pull on the liquor Mya had sequestered off her grandmother. It almost blew my brains out the first sip I had, but at least it left me numb.

"I hate to break it to you," my partner in crime said, "but I'm not exactly sure this is the place to meet guys."

We were down by the river, huddled on a bench. It probably wasn't my brightest idea ever, but I couldn't sit at home, wallowing. Deflecting Mom's incessant questions. It wasn't like I could call Hailee; not when she was off with Jason preparing for the Seniors Night thing tomorrow. At least it was family and close friends of the team only. I wouldn't have to survive sitting there, watching him, remembering how he made me feel... how he trampled all over any hopes of there being something real between us.

Fuck you right out of my head.

He hadn't meant to say the words. I'd seen the surprise in his dark eyes, the flash of panic. Any other girl would have probably slapped him across the face and run a mile. But not me.

What the hell was wrong with me?

"You're in deep with him," Mya said, and my head whipped up to hers.

"Huh?" I slurred.

"I said, 'you're in deep with him'."

"I'm not... I wasn't supposed—"

"Girl, we both know it doesn't work like that. You don't get to decide who you fall in love with."

"I'm not in love with him."

"Maybe not now. But it's there, inside you. You want him."

"I do," I admitted, my eyes darting to the ground beneath me. "He's different with me."

"They always are," she sighed, her voice distant.

"Your ex?"

She gave a small nod. "Reeled me in before I could even see what was happening."

"He hurt you?"

"He didn't just hurt me," Mya gave me a sad smile, "he completely destroyed me. Jermaine was my best friend growing up. Our momma's were girlfriends, got pregnant together, raised us together. We were all tight."

"What happened?" I asked, surprised Mya was finally opening up to me.

"He fell into a bad crowd. At first it was just young boys thinking they be gangsters. But last year, things changed. He changed. He was the same old Jermaine when it was just the two of us, but he started running for a crew. I begged him to stop, but money talks and he thought he was invincible."

"Sounds like someone I know," I grumbled.

"Jermaine wasn't involved in some high school football rivalry, Felicity. He was running drugs and errands for the kind of people you don't say no to."

"Oh." My cheeks heated.

"I know this rivalry has you all on edge," her expression softened, "but it's not life or death."

"Did Jermaine—"

"Die? No, but he did get taught a lesson after he screwed up, and I..." Mya gulped, her whole demeanor turning dark. "I was collateral."

My eyes grew to saucers. "You mean you were... *hurt?*"

She nodded slowly. "My mama finally told J we were done and she shipped me off to the ass crack of nowhere to finish up senior year. I haven't heard from Jermaine since." My new friend shrugged as if it was nothing, but pain radiated from her.

"You'll be safer here," I said, as if that mattered.

"Safe but not whole. I spent my entire life with Jermaine at my side. Even though I know it's for the best, even though I know I couldn't stand by any longer and watch him ruin his life, it doesn't make it any easier. If I'm not there, who's going to protect him?" A single tear slipped from the corner of Mya's eye, but she quickly swallowed the rest down, and I couldn't help but wonder what she'd been through to have hardened so much.

"He'll be okay," I added.

She gave a little shrug. "It doesn't matter anymore."

But something told me it did. She was lying to herself. Just like I'd been lying to myself. About Jason. About my perfectly mapped out future courtesy of my parents.

"So what's the history between you and Jason?"

"That is a story for another day."

"I'm not going anywhere." Mya gave me a pointed look.

"Jason is ... well, he's complicated. He's always been this asshole, you know? Untouchable. Cold. Cruel. He made Hailee's life hell ever since she moved to Rixon. I never liked him, hated what he stood for, how he treated her."

"What changed?"

"Everything." I smiled sadly. "Everything changed. I started to see glimpses of behind his mask, and I was so sick of being the good girl. Of being the girl always overlooked. And he'd look at me with this intensity... But it was nothing more than a game."

A game I'd lost.

Silence descended over us while we both got lost thinking about the guys in our life we wanted but couldn't have. I grabbed the bottle of liquor and took another mouthful, wanting nothing more than to erase the pit in my stomach.

"You're vibrating," Mya said after a couple of minutes. "It's Hailee."

"Let it go to voicemail." I waved her off, tracing patterns into the fluffy white clouds drifting across the dusky sky. The vibrations finally stopped, only to start again seconds later.

"She's calling again."

"She probably just wants to tell me all about Cameron. He's always doing cute things for her."

"He seems nice."

"He's the best," I sighed dreamily.

"Makes you wonder why a guy like him is friends with a guy like Ja—"

214

"Nope." My head snapped over to Mya. "You promised. No talking about him."

"I know, but—"

"No buts, Mya, please."

"Okay." She held up her hands. "I'm sorry. I didn't mean to upset you."

"I'm not upset, I'm just..."

What was I? Hurt? That was a given. Embarrassed? Dreadfully so. But most of all, I was annoyed at myself. At how easily I'd given in to Jason's charms, when all along I knew it was a game. A game that, once upon a time, I had no intention of playing.

Gah. I was so stupid. Jason had played me hook, line, and sinker. Letting me believe I had the upper hand, that I was calling the shots, only to rip the ground out from beneath me.

"She's still calling," Mya's concern perforated my bubble. "Maybe you should take it?" She handed me my cell.

"Hey, Hails," I tried my best at sounding sober.

"Thank God," my best friend sounded fraught. "I've been trying to call you for the last five minutes."

"Sorry, I was just... downstairs getting a drink." It was almost true.

Mya shot me a bemused look. "What?" I mouthed, shrugging. She rolled her eyes and went back to whatever—or whoever—had her attention on her cell.

"The portraits..." It was only then I realized she sounded upset.

"What happened?" I bolted upright, dread creeping up my spine.

"Thatcher, he... he completely trashed the studio."

"He didn't?" I gasped, my eyes growing to saucers. Hailee had slaved for hours over the Seniors Night project. "How bad is it?"

"Pretty bad." She sniffled and I knew she was probably putting on a brave front. "The guys helped me tidy up most of the mess but at least two portraits are ruined."

"Oh God, Hails, I'm so sorry."

"Yeah, it sucks. Mr. Jalin thinks we can still pull something off in time for tomorrow, but I'm not so sure."

"How's Ja—" His name stuck in my throat.

"He's acting surprisingly cool. But I know he's already plotting revenge. He just has this look, you know?"

Her words sent chills through me.

"Yeah," I whispered.

"Anyway, we're all heading over to Bell's. I think they want to cheer me up."

"That's nice."

"So, you'll meet us there?"

"I..." Mya must have overheard Hailee because she was shaking her head mouthing, "No," at me.

"Sure. Why not. I'm with Mya so it'll be the two of us."

"Okay," Hailee said. "I need a drink. Something strong."

Liquor sloshed in my stomach at her words. I needed water. But she didn't need to know that.

"We'll see you soon." I hung up and downed the rest of the liquor.

"This is a bad idea." Mya glared at me.

"I know." I clambered to my feet, swaying slighting as the cool air wafted around me. "But didn't you suggest I should add crashing a party to my list?" My lip curved deviously.

"This is *not* what I had in mind. I won't say I told you so when things go to shit because it's not my style, but I will say this: I think you should call Hailee back and say you've changed your mind."

"Noted." I gave her a defiant nod.

Mya rolled her eyes. "Fine, come on. Let's go cause some trouble."

"Trouble?" My lips curved into a thin line. "Who said anything about trouble?"

But she was right. I was drunk. And Jason was an asshole.

This couldn't possibly end well.

———

"Hails," I called across the bar. It was crammed for a Thursday, but I figured someone had told everyone that Jason, Asher, and Cameron were here, and like bees to honey they couldn't resist.

Very sexy, very lickable, very bad-for-your-heart honey.

"Are you drunk?" Hailee's eyes narrowed, her forehead crinkling like old lady skin.

"Who, me? Never!" I flashed her a mischievous smirk.

"Do I even want to know?" She cut me out, going straight to Mya.

"She called me." The traitor held up her hands. "I'm merely the wingwoman."

"And the liquor thief," I mouthed.

"Liquor thief?" Hailee looked really worried now. "Did something happen?"

"Happen? What could have possibly happened?"

She grabbed my arm and pulled me close. "Flick, talk to me. This isn't like you."

Lots of things weren't like me nowadays.

I let out an exasperated breath. "I just need to cut loose. Blow off some steam. Have a little fun." I waggled my brows suggestively.

"Are you sure you're okay? Maybe we should—"

"Fee, baby," a voice came from behind Hailee. "Get your cute ass over here."

I went to move around her, but she cut me off. "Flick, talk to me."

"I'm sorry, Hails," pulling her into my arms, I hugged my best friend tight. "I'm so sorry."

"Sorry?" She eased back. "For what?"

"The portraits of course."

Mya shook her head discreetly, but I levelled her with a look that told her this was between me and my best friend.

"You're sure you're okay?" Hails asked.

"Just feeling the pressure of senior year is all. You know how the parentals can get."

"Your mom—"

"Is the last thing I want to talk about. Let's forget all about parents and jerk face football players and just enjoy ourselves."

"You do know it's a school night?"

I shrugged. "One night won't hurt."

"Flick—" But I was already gone; weaving my way through the tables to where Asher and Cameron sat.

"Something you want to tell us?" Asher asked me as I slid into the booth next to him, a goofy grin plastered on my face.

"We're here to take Hailee's mind off things, right?" I arched my brow. "I figured what better way than to let loose a little." My gaze landed on Asher's beer and it was his turn to arch a brow.

"Seriously?" he asked, but I was already snatching his bottle away and bringing it to my lips. "Well, okay then."

"Flick," Hailee and Mya finally caught up to us. "Is that really a good idea?"

"It's on my list remember," I said giving her my best puppy-dog eyes.

"No way, you don't get to pull that crap with me, not tonight."

"Ah, the elusive list." Asher's arm went around my shoulder and I leaned into him slightly. He wasn't Jason, but he smelled good and the weight of his arm around me was nice.

Too nice.

"When do we get to find out what's on the list?"

"Never." I grinned at him.

"Bet I could persuade you to tell me."

"Oh yeah, and how do you plan on doing that?" I was flirting... with Asher and it felt good. He'd moved closer but so had I.

"I'm pretty creative, I'm sure I can think of—"

Someone cleared their throat and when my head lifted over to where the sound had come from, I was met with an icy cold stare that didn't just give me chills, it froze the blood running through my veins.

"What took you so long?" Asher asked, edging away from me but not removing his arm.

"Jerry wanted to shoot the shit." Jason's eyes didn't leave mine for a second but then moved to where Asher's hand rested on my shoulder. If looks could kill, I was pretty sure we'd both be dead.

"Mya, right?" he asked sliding in beside her. "You know who I am?"

"Everyone does." She shrugged, sitting a little straighter. I mirrored her action, desperate to see what he said next. Jason leaned in, his mouth dangerously close to her ear, and whispered something. Her gaze widened and then narrowed.

"Thanks," Mya said coolly," But I couldn't be less interested if I tried." She shot me a reassuring look, but the damage was done. Jason had flirted with her... right in front of me. Acting like it was nothing.

Like *I* was nothing.

Just like you're doing with Asher.

"I'll be back," I said to no one in particular as I hurried from the booth. The room began to spin, but I kept going until I was in the hall leading to the restrooms.

"Felicity, wait up," Mya called.

"I'm fine." I waved her off, staggering toward the girls' bathroom.

"It's okay," she said, gently grabbing my arm. "He's just trying to make you jealous. I would never—"

"I know." I finally met her eyes.

"Look, from one broken girl to another; you can't let him win. You deserve more. You deserve everything he won't give you."

"I know," the repeated words came out a whisper.

"So act like it," Mya said. "Throwing yourself at his best friend is only lowering yourself to his level. You're better than that. You're better than him and if he's going to get another chance with you, make him earn it."

"Earn it... right?" I half-smiled. "And how do I do that again?"

"Make him think you don't need him."

"By *not* flirting with Asher?"

"His friends are definitely off-limits but I didn't say anything about other guys." Mya grinned mischievously. "So what do you say? Shall we get back out there, find us a couple of cute non-football players, and make your guy crazy jealous?"

My guy.

As if Jason would ever allow himself to belong to anyone.

"I guess."

"Not good enough," her expression darkened, "If I can survive leaving my home and the guy I've loved since I can remember, I'm sure you can survive a night of harmless flirting in the name of making Jason Ford realize what he's missing."

"Ssh." My eyes darted around the hall. The last thing I needed was the wrong person overhearing our conversation —or any person for that matter.

"Okay, that's it." A look of determination flashed across her face. "I was ready to drag you out of here screaming and kicking but I can see it's worse than I thought. So one night. You get one night."

"One night?" I had no idea what she was talking about.

"Less talking," Mya grabbed my hand, "And more drinking. We've got work to do."

20

Jason

"Bro, if you clench any harder, your jaw is going to break." Asher chuckled, taking a long pull of his beer.

"She drives me fucking insane," I ground out, watching on as Felicity and some douchebag from the soccer team laughed like they were old friends.

"She's a girl. It's what they do. So you and her—"

"Never going to happen."

Felicity disarmed me. Every moment I spent with her, I felt my walls chip away a little more. I couldn't afford to be defenseless, not in a world that would chew me up and spit me out quicker than you could say, 'Go Raiders'.

I glanced over at him and noticed his eyes fixed in another direction... where Mya was also talking to some guy.

"New girl, huh?"

"What?" His head whipped around.

"You and the new girl?"

"I heard you the first time. I just have no fucking clue what you're talking about."

"Of course you don't." I scrubbed my jaw. He was right. If I clenched any harder there was a good chance I'd need emergency dental work. But ever since she returned from the restroom, Felicity had been talking to anyone and anything with a dick that wasn't me.

"Well, aren't we a pair?" Asher just wouldn't shut the hell up. "You won't admit you want Fee and I can't admit I like the new girl."

"So you do like her? Knew it." I smirked.

"She's... different."

"You're not wrong there." I downed the rest of my beer.

"So you and Fee?"

"There is no me and *Fee*." What kind of fucking nickname was that anyway?

"You know I only pushed you before because I wanted you to pull your head out of your ass, right?"

"I know," I grumbled. When Cam and Asher had suggested we all come to Bell's to take Hailee's mind off the mess at the studio, I hadn't anticipated on it turning into a session with *Dr Phil*. All I wanted to do was drink and forget about Thatcher. Numb the burning desire to ram my fist straight into his face.

I would never forget the look on my step-sister's face when she saw the devastation he'd caused. Part of me didn't want to care, didn't want to feel responsible for it.

But I did care.

I was responsible.

And it was a hard truth to swallow.

Asher slung his arm over my shoulder as we watched the girls flirt shamelessly with the two douchecanoes. "I don't know about you, but I'm not going to just sit here and watch this shit." He gave me a pointed look, one that should have had me following him as he cut across the bar to them. But I didn't go.

I couldn't.

Because going would be admitting something I wasn't ready for.

So I sat there like a fucking statue watching the girl who had completely flipped my world on its head as she batted her eyes and twirled a strand of hair around her finger.

My hand curled around the table. *Walk away*, I silently willed the douche to excuse himself. Because while I couldn't go over there and stake my claim, I wasn't sure I was strong enough to stand by and watch someone else make a move on Felicity. Not when I could still taste her on my lips, remember how good she felt bouncing on my dick, how fucking easy it was to lose myself in her.

"Penny for your thoughts?" Hailee came up beside me.

"Just chillin'."

"I don't think I've ever seen her like this before," she said, guilt ripping through me. "Did something happen between the two of you?"

"Hailee—"

"I know, I know. But I know Felicity and this isn't her."

"I can't be who she needs."

"I want to agree. I want to tell you to walk away and save her the heartache. But something tells me you're both already in too deep for that." My step-sister looked at me as if she could see right through me.

I hated it.

"You have to make a choice, Jason," she went on. "Take a chance on her or let her go. Because this—whatever this is that you're doing right now—it's hurting her. And I won't stand by and let you hurt her, I just won't."

Pressing my lips together, I gave her the silent

treatment. I wasn't having this conversation. Not here. Not now. And most definitely not with her. My step-sister. Hailee fucking Raine; the girl I'd hated for so long I didn't know how to deal with my newfound concern for her.

"Hey," she laid her hand on my arm when I didn't reply, "I'm not your enemy, Jason."

Slowly, I slid my hard gaze to hers. She was right. The lines had been redrawn and somehow, we were on the same side now, but it didn't mean I had to like it, or even accept it.

"Yeah, whatever." I shrugged her off, finding Felicity in the crowd again.

Maybe I couldn't go claim her, but I could sit here and watch. I could make sure that douchecanoe kept his hands firmly to himself.

"I hope you know what you're doing," Hailee let out a heavy sigh. "I'm going to find Cameron."

"You do that," I grunted. "I need another beer." Catching Jerry's eye, I tipped my empty bottle toward him. He gave me a terse nod, disappointment glittering in his eyes. He could judge all he wanted. Jerry didn't know what it was like to shoulder the expectation of an entire town... your classmates... teammates. He didn't know what it was like to want something so bad you had to give up everything else.

No one did.

———

"Are you going to handle that?" Asher asked me sometime later, "Or am I?"

Inhaling a deep breath, I watched Felicity sway on her

feet as she attempted to make Hailee and Mya dance with her. It had been the same for the last hour; Felicity trying to coerce the girls into dancing, them telling her no.

"Shit, she's going to—"

Mya caught her fall.

"Someone should have taken her home an hour ago," I said.

"Hailee tried. Mya too. She's on a mission, man."

Hailee caught my eye across the bar, her expression full of challenge. *Are you going to step up?*

I rubbed my temples, exhaling a shaky breath, holding her steely gaze. It was a bad idea—the fucking worst. But I couldn't take another second of Felicity flashing her bedroom eyes at some random guy or dodging advances from some dickwad who didn't deserve to touch her.

"Here." I thrust my bottle of water at Asher. I'd stopped drinking a while ago, right around the time Felicity began to try—and fail—to turn Bell's into a club.

"Good man." He clapped me on the shoulder. "Just go easy on her, she's wasted."

"Yeah, yeah. See you tomorrow." Our eyes connected and I saw his concern. Asher might have had a crush on the new girl, but he cared about Felicity, and I couldn't decide if I was relieved she had him in her corner, or insanely jealous.

Maybe both.

Hailee and Mya noticed me first. "Oh it's you," Felicity slurred, her body falling limp against me. "I'm not sure I like you anymore." Her hands pressed against my chest, my body vibrating with heat.

Jesus, even her touch was magic.

"House key?" I asked Hailee over her shoulder.

"Pocket I assume."

"If her parents wake up and discover me in their house, you'd better have a damn good cover story ready." I kept my voice low.

"We can take her," Mya said over my shoulder. But I ignored her, slipping my arm around Felicity's waist and tucking her into my side.

"I'll see you back at the house." I gave her a tight nod. Hailee returned it, amusement dancing in her eyes. But it was nothing compared to the curious stares aimed at us as I herded Felicity out of the bar. I was just relieved that Jenna and the gym team were nowhere to be seen because that was one shitshow I didn't need right now.

"Jason?" Felicity murmured.

"Yeah?"

"Whatever you're doing, stop. I hate you." She sucked in a shaky breath. "And I hate myself for ever thinking you could change."

"Yeah, yeah, Giles. You hate me, I get it. Now get your drunk ass in the car."

———

Fifteen minutes, and one emergency stop later, thanks to Felicity thinking she was going to puke all over my car, we were at her house. I dug the key out of her pocket, Felicity cradled in my arms, and unlocked the Giles' front door. She let out a soft moan when her head bumped the wall as I slipped inside.

"Ssh." My fingers traced her cheek. The last thing I

needed was Mr. Giles to find me carrying his daughter upstairs but yet again, all rational thought had flown out of the window.

Thankfully I remembered the layout of her house so I didn't have to worry about walking in on her parents sleeping.

"Okay, let's get you into bed." I dropped her down onto the mattress and began the torturous task of undressing her.

"No," she murmured, trying to fumble with her clothes. "I can do it."

"You can barely talk, let alone get undressed." My fingers peeled hers away. "Let me do it."

"Why?" she murmured, her head rolling like a rag doll. "I'm no one. Nothing."

"You're not nothing." I brushed the hair from her face, fighting a smile, and ignoring the giant lump in my throat.

Couldn't she see she was someone to me? That she was slowly becoming too important, which is why I had to walk away? Before we were both in too deep and things became too messy.

Felicity relented, her body pliant as I peeled her shirt and jeans off before tucking her into bed. Her eyes were closed, her breathing deep and steady. She'd drunk a lot tonight. Too much. And I knew it was my fault for how things went down earlier.

"Fuck," I muttered, stepping away from her before I did something stupid. Something more stupid than sneaking into her house on a Thursday night while her parents slept down the hall.

But I couldn't seem to drag myself away either. Because in that moment, with her passed out on the bed, I could pretend. Pretend she was mine and I was hers. Even if it was only a dream. One I knew could never become reality.

Leaning against her desk, something caught my eye. Reaching for the stack of papers, the familiar crest stared up at me. "What the..." My eyes squinted as I snatched up the college application, a sinking feeling tugging at my stomach.

There was no way.

No way she was applying to Penn, *my* fucking school.

Yet, there it was, staring me in the face, like a giant screw you from the universe.

"J- Jason?" Her soft voice hit me dead in the chest. "Are you still here?"

I wanted to go to her, to reassure her everything was okay. That she was just disorientated from all the liquor in her bloodstream. But I was paralyzed by the papers in my hand. At what they implied.

Penn was Ivy League, one of the best colleges in the country. What were the chances that Felicity also had plans to go there?

Unless... no. She wouldn't pull that kind of crazy shit.

Would she?

Suddenly I couldn't breathe. My chest tightened around my lungs like I'd been sacked by a hulk of a linebacker. Quietly hurrying to the door, I glanced over at her one last time before ducking out of her room and retracing my steps out of the house.

Felicity was never supposed to be a distraction. She was never supposed to bury her way under my skin.

Only she had.

And for as much as I'd resisted, for as much as I knew it was a terrible idea, deep down, I had been coming around to the idea of exploring this thing between us. The inexplicable pull. But I wasn't looking for anything serious. Didn't have time for it. Not now. Not when I went off to Penn next fall. So the idea she would be there, on campus, showing up all over the place... I couldn't deal with that shit.

It was better this way.

Better she hated me.

Better she got all ideas of her and me out of her head.

Felicity deserved Prince Charming, not the misunderstood Knight with a chip on his shoulder and hate in his soul.

The vibrations of my cell pulled me from my thoughts and I dug it out my pocket. "Yeah?"

"Check your snapchat," Grady said. "We've got a problem."

"Do I even want to know?"

"I think you'll want to see this, Cap."

"Fine," my jaw clenched, "thanks for the heads up."

I waited until I was in my car to open up Grady's message and when I did, I knew only one person was responsible.

Thatcher.

21

Felicity

"I THINK I'M IN HELL."

"No," Hailee said, "that's just your hangover talking."

"Don't say that word. It's evil."

"What did your mom say?"

"Oh, I hid out in the bathroom until she left for work. But if I don't make it through the day, I'm ready to fake a stomach flu. So ready."

"That was some impressive display last night." She gave me a pointed look; one I felt all the way down to the pit of my stomach.

"Honestly, I don't know what to say." My cheeks flushed.

"You could start with the truth."

"I'm not sure you're ready to hear it." I peeked over at her while the rest of the student population filed down the hall, moving to their classes.

"Hey," she grabbed my hand, "It's okay. You don't need to protect me. I know you like him. I know he likes you—"

"He doesn't like me, Hails." My head shook side to side. "I'm just a game to him."

A game I could never win.

"So what was last night then?"

"What do you mean?"

"I mean, why did my pig-headed step-brother pretty much carry you out of Bell's—in front of everyone might I add—if you're just a game?"

"He did?"

I had hazy memories of being wrapped in his arms but I hadn't considered what it meant. That he'd done it in front of other people. Our classmates. Hailee was staring at me like she expected an answer, so I said, "Because he's trying to win student of the year? I don't know."

"God, you're dense sometimes. He likes you. It's written all over his face every time he looks at you."

"Hails, I don't know what you think you know, but Jason doesn't like me." At least, not in the way I wanted him to.

"Come to the Seniors Night thing tonight."

"I can't. It's family and friends of the team only."

"Well I'm a guest of honor *and* I'm family. You can be my plus one."

"I don't think it's a good idea."

"Look," Hailee pulled me closer to the locker bank. "Jason is as stubborn as he is good at football. But he's different with you. I can't explain it, but ever since New York, he's been different. Come tonight, be there for him. And maybe after, the two of you can talk."

"You really think it's a good idea? He made it seem like..." My voice trailed off before I revealed too much.

Everything was so confusing. He said one thing but was constantly doing another. And despite my head knowing it was better—easier—to walk away, my heart didn't want that.

"Don't you at least want to know where you stand?"

"I guess..."

"So come."

"Fine, I'll come." I was going to the game anyway and even if Jason didn't want me there, Hailee, Asher, and Cameron would make me feel welcome.

Butterflies tickled my insides. I didn't want to get my hopes up again, not where Jason was concerned. But I had hazy memories of last night. Of him undressing me and tucking me in. Of his fingers tracing my face as if I was the most precious thing in the world. He could be so gentle and tactile and warm with me. A stark contrast to the cold icy version everyone else got to see.

"Don't look so worried." Hailee squeezed my hand, offering me a reassuring smile.

But this was Jason she was talking about.

Which meant I didn't need to be worried.

I needed to be terrified.

———

I should have known the night was doomed when the Raiders lost. The entire game had been like pulling teeth. We scored a touchdown. They got one back. We sacked their QB, they took down ours even harder. Jason was off his game, so much so we'd all witnessed Coach Hasson chew him out on the sideline more than once. It was a shitshow and everyone felt the tension on the field.

By the time we arrived at the Hassons', nervous energy coursed through my veins.

"Relax," Hailee said. "It's going to be fine."

"Did you watch the same game I did?" I asked incredulously. "We practically got our asses handed to us."

"It was one game and it isn't like they needed the win or anything."

"Hails, you have so much still to learn."

She chuckled, cutting the engine. "I know I talked you into coming tonight for Jason; but confession time, I partly did it for me."

"Hails, he's seen the portrait. He knows how good you are."

"I know but this is different." Her voice cracked. "It's like baring myself to everyone, and that terrifies me."

I twisted around to her. "You are so talented, babe. You have nothing to be worried about. Mr. Jalin managed to fix the damaged portraits and everyone is going to love them. *All* of them. This is your time to shine, Hails."

She gave me a slight nod, but I could see the fear in her eyes. Reaching over, I squeezed her hand. "You've got this."

"*We've* got this." Her smile grew.

"Ride or die."

"Ride or die." Hailee gave me a small nod, before we got out of the car and made our way around the side of the house. The team were already there, their expressions somber, the mood still tense.

"Ah, Miss Raine," Coach Hasson made his way over. "Just the person I wanted to see."

"Hi, Coach, tough game."

"Hmm." His lips pressed into a thin line. "We're not going to dwell on that tonight. We're here to celebrate our seniors and your talent. Mr. Jalin informed me of the *incident.*" The way he said it suggested he knew there was more to it than what he'd been told.

"Unfortunate to have happened the day before the presentation," he added.

Hailee tensed but kept her expression neutral. "These things happen. I'm just relieved Mr. Jalin had the foresight to take photographs of them."

"Indeed. Now if I could borrow you for a quick moment to run through the plan."

"Hmm, sure." Hailee looked to me and I nodded.

"Go, I'll be fine." Glancing around the Hassons' yard, I spotted Asher and Cameron with their parents. The rest of the players were standing with their families.

But not Jason.

He was sat in a chair on the edge of the gathering, drinking a beer. Jenna Jarvis sat proudly on his lap, like the Queen Bitch she was. A potent mix of anger and jealousy skittered up my spine when her eyes lifted to mine and glittered with victory.

"Flick, what's... Oh." Hailee reappeared. "What the hell is he playing at? She isn't even supposed to be here, it's a closed event," she mumbled beneath her breath.

"It's fine," I steeled myself, ignoring the ache in my chest. "Let's go get our seats."

"You're sure?"

"I'm here now, aren't I?" And it wasn't like seeing Jenna all over Jason was new to me. I'd been there and done that enough times, I didn't just own the t-shirt, I had that crap trademarked.

I trailed after Hailee, keeping my eyes ahead. If Jason noticed me, he didn't let it be known. Asher on the other hand, beamed at me as we approached the long table. They had been arranged in a giant U shape with the lectern at the front surrounded by Hailee's portraits behind in a sweeping arc, and rows behind for the rest of the guests.

"Fee, baby, this is a surprise," Asher said quietly, his gaze moving past me, probably to Jason.

"Hailee invited me as her plus one."

"Screw that, you can be my plus one. Come on." He patted the seat beside him.

"Isn't someone sitting there?"

"You." He smiled and some of my nerves subsided.

"Hey, Felicity," Cameron added once I was seated. "How are you?"

"I'm good. Sorry for gate-crashing." I gave him a tight smile.

"Never. You're Hailee's best friend which makes you one of us. Besides I think Mrs. Hasson got carried away with all the food. The more the merrier."

"Thanks." Before I could stop myself, I'd lifted my gaze over to where Jason and Jenna sat. He looked indifferent, barely touching her, but she was wrapped around him, hands splayed on his chest, her body turned into him slightly, sending a clear signal to everyone—*to me*—that tonight, Jason belonged to her.

"He's pissed we lost," Cameron said.

"Nah, he's pissed his head wasn't in it and that's *why* we lost."

"Ash," Cam warned.

"He needs to figure his shit out before the play-offs or we can kiss State goodbye."

"What?" I asked, the three of them staring at me.

"You should talk to him." That was Asher.

"She's going to, right, Flick?" Hailee added. "After the presentation."

"I, uh, I guess." My eyes found him again only this time he was staring back. His eyes narrowed and dark. Anger rippled off him, palpable even from our position all the way across the yard.

"Ignore her." Asher leaned in.

"Easy for you to say." I tried to give him an easy smile, but I knew it probably looked strained.

"He doesn't want her. She's just convenient. Or a bad habit. Yeah, she's a bad habit." His lip kicked up.

"You know what they say about bad habits, right?" I said. "They're hard to break." My stomach sank.

"Don't give up on our guy yet. I don't know what happened today but something's eating at him." I gave him a pointed look and he added, "More than usual."

"You really want me to do this?" The words flew out of my mouth. "Me and Jason?"

Asher sucked in a harsh breath, his eyes shuttering. But when they opened again, he was looking at me with nothing but understanding. "Did I wish for a second that things could be different? That maybe I'd caught your eye first? Hell yeah, I do." He swallowed thickly. "But you can't help who you fall for and I always knew it was you and him."

"I'm not sure there's a me and him, Asher."

"That's because Jason doesn't know how to let people in. He doesn't know how to trust anyone. But you're changing him, Fee, baby. Which is why you can't give up on him yet. He might not realize it yet, but he needs you. And something tells me, you need him too."

"I..." The words died on my lips. "You're a good friend, Asher Bennet. He's lucky to have you."

"You've got me too." He grinned. "No matter what happens, I'll always be here for you."

"That means a lot. You're going to make some girl very happy one day."

"I'm not so sure about that." He chuckled, but it came out strangled. "Here we go."

I followed Asher's line of sight to where Coach Hasson was standing next to the lectern. Jason had finally moved to an empty seat at the table. Of course it had to be right opposite me. His hard gaze burned into the side of my face as I tried to concentrate on Coach Hasson.

"Okay, okay, settle down." He waited for silence to fall over the yard. "Tonight we celebrate our seniors. Their commitment and dedication, their leadership and talent. But it isn't only a celebration of the past, it's a celebration of the future. Of the young men you're becoming and the doors that await you. I have a whole other speech somewhere," he pretended to check his pockets, "But for now, I'm going to hand it over to a man who knows all about what it takes to be the best. Kent Ford."

Hailee stiffened beside me and I leaned in. "Did you know about this?"

"He never said a word," she whispered.

"Maybe that's why he was off his game." It would make sense. Everyone knew there was no love lost between Jason and his father, despite the united front Mr. Ford liked to present to everyone.

Jason's dad moved to the lectern, brushing down the lapels of his dinner jacket. He looked good, much like an older Jason. Same unruly brown hair, same dark intense eyes. But age had mellowed him, or maybe that was Hailee's mom. Either way, he looked happy. He looked like a man content with life. A man in love.

I found Hailee's mom in the outer row of seats. She beamed at her husband, radiating happiness. "Look at your mom," I said quietly.

"I'd rather not," Hailee groaned.

"Hey." I took her hand under the table. "She's happy. They're happy. I know she hurt you, but you can't help who you fall in love with." God, I sounded like Mya and Asher. I knew Hailee carried a lot of resentment toward her mom and the lies she'd told. But if I'd learned anything over the last few weeks, it was that sometimes your head and heart went to war and it wasn't always your head that came out the winner.

It was so easy to judge, but it wasn't until you were in that situation, trying to do the right thing, that you realized just how powerful the heart was. I mean, here I was, completely aware that Jason didn't want me, not the way I wanted him, but I was willing to put myself on the line one more time to try to reach him. To try to show him that sometimes you had to take a risk.

"Hey," Hailee nudged my shoulder, "Are you okay?"

"Yeah." I flashed her a weak smile. "I'm fine." The lie was so regular now, it rolled off my tongue with ease. Even if every time the two little words spilled from my lips, it killed another little piece of my heart.

22

Jason

I WANTED TO RUN. The urge to get up and walk away from my old man, from Coach, my teammates, and best friends, Hailee, even Felicity, coursed through me. Like deadly poison, it burned, eating away at my soul.

The last thing I wanted to do was sit here and listen to Kent Ford spout shit about hard work and sacrifice and family. Because he was a liar. Sure he'd loved the game, and he was a damn good player back in the day, one of the best, but he didn't know what it meant to make sacrifices. He was a have-your-cake-and-eat-it kind of guy, and like so many players before him, I suspected he loved what the game could do for him more than the game itself.

But still, I didn't move.

People thought I was cold, that I didn't care. Sometimes I wondered if I cared too damn much. I just didn't let people see it.

"Welcome to Seniors Night," his strong voice carried across the Hasson's yard, "The final home game of any season always holds a special place in my heart, but tonight was something else. Tonight, I watched my son continue the Ford legacy in Raider history. It's just a shame his game was off, but what player doesn't have his ups and downs." He

241

gave the crowd an easy smile, even earned a laugh or two. But I wasn't laughing. I wasn't even smiling. Because I knew it wasn't a joke.

He and Coach were pissed we didn't get the win and they weren't the only ones, My old man was telling me in front of everyone I hadn't been good enough tonight and it fucking burned. So much so, part of me wished I'd have gotten up at his wedding and talked about his failure as a father and husband just to see how he fucking liked it.

The feeling of never quite being good enough, even though you thought you gave your all.

But the truth was my head wasn't in it tonight. Too consumed with Thatcher's latest threat. With Felicity's sea-green gaze every time she'd looked my way at school. I couldn't tell anyone about Thatcher though. Until I figured out what the fuck to do, I had to lie and pretend everything was fine.

Everything was not fucking fine.

It was falling to shit around me. The pieces of my carefully constructed world falling apart all because I couldn't keep my dick in my pants and out of the girl who made me fucking crazy.

"I know all about the sacrifice and dedication; the blood, sweat, and tears that go into winning a State Championship," Dad flashed his championship ring to his enthralled audience, "that's why I know you'll bring it home this season. Because you're fighters. Because you're the best. Because you're Raiders. And Raiders—"

"Never quit," rang out around me, reverberating through me, stoking a fire in my soul. Even though I was pissed, even though this was the last place on Earth I wanted to be right now, it didn't matter. Football was in my blood, part of my DNA, and when my teammates and our supporters cheered our name, it called to something inside me.

My eyes found Felicity across the yard. She was watching me, a faint smile gracing her lips. Why she was here I had no fucking idea, but deep down, I wanted to believe she came for me. Not that I could ever tell her that.

"Okay, okay, I'm going to wrap this up so we can get to the good stuff."

"Yeah, Mrs. H's chicken wings," someone yelled, earning him a round of hoots and hollers.

Dad grabbed his drink off the lectern and raised it high. "To the seniors of 2019. May your futures be filled with opportunity, success, and most of all... football."

The place erupted, everyone cheering for the man I hated so much I could barely look at him. It probably wasn't healthy, the amount of resentment and bitterness I carried around with me, but I didn't know how to let go.

I didn't know how to forgive him.

Parents were supposed to set the standard. They were supposed to help shape us into the adults we would one day become. Which meant I could look forward to becoming a cheating son of a bitch who cared more about looking good in front of his town, and getting his dick wet, than his family.

The man of the moment approached me. "Jason," he stuck out his hand. "I'm proud of you, Son. So damn proud."

I stared at his hand, wishing I could leave him hanging.

But everyone was watching, waiting to see the special moment between father and son.

"Thanks," I choked out, grabbing his hand and shaking.

His eyes held so many apologies, but it was too little too late. I wasn't sure we'd ever find our way back to one another. Not after everything.

Coach chose that exact moment to intervene and I breathed a sigh of relief as Dad took his seat. "Thank you, Kent," he said, offering a nod of appreciation. "I know it means a lot to the team to have you here. You're a true inspiration to the guys and proof that dreams can come true.

"Now we move onto the presentation. Every year, I like to give each of my seniors a token gift to remember their time at Rixon High. To remind them where they came from. This year, we've done something a little different. In an effort to work across departments, I approached Mr. Jalin, our arts director, about an exciting opportunity for one of his students. Miss Raine, if you'd like to come up here."

I watched from across the way as Hailee stood up, cheeks flushed and eyes wide, and walked toward the coach.

"What Miss Raine has created for this year's presentation is nothing other than incredible. And I hope you'll join me in applauding her talent. Seniors of 2019, we present your senior year portraits." He and Hailee began uncovering each portrait. The crowd hushed into awed silence. Even I couldn't deny the impact of the nine paintings side by side.

"I think you'll agree they really are something special."

"Thank you," my step-sister said, barely able to look at her audience.

One by one, Coach called up the seniors, presenting them with their portrait. Hailee posed for photos, graciously accepting a chaste kiss on the cheek from each of them, all except Asher who picked her up and twirled her around, and Cam who pulled her into his arms and kissed the crap out of her, audience be damned.

"And last but by no means least, our quarterback and captain, Jason Ford."

The crowd's applause faded into white noise as I got up and moved toward Hailee. She was smiling at me with such uncertainty, I felt like a complete shit. But when I reached her and she wrapped her arms around me, it was my turn to choke. Hailee didn't speak, she didn't need to. That one gesture spoke volumes.

When she pulled away, her smile was no longer uncertain but full of understanding. It only twisted the knife deeper. I'd been such a dick to her: making her life hell ever since she arrived in Rixon. Yet, here she was forgiving me for everything as if it was the simplest thing in the world.

"I hope you like it," she said taking the framed photo down from the easel and presenting it to me.

I'd seen the portrait yesterday, but it had been ruined with red and white paint splashes.

"Well, Son," Coach said, filling the awkward silence. "What do you think?"

"I..." The words lodged in my throat along with the giant fucking lump that had been there for the last couple of minutes.

245

"I think you've stunned him into silence."

Hailee's brows furrowed. "Are you okay?" she whispered.

"It's good, really good," I managed to choke out. "Thanks."

"Okay, now we've got all the formalities out of the way," Coach declared, "let's eat."

Mrs. Hasson and some of the other player's moms began uncovering all the food laid out on a long table at the edge of the gazebo. Most of the guys wasted no time joining the line. But Cam and Asher came over to us. "You've been holding out on us, Hails," Ash said.

"You saw them yesterday."

"No, I saw the mess Thatcher made." I winced at the mention of his name. "You're super talented and I don't know about these two goons, but I'll be hanging mine above my bed."

"Thanks, I think," she chuckled.

"Where's Fee?" he asked.

"She's hmm," Hailee's eyes flicked to mine, "around."

Code for: she didn't know if she should come over here.

My chest tightened.

"Are you hungry?" Cam asked her.

"I could eat." Hailee blushed, and I groaned.

"Seriously, can you two at least pretend to be talking about food." Shouldering past him, I headed for the line, only to be intercepted by Felicity.

"Hi," she said, her smile not quite reaching her eyes.

"Hey."

She winced at my cool tone, but shook it off maintaining eye contact. "I just wanted to say congratulations."

"Thanks." I went to move around her, needing to get away, but she grabbed my arm. "I was hoping we could talk, later, maybe?"

"There's nothing to say."

Hurt flashed across her face. "Jason, please, I came tonight for—"

"Hey, Cap, you gotta try this," Grady yelled, and I took the opportunity to slip away. He shoved a sophomore out the way to make room for me and handed me a plate. "What was all that about?" He tipped his head to where Felicity was still standing, watching us.

"Nothing."

"So last night was..."

"Nothing." I shrugged.

"Doesn't look like nothing from where I'm standing. It looks like you got yourself a stage five clinger."

"She's Hailee's best friend," I deadpanned.

"Never shit where you eat, man." He slung his arm around my shoulder.

"It isn't like that."

"For you, maybe, but she's got that look." He glanced back again but I didn't look, not this time. "And we both know you don't need that shit right now."

"Do me a favor, Grady?"

"Yeah?"

"Shut the fuck up."

His expression fell. "Sorry, man, I'm just yanking your chain." We moved up the line, loading our plates with barbecue. "Did you decide how to deal with the Thatcher problem yet?"

Shaking my head, I glared at him. Hard.

"Shit, my bad. I'm just concerned he's going to lure you into doing something real fucking stupid."

"Why don't you worry about you and leave Thatcher to me, yeah?"

"Sure, Jase, I just—"

"Let. It. Go," I hissed.

"Whatever you say, man." He held up his hands. "This barbecue looks good."

"So let's eat."

And forget all about Felicity and Thatcher.

———

After everyone had stuffed their faces, we all settled down again. The clink of Coach's fork against his glass ushered everyone into silence. I pulled at the collar of my shirt. It felt like it was getting tighter by the second, squeezing the air from my lungs and making it difficult to breathe.

"You've got this," Cam mouthed at me.

"Now that you've all filled your bellies, I'm going to handover to Jason. Before I do though, I wanted to take this opportunity to say a few words about this young man."

Silently groaning, I buried my face in my hands.

"Jason Ford came to me an angry, hot-headed young man. He pushed every boundary I set, broke every record before him, and worked harder than any other player I've ever had the pleasure of working with. But with great talent comes great responsibility, and four years ago, if someone asked me if Jason had what it took to be QB One, I would have had to think about it.

"You see being quarterback requires leadership; it

requires a player who understands the importance of teamwork, someone who calls the plays but might not always get the glory in the end zone. Jason had talent in spades. Still does. In fact, I'd go out on a limb and say I've never seen a senior player command the field the way Jason does." His eyes landed on me and he gave me a nod of encouragement. "But talent is only part of it. If you want to go all the way, you have to keep your eye on the prize. You have to forget all the other crap off field, the rivalries and drama, the girls and parties. You have to leave all that at the door and give one hundred and ten percent every time you step out on the field. Jason isn't perfect and he still has a way to go, but if anyone can go all the way, it's him. Which is why I want to present Jason Ford the Rixon High School 2019 MVP *and* Coach's Player of the Year Award. It has been my pleasure watching you grow into the player you are today, Son. Now you go out there and make Rixon proud."

His compliment swirled around me, weighing heavily on my shoulders as I went to him, accepting his firm handshake and the two trophies. But Coach went one step further, pulling me into a hug. "I'm proud of you, Kid. Real damn proud. Just don't forget where you came from when you go off and dominate the NCAA."

"Thanks, Coach." I stepped up to the lectern, adjusting the mic. "Hey everyone, I'm Jason."

A few snickers rang out and Grady flipped me off.

Fucker.

"Coach asked me to say a few words, but public speaking isn't exactly my forte. I prefer kicking ass on the field."

The guys burst into hoots and hollers and Coach had to step in to quiet them down.

"Being QB One for the last four years has been a privilege. Football is my life. It's all I've ever wanted to do. All I can ever imagine doing. And I'm grateful to have had the opportunity to work with Coach and his team.

"But Coach is right; being a Raider is more than just football, it's family, and I love you guys like brothers. Well, most of you; the jury is still out on Mackey." I smirked at the sophomore watching me with hunger in his eyes. Hunger I remembered. He wanted to be me one day. To be standing here addressing his teammates, his brothers. But he was too distracted by the girls and parties and the god-like worship we received every time we walked the halls at school.

"Coach talked a lot about sacrifices." My eyes found Felicity. "But when you want something bad enough, when it's all you can see, there isn't any price too high to pay. Mark my words Raiders, one day, it'll be my name in the Hall of Fame. One day, you'll all get to say you knew an NFL legend."

It sounded arrogant; a pipe dream that might never come true. But I didn't work in what ifs and maybes, I worked in hard facts. And I was going all the way.

No matter the sacrifice.

———

"Here he is, the man of the hour." Dad grabbed my shoulder and pulled me into his side. "We're proud of you, Son, real damn proud."

I smiled tightly at the group of men gathered around my old man.

"Must be something, Kent, watching your kid follow in your footsteps."

"It's something all right." His hand tightened. "The question is though, does he have what it takes to go all the way?" It came out lighthearted but I didn't miss the lingering bitterness.

"Coach seems to think so, and I for one, am rooting for you, Jason." Grady's dad chimed in, tipping his beer in my direction. I gave him a small nod of appreciation.

"He just needs to learn to rein in his emotions. Take tonight for example..."

I tuned out, my teeth grinding behind my lips. I didn't want to hear about how I messed up or how I threw away the team's perfect season.

"Excuse me," I said, shucking out of his grip. "But tonight is supposed to be a celebration, so I'm going to do just that, celebrate." Stalking away, I didn't expect to hear him call my name.

"Jason." I turned slowly, narrowing my eyes on my old man. "I was just shooting the shit with the guys, you know how it is."

"Whatever," I grumbled.

"You're annoyed."

"I'm not annoyed, I'm just... It doesn't matter." I let out an exasperated breath.

"I think it does." His audience had dispersed, leaving the two of us and a boat load of shit I didn't want to deal with.

"You know," he stepped closer, hands jammed deep in

his pockets, "I remember what it was like to be young. To have the world at your feet. To think you're invincible." Pain flashed in his eyes. "But we're all human, Jason. We all make mistakes."

"You are such a fucking hypocrite," I spat the words. "Standing up there tonight to talk about sacrifice and dedication and what it means to be a team."

"Watch your tone, Son," he said coolly, glancing around to make sure no one had overheard me. Because God forbid someone actually saw the real us, the father and son behind the fake smiles and state records. "I know you're still upset over me and Denise—"

"Upset? Is that what you think? That I'm upset about you and Denise?" Bitter laughter rumbled in my chest. "I'm not upset about you and Denise; you two deserve each other. You have no fucking idea what it's been like growing up in your shadow, a man respected and revered by an entire town. Knowing that without you, I probably wouldn't be where I am today, but at the same time, knowing I'm *who* I am because of you. Cold. Callous... Cruel."

"Jason, I—"

"Save it, Dad," I ground out. "You have everything you need now, right? You have Denise and a son you can live vicariously through. And me? I've got football. At least I know the game will never disappoint me."

23

Felicity

"Have you seen Jason?" were the first words out of Hailee's mouth as she hurried over to us.

"No, we've been here the whole time," Asher said.

"Crap, he and his dad got into it and Jason stormed off. He looked pretty pissed. I was going to go after him but someone stopped me to talk about the paintings."

"Fuck," Cam grumbled, pulling Hailee onto his lap. "This is the last thing we need."

"You should go after him," Asher said to me while I obsessed over how his best friend held my best friend. Intimately. Tenderly. As if she was the most precious thing in the whole world.

"I don't know," I said, dejection crawling up my throat like a cockroach, "he didn't seem pleased to see me earlier." In fact he'd acted like seeing me was the last thing he wanted. "Maybe I should just leave."

"Ride or die, remember?" Hailee said, her eyes pleading with me. "At least try to talk to him. He looked really upset."

My heart ached for Jason and I wanted to go after him, I did, but I wasn't sure my heart would survive another rejection.

"He needs you, Fee." Asher gave me a half-smile. "Besides, if you don't go after him, one of us has to and I'm sure he'd rather see a pretty face than Cam's ugly mug."

"Fine, I'll go." I stood up. "Any ideas where I should try to look?" Coach Hasson's place was like a maze.

"Try the boat shed or down by the river."

"Okay, wish me luck."

The three of them smiled. "Good luck," Hailee said. "And don't take no for an answer."

On shaky legs, I crossed the Hasson's yard, taking the path away from the main patio down to the river. It was dark out, nothing but the silvery hue of the moon lighting the way.

"Jason?" I whisper-hissed. "Are you down here?"

Met with nothing but silence, I kept walking, bypassing the boat shed. There was no one down here. I dropped down onto a rickety bench, watching the river shimmer and dance in the distance.

All night Jason had avoided me. But despite his cold shoulder, Hailee was right. I needed closure. I needed to know once and for all where I stood. Whether I'd dreamed up the growing connection between us. Because I knew what I felt, and Jason liked me. He just didn't know how to handle it.

The seconds ticked by, the air like cold fingers ghosting over my face and neck. Shucking into my jacket, I stood up, ready to admit defeat and return to my friends when I heard a rustle. "Jason?" I called.

"You shouldn't be down here," he said from the shadows. I stepped closer, the sliver of moonlight bouncing off his hard profile, making him look even more intimidating than usual.

"I came to see if you're okay. Hailee said she saw you arguing with your dad."

"Hailee needs to learn to mind her own fucking business." His tone matched his eyes.

Cold.

Guarded.

Completely devoid of emotion, despite the anger rippling off him in dark waves.

A shiver skittered along my spine and I hugged myself tight. "Jason, come on, talk to me, please."

"And say what? I thought you got the memo yesterday."

"So that's it?" I stuffed down the sting of his harsh words. "You're just going to walk away and pretend this, *us*, is nothing."

"It *is* nothing," he ground out. "I don't know what else I can do to make you see that. You said it yourself, Giles; you were nothing more than a game. A game I won, and now I'm done with you."

Tears pricked the corners of my eyes, but I would not cry, not in front of him. He didn't deserve my tears.

Not a single one.

"Why are doing this? Why are you being so cruel? You care, Jason," I said, steeling myself, "I know you do. You're just scared. Scared of letting yourself feel something. Well, newsflash, I'm scared too. But I'm here. I'm willing to take a risk on you. On us." My chest heaved with the weight of the words but Jason looked unaffected.

Indifferent.

"There is no us." His sharp words made me flinch. "Why can't you just accept that?"

"Because I don't believe you. Last night—"

"You think last night meant something?" He sneered, the harshness of his stare like a hundred tiny daggers cutting into my skin. "I was doing Hailee a favor and saving everyone anymore embarrassment. You were a fucking mess."

The words crashed over me, making my heart lurch into my throat. Blood pounded between my ears.

A fucking mess.

He hadn't saved me because he cared... he'd saved me out of pity.

"God, I'm stupid." *So stupid.* "I let them all convince me you liked me, that you needed me. But you don't need anyone."

People with no hearts didn't have room to care about others let alone *need* them.

"Finally figured it out, huh?" He scratched his jaw absentmindedly.

"I hope you find what you're looking for, Jason," I said with nothing but quiet confidence. I might have been breaking inside, but he wouldn't see me crumble.

Jason didn't say anything as I turned and started walking away. But then his voice perforated the heavy silence. "Oh and Giles..."

"Yes?" I snapped over my shoulder, barely hanging on by a thread.

"You might want to think about applying to another school. Penn isn't big enough for the both of us and I don't know what crap you're trying to pull but I don't want you there."

My lips parted on a pained gasp. I wanted to argue, to tell him me applying for UPenn had nothing to do with him and everything to do with my parents, *my* future, but a figure burst from the shadows.

"Hey, baby," Jenna said, sidling up to Jason as if I wasn't standing right there with tears in my eyes. "Miss me? Oh, hey, Felicity, I didn't see you there."

She saw me all right.

She just got great satisfaction over watching the blood drain from my face.

"You might want to run along now, unless you want to see the show, if you know what I mean." She smirked before pressing her lips to Jason's, making sure I got a front row seat.

He wasn't invested in it; he wasn't touching her or kissing her back. He was watching me. His hard eyes silently daring me to call him out.

It took everything I had not to jump on her back and tear her away from the guy who had unknowingly stolen my heart.

No, that wasn't right. He hadn't stolen it. I'd handed it over willingly. Secretly hoping it was enough.

That *I* was enough.

When all along, I knew wasn't.

Jason Ford was the devil in sheep's clothing and I was nothing more than a game wrapped up in a pretty package.

Something to pass the time.

A game he'd already grown tired of.

"I never had you down as a voyeur," Jenna's voice snapped me from my morose reverie. "But if you want to watch, maybe you'll learn a thing or two." She snickered into Jason's shoulder.

Damn that hurt. I didn't want to believe he'd told her that I'd given up my v-card to him, but at this point, anything was possible. Because I didn't know Jason.

Maybe I never had.

"You're welcome to him." I barely managed to choke out the words.

Just for a brief moment I thought I saw a flash of regret in Jason's gaze, but then he captured Jenna's mouth and closed his eyes, losing himself in the kiss, showing me he hadn't changed at all. He was still the cold-hearted bastard he'd always claimed to be. Only it was too late. He'd reeled me and then spat me out, not caring that he'd smashed my heart into a thousand pieces.

Pieces I knew would never heal right.

Somehow, despite the gaping hole in my chest, I managed to turn and walk away from them with my head held high.

From Jason.

For what I promised myself would be the final time.

———

"This is nice," Mya said as we ate cookies and ice cream and watched cheesy movies. It had been Hailee's idea after the disastrous end to last night.

I hadn't even stopped to tell them I was leaving, I just needed to be far, far away from Jason and his poisonous words.

"I can't remember the last time I had a girls' night."

"Pre-Cameron we did this a lot. Although most of our sleepovers ended up with Hailee plotting revenge on Jason."

"Hey," Hailee said, "We still hang out. You make it sound like now I have Cameron, I'm not around."

"I'm joking, Hails. I'm happy for you, I am. After everything they put you through, you deserve all the happiness."

"Your brother sounds like a grade-A asshole." Mya's eyes crinkled.

"My *step*-brother is an asshole. But he's different lately." Her gaze flicked to mine.

"Yeah, well, different or not," I sighed, "he's still a cold-hearted bastard."

Mya and Hailee both looked at me with sympathy in their eyes. "Please don't do that; don't look at me like he ripped out my heart and trampled all over it. I wanted closure and I got it."

"Yeah, but I still can't believe he did that. And with Jenna, of all people."

"Really, Hails? Because this is Jason we're talking about. He's disappointed me at every turn, why should last night have been any different?"

"I just thought that this time he would..." She swallowed the words.

"I know," I said quietly, "me too."

Although I knew exactly who Jason Ford was, part of me had still foolishly hoped he had changed. That I'd changed him. I had managed to convince myself I was different to the Jenna Jarvis' of the world when all along I was exactly the same.

It was a bitter pill to swallow. But at least I'd seen his true colors once and for all. I could move on knowing I'd tried to smash through Jason's steel walls. Even if it did suck that I failed.

"If you ask me, you're better off without him. Jason Ford loves only two things: himself and football."

"You're not wrong there." Hailee leaned over to high five Mya.

"Anyway, enough boy talk. I thought this was supposed to be girls' night. What are your plans for after high school, Mya?"

"Ooh straight into the heavy stuff, I like it." She crossed her legs in front of her and pushed her spiral curls from her face. "I always wanted to do something to help people, you know. Like drugs counselling or a school guidance counsellor."

"Psych major?" I asked.

"Maybe, or education. I haven't really narrowed it down, but I'm applying to Montclair State and Michigan. I want to go out of state but not too far away."

"Me and Cameron are headed to Michigan."

"No way."

Hails nodded. "He was supposed to go to UPenn with Jason, but—"

"But he realized he couldn't bear to be apart from Hailee and applied to Michigan instead." The way my best friend blushed at my words was so darn cute.

"Wow, that's... serious."

Hailee shrugged. "I couldn't imagine going without him."

"I miss that," Mya sighed. "Having someone to make

plans with. What about you, Flick? Given anymore thought to your plans?"

"I thought the plan was to study business." Hailee frowned at me.

"It was... I mean, it is."

"But..."

"But I might be having teeny tiny second thoughts."

"Oh shit, do your parents know?"

"What do you think?" My eyes rolled dramatically.

"I thought you were happy applying to UPenn and following in their footsteps?"

"I mean, yeah, I was. It's always been the plan. Instilled in me from day one. But now, now I'm not so sure it's what I want."

Jason's cruel words from last night filled my head. He thought I was applying to UPenn because it was where he was going, but it couldn't be further from the truth. I was applying because it was expected. Because my parents wanted me to follow in their footsteps and continue their legacy. The exciting world of white-collar employment. And until recently, I had been all too happy to make them happy.

"You never said anything," Hailee sounded dejected, her expression crestfallen.

"You know me, Hails," I gave her a tight smile, "I'm a people pleaser, not a rulebreaker." Until Jason. I left that strictly to Hailee and her vendetta against the guys.

"But this is your future. You can't do something just because your parents want you to."

"I know." It had just taken me a while, and a little push from Mya, to find the courage to pursue my own path.

"So what are you going to do?"

That was the million-dollar question. I could pursue business at UPenn and make my parents happy or I could go after what I wanted. Chase my dreams.

The only problem was; I still didn't know what they were.

"I'm going to work on my list."

"Your list?" Hailee groaned. "Hasn't that already caused enough trouble?"

"Actually, Mya helped me rethink a few things. I think it could be good for me to work toward completing it, and who knows, maybe I'll figure out exactly what I want to do with my life."

"Now that sounds like a plan I can get on board with." Mya grinned, her eyes sparkling with eagerness, as if I was a project she just couldn't wait to get her hands on.

"You know I've got your back, whatever you decide," Hailee added. "Just because I have Cameron now, doesn't mean I'm not one-hundred percent here for you."

"Thank you. But first things first..." I dug my cell out of my pocket and found Jason's number.

"Is that what I think it is?" Hailee craned her neck to get a better look.

"Yep. I need to draw a line under Jason and his games." My thumb hovered over the 'delete' button. Drawing in a deep breath, I closed my eyes, and pressed it.

"To new beginnings." Mya declared, raising her soda in the air.

"New beginnings," I echoed, clinking my glass against hers.

But the sound of Hailee clearing her throat cut through

our soft laughter. "Now are you going to fess up about what *really* happened between the two of you?"

Well, damn.

"Seriously? You want to know? I figured you were mentally scarred from New York."

"I don't want to know the graphic details, but yeah, I want to know." She gave me a tentative smile. "After all, I need to know how badly I need to get him back for hurting you." Her mouth curved into a devious smirk and soon the three of us were falling around my bedroom floor in fits of laughter.

And the ache in my heart faded.

Just a little bit.

24

Jason

"Are you going to drill daggers into my head all morning?" I finally dragged my eyes to Hailee's, and she clucked her tongue in disgust. "Whatever's on your mind, just spit it out so I can finish my breakfast in peace." I all but growled the words.

"I'm just wondering what made you this way. I know you have Daddy issues, but join the fucking club. Most of us have parent issues. Which makes me think there must be something else. A reason you're so... so cruel."

"I don't have to answer to you." My eyes narrowed.

"You're right, you don't. But I'm asking anyway." Hailee glared right back. "Why? Why did you do that to her?"

"Am I supposed to know what the fuck you're talking about?"

Her nostrils flared, a streak of pink coloring each cheek. My step-sister was pissed and instead of trying to cool the flames, I was stoking them. But she didn't have the first fucking clue about why I did the things I did.

No one did.

"Felicity came to Seniors Night for you," she hissed. "To be there for you. And you went and threw it back in her

264

face. I know the two of you have been meeting. I know she slept with you... again. I know everything."

It wasn't her harsh tone that had me internally flinching, it was the fact Felicity had told her everything. Things I'd thought had been just between the two of us. Not that it mattered now.

None of it did.

"Yeah, well, it's over."

"Are you even listening to yourself? You were seeing her in secret... why?"

"I don't—"

"Because you care about her. Stop pretending you don't. You think we don't all see the way you look at her? Even Thatcher and his goons noticed. You watch her. You watch her when you think no one is looking, so don't stand there and tell me whatever was happening between the two of you was nothing." Hailee slammed her hands down on the table, making the breakfast bowls clatter.

"So I care?" I yelled back, my thin rope of control snapping. "It doesn't matter. None of it fucking matters. I can't afford any distractions next year."

"If you care about someone, they're not a distraction, Jason," her voice softened a fraction, "they're a support."

"It doesn't matter."

"Stop saying it doesn't matter. It fucking matters," she roared back, her chest heaving with the strain of her words. "Felicity deserves better. And you promised; you promised me you wouldn't hurt her..." Tears pooled in her eyes, twisting my gut.

"No, I didn't," I said coolly.

"Yes, you did."

"No, I didn't. I promised to only ever do what I think's best for her, and this... this is what's best."

Hailee shook her head, cussing under her breath. "That doesn't even make any sense. If you wanted to fuck Jenna, you could have at least waited until Felicity left. She was right there and you rubbed Jenna in her face. So tell me, Jason, how is that what's best for her?"

"She needed to know we were done." The words almost got stuck in my throat and I sucked in a harsh breath.

"Oh my god, listen to yourself. You make me sick." She slumped back in her chair defeated. "I really thought you were changing. I thought you'd finally shed that hard shell of yours. But it really was a game, wasn't it?"

I gave her a dismissive shrug.

"You think the whole world revolves around you. That just because you're some football god you can do whatever the hell you want. But this is high school, Jason. Soon you won't be at the top of the food chain anymore and I hope you get a taste of your own medicine."

"Are you done?" I growled.

"Done?" She smirked. "I'm only just getting started. You're so self-centered you can't even see what's going on around you. You didn't stop for a second to consider Felicity's feelings. It never even occurred to you that maybe she has her own shit going on. You automatically assumed she was applying to UPenn to follow *you* there. Jason Ford. Football star and epic asshole." bitter laughter spilled from Hailee's lips, "but you couldn't be more wrong."

"What the hell is that supposed to mean?"

"Maybe you should have pulled your head out of your

ass for five seconds and asked her about her own life. But now you'll never get the chance."

"Yeah? Why's that?" I sounded composed but her words had completely disarmed me.

Hands pressed firmly against the table, Hailee stood slowly, the chair scraping against the tiles, the sound cutting me right to the bone. "Because, dear brother, you might have won *the game* but the only real loser here is you." She walked to the door, glancing back at the last second. "And Jason?"

"Yeah?" I croaked.

"If you know what's good for you, you'll stay away from Felicity. She doesn't need you back complicating her life anymore than it already is."

Her warning hung between us, and I knew whatever progress we'd made in patching up our relationship had just been torn wide open again.

And I only had myself to blame.

———

"Hey," Cam said as I entered the gym. We had morning practice, and I'd been bracing myself for his tirade. So his greeting was unexpected to say the least.

"You're still talking to me then? Because after the lecture Hailee gave me this morning, I wasn't sure if I should wear body armor."

"Come on, Jase," he let out a heavy sigh, "you had to know it wouldn't end well. You really hurt—"

"Yeah, yeah, save me the speech. I already heard it." We moved over to the chest press and started adding weights.

"So what happens now?"

"Nothing happens. It's done, we're done. Felicity knew what she was getting into."

"But—"

"There are no fucking buts," I ground out, irritation swimming in my veins. "It's done. Over. Did you know she applied to Penn?" My brow rose.

"Hailee mentioned it, but I didn't, no. You think she did it because she knew you were going there?"

"I don't know what the fuck to think, but she can't go there."

"Jase, you can't tell someone where they can or can't go to college, man. It's her future and Hailee said something about her parents being alumni."

"I don't care if her parents are best friends with the Dean, she can't go there." *I can't have her there, everywhere I turn.*

When I met Cam's eyes again, he was scrutinizing me. "What?" I barked.

"What's really going on with you?"

"Save the *Dr Phil* routine, I had enough of that from Asher."

"You called?" he appeared out of nowhere.

"Great, now I have to listen to the two of you bitch."

"Nope." Ash held up his hands as I got situated on the bench. "No bitchin' here. The way I see it, now you've cast Fee aside, she's fair gam—"

"Don't even fucking think about it." My chest rumbled.

"About what?" He played dumb.

"Ash, don't push him."

"Push him? How could I possibly be pushing him when

he chewed her up and spit her out like she's nothing?" His smile was easy, but his tone was cool.

Yeah, Asher was pissed and I couldn't blame him.

"You want my sloppy seconds, Bennet?" I swallowed the guilt crawling up my throat, and doing what I did best, I dialed up my asshole meter. "She's all yours."

"You're a heartless fucker, you know that, Ford?" he said before storming off.

Cam shook his head, rubbing the back of his neck. "Was that really necessary?"

"He's wanted her since day one."

"And you'd be okay with him being with her? Because you know he'll probably go after her just to prove a point."

Shrugging, I pushed the press harder, grunting with exertion. "Like he said, she's fair game." The words snaked around my heart.

"I don't believe you," Cam said. "You're a cruel motherfucker but you care about her."

"Yeah, well I don't care enough."

I half-expected Cam to take a page out of Asher's book and storm off, but he didn't. Cameron was loyal to the bone. It's why it had taken him so long to go after what he really wanted: Hailee. Still, he wasn't impressed with my attitude and for the next ten minutes, we worked in painful silence. All while he studied me, trying to see past my icy exterior. But if anyone was an expert on keeping their emotions locked down, it was me. I'd had years of practice and I wasn't about to open up now.

I had more important things to think about.

———

By the time lunch rolled around, all I wanted was to eat my turkey sub in peace. But even that was too fucking much to ask.

"You know, if you want to go over there, I'm sure they wouldn't—"

My head snapped up to Grady and I levelled with him a hard look. "Jeez," he breathed out. "Someone has a giant stick up their ass. I'm just saying—"

"Well, don't."

As if they heard our argument, Asher and Felicity both looked over at us. Ash held my stare, a silent 'fuck you' glittering in his eyes. I let my eyes run right over him to her. The blood drained from Felicity's face as she tried to remain unaffected, but I saw the tell-tale signs. Wide eyes, the way her breath hitched, and I knew if I was close enough, if I ran my fingers up her neck, her skin would be warm.

Felicity wasn't the only one affected though. My heart was racing like I'd just done an hour of cardio. It beat so hard I felt it in my skull. Curling my hands into fists, I pressed them into my jeans, urging myself to calm the fuck down. She saw it though. She saw it and instead of letting it go, she decided to bait me. Sliding closer to Asher, Felicity leaned into him, laughing at something he said.

"Easy, bro," Grady said under his breath. "Before you break something." He got all up in my face, blocking my view of Asher and Felicity. "It's not worth it," his voice was low.

"Yeah, I'm cool." I sat back, forcing my hands to uncurl.

"Eyes on the prize, remember?" Grady moved back,

squeezing my shoulder. "You need to get laid, work off some of that tension, Cap."

"Did someone say my name?" Jenna appeared, a seductive smile on her face. "Hey, baby." She made a show of wiggling onto my lap, draping her arm around my neck like she belonged there.

Like *I* belonged to *her*.

"S'up?"

"You, if I have anything to say about it." Dipping her hand between us, she grasped my junk.

Grady bellowed with laughter, high-fiving a couple of the players. "Yo, Jenna, where's the rest of you?"

"The girls will be here soon enough." She shot him a suggestive wink.

"Mr. Ford, Miss Jarvis," Principal Finnigan appeared out of nowhere, clearing his throat. "Please keep it clean. This a school cafeteria, not a strip club." His narrowed gaze fixed right on me, his disdain for everything I represented etched into every line of his face, and there were plenty. "All set for Friday?"

I gave him an imperceptible nod.

"Well, I look forward to it." He stalked off to his next unsuspecting victim.

"Dude needs to get laid," someone said, causing our table to break out in laughter.

"He really doesn't like you, does he?" Mackey asked.

I shrugged. He didn't like me, but it didn't matter. Soon the season would be over and then he couldn't touch me.

Grady threw me a look, but I shook it off. I wasn't about to do anything stupid, anything to jeopardize the team's shot at the Championship. But after that, Thatcher was mine.

All I had to do was keep my cool and refuse to be drawn any further into his games.

Jenna swept her hair off her shoulder and dipped her mouth to my ear. "I want you, let's sneak off to the locker room."

It would have been so easy to say yes.

So easy to let her drop to her knees and help me forget all the bullshit.

"Jason, what do you say? Shall we get out of here?" She nipped my ear, but I was too busy watching Felicity.

Watching her watch me.

"Maybe later, yeah?" I gave Jenna an easy smile, sliding my eyes back to Felicity.

But she was gone.

25

Felicity

"Okay, well thanks for getting back to me. Please keep me in mind if anything comes up." I hung up, rubbing a hand down my face.

"No luck?" Mya dropped down beside me.

"No. I called every veterinary clinic within a fifteen-mile radius."

"Well, that sucks. What about pounds?"

"There's only two locally. One does offer volunteer positions, but they have no vacancies and the other one is undergoing a restructure so they're not taking on new staff at the moment."

"You could widen the radius."

"I could but anything further and my parents will get suspicious."

Mya nudged my shoulder. "You could always just tell them."

"I could but I want to be sure first. If I tell them and it doesn't work out, I'll be causing a lot of heartache for nothing."

"You really think they'll be that upset? Veterinary school is a solid plan."

"But it isn't *their* plan and it's at least eight years in school."

"But do *you* want it?"

"I think so. I mean, I've taken all the right courses and I love animals. But I'll need to talk to Miss Hampstead about changing my application and I'll definitely need to find some hands-on experience."

"Ooh, you could do some dog walking for your neighbors or run a doggie day care service on the weekend."

"Oh yeah, my anti-pet parents would love that while they overreacted every day that I was going to get Tetanus, or the house invaded with fleas, or the neighbors complain about barking."

"Okay I get it, over-cautious parent alert. There must be a vacancy somewhere for you."

"Hey, what are you two doing out here?" Hailee's brows bunched. "I went to study hall but you weren't there."

"I wanted to get a head start on calling local veterinary clinics and Mya found me out here."

"Any luck?"

"Nothing yet. I may have to figure out a plan B."

"Have you tried the clinic in town?" she asked.

"No, it's too close to home. If Mom and Dad find—"

"You don't have to tell them why you're doing it yet, just that you want to try new things."

"I don't know... it would be ideal being so local." I wouldn't have to worry about travel time and maybe I could help after school.

"You should call them," Mya said, handing me her phone, the clinic's number already punched in.

"Now?"

"Can you think of a better time?"

Hailee sat down beside me, the two of them giving me expectant stares.

"Fine, but I bet they have nothing." I'd left it too late to try to find something.

I hit call and waited.

"Hello, Rixon Veterinary Clinic, Regina speaking. How can I help you?"

"Hmm, hi, Regina. I'm a senior at Rixon High School and I was wondering if you have any volunteering opportunities? I'm considering studying animal science at college and really wanted some hands-on experience."

Mya gave me a little thumbs up.

"I didn't catch your name?"

"Oh? I'm sorry, it's Felicity."

"Well, firstly thanks for thinking of us, Felicity. I'd love to be able to tell you we have something right now, but unfortunately—"

"You don't." My shoulders slumped. "I expected as much."

"I'm sure you can appreciate, we have a rigorous process in place for all of our volunteers and we only recently recruited."

"Of course, I completely understand."

"That said, I might be able to arrange you a visit to our sister-center across town."

"The pet rescue place?" I asked.

"Yes, A Brand New Tail. There's no permanent volunteer spots at the minute but I'm sure George, the manager, wouldn't mind showing you around."

"That would be great, thank you."

"Excellent. Drop me an email and I'll forward it to George. We can also add you to the waitlist should anything come up..."

"Thank you so much." We said goodbye and hung up.

"So..." Mya asked.

"They can let me look around, but they don't have anything permanent right now."

"Well, it's a step in the right direction." She gave me a reassuring smile. "And who knows. Maybe you can work your magic on George and get him to give you a shift or two?"

"Mya!" My cheeks burned. "I would never—"

"Relax, I'm joking. But it's good to see you smile, girl."

It felt good to smile. Until I spotted Cameron, Asher... and Jason heading in our direction. My breath caught in my throat. Even now, after everything, my heart still wanted him. The rest of me wanted nothing more than to watch him combust into flames, but my heart, well it wasn't quite there yet.

Before they reached us, Jason split away from his friends and took off toward the gym. I let out a little sigh of relief, ignoring the way my stomach sank, and pasted on the brightest smile I could for Cameron and Asher.

"Ladies," Asher said. "We missed you at lunch." His eyes settled on mine, asking me things I didn't want to answer.

"We had a... thing." Mya winked at me.

"A thing. I like things. You could have invited me."

"Asher," Hailee warned.

"It's okay, Hails. You don't all have to pretend this isn't awkward. But I'm fine. Truly."

"That's the spirit, Fee, baby. So what's happening?"

"Felicity is trying to figure out her future," Hailee said.

"Sounds interesting. Anything we can help with?"

"Not unless you know of a veterinary clinic taking on volunteers."

"Huh." Asher's brows pinched. "I never had you down as a cat lover."

"Hey, I like dogs too. Anything soft and cute really, I don't discriminate."

"You've tried the one downtown?"

I nodded. "They have nothing. I'll figure something out." I waved him off, hoping to deflect the attention from me to someone else. The last thing I needed was Asher on the case. He was worse than a dog with a bone.

"We should probably head to practice before Coach comes looking for us." Cameron reached for Hailee, pulling her to her feet. "I'll miss you."

"Miss you too," she said, kissing him.

"Miss you three," Asher added around a grin.

Cameron flipped him off behind Hailee's back.

"You'll be at the game Friday, right?" Asher turned his attention to me and Mya.

"Actually," I tucked my long bangs behind my ear, "I don't think so."

"What the fuck? You have to come. It's our final game before the play-offs."

"Hails will be there, right, Hails?"

"Yes, she will," Cam answered for her.

"See, you have to come."

"Hailee can hang out with Cam's parents." His mom

and dad were making the trip to Brennington since she was finally feeling a little better.

"What about you, Mya? Can I count on you to be there, cheering us on?"

"Oh shoot, did you say Friday? I think I'm washing my hair."

"*I think I'm washing my hair,*" he muttered beneath his breath, rolling his eyes. "If you don't come, you can't come party with us afterwards."

"Whatever will we do?" Mya clutched my hands, feigning disappointment.

"We could always hang out at The Alley?" I suggested. "Or maybe get drunk down by the river again, that was fun. Oh, I know, we could—"

"Okay, okay, you both made your point. But let's face it, whatever you do, wherever you hang out, it's not going to be half as much fun as being with me." Asher's amused gaze lingered on Mya until he winked and walked off, not bothering to wait for Cameron.

"You really shouldn't encourage him," he remarked.

"He can handle it," Mya scoffed, her eyes tracking Asher's retreating form. She could play down the chemistry between the two of them, but she wasn't fooling anyone.

Jealousy stirred in my chest, which was crazy. Because I didn't want Asher like that. But I couldn't deny his attention softened the blow of Jason's rejection somewhat. Not to mention the part of me that worried if Mya and Asher hooked up, I'd lose my two closest friends to Raiders.

"Hey, are you okay?" Mya nudged me again and I flashed her a weak smile.

"Me? I'm good."

"Everything's going to work out, Flick. I can feel it in my bones."

"Speaking of bones," Cam cleared his throat, "I'd better go before Coach breaks some of mine for being tardy. I'll see you tonight?" he asked Hailee.

"Of course. Bye."

He pulled her in for one last kiss and disappeared after Asher.

"What?" she said, noticing us both glaring at her.

"You two are so cute it's disgusting." Mya grinned.

"So disgusting," I added around a smirk despite the sinking feeling in my stomach.

I wanted that.

Wanted someone to look at me the way Cameron looked at her.

But I would never get it so long as I was stuck on Jason.

———

"Felicity, sweetheart, is that you?" Mom's voice filtered down the hall as I kicked off my shoes and dropped my keys on the sideboard.

"Hey, Mom." I entered the kitchen.

"How was book club?"

"Good, thanks. No Dad?"

"He needed to stay late at the office."

"Again? He's always working."

"Sure is. You know how it is, got to keep that roof over our heads. Well, you will soon enough." She chuckled.

"So I've been thinking," I said, sliding onto one of the

stools. "Since its senior year and all, that I might like to do some volunteering."

"What a wonderful idea." Mom came over to the breakfast island to join me. "I'm sure me or your father can arrange some work experience with—"

"Actually, Mom, I was thinking I might do something else."

"Something else?" Her brows pinched. "I'm sorry, I'm not sure I understand."

"I just realized there's so much I've always wanted to do and time's running out, so I thought now might be a good time to experiment."

"Hmm, that sounds kind of distracting, sweetheart. You have book club; that's outside the box."

Dear God, if she though book club was outside the box, I had no hope getting her on side for my new plan.

"It's not exactly giving me major life experience though, Mom. I want to learn something new, try new things. Before I know it, college will be here, and I'll have a full schedule of classes. I don't want to leave high school with any regrets."

"No, you're right, you're absolutely right." Her bright smile gave me a smidgen of hope. "I bet if your father speaks to Killian at the bank he could help out or I could ask Mrs. Fenton if she has anything suitable."

My bubble burst almost as quickly as it began inflating.

"Mrs. Fenton from the care home?" Disbelief filled my voice.

"That's the one. I'm sure the residents would love to have a visit from you."

"That wasn't quite what I had in mind, Mom. I was

thinking something more along the lines of working with... animals."

"Animals?" she barely contained her surprise. "But why on earth would you want to work with animals?"

"Well, I did always want a pet, remember? And imagine how much fun it must be working with all cute little puppies and kittens."

"Cute and dangerous, Felicity. And don't even get me started on the allergies."

"Mom, I don't have allergies."

"Because we raised you in a pet free environment."

"I'm not sure it works that way."

"It seems like an awful waste of your time when you could be getting real hands on experience in the workplace."

She didn't get it. She never had. Which is why I'd never veered from the plan. *Their* plan.

It was just easier that way. But now I'd considered a different plan, I couldn't just switch it off. If my brief time with Jason had taught me anything, it was to go after what you wanted.

"I think it'll be good for me," I said defiantly, feeling something stir in my chest.

"I'm not sure I agree, sweetheart. And I can only imagine what your father will say; but if it's something you really want to do," she gave a resigned sigh, "then I suppose it would be okay, as long as we've checked out they have up to date health and safety policies."

"Really?"

"You've worked hard for the last three years, Felicity. You deserve some downtime."

It wasn't exactly a gleaming endorsement, but I'd take it.

"Thanks, Mom, it means a lot to have your support." Whether or not she'd feel the same if she knew the truth was another matter.

"Sweetheart, all I want is for you to be happy," she reached over the counter, "you know that, right?"

I nodded over the lump in my throat. She wanted me to be happy... doing what had made her so happy. But I wanted more. I realized that now. I wanted to chase my own dreams even when they led me down the wrong path. I wanted to make mistakes and learn from them. I didn't want to settle for average anymore; not when I could have amazing.

There was still one fatal flaw in my new plan—I wasn't sure I would ever be brave enough to tell my parents.

26

Jason

"LET'S GO NUMBER ONE, you're slacking," one of the assistant coaches yelled across the field. I cussed under my breath, pumping my legs harder, pushing through the wall of pain closing in around me.

I was fucking tired.

Thanks to Thatcher and the shit with Felicity, I was barely sleeping. My muscles ached and my head pounded but it was practice and I had a job to do. Giving anything less than one-hundred and ten percent was not an option.

"That's it, QB, keep it up."

I felt eyes on me as I ran the drill again. Looking around, I found Asher glaring at me. The little shit was still pissed over our last conversation about Felicity and it sucked that I couldn't tell him the truth. But he'd get over it. He always did.

"Hey," Cam said, jogging over to me. "You okay?"

"I'm good. Ready to kick some Brennington ass Friday." It was our last game and we were playing at their place. Then we had a rest week before the first round of the play-offs.

"You and your dad figure things out?"

We'd barely spoken since Seniors Night but that was nothing new.

"Not really."

"I know you're angry at him for everything but maybe—"

"I appreciate the advice, I do." I grunted as my hands closed around the pass from Grady. "But I'd rather not do this. You're with Hailee now, save it for her."

"I can be here for both of you. Besides, Hailee and her mom are patching things up."

My brow arched. "Guess we're not so similar after all." Because I could barely look at my old man for his indiscretions, let alone try to smooth things over.

I guess it was different for me, though. I'd known for years who my father really was. Long before Denise and Hailee came on the scene. She was just the final straw where my mom was concerned.

So no, I wasn't in a hurry to forgive the man who had ruined our family. But I was in a hurry to get the hell out of this town. A clean break. That's what I wanted. To escape out from under the shadow of Kent Ford and forge my own legacy.

"Heard anything more from Thatcher? I was thinking perhaps we should have told Coach—"

"You think he doesn't know exactly what happened with the art project? He's not an idiot. But he can't afford Finnigan sticking his nose where it doesn't belong."

"Has he said anything to you?"

"No, but he's hinted at it."

"So what are you going to do? Thatcher won't—"

"If Thatcher knows what's good for him, he'll stay across the river until after the play-offs."

"You really think he'll do that, after everything?"

I didn't, but there was no use telling Cam that. Not when he wanted to run off and tattle to Coach.

"I don't know how many times I have to say it," I ground out, "I can handle Thatcher."

Cameron didn't look convinced, but I was done arguing over something that I couldn't change. Thatcher wouldn't stop coming until he got what he wanted.

Me.

So it was my plan to lie low and stay out of trouble at least until we were crowned State champs.

"Jase, get over here, Son." Coach beckoned me over with his usual crooked finger.

"He doesn't look too happy."

"I'm sure it's nothing," I grunted, ripping off my helmet and shouldering past Cam to head for where Coach and one of the assistant coaches were talking.

"What's up, Coach?"

The assistant coach excused himself and left us to it. Coach Hasson gripped my shoulder. "Walk with me."

We looped around the guys and walked to the other end of the field. The air was frigid, the first signs of winter evident in the dewy grass. "Talk to me about what happened with Miss Raine's art project."

"We told you, Coach. It was an accident. We were moving the—"

"I know what you told me, Jase, but I'm asking for the truth." He gave me a pointed look. "There are rumors circulating that the Eagles had something to do with it. Wouldn't happen to know anything about that would you?"

"Not me, Coach." I jammed my hands into the waistband of my pants and kept my expression neutral.

"Jase, level with me. If it comes out Thatcher and his band of idiots from across the river were responsible, I won't be able to protect you from Principal Finnigan and we both know he's just waiting for an excuse to pull you from the team."

"I don't know what to tell you, Coach." Rubbing the back of my neck, I gave him a half-smile.

"This rivalry will be the death of me." He shook his head with frustration. "I'm going to miss the hell out of you next year, but I can't say I'll miss you and this Thatcher kid going at it every time I turn my back."

"I'm so—"

"Listen to me and listen to me good, Jason. Four more games. That's all that's standing between you and the championship. It would be a damn shame if you ruined what has been a near perfect season because you didn't know when to quit it. Keep your head on straight, you hear me?"

"Yes, Sir."

"I mean it, Son. If I find out you're planning a retaliation on the Eagles, you won't have to worry about Finnigan because I'll be the one making you sit out. I've turned a blind eye for too long where the two of you are concerned. Stupid high school pranks are one thing, but when it starts affecting the people around you, that's when it's time to call it a day."

If he wanted to make me feel guiltier than I already did,

he'd succeeded. It slithered through my gut, twisting and tightening.

"You're a good kid, Jason. I meant every word I said at Seniors Night, but sometimes you're blinded to the game and that makes you your own worst enemy. From someone who remembers what it's like to want it so bad you can't see anything else, it's a big old world out there, and there is room for more than just football. It doesn't feel like it now, when you're on the precipice of greatness, but trust me when I say, it's true." He gripped my shoulder again. "Now get out of here. I don't want to see you again until we're boarding the buses for Friday's game, okay?"

"But, Coach, that's still two days away."

"I'm giving you all some well-deserved downtime. I'm not worried about Friday and neither should you be. It's what comes after that matters. You've worked hard this season Jason, try being an eighteen-year-old kid for once; you never know, it might suit you." Coach winked at me, before straightening his ball cap and strolling off toward the gym.

Downtime?

It didn't figure into the equation. There was always something to be working toward, training for. Even when the season was over, I was in the gym working out, or working with the guys on drills. Perfecting the play, strengthening any weak links in the chain.

"Well?" Cam strolled over to me. "What's the verdict?"

"He wants us to take some downtime."

"Downtime? Sounds good to me." He grinned.

It was in that split second, I realized how much we'd changed. Maybe it was Hailee or his mom being sick or the looming future, but football was no longer the most important thing in Cam's life anymore.

Maybe it never had been.

I didn't ever think anything would come in between us, our plans, but it had. Yet, I couldn't blame him. I'd never seen him as happy as he was with my step-sister.

It had never been in my plan to meet someone, to let someone in. To distract me.

Then *she* came along.

Felicity Giles.

Fuck, had she taken me by surprise. A dark-haired angel with no filter and crazy fashion sense. She was everything I didn't want or need, and yet, she'd infiltrated my steel exterior before I even had time to realize what was happening.

"You're thinking about her, aren't you?" Cam's voice burst my daydream.

"Who, Hailee?" I quipped.

"You know exactly who I mean." He smirked.

"Doesn't matter."

"You keep saying that..."

"Because it's true. We're done." We had to be.

"If you say so."

I did.

Even if it was the biggest lie of all.

———

"And that's how it's done, ladies," Coach yanked off his ball cap and thrust it in the air. "A damn near perfect season." If we hadn't have blown our last game.

It was a bitter pill to swallow, but it didn't matter. We were in the play-offs. One step closer to the end goal.

"Get showered and get changed. I want to get out of here and back home stat."

A chorus of 'Yes, Coach' rang out around me, the buzz of the win still crackling in the air.

"Hey, Cap, check it out," Grady flashed me his cell.

*@**ThatcherQB1:** Raiders might have made the play-offs but Ford is going down #youredone #watchyourback*

"He's just pissed the Eagles are out and we're in," I said, feeling my stomach knot. "Let him talk shit, we all know who's the better team."

"I still think we should go across the river and show him who's boss." Ash slung his towel over his shoulder.

"You over your tantrum?" My tone was cool.

He shrugged as we hit the showers. "I figured if anyone's going to show to the party later, I need to make the peace."

"Oh, so it's like that, huh?"

Asher's mouth curved. "What can I say, gotta give the people what they want."

"Fucker," I muttered under my breath.

After a quick shower, we got dressed and gathered by the buses where Hailee and some other fans hung around to congratulate us. "Great game," she said to Cam and Asher, completely ignoring me. I edged away, hitching my bag over my shoulder. It was on the tip of my tongue to ask where Felicity was, but that would suggest I cared.

"Hey, Jase, we're going to ride back with Hailee. You want a ride?"

My eyes slid to hers in question, and she gave a dismissive shrug.

"I'll ride with—"

"Just get in the damn car, Jason," she sighed.

"You heard the woman, *Jason*, get in the damn car." Ash winked, and I flipped him off. He was so smug I wanted to tell him to fuck off. But I didn't. Instead, I gritted my teeth behind my lips and got in the car.

Wondering when I became such a pussy.

———

Two hours later, everyone who was anyone was crammed into Asher's house.

"Okay fuckers, quiet down." He jumped up on the breakfast counter and thrust his beer in the air. "Now I know Coach said it all last week at Seniors Night, but this is my house and I want to say a few words."

A couple of the guys cheered while Grady balled up a napkin and launched it at him. "Get on with it," he yelled.

"This won't take long," Ash grinned at him, waggling his brows, "just like Mackey in the sack." Another round of hoots and hollers broke out around me.

"Last year should have been ours; we should have been in that championship game, bringing home the crown. But this year... this year it's ours. I love you guys and I don't know what I'm going to do when the season's over. So raise your drink in the air and let me hear y'all. Who are we?"

"Raiders."

"And what are we going to do?"

"Win!"

"Damn right we are. Now let's celebrate like the winners we are and get fucked up." He chugged his drink down and thumped his chest like Tarzan. Cam laughed beside me, but I barely smiled. Because celebration or not, something was missing.

I followed Cam outside to our usual seats where Hailee joined us. "Everything okay?" Cam asked her as she slid onto his lap.

"Yeah, fine."

"They're not coming?"

She shook her head, her eyes finding mine. "I don't think so."

"Maybe it's for the best," Cam said quietly as I focused on my beer, scratching off the label with my thumbnail.

"Yeah." Hailee's eyes burned into the top of my head.

"Shots," Asher appeared with a tray of Jell-O shots.

"Nah, man," I grumbled, not in the mood.

"Aw come on, man, we made it. A near perfect season and State in our sights." He thrust a cup at me, waiting for Cameron and Hailee to take theirs.

"I can't believe this is almost the end." Ash's expression fell as he raised his cup in the air. "It's been the best four years of my life. To good friends, football, and the future, whatever it may hold." Something flashed over his face, but it was quickly gone as he downed his shot.

"Pittsburg won't know what hit them," Cam said, tossing his empty cup on the tray.

"Yeah," Ash shrugged, "but it won't be the same will it?"

A good friend would have reassured him, would have promised things wouldn't change.

But he was right.

Come graduation nothing would be the same anymore.

27

Felicity

"You must be Felicity. I'm George, welcome to A Brand New Tail."

"Hi," I smiled at the man. He was younger than I expected; with sandy blond hair and a bright smile. He couldn't be a day older than twenty-five.

"Thank you so much for this."

"No problem. Regina said you're thinking of applying to study animal science at college?"

"It's a possibility but I know it's super competitive and some hands-on experience would really help my application."

"Can I ask why now? Most of our volunteers from high school start with us in junior year."

"I've always loved animals and vet school is something I've always had in the back of my mind, but my parents... well, they have a different idea where my future is concerned."

"Ah," he smiled. "Say no more. My parents wanted a doctor and got a vet tech instead."

"How'd they take it?"

"It was a shock at first, but they came around to the

idea. In the end, I think all our parents really want is for us to be happy. Shall we get started?"

"I'd love that."

For the first time since Mya talked me into this whole thing, I felt a seed of hope blossom in my chest. George got it. He'd been where I was now and come out the other side without too many bumps and scrapes if his senior position here was anything to go by.

"First things first. This is Serena, our front of house manager." He motioned to the pixie-haired woman manning the desk. "Serena, meet Felicity. I'm giving her the grand tour."

"Hey, doll," she smiled warmly. "High school junior?"

"Senior, actually," George corrected. "She's a bit of a late starter."

"No time like the present. Don't let him scare you off, Felicity, was it?" I nodded. "George is all bark and no bite. Excuse the dog pun, you get a lot of those around here." She gave me a wink and went back to whatever had her attention behind the desk.

"Don't mind her," George said, leading me through a door into a long hall. "So out there was what we call, 'the floor'. And everything beyond this door is what we refer to as 'the back'."

"Got it."

"I figured we'd start with the fun stuff and work backwards."

"Sounds good to me." The place had a very distinct smell. I couldn't quite put my finger on it, but it was there.

"We have a permanent staff of four. Me, Serena, Joseph, and Maggie, and a team of five volunteers who help us out on a week-to-week basis depending on how busy we are." George kept walking, leading me to the far end of the hall. "Serena handles front of house, all customer enquiries, and adoptions. Maggie and I deal with new arrivals; we run full check overs, update vaccination boosters, administer medication and treatment in any cases requiring it. And Joseph is our resident animal whisperer."

"Animal whisperer?"

"It's what we like to call him. It's his job to look after the animals day-to-day, but the guy has a rare gift with them, even the most severe cases we see. In my five years being here, I haven't seen a case he hasn't been able to crack."

"Wow, he sounds wonderful."

"He's really something. Unfortunately, he's taken a rare day off, so you won't meet him today."

Disappointment settled in my chest, but I tried to shake it off, remembering Hailee and Mya's words of encouragement. This was a positive step in the right direction.

"And here we are. This is what we like to call, 'the zoo'."

The second George opened the door, I realized why. Assaulted with overzealous barks and wary purrs, I stepped into the room. Even a few growls greeted me.

"Okay, okay, quiet down." George dragged his keys along the nearest cage. "I brought someone to meet you all, but you have to promise to behave."

"There are so many."

"We don't just take cases from Rixon. We cover the surrounding areas too, so things can get pretty crazy. We're almost at capacity right now. Twenty-five cats, eighteen dogs, and Earl."

"Earl?" I asked, my eyes wide as I observed the vast room. It was clearly divided into cats and dogs with an examination table and apparatus set up in the middle. The crates were big and spacious, each equipped with food and water bowls and scratching posts for the cats, a few toys for the dogs.

"Our rabbit. We technically only take cats or dogs, but he was found in the alley behind the building and Serena begged us to take him in.

"Someone just left him there?"

"You'd be surprised where people dump their unwanted pets."

My heart clenched as I found the long-eared rabbit in a special cage away from the other animals. He was so cute and defenseless; the idea someone could just toss him away made my heart ache.

"So when an animal first arrives, the first port of call is a full health check..." For the next ten minutes, George explained how they processed new animals and how they used a digital matching service to try and rehome as many animals as possible.

"The average stay with us is eleven weeks, which means we're doing a fairly good job of finding animals new compatible homes. We have a thorough screening process and insist potential adopters attend one of our information sessions before jumping headfirst into anything. And we're proud to hold an eighty-five percent rehoming success."

"Eighty-five percent? But what happens to the other fifteen percent?"

"Oh, they usually become lifers here or we transfer them to a more suited center." He moved over to a cage and crouched down. "Now this is Boomer. He's a black lab who's been with me since the beginning."

The dog stared up at me, leaning up to sniff the air around me. "Hi there, boy."

"You want to meet him? He's as friendly as they come."

"I'd love to." A little thrill shot through me as George unlocked the cage and pulled open the front gate.

"He's a little unsure of new faces so give him a minute."

"Hey, Bo—"

The huge dog leaped toward me, knocking me back onto my butt.

"I think you have a fan," George chuckled but I had my hands full of dog as Boomer nudged and licked my face, coaxing me to run my hands through his soft, glossy fur.

"And George said you were shy." I glanced over at him and he blushed a little. He was kind of cute, made ten times cuter by the fact he cared for all these animals.

But I wasn't here to crush on George, I was here to soak up everything I could about what it entailed to work in a place like A Brand New Tail.

"You like that, huh?" I scratched under Boomer's neck and he lifted his head from side to side so I could get better access.

"Okay, Boom, back in you go. Joseph isn't on shift today, but I'll make sure you get to stretch those legs later." He patted Boomer on the head before gently herding him back into his cage.

"They all get daily exercise?"

"They do. Twice a day. And then Joseph usually has them out in small groups in the yard. It's important for socialization and preparation for their new homes."

I nodded, eagerly soaking up every word. "I always wanted a dog or a cat, but my mom was concerned about allergies."

"I have three pets." George scooped a handful of doggy treats out of a jar and began working his way down the low row of cages. "A spaniel and two cats."

"Where did you study?"

"I did animal science at Penn's School of Veterinary Medicine. I graduated last year, got my licenses, and Regina offered me the position of center manager."

"Wow, that's amazing."

"I always imagined I'd work at a veterinary clinic, but once I started volunteering here, I couldn't imagine being anywhere else. There's something magical about bringing together a rescue pet and a new owner." Pride radiated from every word and I realized I wanted that. I wanted to make a difference to animals *and* people.

"You have that look," he observed.

"I do?"

"Yeah," he smiled, "The newbie sparkle. I remember it well. It looks good on you." His eyes widened at his slip of the tongue, and I smothered a giggle.

George was flirting with me. It was probably unintentional and harmless, but it felt nice all the same.

"And that was really inappropriate. I'm sorry. Sometimes I speak before I think. I can assure you, I'm usually much more professional."

"It's okay."

Awkward silence stretched out before us despite the little flutters in my chest.

"So, hmm, yeah this is the 'zoo'. We also have a surgical

room, a recovery room, and a couple of isolation pens for the worst cases."

"It hurts my heart knowing people can be so cruel to something so cute."

"We see it all here. It's definitely not for the faint of heart, but it only makes it all the more rewarding when a dog who has only ever known neglect and abuse finds a loving home. You want to see the rest of the place?"

Nodding eagerly, I said, "I'd love to."

———

I ended up staying most of the afternoon. George was happy to talk shop and I was more than willing to listen. It couldn't have gone better... until he reminded me there were no volunteer openings, and the bottom fell out of my happy bubble.

"Of course, I understand," I said, wringing my hands in front of me.

"I think you'd really fit in here." A gentle blush creeped into his cheeks again and there was no mistaking he was flirting. "But my hands are tied. Hopefully you got a real feel for what it's like though?"

"I did, thank you."

"Well, it was nice to meet you, Felicity. If you have any questions or need any help with your application, just give me a shout." He fumbled in his pocket. "Here's my card."

"Thanks." I plucked it from him and held it close to my chest as if he'd just offered me the universe. "I should probably let you get back to it. Wouldn't want to keep them waiting." My head flicked over his shoulder.

"Yeah, I have big shoes to fill today since Joseph is on vacation."

"I'm sure you'll do a great job."

"I'll try."

Neither of us made any effort to move but it was starting to feel awkward, so I gave him a small wave and walked away. It had been such a bittersweet experience; confirming my unexplored desire to work with animals but tempered by a sting of regret. Frustration because I hadn't been braver to go after what I wanted last year or whenever my mom and dad brought up college.

And knowing it might have been too late.

28

Jason

I WAS on the way out when Hailee's voice stopped me in my tracks. "Maybe you should call George and see if he can..." The conversation became muffled but I caught the odd word.

Flick.

Ask.

Risk.

"George?" I doubled back and breezed into the kitchen.

"Good morning to you too," my step-sister grumbled as she poured herself a glass of juice.

"So who's George?" I leaned against the door jamb casually.

"No one."

"You make it too easy sometimes, you know that, right?"

"And you make it so easy to hate you." A smirk spread across her face. "Don't you have to be at school bright and early for practice?"

"They'll wait for me."

"So arrogant."

"So prickly," I shot back. "So, George?"

"Is no one."

I didn't like the way she was deflecting. Hailee only

usually did that if she didn't want me to know something. And right now, there was only one person she didn't want me to know about.

Felicity.

"I'll find out, *little sis*," I warned. "One way or another, I'll find out who George is." Grabbing an apple from the bowl, I bit into it, sending her a pointed look.

"You don't care remember? So why would you possibly want to know who George is?" I glared harder and she chuckled. "Not so arrogant now, are you?" Her brow shot up.

Without another word I stalked out of the kitchen, the muscle in my jaw working overtime.

Fucking George.

It shouldn't have mattered who he was. He could have been the Giles' new pool boy or a family friend for all I knew. But it didn't stop my mind zipping off in a hundred different directions, all of them ending at the same point. George wasn't no one.

He was someone, and I fucking hated it.

By the time I'd arrived at Asher's house, George had taken on a life of his own. Snowballing into Felicity's life. Maybe they were dating. Maybe he was an ex looking to rekindle their relationship. Or maybe Felicity was pursuing him. That one especially stung.

"Good mornin'." Asher took one look at me when he climbed into my car and let out a low whistle. "What happened now?"

"Who's George?"

"George? Is this some kind of test? Am I supposed to know who George is?"

"Just answer the fucking question."

"Curious George? George Foreman? George Clooney?" Asher mocked, and I stared at him blankly. "No? Well, in that case I have no idea who George is." My hands tightened around the wheel as I took the turn for school. "I'm guessing from the way you're strangling the life out of your steering wheel that wasn't the answer you wanted?"

"It's nothing."

He snorted. "If you say so."

A beat passed. And another. Until I finally choked out, "I heard Hailee on the phone to Felicity."

"And what? You're worried George is swooping in to mend her broken heart? I'd call that a sweet dose of 'I fucking told you so'."

My chest rumbled with indignation as I swallowed my reply. It pained me to say it, but Asher was right.

"What, no comeback?" he added.

My eyes slid to his, silently pleading for him to drop it. But I'd picked the wrong friend to confide in for that.

"Didn't I tell you this would happen?" Ash ground out. "Felicity is a catch, bro. If you weren't so hung up on her, I wouldn't have hesitated to try my luck there. But there are a lot of other guys out there, Jase."

"I know. Fuck, you think I don't know that?" The words came out strained.

"So what happened?" Out the corner of my eye, I watched as he twisted around, running a hand through his messily styled hair. "Talk to me; let's try to fix this before it's too late."

"Coach is going to be pissed if we're late," I said, deflecting.

303

"Jase, man, come—"

"Just do me a favor and look out for her, yeah?" I lowered my voice, finding an empty parking spot. Cutting the engine, silence descended on us.

Asher wanted to say more, to argue I was making a huge mistake, but I'd already made my bed. This morning was just a blip. Surprise at hearing her and Hailee talk about another guy so soon. But it was bound to happen eventually. Felicity might have been quirky, but she had a caring personality and the kind of smile that lit up an entire room. Any guy would have been lucky to have her. *I* would have been lucky to have her. In another life, maybe.

I shouldered the door, not even bothering to wait for Ash, and headed for the locker room. I needed to hit something. I needed to hurt.

But most of all, I needed to forget.

———

Practice didn't help much. I skulked through two classes, barely listening to the teachers, before joining my teammates at lunch. They chatted around me, excited for a week's rest before the first play-off game next weekend.

"I come bearing good news." Asher dropped his tray down and sat beside me. "George is no one." He leaned in, keeping his voice low. "Well, he's someone, but he's no one for us to worry about."

"Us?" I said coolly, irritation shooting up my spine.

"Who knew you could be so possessive?" He pinned me with a sarcastic look. "Anyway, George is the manager at a pet rescue place Felicity is trying to get some volunteer experience at."

"What the hell does she want to do that for?"

"I heard Hailee telling Cameron she's thinking of a switching her degree to animal science or something. But she needs hands-on experience for her application."

So George wasn't some new guy she was dating. I should have felt relief coursing through me.

I didn't.

Because I couldn't help but wonder if her change of plans had anything to do with my knee-jerk reaction to finding out she had applied to Penn.

"Okay," I grunted.

"Okay?" Ash drawled. "I bring you the four-one-one and all you can say is, 'okay'?"

"Like I said before, it doesn't—"

"Matter, yeah, I got the memo. Guess you won't be interested to know George gave Flick his card and told her to call him if she needed *anything*. I don't know about you, but that sounds a lot like code for—" Asher groaned with pain as my elbow jammed into his ribs. I casually went back to my sub, pretending like he hadn't just blown my world wide open.

So George wasn't a new guy she was seeing. But by the sounds of it, he wanted to be.

I'd pushed her straight into his open arms.

And I didn't know what the fuck to do with that.

My mood only got worse as the day went on. So when my cell vibrated as I was walking to my car at the end of the day, and I opened the incoming Snapchat message, I almost saw red. The grainy image was accompanied by only two words.

Time's up.

Fuck.

Thatcher wasn't backing down, and I wasn't sure how much longer I could avoid him. Maybe it was better to end it now. Him and me. One on one.

Against my better judgment, I typed back.

Name your time and place.

His reply was instant.

No man's land... Friday after sundown.

It was a stretch of land down by the river not far from The Alley. We used to hang out there when we were kids, before the rivalry between The Raiders and The Eagles became more than just a few harmless high school pranks.

. . .

Done. Just you and me.

Oh you know it. I'm going to enjoy making you bleed.

Big words for a guy who's waited almost eight months to get revenge.

All good things come to those who wait.

I didn't reply. There was no point. We could go around in circles all day about the fact he was choosing now to strike, but it wouldn't change anything. I just had to figure out a way to walk away from this thing in one piece. Because while he had everything to gain, I had everything to lose.

———

I was sitting in the yard, drinking a beer, when Hailee found me. "Out here drinking all alone, it must be bad."

"Just needed some air."

"Want to talk about it?"

"No, I really don't. But thanks for the offer," I tacked on the end.

"Someone hold the phone, hell must have frozen over,"

she chuckled, dragging another chair over to mine. "You must be excited for the play-offs."

"I'm ready. It's like my whole life has been leading up to this point, you know?"

"I really don't." She gave me a hesitant smile. "But I've been around you long enough to know how important this is to you."

"So what? We're friends again?"

"I'm not sure we were ever friends, but I'm done holding onto so much hate and bitterness. I want to enjoy the rest of senior year."

"To non-friends?" I held up my beer and Hailee frowned. "Here," passing her an empty, I clinked the neck of my bottle against hers.

"Truce?" she added.

"I think I can agree to that."

"I know I gave you a hard time about Felicity and I'm not going to lie, I spent a couple of days planning on ways to make you pay, but I think I've realized it's for the best."

Her words coiled around my lungs making it difficult to breathe.

"Yeah?" I barely managed to choke out.

"Yeah. The two of you are from completely different worlds, and football will always be the most important thing to you. And that's okay. Felicity needs someone solid, someone who can put up with her brand of crazy."

"Someone like George?" The words were out before I could stop them.

"Oh God, please don't tell me you're jealous of George?"

"Should I be?"

Her expression fell. "I really don't know how to answer that."

"So she wants to be a veterinary doctor or something?"

"Yeah, it's all kind of new. She was supposed to be studying business like her parents both did. But she made this list and it pushed her to reassess things, to go after things she wouldn't have before."

"Like asshole football players who don't know what they want?"

"Exactly like that." Hailee burst into quiet laughter. "Maybe in another time and place you two would have figured things out."

"Maybe." I liked that idea; Felicity and me together in a few years' time. Me the hotshot NFL player and her the big-hearted animal doctor.

"How did you know Chase was the one?" I asked even though I felt fucking stupid the second the words left my mouth.

"It wasn't really a case of knowing. It was just a realization that life was better with him around than not, and when things went bad with his mom, I wanted to be there for him. I wanted to be his person."

I took a long pull on my beer mulling over her words. "I always thought I was his person." My lip curved in a half-smirk despite the knot in my gut.

"One day, you'll get it. Maybe not now but one day..."

"I almost had it once you know."

"Aimee?"

"Yeah." I stared off into the distance remembering a time that felt so long ago but wasn't that long at all.

309

"What happened?" Hailee asked. "I mean, I know a little, but I'd rather hear it from you."

Sliding my eyes to hers, I let out a weary sigh. "Aimee was... different. Special." At least I'd thought she was. But that was before I knew the truth. Before I ever met Felicity and realized what I felt for Aimee was nothing but puppy love.

"She hurt you?"

"She didn't just hurt me, she completely fucking destroyed me."

29

Felicity

I WOKE to the sound of my cell vibrating. Leaning over, I fumbled to find it, and lifted it to my ear. "Hello?"

"Felicity, it's George."

"George?" I rubbed the sleep from my eyes unsure I'd heard him correctly.

"George from New Tail. I hope I didn't wake you?"

"Is it that obvious?" A soft chuckle left my lips.

"Sorry, I figured with it being a school day you'd be up and at it."

"I'm not really a morning person."

"I remember it well." I heard his smile. "Anyway, I just wanted to call and let you know that a position came up, so if you're still interested—"

"Interested?" I bolted upright. "I would love to."

"Well, that's great. When can you come down and fill in the paperwork?"

"Today, I can come today," the words spilled out in a frenzy. "I have classes until three-thirty, but I'm free after that."

"I'll need to check what we have going on today, but I can't see it being a problem. I can email you later to confirm," he hesitated, "or shoot you a text?"

"Either is fine." Excitement danced in my tummy. "I'm just relieved and excited, definitely excited. You were so certain nothing was available, I'd kind of given up hope."

"Well, I'm glad to be calling with good news." George gave me a list of what to bring in with me later before we said goodbye and hung up.

I leaped out of bed with a spring in my step, and quickly shot a text to Hailee and Mya.

Me: George just called... there's a position for me.

Hailee: That's amazing, I'm so happy for you.

Mya: That's great. All that flirting must have paid off.

My stomach knotted. Is that why George had suddenly found me something? Because he liked me? I didn't want to owe him anything.

Dammit.

I typed another quick text to Hailee.

. . .

Me: You don't think George found me something because he thinks I'll owe him now, do you?

My cell rang and I hit answer. "Mya seems to think he's doing this because he likes me," I rushed out.

"Good morning to you too," Hailee laughed softly.

"Sorry, I was just so happy and now I'm panicking."

"Did he give you that vibe just now?"

"I don't know. He was friendly, but he seemed like a nice guy."

"He knows you're in high school, right?"

"Of course."

"So he's probably just doing a nice thing. You said he's fresh out of college himself, so he probably just appreciates how much this means to you. This is a good thing, Flick."

"You're right," I breathed a sigh of relief. "You're totally right. It's Mya's fault."

"She likes to mess with your head. But she means well."

"I know. Thanks. I should get ready for school. Do you want a ride?"

"Cameron's picking me up, but you can ride with us?"

"Is Jason... actually, don't answer that. I'll meet you there. I think I have to get Mya anyway."

"Okay, and Flick?"

"Yeah?"

"I think Mya's right. I think this could be a really good thing for you."

"Thanks, I'll see you at school." I hung up and let out a

shaky breath, nervous energy radiating through me. Getting this break at A Brand New Tail was a good thing but it meant pulling the plug on my parents' dream for me.

Something I didn't relish doing.

———

"Hey," Hailee chased me down after class. The day had flown, my head too consumed with George's early morning call to concentrate. "Are you headed straight there?"

I nodded. "I didn't want to risk going home and running into Mom. This way I can hopefully calm my nerves before I get there."

"And what has you all worked up?" Asher peeked over Hailee's shoulder, grinning at me.

"The pet rescue place called Flick; they have an opening for her."

"Georgie boy pulled some strings, did he?"

"How do you know about George?" My brows bunched together.

"I, uh," he stuttered, guilt swimming in his eyes. "I overheard Hailee telling Cam all about it."

"Okay."

"I'm proud of you, Fee, baby." He hooked his arm around my neck and pulled me in. "Those furballs are going to love you."

"I hope so, I could really—" Asher yanked his arm free and jerked away from me.

"Hey, guys," Mya said, joining us.

"Mya," he said smoothly, the reason for his sudden change apparent. "Nice shirt."

"This old thing." She pulled at the frayed t-shirt and chuckled. "Thanks, I guess."

Hailee and I watched the two of them. Asher was smitten, his eyes tracking Mya's every move. But she seemed indifferent to his attention.

"So what are you girls up to later? I know Flick is heading to puppy heaven but what about you, Hailee? Mya?"

"Me and Cam promised Xander we would take him to Ice-T's."

"Just don't feed that little shit any of the candy. We made that mistake once."

"I think we've got it covered." Hailee smiled.

"Mya?"

"I'm living the dream tonight with Mr. Galveston's homework."

"History?" Asher winced. "Ouch."

"Do you even do homework?" She threw back.

"I do it... occasionally," he added. "But just because I play football doesn't mean I'm a dumb jock. You're looking at a GPA of 3.33 right here."

"Athletic and book smart. I am impressed."

"You should be."

"Okay," I interrupted. "Not that I'm not enjoying watching whatever this is," I wagged my finger between them, "but I need to go. I don't want to keep George waiting."

"Call me as soon as you get done," Mya said, "I want to hear all about dreamy George."

"Dreamy George?" Asher frowned. "Isn't he the manager of the place?"

"The very young, very cute manager," Mya nodded. "Flick's words, not mine."

"You have a crush, Fee, baby? I'm wounded."

"I do not have a crush." Heat spread along my neck and into my cheeks. "George is... nice. He's also going to be my boss so..."

"Kinky." Asher grinned, his eyes dancing with amusement.

"Gross," I hissed, waving him off. "Right, I'm out of here. I'll call you both later. Asher, it was a pleasure as always."

"The pleasure is all mine," he called as I left them to it. "Oh and Fee? Make sure George keeps his paws to himself. See what I did there... paws." He exploded with laughter as I rolled my eyes and headed out of the building.

Wondering what I was getting myself into.

———

Turned out, I had nothing to worry about. When I'd arrived at the center, Serena had welcomed me, handing me a stack of paperwork to fill in. Then she traded me the papers for a volunteer handbook which she left me to study while she dealt with some clients. George eventually showed up to walk me through the volunteer schedule and list of duties. I'd missed the latest round of volunteer training, so for now I'd have to learn the ropes as I went, but I was just relieved to be there.

"I had no idea there was so much involved in pet adoption," I said, shadowing George as he scrubbed a new arrival: Benji, a cute one-year-old puppy, brought in by his parents who were getting a divorce and no longer wanted him. He was so frickin' cute, with big, round eyes and thick soft fur, the color of the sand.

"Our matching process is rigorous and time consuming, but it means better success rates. Something we're very proud of."

"I'm so excited to get started."

"And we're excited to have you. You'll get to meet the other volunteers over the weekend. I think Sandie, Hale, and Lisa are in Saturday, and then Tom and Beth are down for Sunday."

"There's five of them?" I asked, confused.

"Yes, didn't I already explain that?"

"You did, but I'd just assumed someone had left since the position came up." And I definitely remembered him telling me there were at capacity.

"Ah." George flushed bright red. "We shuffled things around and managed to find you some hours after all."

"Wow, that's... wow."

"It's actually great timing as Sandie recently announced she's pregnant, so she'll be looking to drop her hours as her pregnancy progresses."

"Oh, okay then, if you're sure." I couldn't shake Mya's insinuation George's motives weren't entirely innocent.

"There's nothing to worry about, I promise. I know how important hands-on experience can be for a college application, so if we can do our bit to help you..." He let his words hang.

"Thank you, that's very kind."

He beamed, the color in his cheeks returning to normal. "You want to takeover while I grab the rest of the supplies?"

"For real?" I started pushing my sleeves up.

"Of course, get in here. Benji is one of our friendlier arrivals."

"He's so cute. I can't wrap my head around the fact they no longer wanted him."

"He'll be rehomed in no time. He's one of the better cases, trust me. Okay, if you get in here," George held onto Benji but stepped back letting me slip around him, so I was closest to the tub and the puppy, "that's it. Now slide one hand to his collar." Our fingers brushed as he withdrew his hand and it was my turn to blush. George cleared his throat and jerked back.

"You can start rinsing him off and then dry him with that towel." He flicked his head over to the counter and a stack of towels.

"Rinse and dry, got it."

"Excellent, I'll be right back."

George left and I took my time washing Benji. He was a placid thing, letting me scrub and run my fingers through his soaked coat. "You like that, boy?" I cooed earning me an eager lick to the face. Laughter bubbled up, the smile on my face so wide it hurt. But there was something so right about being here, that I felt happiness wrap around me like a warm blanket.

"We good in here?" George's voice perforated my bubble.

"We're fi—" Benji chose that exact moment to shake off his fur, spraying droplets of water everywhere. "Oh my..."

George handed me a towel. "Here, get dried off while I pat him down."

"Does that happen a lot?"

"Yep, hazard of the job I'm afraid," he chuckled.

"It's funny," I said toweling myself off, "I've kind of drifted through high school, never being sure what I wanted to do. Happy to go along with my parents' plan for me. But being here, it's like I know this is what I want to do. Gosh, I bet that sounds so cliché."

"It doesn't. I felt the same, back in the day. I knew being a doctor was what my parents wanted for me. But I'd be at the hospital, visiting my gran when she was sick, or hanging out with my dad on his rare day off, and I never felt that connection. I knew it would be rewarding, to heal people, save lives. But it never felt like what I was destined to do."

"How am I going to tell them?" I whispered the words.

"If it makes you happy, eventually it'll make them happy."

He made it sound so easy.

"Look at it this way, you could spend the next four years of your life at college, surfing along studying a course that's okay, or you could spend the next four years of your life studying something that excites you. Something you feel passionate about. Who knows where the future will take you, but wouldn't you rather be on a path you choose? Sorry," George added. "Like I said before, sometimes things just spill out before I can stop them."

"I admire it actually. It's nice to meet someone who understands where I'm coming from."

"Surely there must be someone? A best friend? Boyfriend?"

"Best friend, yes. Boyfriend, no." My stomach dipped. "But I'm not sure Hailee really gets it. She's always known what she wanted to do."

George's expression had changed, his eyes fixed on mine, searching for something.

"George?" I asked, breaking the strange tension that had descended over us.

"What? Sorry." He shook his head. "It's been a long day. Where were we?"

Benji chose that moment to shake his fur again, soaking George. I grabbed some towels and hurried over to them. "Thanks," he said, "that'll teach me for not paying more attention."

The moment between us had passed, but I couldn't help but wonder what had him so distracted in the first place.

30

Jason

"You're sure about this?" Grady asked for the twentieth time that week.

"This thing needs to end now."

"I'm not disagreeing, I just don't understand why you're not taking Bennet and Chase for back up. Well, Chase I kind of get. If Thatcher had come after my girl the way he went after Hailee, I wouldn't be able to—"

"Grady..."

"Shutting up," he groaned. "So we're really doing this?"

"*I'm* doing this. I just need you there in case things go south."

He let out a low whistle. "And you're sure we can't hold off doing this until after we win State?"

"It has to be now."

"If Coach—"

"Coach won't find out." Thatcher was many things, but he wasn't a snitch.

"I could call a couple of the other guys—"

"If you're having second thoughts, man, I'll go alone."

"Nah, I've got you. I just think this is a bad idea. A really bad idea."

I didn't disagree but Thatcher wanted his pound of

flesh and he was determined to get it one way or another. At least this way, if I met him one on one, it would be a fair fight. Besides, it wasn't the first time we'd rumbled. I knew I could take him.

"Noted. I'll see you in ten."

"Yeah, yeah. See you there." I hung up and grabbed my keys off the sideboard. It was almost sundown. Cameron was out with Hailee, and Asher's parents were in town for a flying visit and had insisted on taking him for dinner. Dad and Denise were off doing whatever the fuck they did on Friday nights. The coast was clear.

Until I walked out of the house.

"Aimee?" I stared at the girl who had screwed me over once upon a time. "What the fuck are you doing here?"

"Hey, Jason," she gave me a tentative smile, "it's been a while."

"Not long enough." My teeth ground together. "Let me guess, your brother sent you."

"Actually he doesn't know I'm here. If he did..." She trailed off, her eyes darting to the ground. "Can we talk?"

"You can say whatever you came to say, yeah, and then you can get the fuck off my property."

"Jason..." she let out a heavy sigh, running a hand through her hair. When I didn't respond she added, "That's fair enough. I guess I earned that."

"You've got to be fucking kidding me," I mumbled beneath my breath.

Aimee lifted her eyes to mine again, sympathy and regret swimming in her brown irises. "I suppose it's too late to say I'm sorry?"

"Apologies mean nothing out of the mouths of liars."

"I never meant to hurt you... it just all went too far and—"

"Save it," I snapped, my chest heaving with frustration.

There had been a time when I'd wanted the girl standing before me. Wanted her so bad, I let down my walls. Opened up to her. There wasn't an inch of her skin I hadn't tasted. A dip or curve or blemish I hadn't trailed my lips over. I thought I'd known everything there was to know about the quiet girl from across the river... until I'd found out she was none other than Lewis Thatcher's little sister.

Anger rushed through my veins, igniting a firestorm in my chest. There had never been any love lost between me and Thatcher, but Aimee had changed everything. Turned our rivalry into a war that spilled off the field and into our lives, affecting everyone around us.

"You got your revenge, Jase, isn't that enough? What you did to me—"

"Don't fucking talk to me about what *I* did. You reeled me in for weeks, let me believe what we had was real. I felt things for you I had never felt before and it was all a lie."

I had been falling in love with her. I couldn't pinpoint the exact moment it happened. Even at the time I hadn't realized. It was *after*, when I learned who she really was, that I understood how deep my feelings ran for Aimee Thatcher—my enemy's sister.

"It wasn't," she cried, swiping at the tears falling from her eyes. "What we shared was real. It was real. It wasn't supposed to be, but I couldn't help it. I couldn't help falling for you."

Closing the distance between us, I stopped right in front of her. Looming over her, my eyes narrowed to deadly slits.

"You played me, Aimee. You made me weak and defenseless and then, when I was completely at your mercy, you stabbed the knife in my back and watched me bleed out."

"Jason..." Aimee's voice trembled as she craned her neck to look at me. "I'm sorry, I'm so sorry."

"Yeah? Well, I'm only sorry I didn't completely destroy you." The words came out low and deadly, laced with the pain of our past.

When I'd found out who she was and what she'd planned with her brother, I'd concocted a plan of my own. I would never forget the look on Thatcher's face when he opened the video message of me fucking his sister. It had been all the revenge I'd needed, but it had been the catalyst for everything since.

"You were always mean, Jason, but I'll forever regret turning you into... *this*." A violent sob spilled from Aimee's lips as she stepped back, putting some much-needed distance between us.

"I only came to warn you," she added. "Lewis is out to destroy you. He wants to make sure you never see the play-offs. If you have any sense, you won't go."

I ran a hand over my head and down the back of my neck, the weight of her words pressing on my chest like a ton of bricks. "Is that all?"

"I mean it, Jason," she warned, "he's out for blood. *Your* blood."

Another time, another place, I would have replied with some cocky statement about him being all talk and no action. But the stakes had changed. I went after his sister and he'd come after mine, but I hadn't retaliated then. I'd been biding my time, waiting for the right time to go after him.

But my time was up.

I had to decide.

Fight.

Or flee.

Something Hailee once told me flashed in my mind, and I couldn't help but think, no matter what I decided, there would be only one loser at the end of this.

Me.

"You should go, Aimee." Shouldering around her, I headed straight for my car. The sooner we got this over with, the better.

"Jason, don't do this..." Her cries bounced off the window like rain against glass. Aimee made it sound like I had a choice but running was never a choice, and my mind was already made up.

Grabbing my cell phone, I shot Grady a quick text before firing up the engine and gunning out of the driveway. Aimee's defeated figure shrank in the rear-view mirror. I'd played in my fair share of dog fights. Football games where players broke the rules and cared more about hurting each other than scoring a touchdown.

As far as I was concerned, this wasn't any different.

Thatcher wanted my blood?

Fine.

But I'd make him work for it.

It was quiet down at No Man's Land when we arrived. Grady sat tense beside me, tapping his fingers against his thigh.

"Nervous?" I asked, surveying the stretch of land in front of us. It was right beside the bridge, sheltered by the huge cement pillars. Part of it ran underneath, only accessible when the river ran low. Which wasn't often. When we were kids, we'd hang out down there, daring each other to try to make it across. Kids doing the kind of shit kids do.

This wasn't like that though.

This was different.

"What's the plan?" Grady ignored my original question.

"Plan?" I side-eyed him. "I'm going to beat the shit out of him and send him crawling back across the river with my initials scratched into his fucking skin."

"Jesus, Cap." Grady let out a low whistle. "Are you sure we shouldn't call—"

"The less people involved, the better. If you want to walk, walk. I won't hold it against you." I wasn't scared; I was fucking furious. It burned through me, liquid fire in my veins.

"Fuck that. I'm staying. Just promise me if things get too messy, we'll leave."

"Yeah, whatever." The lie rolled off my tongue. No way was I leaving until Thatcher got the message loud and clear not to mess with me and mine.

"Shall we then?"

We climbed out, the bitter fall wind slamming into us. "Shit, it's cold."

"Grow a pair, Grady." I smirked as I flexed my arms

either side of me and took off toward the riverside. Thatcher was waiting but he wasn't alone.

"Surprised you came," he drawled.

"I'm a man of my word."

"Interesting." He inclined his head, scratching his jaw. "You didn't come alone." Thatcher's hard gaze moved to Grady.

"Neither did you." My eyes went to the goon at his side.

"Didn't want to miss you get your ass handed to you, Ford," Gallen said, stepping up to his teammate.

Anger shot up my spine knowing that he'd put his hands on Felicity.

"Yeah, yeah, are we doing this or what?"

"Oh, we're doing it. But you really should have brought reinforcements." His lip twisted as a handful of other Eagles' players stepped out from the shadows.

"Whoa, this isn't what was agreed," Grady said, edging closer to me.

Thatcher shrugged, yanking his hoodie and shirt clean off in one. "Yeah, well, the game just changed."

My eyes ran over each of them; players I recognized. Players I'd gone head to head with on the field more times than I could count. Players who I knew would do anything for their captain and quarterback.

Even if he was a complete dickwad.

"The difference between me and you?" I said. "I refuse to take my players down with me."

"The righteous Jason Ford everyone," Thatcher swept his arm around him, "how fucking poetic."

Letting out a fake yawn, I glanced at Grady. "Bored yet? I know I am." Grabbing the hem of my hoodie and jersey, I pulled them off, throwing them down at my teammate's feet.

Thatcher glanced back at his audience, ready to showboat a little more, but I was done talking. Head down, shoulder cocked, I tackled him to the ground. We landed with a *thud*, his grunts filling the air while I rammed my fists into his side.

"Motherfucker!" He roared, bucking and thrashing against me. His fist came up hard, crunching into the soft flesh of my neck and I rolled away, momentarily winded.

"Cheap shot, Ford," he gritted out, clambering to his feet.

Before I could anticipate his next move, two of his teammates wrestled me to my feet, restraining my arms behind my back.

"Hey, hey," Grady rushed over to us, "that wasn't—" His head snapped back as Gallen's fist caught his cheek, and the two of them began going at it.

"Is this how you win?" I seethed, "by playing dirty."

"No," Thatcher grinned, "this is how I end your season." His fists slammed into my ribs. Over and over. Knocking the air clean out my lungs. Pain ricocheting through me. The hands restraining me loosened their grip and I dropped forward onto my knees, my hands breaking my fall.

"What's the matter, Ford, cat got your tongue?"

Thatcher edged back, giving me space to clamber to my feet. I could already feel the bruising around my ribs, the damaged tissue. But I was used to a little pain, I thrived on it.

Wiping my bloody lip with the back of my hand, I lifted

my chin in defiance. "It'll take a lot more than that to put me down." I threw all my weight up and forward, our bodies crashing together, bone on bone, skin on skin. Pure hatred on pure hatred.

"You're a fucking lunatic," I spat the words at him as he slammed his head into my mine, missing my nose and grazing my jaw. It stung something fierce, but I forced down the pain, locking it away where I'd deal with it later.

I'd had worse. Thatcher could do his worst but there was only one of us walking away from this in one piece, and it wasn't him.

31

Felicity

"WE HAVE GOT to find somewhere new to hang out on a Friday night," Mya grumbled, her eyes running around The Alley.

"Hey, it's not that bad."

"Not that bad? Girl, I just watched two man-boys get excited over winning at air hockey. Not sexy."

"I don't know." My shoulders lifted in a small shrug. "I kinda like it." The Alley was familiar, like your favorite pair of sneakers. The ones you couldn't bear to throw out no matter how worn and stinky they were.

"One day, I'm going to take you to the city." Mya's eyes lit up with promise. "Oh yeah, we could hit a club or two and find us a nice pair of—"

"You guys have got to come see this." A guy rushed into the diner, breathless and red-faced. "Jason Ford and Lewis Thatcher are down by the river, beating the shit out of each other."

The room spun, my hands gripping the edge of the counter so tight the blood drained from my fingers.

"Flick, breathe," Mya's voice called to me. "Just breathe." Snapping out of my trance, I met her worried gaze. "It's probably nothing. You know how rumors fly around here."

It wasn't nothing.

I felt it in my bones.

Just then, my cell phone blared to life. "It's Hailee," I said, staring at the screen, willing her to tell me it wasn't true.

"Hails?" her name came out strangled.

"We're on our way there now but you're closer."

"I can't... I'm not..."

"Fee, baby," Asher came over the line. "How're you holding up?"

"I don't... It's true? He's down there *fighting* Thatcher?"

"We're not too sure what the fuck is happening right now which is why we need you to go down there. Now, Felicity."

I couldn't speak, the words lodged up against the giant lump in my throat.

"Asher? It's Mya. She's spaced out or something. Yeah, okay. We can do that. Should we call... No, okay. Got it." She thrust the cell phone back at me.

"We need to leave, now."

"But—"

"Pull yourself together, your man needs you."

"He's not—"

Mya slammed her hands down on the table, leaning over to shove her face in front of mine. "You need to get it together, okay?" I nodded. "Jason can hold his own, but Asher is worried... it doesn't matter. We need to go stat. You can either stay here and freak out, or you can come with me and hope to God you can talk some sense into him before it's too late."

"The play-offs," I shrieked, leaping to my feet. If Coach or Principal Finnigan found out about this, Jason could be forced to sit out of the play-offs.

Mya rolled her eyes dramatically. "Now she gets it. Come on, we're wasting time." She'd rolled up the sleeves on her jacket and pulled her spiral curls into a messy ponytail which made me wonder how often she did this kind of thing for Jermaine.

"Too many times," she said as if she heard my thoughts. "Now let's go. Jason needs you."

I could barely see for the sea of people—Rixon and Rixon East kids—all mingled together, desperate to get a glimpse of Thatcher and Jason, their quarterback Kings going at it.

"What the hell are we supposed to do now?" I asked Mya, clutching onto her hand like it was my lifeline.

"Flick, over here," Hailee's voice settled some of the unease swimming in my stomach.

"Thank God," I all but fell into her arms, taking comfort from her hug. "This is crazy. Hey, how'd you get here before me?"

"Asher drove like a crazy person." She gave him a scowl. "But we're here now, and the guys called the cavalry."

"The cav—" the words died on my tongue as the entire team filtered in behind Asher and Cameron.

"We need to disperse this crowd," Cam said, his brows pinched with concern. "Any suggestions?"

"Leave it to me," Asher said, grabbing a couple of the guys and whispering in their ears. Soon they had disappeared into the crowd.

"Come on," Cam grabbed Hailee's hand and motioned for us to follow. We had to push and shove our way through the wall of bodies, but when I finally saw Jason, I froze. The sight of him shirtless and bloody was sensory overload.

"Flick?" Mya yelled over the noise: the grunts and groans from the two fighters in the middle of the crudely formed ring, the bloodthirsty cheers from our classmates. "Hold it together," she scolded, yanking on my arm, jerking me into action. "He's okay, see? You need to really worry when—"

Thatcher got in a good hit, the crack of bone on bone reverberating through me so violently, my stomach lurched, bile rushing up my throat. I swallowed, dragging in a lungful of fresh air. "Someone has to do something."

"We are, if you'll just keep moving."

"Thank fuck," Grady rushed over to us, sporting a black eye of his own.

Cam shook his head at his teammate, disapproval written all over his expression. "Save the lecture, man, I'm fully aware of what a clusterfuck this is," Grady winced.

"I'll deal with you later," Cameron seethed. "Right now, we need to figure out how to end this."

"I've tried, twice. This is the thanks I got." He pointed to the ugly bruise forming around his eye.

"Okay, go find Asher and help with the crowd. We've got this."

We did?

Because my legs felt ready to give out on me as I clung to Mya.

"Okay," Asher reappeared, breathless and flushed. "I'm here, what's the plan?"

"I'm thinking you two should get in there before you lose your quarterback for the play-offs," Mya deadpanned.

"Man, I love a woman who tells it like it is." Ash grinned at her. "Yo, Thatcher," he sauntered toward them, "Having all the fun without me?"

"Fuck off, Bennet, this is between me and Ford." Thatcher wasn't unscathed, blood trickling from a cut in his lip, another under his eye. He also had a nasty bruise ripening around his ribs.

"Sorry, bro, but we kind of need our QB for the play-offs; you know, the ones you didn't make this year."

"What the hell is he doing?" Mya lurched forward but Cam cut her off with his arm.

"He's got this."

"The hell he does, look..." She flicked her head to where a couple of Eagles' players were closing in on him.

"Fuck, okay, you three stay here."

"Cam," Hailee said, "I'm not sure this is a good idea. Maybe we should call the police?"

"If it comes to that, we will, I promise. But for now, just stay here." He levelled her with a look I rarely saw from him.

"That boy has more restraint than me," Mya remarked.

"That's what I'm worried about." Hailee reached back for my hand and we stood there, the three of us, watching while the guys we cared about faced off with Thatcher and his bunch of goons.

"Whatever Asher did, it worked. Look, people are leaving."

We glanced back to find the crowd slowly dispersing, being herded away by the remaining Raiders.

"It's over, Thatcher," Cameron stepped between him and Jason.

"You think just because you showed up with your girl in tow that it's over? It's over when I say it's fucking over." He was incensed, anger rolling off him like a tidal wave. "In fact, since she's here," his eyes found Hailee, "why don't you come over here and experience what it feels like to be with a real ma—"

Cameron's fist drove straight into his face. Thatcher grunted in pain, staggering back, but he quickly righted himself, spitting blood onto the ground. "So you do have balls, Chase? I was beginning to think you didn't after you let me and the guys mess with your girl time and time again."

"Cameron, don't." Hailee tore her hand free, moving toward them, but before she got there, Grady appeared and scooped her up, bringing her back to us.

"Stay out of this, Hailee, trust me."

"Aw, you don't want to play? What about your girl, Ford, does she like to play? It sure looked like it from the—"

"Thatcher," Jason's tone was icy cold.

A chill ran up my spine watching them. There was so much anger and hatred between them, I knew I was missing some of the pieces of the puzzle.

"Lewis, stop," a girl's voice shattered the tension.

"Aimee, I thought I told you to stay the fuck out of this?"

Her dark hair whipped around her as she ran toward them, putting herself in front of Jason as if she was shielding him.

"Hailee," I asked, the knot in my stomach tightening, "who is that?"

"I think that's Aimee."

"Aimee?"

"Yeah, Thatcher's sister, Jason's ex."

Jason had an ex?

I had vague lust-haze filled memories of him mentioning a girl, but he hadn't gone into detail. She hadn't even been a blip on my radar, but now she was there; a real-life person. And she was standing in front of Jason like he was hers to protect.

"Oh, shit, Flick, I didn't..." Hailee's voice became white noise as I watched the unfamiliar girl face off with her brother. She hadn't frozen on the side lines or stood by and watched; she'd run straight into the fray.

To protect Jason.

But why would she do that? Unless...

"Hey, you don't know anything yet, so stop thinking whatever you're thinking right now." Mya nudged my arm, giving me her trademark death stare.

"I'm not leaving until you walk away, Lewis. This has gone too far. Jason only did what he did because he was hurt."

"You think I give a shit about that? He sent that video to—"

"Hurt me. *Me*, Lewis. If anyone should be standing here demanding revenge, it's me." Aimee's expression turned sad. "Look, I know you only want to protect me, to get back at him, but this is his future."

Thatcher's jaw clenched, his eyes burning with hatred for the guy I realized I knew nothing about. Not really. I thought he'd let me in, let me see a side of him no one else got to see, but Jason was a locked box.

Maybe he always would be.

Tears burned the backs of my eyes as I slowly began to edge away from my friends.

"Felicity, where the hell are you going?" Mya hissed, trying to reach for me, but I shrugged her off.

"I can't be here." I couldn't see Jason's past play out right in front of my eyes. It hurt too much to see their history.

To *feel* it.

"Don't run, not now. Not when he needs you."

"Jason doesn't need me, Mya." I smiled sadly, letting the tears fall freely now. "He never did."

Without a second glance, I walked away. Ignoring her calls, Hailee's too. Blocking out the sound of Aimee's voice as she tried to reason with Thatcher. The low rumble of whispers as the Raiders and Eagles stood guard.

But most of all, I ignored the sound of my heart breaking.

32

Jason

"THIS ISN'T OVER," Thatcher spat as he finally relented, letting Aimee slip her arm around his waist and lead him away. She glanced back, her eyes saying things I didn't want to hear.

Cam and Ash were on me in a second, helping me stay upright as they guided me over to our friends and teammates.

"Fuck, man, you're a mess," he released a shaky breath. "You need the ER?" I threw Grady a 'fuck you' expression, and his hands went up. "Is it too early to say, 'told you so'?"

"Grady?" I hacked up a mouthful of blood, leaning on Ash for support. My ribs burned like a motherfucker and I wasn't one-hundred percent sure Thatcher hadn't broken something.

If he had, I could kiss the play-offs goodbye.

That was assuming this didn't land on Principal Finnigan's desk first thing Monday morning.

Fuck.

I'd really fucked up. But I'd been caught between a rock and a hard place.

"Yeah, Cap?" Grady asked.

"Shut the fuck up."

"Come on, we should probably get out of here before the cops show up." Cam barely met my eyes, disappointment radiating off him.

But screw him.

He didn't know the whole story yet, no one did.

I'd tell them eventually, but first I needed a shit ton of Advil and a bottle of Jack.

I managed to crawl into the back of Asher's Jeep, Mya climbing in behind me while Cam and Hailee sat up front. There was no sign of Felicity, but I was almost certain I'd seen her there, standing with the girls.

Maybe I dreamed it up.

A mirage in the middle of one of the worst fucking beatings of my life.

A beautiful angel in the middle of my own personal hell.

"Guess the rumors are true," Mya said, studying me intently.

"Yeah, and what do they say?" It hurt to fucking breathe let alone talk, but there was something about the way she looked at me that had me intrigued.

"You're not just a pretty face." Her lip curved. "Before you pass out, tell me one thing. Was it worth it?" She kept her voice low, as if we were sharing some big secret.

"So worth it." I sank back against the leather, swallowing a groan and closing my eyes. "So fucking worth it."

Her hearty laughter was the last thing I heard.

———

"What the fuck were you thinking, bro?" The veins in Asher's neck throbbed with frustration. "We're this close to State and you go and screw it all up and for what? To say you have bigger balls than Thatcher? It makes no sense, none."

"Ash, leave it," Cam said coolly, his eyes hard on me.

"Leave it? Are you fucking kidding me? He's out. When Coach gets wind of this, and he will, he'll have no choice but to pull your," he jabbed his finger at me, "ass from the team. All that hard work for nothing. I just don't get it. You told us all to leave it, so then why the fuck did you—"

"ASH!" Cam roared, and his eyes grew to saucers.

"What?"

"I said, leave it."

"Yeah, whatever, I'm out. I need a beer or something." He stormed from the room, the door slamming behind him.

"That went well," I smirked, the pain meds and whisky slowly working their way through my system.

"Jase, come on, cut him some slack. He's only worried. We all are."

"Yeah, yeah, save me the Mother Teresa routine. I knew what I was doing when I went down there."

"So why'd you do it?"

"Like you don't already know."

"For her?" His brow hit his hairline. "But why?"

Why?

That was the question I'd asked myself over and over since getting back to Ash's house.

"Because the thought of him hurting her any more than he already had kills me."

A slow smile cracked his face.

"What?" I asked.

"Took you long enough."

"Doesn't change anything," I groaned, pain burning through every part of me.

"I think it does. I think it changes everything."

"I'm not that guy, Cam. I'm not like you."

"You just got your ass handed to you... for a girl. I think you're more like me than you give yourself credit for."

I snorted. "I had him." There was no way Thatcher had the upper hand on me. Sure, I was bloody and bruised but so was he. My knuckles were busted wide open to prove it.

"So in the end you risked everything... for a girl."

"Not just any girl." My head dropped back, my eyes shuttering as the reality of everything sank in.

Asher was right. I'd blown everything I'd ever worked for. But it wasn't for nothing.

It was for her.

And I'd do it again. Over and over, if it meant protecting Felicity from the likes of Thatcher and his goons.

"He has some images of her... *us*." I groaned the words, guilt slamming into me. It was all my fucking fault. Thatcher might have been unhinged but I'd given him the ammunition he needed to come after Hailee and then Felicity. All this time, I'd thought by not caring, by not giving a crap about anyone around me, I was protecting myself. But they weren't the weak link.

I was.

"Images, what kind of... oh, shit."

"Yeah," I breathed out. I still had no idea how he got them, but I'd seen them with my own eyes; me and Felicity in my car down by the lake. "He threatened to send them viral unless I agreed to the fight."

"Did Aimee know? She was the one who messaged Asher."

"I have no idea why the fuck she was there. She turned up at my house to warn me it was a setup, that Thatcher intended on fucking me up enough to ruin my shot at playing in the play-offs."

"First Hailee, now you and Felicity. This isn't just some harmless prank, Jase; it's more serious than that."

"You think I don't know that?"

"We have to report him."

"I started it." I ground out. "None of this would ever have happened if it wasn't for that video I sent him of me and Aimee."

"True but that was between the three of you." Cam rubbed his temples. "You never passed that shit around. He's out of control and there's still nothing stopping him from sending those images to everyone. We have to report him."

"Give me some time to figure this out, yeah?"

"Jase..."

"Twenty-four hours, that's all I'm asking."

"Fine. But if you don't handle this the proper way, I will. Coach and Principal Finnigan are going to blow a gasket when they find out about this, maybe the truth will soften the blow."

I didn't share his optimism, but it was hard to worry about the play-offs when I currently felt like I'd never lift a ball again.

"You look like shit. You sure I can't take you to the

ER?"

"Nah, I'm good. Got everything I need." I flicked my head over to the bottle of Jack and box of pills.

"Okay, get some rest. If you need anything..."

"Thanks, and Cam?"

"Yeah?"

"Was she there? I mean, I think I saw there but it's all a bit hazy."

"She was there," he hesitated, "but she left."

"Right." His confirmation hurt more than any bruise caused by Thatcher's fist.

"She'll come around." He lingered by the door.

"You think?"

"I know so." A faint smile tugged at his mouth.

"How's that?"

"Because that's what you do when you love someone." Cameron slipped out of the room as if he hadn't just delivered a bomb.

He thought Felicity loved me?

After everything I'd done to her, the way I'd treated her.

It wasn't possible.

Was it?

Did I even want her to love me?

It was crazy.

Her and me.

I cared about her, sure. I wouldn't have done everything I had for her if I didn't.

But love?

I wasn't in love with her.

She was nothing like my usual type. Quirky and irritating. Unapologetically weird with her lists and lack of filter. But she was also kind and compassionate and she didn't take herself too seriously. And she had a banging body hiding underneath those god-awful overalls she wore.

My heart began to crash violently against my ribcage, my palms growing clammy. I was having some kind of reaction. A moment of complete 'oh fuck' clarity.

I was ass over elbow in love with Felicity Giles.

———

When I woke up the next morning, I was pretty sure I was in hell. So when a knock sounded on the door, I croaked, "Come in," hardly caring who it was. I just needed some damn pain meds.

The door swung open and Hailee's head peeked into the room. "Oh my god," she hurried over to me, unshed tears in her eyes.

"I hope you're not going to cry on me," I said gruffly, "because I don't do tears."

"What the hell were you thinking?" Perching gingerly on the edge of the bed, Hailee grabbed the box of pain meds and gave me two, handing me a glass of water to wash them down with.

A pained groan rumbled in my chest but I stuffed it down. "Thanks."

"Are you sure I can't persuade you to go the ER?"

"Not gonna happen. But I'll go see our physician Monday."

"Coach is going to lose his shit."

"It is what it is."

"Jason don't do that. Don't downplay the fact you just threw away the play-offs to try to defend my honor."

"Of course you think this about you, little miss 'look at me'." Even though it hurt like a bitch, I chuckled. The look on Hailee's face was just too damn priceless.

"You mean, you didn't do this to get Thatcher back for trashing the portraits?"

"Oh, I definitely got a couple of hits in for that." I managed a wink despite the bruising around my eye. "But no, it wasn't about you."

"So what the hell... Felicity." Her eyes widened. "This was all for Felicity."

"How'd you guess?"

"Because this isn't you. Well, it is, I mean you're not exactly known for your cool headedness. But you wouldn't risk everything, the play-offs, if it wasn't important." The understanding in her eyes was almost too much to bear. "What did he threaten to do?"

"He has some photos of us. Threatened to send them viral if I didn't agree to the meet. I couldn't do that to her, not after everything." Flopping back onto the pillows, I stared up at the ceiling.

"So all this? Pushing her away, shoving Jenna in her face, acting like you didn't care, it was all to distance yourself? To protect her?"

My eyes slid slowly to hers. "He knew she was someone to me. He knew she was my weakness, so yeah, I thought if I pushed her away, if I pretended I didn't care, he'd forget about her. I didn't know he had the images. He must have had one of his guys keeping tabs on me."

"Oh, Jason." Hailee did something she'd never done

before; she grabbed my hand and squeezed gently. "You care. All this time you cared. You know you have to tell her, right?"

I gave her a pointed look.

"Jason, come on, she thinks you and Aimee—"

"Aimee is nothing to me."

"I know that, but Felicity saw the way she jumped in to protect you. Put yourself in her shoes. She didn't even know you had an ex."

"Fuck," I breathed out, pain splintering through me. Only this time, it wasn't just the physical kind.

Everything was so fucking messed up.

"You have to fix this. Otherwise, it was all for nothing."

That's where she was wrong though.

It wasn't all for nothing.

Because if I knew anything about relationships, about love, it was that you protected the people you cared about. You stood up for them and made sacrifices.

And I'd just made the ultimate one.

I'd sacrificed the one thing I wanted more than anything. But even now, even knowing I probably wasn't going to see a single play-off game, I didn't regret it.

I only regretted not choosing Felicity sooner.

33

Felicity

I WAS IN DREAM HEAVEN. Jason's greedy lips tracing featherlight kisses up the slope of my neck, the heat of his body radiating around me, his delicious scent assaulting my senses.

"Open your eyes, babe,"

"I don't want to," I murmured, feeling desire swirl low in my tummy.

"Felicity." His voice was so real. "Open your eyes."

"No, don't make me. I don't want this to be over." It was too nice here. Wrapped in his arms, safe and protected. Cherished. I snuggled my face into his shoulder, breathing him in.

"Jason," I sighed, his name sweet on my tongue.

"Yeah, babe?"

"Make love to me, please." I wanted him. More than I'd ever wanted anything. Certain, if he didn't touch me soon, I'd drown in the flames raging inside me.

A throaty groan filled my ears as his lips brushed the shell of my ear. "Open your eyes and ask me again."

Damn him. Even in my dreams he was insufferable.

"Fine, all good things have to come to an end

eventually," I mumbled to myself because I knew the second I opened my eyes—

"Jason?" I grabbed the sheets, my body paralyzed as he loomed over me. "B- but what are you... *Jason?*"

"Hey." His swollen lip curved into a hesitant smile. "I'm sorry I scared you."

"Scared me?" I sucked in a harsh breath, my back plastered against the pillows. "You almost gave me a heart attack."

"Among other things." A faint smirk played on his face.

"Oh God," I mumbled, turning my face into the pillow. It hadn't been a dream at all. Jason was here, in my room.

He'd kissed me... and I'd begged him to make love to me.

The universe owed me some good karma in the future after all the shit it had put me through lately.

Sensing my impending meltdown, Jason backed up, giving me some space. My eyes adjusted to the darkness, revealing the extent of his injuries. I reached for him instinctively, ghosting my fingers over the dark bruises around his eyes. He leaned into me, exhaling a shaky breath.

"Why, Jason? Everything you've worked for..." my voice trailed off, the weight of what had happened on Friday night settling over us.

"For you," he whispered.

The words were like a gunshot to my heart.

Two little words I'd never in a million years expected to hear.

"Me?" I choked out, my eyes searching his for any signs this was a joke. That it was all a part of his cruel game.

"We should probably talk."

"Talk... you broke into my house in the middle of the night... to *talk*?"

"I was supposed to wait." He raked a hand through his unruly brown hair, letting it fall haphazardly around his face. "Had it all planned out and everything. But I was lying in bed, trying to ignore the pain, and I couldn't wait another second longer. I had to see you now."

"You did?"

I'd spent all weekend fretting over him, greedily absorbing any minute details Hailee would feed me.

Jason nodded, a small uncertain smile lifting the corner of his mouth. He winced at the involuntary action.

"It hurts?"

"Like you wouldn't believe. But not as much as it hurts knowing I might have screwed things up between us."

Us.

He thought there was an us still?

Maybe I was still dreaming, stuck in some beautiful nightmare.

"Is this real?" I asked quietly. He leaned in, cupping my face, brushing his thumb over my lips. Raw desire blazing in the depths of his eyes. "Does this feel real?"

"Honestly, I'm not sure." I could barely think straight with the way my heart was galloping in my chest, crashing against my ribs looking for a way out.

"What about this?" Jason moved closer, his lips touching mine.

"I'm still not sure, you should probably do it again. Just so I can be certain." I fought a smile and he chuckled, the sound like a salve to my battered heart.

Slowly, he threaded his fingers into my hair, tilting my

face ever so slightly to align our mouths at the perfect angle. "Jason," I pleaded, desperate for him to kiss me, to show me this was real. But he hovered there, staring at me with such intensity I thought my heart might explode. His eyes were dark and hooded and filled with so much emotion, I couldn't breathe.

I couldn't do anything but wait.

"You are the single most important thing in my life, and I'm sorry. I'm so fucking sorry," he said with complete conviction.

Then he kissed me.

But it wasn't just a kiss at all.

It was Jason willingly handing over his heart. With every press of his lips, every stroke of his tongue, he silently told me everything I'd so desperately craved to hear from him as his mouth moved over mine. He might have been the one in control, setting the pace, but I was the one with the power. It simmered between us. An unspoken admonition. He was apologizing to me through actions, not words, but the ball was in my court regarding what happened next.

"Jason, wait," I said, physically forcing myself to break the kiss.

He dropped his forehead to mine, letting out a pained groan. "Hey," I said, sliding my hands gently against his cheeks, forcing him to look at me. "I'm here, I'm right here, but you're right, we should talk."

There was so much we needed to figure out. Things I needed to know before I let him off the hook.

"I can come back later," he started to pull away, "when it's—"

"Jase?"

"Yeah, Giles?"

"Shut the hell up and lie down with me." I shuffled over to make room for him and threw back the cover. His brow went up but his expression quickly softened.

"You're sure?"

"Get over here before I change my mind." My parents were sleeping right down the hall, and I didn't want to think about what my dad would do if he found me with a boy in my bed, let alone a Raider, but I wasn't about to give up the chance to have Jason here like this. In my bed, heart on his sleeve and ready to talk.

He kicked off his sneakers, his hoodie going next, before slipping in beside me. We lay on our sides, facing one another. "What did you mean, you did it for me?" I asked.

"Thatcher knew you were someone to me. He sent me some messages, threatening to come at me through you. So I distanced myself." His eyes shuttered. "Pushed you away."

"I see." I shuddered thinking about everything we'd been through the last few weeks, everything he'd put me through.

Jason pulled the covers up around us, refusing to let me escape from the conversation. "But it didn't matter because he knew the truth and he already had his ace card up his sleeve," he hesitated, guilt swimming in his eyes. "He had some images of us, down by the lake that day."

"No!" Panic flooded me, embarrassment flaming my cheeks, as my thoughts shot off in a hundred different directions.

"I'm so fucking sorry. I still can't figure out how he got them, but he threatened to make them viral unless I agreed to meet him."

"He has images... of me. Us?"

"I'm going to go to the authorities. It's gone too far. I realize that now. I will do everything in my power to make sure he doesn't release those photos."

Tears pooled in the corners of my eyes. I wasn't a slut. I didn't sleep around or date guy after guy after guy. But I'd done things with Jason... things I didn't want anyone to know about, let alone *see*. "Oh God, if my parents—"

"Hey, hey," he pulled me into his arms, tucking me against his solid body. "It won't come to that, I promise."

Hands pressed against his chest, I closed my eyes and inhaled a shuddering breath.

"I'll fix it, Felicity, you have my word." I didn't just hear the words, I felt them. Jason meant every single one. He'd done all this for me, to protect me. It was a lot to process.

Suddenly, a thought popped into my head. "What about Aimee?" I craned my head back to look at him.

"Aimee is no one."

"Jason..."

"She was someone, once upon a time. But that shit was over a long time ago."

"She's Thatcher's sister?" He nodded, his fingers tracing up and down my spine, making it difficult to concentrate. "You were together?"

"You really want to know this stuff?" he asked, and I gave him a weak smile, nodding. "I hadn't seen or spoken to Aimee in months until yesterday."

"Oh, that makes me feel better."

"Good, I don't want you to ever worry about other girls. There is no one but you."

"Jenna?" my brow rose accusingly.

He snorted. "A means to an end."

"Whatever happens next between us, promise me you'll never ever refer to me as a means to an end."

"You're not a means to an end, Giles. You're endgame."

If I wasn't already head over heels in love with Jason Ford, those three little words would have spun my world.

"Endgame? Sounds... serious?"

"Oh it is." He pecked the end of my nose. "Dead serious."

"I'm not entirely sure I understand exactly what it means, you might have to break it down for me." I fought a grin.

"It means you're mine."

"I'm yours, okay, I think I can get on board with that." Warmth spread through me. He said the words as if they were the simplest thing in the entire world. And I loved it.

I loved him.

I had for a while now. I'd just been too scared to admit it.

"Anything else?" I lowered my head, looking up at him through my lashes, acting coy.

"Yeah, I think it means come game day, there's only one number you'll be wearing." He captured my lips in a bruising kiss. "Mine."

———

The next time I woke was to my alarm and a very hard, very warm chest. I untangled myself from Jason's embrace and reached behind me, desperately trying to locate my cell to make the noise stop.

"What the—"

"Sorry," I whispered, "Alarm."

"Shit," he bolted upright and quickly sank back down, groaning in pain. "I didn't mean to fall asleep."

"I'm glad you did." Pushing my bed hair out of my face, I smiled at the sight of Jason sprawled out in my bed. At some point in the night, he'd taken off his jeans and jersey and climbed back in beside me, sliding his bare legs against mine.

It had been heaven.

"How long do we have before your parents surface?"

"Not long." I'd had the foresight to set my alarm thirty minutes earlier than usual so he could sneak out before they got up.

"Come here." He hooked his arm around my neck and pulled me down to him, his lips finding mine in a clumsy kiss.

"Ew, morning breath," I complained.

"You think I give a shit about that? Lips, now," he growled the words, fixing his mouth over mine, making a show of pushing his tongue deep into my mouth and tangling it with my own. My tummy clenched; a delicious ache spreading through me.

"How long did you say we have again?" Jason rolled onto his side, sliding my leg over his hip and rocking his erection into me.

"Not long enough." A soft moan spilled from my lips as he continued grinding against me. "Oh God, that feels..."

"Fuck, I need to stop. I need to—" A knock at my bedroom door had us both freezing.

"Morning, baby, are you awake?"

"Uh, yeah, Mom," I croaked, barely able to form words as Jason pressed into me again, a smug smirk gracing his bruised face.

"I'll make coffee. See you down there."

I waited a second to make sure she had left and then swatted Jason's chest. "You're so bad," I scolded, but his expression was twisted with pain. "Crap, I'm sorry. Where does it hurt?"

"Everywhere, but nowhere as bad as here." He grabbed my hand and closed it around his rock-hard dick.

"Jason!"

"You're telling me if I do this," he slipped his fingers inside my panties, "I'm not going to find you wet?"

"Oh God..." I pressed my lips together as he rubbed back and forth, sliding through my wetness. "We can't..." I moaned, lost in sensation.

"For once, I'm inclined to agree." His fingers disappeared and my eyes fluttered open, only to find him sucking them clean. "Later." Promise burned in his eyes as he leaned in, kissing me. Swirling his tongue around mine, letting me taste myself on his lips.

"How will you sneak out?" He could barely sit up, let alone execute a stealthy escape plan.

"Who said anything about sneaking out? Moms love me, remember?" My eyes widened to saucers and his face broke out in a wide grin. "Gotcha."

"Haha, now go, before my dad wakes up."

Jason climbed out of bed and grabbed his clothes.

"Your ribs," I blanched at the huge purple bruise painted along his side.

"It's nothing," he played it down, but I saw how

carefully he pulled on his jersey and hoodie, pain behind his eyes with every movement. "I'll see you later, okay?"

It was on the tip of my tongue to ask what happened when we got to school, but Jason had already slipped into the hall. He glanced back, his eyes saying all the things we were yet to say.

Things I never thought we'd get to say.

And I knew in that second, this time it wasn't a game or some cruel prank.

It was real.

Jason Ford, Rixon's golden boy of football, was mine.

34

Jason

"ARE YOU SURE ABOUT THIS?" Cam asked me as we made our way into school. Everyone was looking; kids, teachers, even the few parents doing the morning drop off. I knew what they saw.

Jason Ford.

Star football player.

Cocky arrogant troublemaker.

People usually turned a blind eye. Usually excused my antics as 'boys being boys'. But not this time.

This time, people had gotten hurt.

I'd gotten hurt.

But they didn't know the truth. They didn't know I'd done what I'd done out of a need to protect Felicity. To stand up for the girl who consumed my every waking thought.

They didn't know at all.

As far as I was concerned, it could stay that way. I hadn't fought Thatcher for glory or in the name of the Raiders reputation, or even my own. I'd done it because when it came down to it, I was just a guy who loved a girl and refused to let some fucktard like Lewis Thatcher ruin her because of his beef with me.

I spotted her first. She was talking to Hailee and Mya near their locker bank, ignoring the rumble of whispers and gossip flying up and down the hallway.

"So did the two of you talk about what happens now?" Cam asked me as we slowly approached them.

"Nope." I couldn't tear my eyes away from her to answer him. Felicity was wearing boy jeans, slung low on her hips, a slither of skin on display where her shirt didn't quite meet the waistband. It was baggy around her midriff, tight over her chest, and hung off one shoulder. Her long brown locks were swept over one shoulder, her face void of makeup, her expression animated as she talked to her friends.

"So what's the pla—"

But I was already gone. Cutting through the stream of kids. Hailee noticed me first, her lips breaking into a wide grin. Mya was next, smugness dancing in her eyes, as if she knew this was a forgone conclusion. I gave zero fucks about their reactions though. The only girl I cared about still hadn't noticed me as I moved up behind her. Sliding my hands around her eyes, I leaned in and whispered, "Guess who?"

"Hmm, Asher?" She chuckled as I spun her in my arms and glared at her.

"Try again, Giles."

"Hi," she said around an uncertain smile.

"Hi."

Hailee and Mya backed up, giving the two of us space. The whole school seemed to have stopped around us, everyone watching their King fall for his Queen.

"Is it me or is everyone watching us?" Felicity cast a quick glance around.

"They're waiting to see if the rumor is true."

"Oh yeah?" Her smile grew. "And what rumor would that be?"

"That QB One is officially off the market." I inched closer to her.

"And is he?" She matched my step.

"I think it's pretty safe to say, he's taken."

"Damn, just when I'd finally plucked up the courage to tell him how I feel. Ah well, I guess I'll have to wait until whoever it is dumps his sorry ass."

"Did I ever tell you, you're so fucking weird?" I lowered my head to hers.

"Did I ever tell you, I have a serious thing for football players?"

"Players, plural? Because I know a couple of the guys who would love to hook—"

She swatted my chest. Before she could move her hands, I captured her wrists, keeping them pressed there.

"Something you want to tell me, Giles?"

"You first, Ford, I have a reputation to protect." She winked and I let out a hearty chuckle. This girl...

This fucking girl.

Leaning in, I brushed my lips over her ear and whispered, "I am so fucking gone for you."

Felicity eased back to look right in my eyes. "Is that your way of telling me you love me?"

Swallowing thickly, I nodded, aware this wasn't exactly how I planned to tell her.

"Good job, because I am completely and utterly gone for you too."

I didn't care we had an audience. I didn't care people had their cell phones out recording the moment QB One publicly handed over his balls to a girl.

I didn't care one bit as I pressed Felicity against the lockers and kissed the ever loving shit out of her. People would just have to get used to it because she was mine, and I was hers, and I intended on reminding her of that every second of every day.

———

"Ford, my office, now!"

All eyes went to me as I stood up and padded across the locker room. A couple of guys clapped me on the back, silently offering their support. But this was my burden to bear, and mine alone. Until I stepped inside his office to find I wasn't alone.

"Coach," I said coolly, waiting for the shit to hit the fan, sliding my eyes to the silent figure already seated in front of his desk.

"Sit," he barked, and I took the other empty chair. "I don't think I even need to ask my next question to know the answer. You're a mess, Son. A real damn mess."

I shifted uncomfortably on the plastic chair, trying to find a position that didn't make my lungs feel like they were on fire.

"As soon as we're done here, you head straight to medical. You hear me? If you've broken anything so help me God..."

I nodded, knowing this was one of those times Coach wouldn't appreciate a smart assed reply.

He tore off his ball cap and rubbed his head with sheer frustration. "Four more games, that's all I asked for. And you couldn't just listen. You know I'll have to go to Principal Finnigan with this, right? If he hasn't already found out since it seems to be the only thing on kids' lips this morning."

"Sorry, Sir." It sounded so lame in comparison to what was at stake, but it was all I had.

"So you're confirming his story?" he looked to Asher who rubbed the back of his neck.

"I, uh..."

"It's okay, bro. I already confessed I screwed up by goading Thatcher into that fight and you had to come save my sorry ass."

What the fuck?

I stared at Ash like he'd lost his goddamn mind. Or maybe I had. Because nothing he was saying was making any sense.

"Well, Jason, what do you have to say for yourself?"

"I, hmm, I..."

"It's okay," Ash whispered and my eyes slid back to his in question. He nodded, his eyes hammering home everything I didn't want to believe.

He was taking the fall.

For me.

My teeth ground together behind my lips as I tried to figure out what the fuck to do. If I let him take the fall, chances were his season was over. But if I told Coach the truth, my season was over, and maybe Asher's too for the fact he tried to save my ass.

Fuck.

"I haven't got all day, Son."

"It's okay, Jase, just tell him."

I couldn't do it. I couldn't be that guy. Not after everything.

"Sorry, Coach, but I have to tell you the—"

"The truth is, Coach," Ash cut me off, "Lewis Thatcher is a sick fuck who has spent the last three months coming after Jason through his friends and family. Jason didn't want to tell anyone to protect his step-sister and girlfriend."

"Girlfriend?" Coach frowned, rubbing his jaw.

"Felicity Giles, you may know her?"

"The name does ring a bell."

"Thatcher threatened to hurt Felicity over and over, but Jason refused to take the bait. His final threat was more persuasive," Asher threw me a sympathetic glance. "I knew if Jason found out about the threat he'd go after Thatcher, so I arranged the meet."

"And what exactly did you expect to achieve, Son?"

Ash shrugged in that easy way of his. "World peace?" I snorted. "Fuck if I know. But I couldn't just sit around and do nothing. Anyway, the whole thing was a set up. They jumped me and I had no choice but to call for back up."

"Which is when you intervened?" Coach cocked his brow at me.

"I... yes."

"To save your teammate's hide?"

"Yes, Sir."

"But we played straight into Thatcher's hand because he'd wanted Jase there all along."

"I see, and the rest of the team? How do they figure in all of this?"

"I took them as back up, but that was it." I ran a hand over my face.

"You have proof of Thatcher's threats?"

Asher nodded. "I have screenshots of everything."

"You do, since when?" I asked.

"Since I knew that one day we might need them."

"There's also a video and some photos, Sir. But they're hmm, quite graphic."

"You should have come to me with this. You should have come to me the second Thatcher upped the ante."

"Yes, Sir," we grumbled in unison.

"Will Miss Raine and Miss Giles attest your story?"

I nodded.

"Right, well, I have no choice but to take this to the Principal. Given your history with him, I wouldn't expect him to be on your side. You know what that means?"

Another, "Yes, Sir," filled the room.

Coach let out an exasperated breath. "I'll do my best, but it could be out of my hands. Now go on, get to class, both of you. And damn well stay there until I say otherwise."

We left his office in silence, but the second we were out of earshot, I grabbed Ash's arm. "What the fuck was that in there?"

"That was me saving your ass, so don't be a dick and mess things up. Stick to the plan."

"The plan? You do realize you just took the fall for something that could end your football season?"

"I know and I'd do it again if it means you get to play."

"But... why?" I was stunned.

"Because you're one of my best friends and I know how much State means to you. Besides, Finnigan is just looking for an excuse to come down on you and this could've opened up a whole can of worms you don't need." He went to walk off, but I tightened my grip on his arm.

"Asher, come on, think about this, it's crazy."

"Actually, it's pretty simple. I'm your friend and this is what friends do. You can thank me later." With that he yanked his arm free and strolled off as if he hadn't just saved my dream and let his go up in flames.

———

Later that day, I had another score to settle.

"Jason?" Jenna's eyes widened as I crowded her back into the girls' locker room. Girls gasped, some shrieking as they hugged clothes to their half-naked bodies.

"Everybody out, now," I roared, knowing full well that no one would complain. One by one, Jenna's friends and teammates scurried out of the locker room, leaving her at my mercy.

"J- Jason, you're scaring me."

"Good, you should be fucking scared." I closed the distance between us until I could smell the cloying stench of her perfume.

"What is it, what's wrong?" She tried to regain control

of the situation. Batting her eyes, brushing her hair back to reveal an expanse of tan skin, the curve of her tits.

"Not going to work, Jenna," I seethed. "You see, I had an interesting chat with Aimee Thatcher earlier. Ring any bells?" Her face blanched, her eyes filled with fear. "I mean, you must know her right, since you've been visiting her house, drip feeding Thatcher things about me. About my. Fucking. Life."

"It isn't... it wasn't like that."

"So you didn't spread your legs and let him fuck you while whispering all my secrets in his ear?"

"It's all your fault," she shrieked, thrusting her hands into my chest and beating hard. "You dropped me like I was nothing. And for Felicity Giles, a fucking no one."

"Watch it, Jenna. You might think you're the Queen Bee around here, but I can soon strip you of that title." I could destroy her without even breaking a sweat. But I wasn't out for blood yet, I was out for answers.

"How'd you do it?"

All morning, I'd been pondering how Thatcher got the photos of me and Felicity. I'd assumed he had one of his guys following me, but it seemed a stretch. Even for Thatcher. It wasn't until Grady mentioned he'd seen Jenna talking to some Eagles players Friday as the fight dispersed that my mind began piecing together a more likely scenario. A quick call to Aimee confirmed my suspicions. Thatcher's guy was in fact, a girl. A girl who, against my better judgment, had an up close and personal relationship with me.

"Jason, I—"

"Answer the fucking question."

"I followed you, okay? I'd been watching you, noticed you always texting someone. It didn't take a rocket scientist to figure out who, the way you two sat staring at one another across the cafeteria." Jealousy dripped from her words. "I didn't plan to follow you, but I saw Felicity sneaking out and before I knew it, I'd gotten in my car. It was just a lucky break."

A low growl tumbled in my chest and the blood drained from her face again. "I didn't... that's not what I meant. I just meant it was a coincidence. Please, Jason, what are you going to do?"

I slammed my hand against the wall beside her and ground out, "Only what you deserve."

Then I walked away without a backward glance.

No matter our history, Jenna made her bed when she came after Felicity.

She could fucking rot in it.

35

Felicity

"How ARE we getting on in here?" George's head appeared around the door just as I got Benji back in his cage.

"We're good. I just finished grooming Benji and I was going to get started on Meagan and Frieda next." They were two of the cutest puppies I'd ever laid eyes on; mini Schnauzers I'd have struggled to tell apart if it wasn't for their contrasting collars.

"Actually, you have a visitor." Something flashed over his face.

"Visitor?" I washed my hands and dried them on paper towel. "Here?"

"He's waiting out front."

He?

I followed George out into the hall, my mind working overtime. As we reached the doors separating the front and back of the center, George paused. "I just want you to know you've already made an impression here. You're great with the animals, eager to learn, and Serena loves you, which is always a bonus." He gave me a tentative smile. "The position is yours for however long you want it."

"What are you—" George pushed opened the door and I gasped. "Jason? But what are you...?"

"Hey," he gave me a hesitant smile as he approached us. "Thanks, man," he held out his hand to George, "I really appreciate it."

"Umm, yeah, sure." My new boss ran a brisk hand over his head, guilt flaming his cheeks.

"Wait a minute." My gaze narrowed, sliding between the two of them. "Did he put you up to this?"

"He may have had a hand in it," George admitted sheepishly.

"Let me guess," I let out an incredulous sigh, "you're a Raiders fan?"

His cheeks turned beet red.

"I don't know what to say." I'd thought maybe George had found me a position because he liked me; it had never occurred to me he'd done it because Jason had asked him to.

"Can I borrow her?"

"She's all yours." There was an undertone to George's words that confirmed Mya's suspicion. He did like me. But he knew I belonged to someone else.

I gave him a half-smile. "Thank you. Should I still come by tomorrow?"

"Of course, Felicity. Like I said, the position is yours for as long as you want it."

With a small nod, I let Jason take my hand and lead me out of New Tail. "You have some explaining to do," I said the second we were on the sidewalk.

"And I will." He pulled me in front of him, so we were face to face. "But first..." Jason slid his hands into my hair, tilting my face. His lips brushed over mine, slow and tender at first but it quickly became something else. Jason licked the seam of my mouth, pushing his tongue inside, finding mine. He tasted like mint, taking my breath away, as he explored every inch of my mouth. Branding me.

Possessing me.

Imprinting himself on my very soul.

When we finally broke away, we were both flushed and breathless.

"Hi," he said quietly.

"Hi." I fought a grin, still hardly able to believe this strong, scary football god was mine.

"What?" he asked.

"I just can't believe we're here, after everything."

"Believe it, babe." He dipped his head, nudging his nose against mine, stealing a chaste kiss. "Because you're mine now and there's no escaping me."

"Good job I have no plans to run then. Now," I slid my hands up his chest, "Fess up. What did you say to George to get him to give me a position?"

"It was nothing a few play-off tickets couldn't solve."

I balked. "Tickets. That's all I'm worth? Wait until I see him."

"Don't give him a hard time over it. I think he would have agreed without me throwing in the tickets to soften the deal."

"How did you even know... Asher," realization dawned on me. "Asher told you."

"He was only trying to help." Jason pulled me closer, his lips finding the soft skin beneath my ear. "I missed you."

"It's only been a few hours."

"Too fucking many."

"Is this the kind of boyfriend you're going to be? Needy?"

Jason lifted his head and frowned at me. "Needy? I'd handcuff you to me if I thought it wouldn't cause some serious trouble with your parents."

"Jason!"

"What?" He played dumb. "I can't help it if all I can think about is kissing you, getting inside you."

"Ssh, you can't say things like that to me here."

He leaned back in, brushing the shell of my ear with his lips. "Babe, I can say whatever the hell I want."

He was so bad.

So very bad and so very all mine.

It was going to take some getting used to.

"What did Principal Finnigan say?"

He took my hand and started leading me across the street to his car. "He's yet to make a decision. But it's not looking good for Asher."

"I still can't believe he did that."

"Really?" His brow shot up. "Because when I think about it, it's exactly the kind of crazy shit he would pull."

"He's a good friend."

Jason opened the passenger door for me and I slipped inside, waiting for him to get in. Once the door slammed shut behind him, the air in the car turned thick. "Do you wish it'd been him?"

"What?" I asked taken aback.

"Do you ever wish it was him you'd fallen for?"

"No." I didn't even need to think about it. "There was never a choice, Jason. You don't get to choose who you fall in love with."

"You love me, Giles?" His eyes slid to mine, dark and uncertain and so vulnerable it made my heart melt.

"I love you so much it terrifies me."

"Good." He leaned across and kissed me. "We can be terrified together."

———

Ten minutes later, Jason pulled up to his house, and cut the engine. "Nervous?" he asked, reaching over and tangling our hands together.

"Nervous? What could I possibly have to be nervous about? I've been in your house more times than I can count. Hailee's mom loves me." It came out smug despite the butterflies fluttering in my stomach.

"No one's home, babe." His smooth laughter filled the car.

"Oh," I stuttered, heat spreading through me. "Where are they all?"

"Hailee's with Cameron, and Denise and my dad are off doing whatever the fuck they like to do on an evening. The house is ours for at least the next four hours."

"Oh." This time I gulped.

"Hey," Jason's hands glided up my arm until he was brushing my neck. "You good?"

"Yeah." I blinked over at him. This was Jason. Nothing I hadn't already experienced—*and survived*—before.

"No pressure, okay?" His eyes searched mine. "We can go in there and watch TV and eat our body weight in chips. Or we can go in there and do homework. I just really, really want to go in there... with you."

"Okay."

"Yeah?"

I nodded, finding the courage to step out of his car. I don't know why I was so nervous suddenly. I'd let him claim me in front of half our class today at school. But this felt different.

This felt like coming out to each other, and after everything we'd been through, there was a little voice at the back of my mind whispering for me to be careful. To not jump in headfirst with him in case he had a sudden change of heart.

But it was too late.

I was already in deep waters hoping Jason would throw me a life raft.

Hoping *he* would be my life raft.

We entered the house in silence. It was the same four walls, the same collection of gaudy ornaments lining the shelves, and family photos Hailee's mom had scattered over the walls. Everything was exactly the same.

But I was different.

We were different.

"Is this weird for you?" Jason asked, no doubt sensing my hesitation.

"A little. I just... I never thought we'd get here and now we are and I'm so happy, I am. But—"

"You're worried I'll hurt you again." Shame washed over him. "Wait here." Jason dropped a kiss on my head before disappearing down the hall.

I stood there, arms wrapped around my waist, wondering what the hell could be so important he had to abandon me.

When he returned, he had that sheepish look again. "Jason," I said, "what did you do?"

He was holding a white plastic bag. "I was trying to think of a way to show you I want this. That I'm serious about *this*." He motioned between us. "So I got you something."

I peeked over, trying to see what was in the bag. But nothing could have prepared me for the Penn hoodie he pulled out.

"I wasn't sure of your size." He handed it to me. It felt soft and heavy in my hands.

"I don't understand..."

"Well, you're going to need one come next fall." Nervous energy radiated from him. "I have one too, but mine's black."

"You're telling me you got us matching hoodies?" My heart swelled.

"Well, yeah." He lowered his face, rubbing the back of his neck, looking up at me through thick dark lashes. "Isn't that what couples do?"

I had no words.

None.

I think Jason had stolen them all right around the time he completely stole my heart.

"I know I said I don't want you there, at Penn, but I was just lashing out. Of course I fucking want you there."

"Four years, that's a long time." I smirked. "What if things go south and we have to be around each other all the time?"

"Not possible." He hooked his arm around my neck and pulled me flush against his chest. "I already told you, we're endgame. So if you have doubts, I suggest you run now.

Because I am locking you down for the next four-and-a-half years at least."

"Only four-and-a-half years?"

"When I enter the draft, I might need to cut you loose."

"Works for me, dating a pro football player isn't on my list."

His fingers dug into my sides, tickling and pinching. My laughter spilled freely, filling the space between us, the remaining cracks in my heart.

"I fucking love you." Jason's hand curved around my neck. "I never thought I needed anyone. But I need you, Felicity. I need you so much it hurts." He pressed his head to mine, breathing in sharply.

"So take me," I whispered.

"Yeah?" His eyes were wide and full of wonder.

And hunger.

So much hunger, my legs turned to jelly.

"I'm right here, what are you waiting—" The air *whooshed* from my lungs as Jason hoisted me over his shoulder and carried me up the stairs, ignoring my cries for mercy.

Inside his room, he slowly lowered me to the floor, letting every inch of him press up against every inch of me. We stood there, our eyes locked on one another's, neither of us saying a word. Simply soaking up the moment.

Eventually, I broke away, moving deeper into the room of the most complicated, most gorgeous guy I'd ever laid eyes on.

It was just as I expected. Dark and manly. Slate gray walls with splashes of black and chrome. The bed drenched in black sheets with silver flecks. It reminded me of a storm. Alluring and mysterious from a distance, but deadly if you got too close.

Just like Jason.

"You're the first girl to ever see inside this room except Hailee," he said. I turned to meet his sincere gaze. He'd moved back to the door jamb, leaning against it casually, watching me.

"It's very... you."

Prowling toward me, Jason took an ounce of air from the room with every step, until he was on me, the air gone and my lungs burning with need. "You are so fucking beautiful. I don't deserve you."

I reached up and palmed his cheek, his scruff like sandpaper beneath my skin. "It isn't for you to decide what you deserve."

"The things I want to do to you would definitely make me undeserving."

My lips parted on a soft '*Oh*'.

"Last chance," he warned, his eyes darkening to the color of his sheets.

"I'm not running," I said defiantly.

"Good, because I'd chase you to the ends of the earth. You're mine, Felicity. Every single piece of you."

36

Jason

MY EYES TRACED over her face, taking in the flush of her cheeks; her slightly parted lips, soft and pink and utterly kissable.

"Where to start?" I pressed my palm against Felicity's breastbone, dragging it down her sweater until my fingers found the hem. Slowly, I tugged the material up her body, letting it bunch around her shoulders. "Fuck, I want to taste every inch of you."

"Jason," my name sounded like fucking heaven on her lips. I dropped to my knees, tracing my name on her stomach with my tongue. I wanted to mark her. Brand her in every way possible until we were bound so tight, she could never leave me. Because there was no going back now. I meant every word I'd said to her. She was endgame. I still wanted football, I still wanted Penn, and the NFL, and everything that came with it, but I didn't want any of it if Felicity wasn't right by my side for the ride.

Kissing a path to her bra, I slid my arms around her back and unhooked the clasp. My mouth greedily sucked one of her breasts, and then I gently bit her nipple. Her body jerked with pleasure, so I did it again... and again, until she was writhing in front of me, clawing at my shoulders.

"You're teasing me," she moaned, burying her fingers in my hair and yanking sharply.

My girl had claws and it was such a fucking turn on, I thought I might explode right there and then.

"I'm only just getting started." I climbed up her body, pulling her sweater and tank top off, letting her dusky pink bra slink off her arms and drop to the floor. My own hoodie and shirt went next. Hooking my arm around her waist, I pressed my hand against the small of her back until we were skin on skin, her delicate curves flush against my shredded muscles. Everything about us was different.

Hard and soft.

Rough and smooth.

Cruel and kind.

But we fit to perfection. Two parts of the same whole.

Her hair hung between us like a silky curtain, so I wound it around my fist, gathering it at her nape and pulled gently, forcing her to arch her back. Giving me perfect access to kiss and suck the hollow of her neck. I took my time, tasting and savoring her salty sweet skin.

"More," Felicity's cries filled the room, "I need more." Her nails grazed my shoulder blades.

"I got you, babe." Our lips met, hot and wet and needy; our tongues lapping and stroking and exploring. Her kisses were addictive and I knew no amount of hits would ever be enough.

Felicity became impatient, her hands tracing my abs, painting a torturous path down to the waistband of my jeans. She expertly popped the button and shoved her hand inside, grasping me. "Fuck," I choked out as she pumped me

377

slowly. "This isn't what I had in mind," my voice cracked with raw lust.

"I can't wait. I need you," she breathed, "now."

I wanted to make her wait, to reacquaint myself with every inch of her body, and then all the parts I'd yet to explore, but truth be told, I couldn't wait either. My need for her was like a firestorm raging inside me, burning higher and higher with every touch, every taste.

We made quick work of each other's jeans and underwear, then I scooped her up and dropped her on the bed, not bothering to ask permission. Felicity giggled, the sound so fucking perfect I wanted to bottle that shit for a rainy day.

"Come here." She crooked her finger, scooting up the bed and letting her legs fall open. There wasn't so much as a hint of shyness or uncertainty in her eyes, her love for me blazing in her sea-green gaze.

Crawling over her, I slid between her legs, my rock-hard dick settling at her entrance. "Do I need to stop?" I arched my brow at her, hoping, praying she wouldn't make me.

"There's only ever been you," she said, "and I'm on birth control. But I know you've been with other—"

"No one."

"What?" She blinked up at me.

"There hasn't been another girl since New York."

Confusion swam in her lust-filled eyes. "But Jenna—"

"I never slept with her, I just let you think... Fuck." I dropped my head to her shoulder, regretting so much that happened between us. In trying to protect her, I'd hurt her, and it would always be there, in the background.

"Jason, look at me," her voice coaxed me out of hiding.

"I don't care about what happened before, I only care what happens now and in the future." She hitched her legs higher, almost pulling me into her body. We both groaned at the intimate contact.

"So if I do this." I rocked my hips, pushing another inch inside her, "you're not going to hate me?"

Licking her lips, Felicity looked right at me, a seductive smirk spreading across her lips. "Didn't I tell you? There's nothing more I love than to hate you." Sliding her hands down to my ass, she pressed me further into her.

"Fuck," I groaned, bolts of pleasure shooting off in all directions inside me. "Do you have any idea how good you feel?"

"Show me," it came out breathy.

I rocked forward again, my hand sliding up one of her legs, anchoring us closer, making it so much deeper. My other hand found her neck, my fingers splaying around her possessively as I pulled out before sinking into her heat again.

My lips claimed Felicity's again, my tongue loving her mouth, the way my body loved her. "I love you," I whispered against her swollen lips, "I love you so fucking much."

"I love you too, Jason. I do."

My pace quickened, needing more. Needing everything she had to give. Our skin became damp, our kisses clumsy, all while Felicity met me thrust for thrust.

My partner.

My equal.

The girl who taught me there was more to life than the game.

Who taught me how to love.

The girl I planned on keeping for as long as she would have me.

———

The next morning rolled around too quickly. I'd dropped Felicity off at home last night and then gone home and drunk one too many whiskies. I was so fucking happy things between us were finally good, but there was still a lot hanging in the balance. So when Coach called me and Asher into his office after a grueling practice, I knew the wait was finally over.

"Come in, ladies," Coach motioned for us to take a seat. "Principal Finnigan has consulted with the school board, and in light of everything, they have decided to suspend you from the team, effective immediately."

Asher let out a heavy sigh, leaning forward on his elbows. "And Jase?"

"Principal Finnigan pushed for a suspension but the board felt that since you were coming to the aid of your teammate that a more lenient punishment was adequate." His mouth pulled into a grim line. "You're out for next week's game but if we make it through to the next round, you can play."

I sank back in the chair, running a hand down the back of my neck. I could play. If we made it to the second round of the play-offs, which I had every faith we would, I could play. But it came at a price.

Asher's season was over.

"Coach," I said ready to defend my teammate, my

brother.

One of the best friend's a guy could ever have.

"It's fair," Ash interrupted me. "I won't contest. Besides, maybe they'll let me wear Vinnie the Viking. Go Raiders." It came out drolly despite the defeat in his eyes.

"Ash—"

"It's cool, bro." He shrugged. "I knew what I was doing when I went down there to meet Thatcher."

Coach Hasson watched us, watched me. He knew. Deep down, I didn't doubt he knew the truth, but he was letting it play out this way because sometimes good men had to make sacrifices, and without Asher's sacrifice, the Raiders would be going into the play-offs without their star player.

"I'm sorry it came to this, real damn sorry," he addressed Asher. "You're a good kid, Bennet, and I don't doubt you're going to have a successful career with the Pittsburg Panthers. Principal Finnigan might get the final say on whether or not you play, but it's my team and my field and I expect to see you sitting there on the bench supporting your teammates, you hear me?"

"I wouldn't be anywhere else, Coach."

"Good, now get out of here."

The door clicked shut behind Asher, sucking the air from the room.

"You know, I couldn't sleep last night. I lay there worrying I was about to lose not one but two of my best players going into the play-offs. It's a Coach's worst nightmare."

"Coach, I—".

"You listen up and listen good, Jason," he gritted out,

disappointment rippling off him. "I don't know all that happened with Thatcher and quite frankly, I don't want to know. But you have got to learn to channel your anger, Son. You think I don't know kids like you and Thatcher? Hell, I used to be you. I thought I was untouchable, a god on and off the field. But my old man refused to let me forget who I was and where I came from. He kept my feet firmly on the ground.

"I know you and Kent have issues, I know it hasn't been easy growing up in his shadow, but for the love of God, do not throw away what could be the opportunity of a lifetime for the likes of the Thatcher's of the world. You're better than that. You take all the crap, all the anger and resentment, and channel it into football. Or if that fails, you find yourself a damn good woman to help keep you grounded."

I chuckled at that. I'd gotten to know Mrs. Hasson quite well over the years and it wasn't any secret she kept Coach in line.

"This Miss Giles. You think it could be serious?"

"I think so, Sir."

"Good, you hold onto her and don't let go, you hear me? When you have the world at your feet like you do, girls are a dime a dozen. They'll all want a piece of the action, the glory, but it's a rare thing to find a girl who will see beyond all that. A girl who will stick around long enough to realize there's more to you than football."

"Got it," I said, trying to disguise how deeply his words affected me.

"There's just one last thing before you leave. I thought you might like to know the school board are issuing a full investigation into Mr. Thatcher and Miss Jarvis. They won't get away with this, Jason. But I'm begging you. Let the authorities handle it from here on out."

"I think I can do that, Coach."

"Glad to hear it. Okay, get out of here. We have a game to prepare for. Just because you're out for the first game doesn't mean I don't expect one-hundred-and-ten percent at practice, okay?"

Nodding, I moved to the door, pausing. "Hey, Coach, you ever get into trouble back in the day?"

"Does a bear shit in the woods?" A rare smirk lifted the corner of his mouth. "Now go, before I change my mind."

The locker room had cleared out by the time I was done. Only Asher remained, sitting on the bench near his locker cage. "Hey," I said, dropping down beside him.

"Hey," he mumbled, kicking his sneakers against the floor.

"Why, Ash?" I'd already asked him the question but that was before the sentence had been handed down.

"Because this was always how it was supposed to be; you get the girl and the glory."

"Ash, come on..." I nudged his shoulder with mine.

"It's all good." Raking a hand through his hair, he finally lifted his eyes to me, but his smile was distant. "It's your dream, man, so make it count."

With a small nod, he got up and walked out of the locker room. Leaving me sitting there with nothing but my regrets.

They said heavy was the head that wore the crown. Well my crown was coiled in guilt and shame, and it weighed a fucking ton.

37

Felicity

MY EYES FLICKED to the wall clock for the tenth time in less than ten minutes.

"Felicity, sweetheart, is something wrong with your food?"

"No, Mom, it's great." I forced a smile, pushing the noodles around my plate. "I... umm... it's just, well, there's something I want to talk to you about. Two things actually." I'd hoped to sit down with her and Dad, but he got held up at the office again, and I figured it might be a blessing in disguise. If I broke the news to her first, then she could help break the news to my dad.

"I'm listening." She placed her silverware down and leaned in attentively. "Whatever it is, baby, I'm sure it doesn't warrant all this worry." Her eyes softened.

"So funny story, I—" The doorbell startled me, making me choke on the words yet to come.

"Are you expecting someone?"

I was... but he was fifteen minutes early.

Damn him.

"I'll get that, Mom." I was up and out of my chair before she could stop me, all but running down the hall. Yanking the front door open, I hissed, "You're early."

"Hailee said you might need some moral support." Jase's brow went up. "And I brought back up."

"Back up?"

He pulled his arm from behind his back, revealing a bouquet of hand tied roses. "They're beautiful." I went to take them from him, but Jason snatched them out of reach.

"Actually, they're for your mom. Hailee said they were her favorite."

"Are you sure you haven't done this before?" Stepping to the side, I let him enter. But Jason paused, turning to meet my dreamy gaze.

"Only for you. Only ever for you. You owe me, Giles." He grinned, leaning in to steal a kiss.

"Felicity, sweetheart," Mom's voice filtered down the hall, "is everything okay?"

"Fine, Mom. I'm coming."

"Already?" Jason whispered, tracing his mouth down my neck. "I haven't even touched you yet."

"Behave." My hands pressed into his chest. "This has to go well." Because if it didn't... well, it didn't bear thinking about. I went to go, but he grabbed my wrist, pulling me back to him.

"Hey, it's going to be okay, Felicity. Whatever happens, we'll deal with it, okay? Together."

Any apprehension I felt melted away. Jason might have been new to the whole relationship thing, but so far, he was doing a pretty amazing job.

"Ready?" I asked him, feeling myself fall into his dark intense eyes. Our mouths fused together again, like magnets unable to fight the attraction.

"Felicity?" Mom's voice was closer now.

Crap.

Lips still attached to Jason's, I slid my eyes to the hall to find her standing there, watching us with a mix of mild curiosity and panic. "Hmm, hey, Mom." I finally detached myself from my boyfriend's mouth. "Surprise."

"Surprise? I'm not sure I follow..." her eyes narrowed, moving from me to Jason and back again. "Is that who I think it is?"

"Hi, Mrs. Giles. I'm Jason. Jason Ford." He stepped forward, thrusting the bouquet of flowers at her. "It's a pleasure to meet you."

"These are for me?" She was giving him a serious case of the mom-stares.

"They are. A little birdy told me they were your favorite."

"They're very beautiful. Thank you, Jason." Mom graciously accepted the flowers despite the scowl on her face. "Now would you care to explain why you're in my house, kissing my daughter?"

"About that, Mom. I can explain. Jason is..." The words were right there, on the tip of my tongue, but I froze.

I totally and utterly froze.

Fingers sliding against mine, Jason's touch slowly thawed the panic coiled around my throat. "I'm Felicity's boyfriend."

"B- boyfriend. Oh my... Well, that is a shock. *Boyfriend?*" Her eyes went to mine and I managed a small nod. "I see, and how long has this been going on?"

"It's fairly new," Jason said with an easy confidence, and I was beginning to wonder if there was anything he couldn't do. "But rest assured, I care about your daughter very much."

"That's... good to know." Her hand slid to her neck as if she was having a hard time breathing. "Maybe we should all sit down." Mom spun around and disappeared down the hall, and I slumped against Jason.

"This is not how I wanted this to go," I let out a heavy sigh. "Did you see her face? She's mortified."

"Hey." Jason's fingers slid underneath my jaw, tilting my face to meet his steely eyes. "At least she knows now. She'll come around."

"How can you be so sure?"

"Because she loves you."

"Okay." Inhaling a deep breath, I said, "Let's go finish this." Because her world was about to spin one more time before the evening was over.

I only hoped we all survived.

We found Mom in the living room, sipping what looked like a glass of liquor. Dear God, I'd driven my mother to drink. *There's one for your list.*

"I'm so sorry, Mom. This wasn't how I wanted you to find out. I was trying to tell you over dinner, but the words just wouldn't come out."

"I won't deny it's a lot to process. I had no idea you were even dating; you never said anything." Hurt flashed in her eyes, making guilt snake around my heart.

"I'm not dating, I mean, I wasn't... Me and Jason just sort of happened." My eyes lifted to his. "I didn't plan for any of this."

"Well, if there's one thing I know, it's that you can't help who you fall for. I mean, take me and your father for example." She smiled wistfully. "I just thought you had more sense, sweetheart."

"Mom!" I scolded.

"Forgive me, Jason, I didn't mean to sound so insensitive. I'm sure you can understand I'm not bowled over at the idea of my daughter dating a football player, let alone Rixon's star quarterback."

He stiffened beside me, squeezing my hand a little tighter. "We're not dating, Mom," I said. "I love him. I'm in love with him."

If she'd been surprised in the hall watching me kiss Jason, it was nothing compared to the expression she wore now. "Felicity Charlotte Giles, in love, really?"

"Really."

"And you," she glared at Jason. "What are your intentions for my daughter?"

He cleared his throat and I wanted the ground to open up and swallow me whole. Jason might have signed on for my brand of crazy, but he was about to learn I had nothing on my mother.

"I'll be honest, it's not a question I imagined answering so soon." Strangled laughter rumbled in his chest. "But I love her, ma'am. She makes me want to be a better man. Makes me want things I wasn't sure I ever wanted. I understand you have concerns, I would too. But please know I would never do anything to hurt her."

Mom's expression barely softened. "You've certainly got a charm about you, don't you?"

Oh dear God, despite her stone mask, my mother was flirting with my boyfriend.

I was never going to live this down.

"I try," Jason quipped back, and I stamped on his foot. He smothered a grunt.

"Your father isn't going to like this, sweetheart."

"I was kind of hoping you might help soften the blow." I flashed her my best puppy-dog eyes. "But before you make any decisions, there's probably something else you should know."

"Oh God, you're not pregnant, are you?"

Jason started choking beside me while Mom stared at me expectantly. And I sat there, shrinking into the chair, wondering when life got so complicated. Knowing the answer was simple.

Jason freaking Ford.

———

After I broke the news to Mom that I planned on switching my business degree to animal science, and she'd had a semi-meltdown, I let Jason drag me away to give us both some space. I'd broken her heart but as he kept reassuring me, it would heal. Because that's what hearts did. Sure, maybe they never quite got pieced back together the same way, but they would carry on beating.

"How are you feeling?" he asked me as he drove to wherever it was he was taking me.

"Sad, but mostly relieved. I'm their only child, their baby. I didn't want to hurt them."

"She'll come around, I promise." His hand splayed over my knee, rubbing gently. I covered it with my own, grateful for his reassurance.

"And my dad?"

"Him too. It might not happen overnight, it might not even happen over a few months, but it will happen." I murmured some incoherent reply, too depressed to answer. "You deserve all your dreams, Felicity, and they will realize that one day."

"Where are we going anyway?" I changed the subject. I wasn't feeling in the mood, but Jason had insisted he had something to show me. I never could resist him, and I wasn't about to start now.

When we turned off the main road out of town and took the familiar dirt path down to the lake, I groaned. "Seriously? You brought me here, now? The last thing I want to do right now is bounce on your—"

"Giles?" He cut the engine.

"Yeah?"

"Shut the fuck up and get out of the car."

Well, okay then. Rolling my eyes, I shouldered the door and climbed out. The lake shimmered under a blanket of twinkling stars. "God, it's so beautiful out here."

Jason came up behind me, wrapping his arms around my waist. "A little birdy told me you almost completed your list."

"Almost."

There were only three things remaining: fall asleep under the stars, get a tattoo, and go to Winter Formal with a date. Although I still wasn't sure about getting a tattoo. It seemed so permanent.

"What if I told you, you can tick two of those things off tonight?"

"We're going to sleep out here?" Because I was pretty

sure my boyfriend didn't have his tattoo license, and Winter Formal wasn't for another couple of weeks.

I craned my face around to his, unable to hide my grin. "Only if you want to," he said.

"But it's freezing."

"So technically, I thought we could sleep in the car, but the view is the same."

"It's perfect." I brushed my lips over his. "Thank you. But that's only one—"

Jason shoved something into my hand. I plucked open the note.

Roses are red, violets are blue
I'd really like to go to Winter Formal with you?

Stifling a giggle, I said, "Fess up. Asher wrote this, didn't he?"

"He may have helped a little."

Turning in Jason's arms, I leaned up, touching my forehead to his. "I'm glad the two of you are okay."

"You really think I want to talk about Ash right now?"

"What else did you have in mind?" I asked, coyly.

"First." he dipped his head, kissing my collarbone, sucking the sensitive skin between his teeth. A shiver rolled through me, my eyes fluttering closed. "I want your answer."

"Yes," I breathed, desire humming through me.

"Good." Jason spun me so that my ass hit the edge of his

car. "Now I'm going to make love to you on the hood of my car and then we can cuddle talk about the final thing on your list before we fall to sleep under the stars, sound good?"

Looping my arms around his neck, I smiled. "It sounds perfect."

EPILOGUE

FOUR WEEKS later

Felicity

"My god, I can't watch," I buried my face into Hailee's arm as we watched from our preferential seats. Mya was with us, as well as Jason's dad and Hailee's mom, and Cameron's parents. Asher was on the outs with his parents since the suspension, so they hadn't made the trip.

A collective *'oooh'* roared through the crowd as the Bulldog's defensive end took down Cam for the third time.

"Is it always this tense?" Mya asked, to which me and Hailee both answered, "No."

"Sorry I asked." She held up her hands, grabbing another hand of popcorn.

"Seriously?" I gawked at her.

"What," she shrugged, "I'm hungry."

I couldn't eat. I was too nervous. My heart had been in my mouth for most of the game. I knew how much this meant to Jason. He'd played it down a lot around Asher; trying to smooth the cracks that had appeared between them ever since Asher took the fall about the Thatcher ordeal. But when it was just the two of us, when I was lying in his arms, nothing between us, I felt his fear. Fear of failure, of letting his team down, his coach, the entire town.

But most of all, of letting himself down.

He'd worked so hard for this, they all had, but no one wanted it more than Jason. It wasn't just some high school accolade; it was his legacy. His way of proving himself. So watching him and the rest of the team get their asses handed to them, was almost too much to bear.

"Run," Hailee yelled, "Run."

We both held our breath, waiting for the moment our offense reached the end zone, but a Bulldog defensive player came out of nowhere and slammed into Grady, knocking him clean off his feet.

"Dammit."

"At least he almost got there that time," Mya remarked.

I levelled her with an incredulous look. "Just because your guy isn't out there on the field doesn't mean you can't at least pretend to be interested."

"I'm interested." She sat a little straighter. "And what do you mean, *my guy*?"

"You know exactly what I mean." She and Asher had gotten closer since I got with Jason but they were both still pleading the fifth on whether it was more than friendship.

"We're just friends."

Case in point.

Rolling my eyes, I settled my gaze back on the field, searching out Jason. Pride radiated from every bone in my body. Not because he'd led his team to this point; the whole town knew he'd do it, but for the fact he was mine.

For how far we'd come.

Rixon's complicated, brooding, cruel, star quarterback

was changing right before my eyes. He was warmer and more open, no longer afraid to tell me how he felt. Even less afraid to show me. He'd even made an effort to get to know my parents, although that was a work in progress. My dad was taking some warming up to the idea I had a boyfriend, let alone a boyfriend by the name of Jason Ford who I planned to go off to college with next year.

Of course, Jason still liked to talk dirty and make me blush at every opportunity, but I didn't mind. In fact, I'd grown to love it. He pushed my boundaries and I pushed his right back.

And I couldn't wait for the next summer when we left for UPenn to start the rest of our lives.

Together.

Jason

"Raiders, gather in," I yelled like a general commanding his army. My teammates huddled together, waiting for my words of encouragement. For the profound speech to carry them into the fourth quarter.

"Listen up," it came out breathless. I was running on empty; we all were. "No team ever wants to be in this position; going into the fourth trailing by eight points. But we can do this. I know we can. Forget all the other games, forget what happened last game." When we'd almost fumbled our comfortable win by giving the opposing team room to score a touchdown with two minutes on the clock. Luckily, we were able to get the conversion before the final whistle, but it had been the most stressful two minutes of my life.

"Four years and it all comes down to this. Whatever happens, I'm proud to call myself a Raider, and you should be too. Hands in, Raiders on three."

The huddle grew tighter as my teammates dropped their hands on mine. My eyes found Asher on the sideline and before I could think about it, I yelled, "Yo, forty-two, get your ass over here," giving zero fucks he wasn't supposed to move from the bench. He deserved this as much as the rest of the guys.

"Feeling the pressure, QB?" he smarted as he jogged over to me.

"You deserve to be here." I held his eyes, silently telling him everything I'd been too chicken shit to say.

Thank you.

I owe you.

You're the best friend a guy could ever have.

He gave me a curt nod and then said, "Are we doing this or what?"

"On your word, Ash."

"Raiders on three. One. Two. Three..." Our battle cry rang out around me for the last time, our six-thousand strong crowd echoing the word at us.

It was something to behold, standing there on Hershey Stadium's now tarnished field, the blinding Friday night lights blazing down on us. Making us seem larger than life. Worshipped and adored. The next time I did this, my jersey would be Penn Quaker red, white, and blue, and I'd be a rookie. But I was ready. Hungry for it.

College.

Football.

A fresh start with Felicity.

It couldn't come soon enough. But first, we had a game to win.

Felicity

"Are you sure this is a good idea?" I asked no one in particular as I stared up at the neon sign reading *Ink City*, nervous energy vibrating through me.

"He'll love it," Mya whispered in my ear as the guys jostled one another, the effects of our few celebration drinks showing. "Besides, it's the last item on your list, you can't back out now."

I nodded slowly, watching the guys. They were buzzed, we all were. Still riding the high of the win. The Raiders had done it, in the last minute of play. Cam getting the final touchdown.

"My parents will—"

"*Never* find out about it. Stick to the plan."

"The plan, right." I took a deep breath. Hailee caught my eye and frowned.

"What are you two up to?"

Ignoring her, I moved to the front of our group and grabbed the door handle. "Are you guys doing this or not?"

"Fuck, I love it when she takes charge," Jason smirked, and I rolled my eyes right back.

"Oh, I'm in," Asher bounced on the balls of his feet. "I'm so fucking in. State Champs 2019, here I come."

"I hate to break it to you, *Champ*," Mya clapped him on the shoulder, "But can you claim the title if you didn't actually play?"

"Way to burst a guy's bubble." He scowled but it

quickly melted away. He was too damn wired. We all were. The after-game celebrations had been crazy, everyone rushing onto the field to celebrate with the team. Then there had been dinner at the hotel's restaurant with close family and friends. Afterwards, Coach finally let us off the hook. Officially, we weren't supposed to leave the hotel, but unofficially, Coach agreed to turn a blind eye as long as we all surfaced tomorrow morning for the buses home.

"Either way," Asher went on, "I'm getting it done. No girls at college are going to know I didn't play. They're only going to see 'State Champ' and flock to me like—"

"Flies to shit?" Mya deadpanned.

We all streamed into the store, instantly assaulted with the sound of tattoo guns and rock music. Jason walked up to the desk and did all the talking. "Three?" he called over to us and the guys nodded. But before he could confirm with the receptionist, I called, "Make that four."

"Holy shit, Fee," Asher whistled between his teeth. "For real?"

"Just something small," I said, my eyes sliding to Jason. "It's the last thing on my list."

"Hell yeah, you heard my girl, make that four."

His girl. I don't think I'd ever get used to hearing him call me that.

"Take a seat and Auden will be with you shortly."

Jason came over to me, dipping his head to my ear. "You sure about this?"

I gave him a little nod, not trusting myself to speak. We'd talked about what I might get if I went through with it. After all, it was the only remaining item on my list. But when he saw it, he was going to freak.

I'd already fallen in crazy messy love with him, so I might as well get the crazy messy tattoo to go with it.

Jason

"What's taking them so long." I growled, pacing back and forth outside the room where Felicity currently was, alone with Auden, with his hands on her body, touching her.

"Chill, man." Cam's hand clamped down on my shoulder. "He's only doing his job."

"Yeah, well, she should have let me in there with her."

"Maybe she was worried about passing out or getting sick."

I threw Ash a hard look. Like I gave a shit about that. My favorite version of Felicity was first thing in the morning, hair all mussed up and crazy, her eyes heavy-lidded with sleep, her skin damp from my touch.

I loved sleeping with her, but it usually didn't lead to much actual sleep. It wasn't my fault she was so irresistible, and I was a hot-blooded guy who was powerless against her voodoo magic.

The vibration of the gun behind the door finally stopped. "Thank fuck," I grumbled, moving closer.

A few minutes later, it swung open and Felicity skipped out.

"About time."

"Sorry," she said meekly. "It hurt more than I expected."

"Can I see?" I asked expecting a tiny heart or some script-font life quote girls liked to get. She'd had a few ideas but had been tightlipped about a decision. So when she said, "Don't freak out," the floor went from under me.

"What did you do?"

Felicity glanced around the store, and moved in closer. She lifted her sweater up, yanking the neck of her tank down, and everything slowed down.

"Tell me that says what I think it says." My heart was pounding so hard I thought I might pass out.

"Oh, it says it all right." Asher was beside me, staring at the curve of Felicity's perfect breast like he'd never seen a girl's naked tits before.

There in tiny Varsity font, stamped right across where her heart lay, were four little words that shouldn't have pleased me so much.

Property of a Raider.

"Flick," Hailee gasped, her eyes growing to saucers, "Please tell me that's temporary."

"It's not." She dropped her sweater, meeting my gaze. "Now, no matter what happens, a part of my heart will always be yours."

"Holy fucking shit," Asher slapped his hands against his thigh. "If you don't put a ring on it, I will." He smirked at me and I glared back, sending him a silent message.

Over my dead body.

The End

PLAYLIST

Two Weeks – FKA Twigs
River of Tears – Alessia Cara
Good Enough – Little Mix
Cruel – Glowie
11 Minutes – YUNGBLUD, ft. Halsey
Gotta Get Up – Moody
Better – Khalid
If I Go – Ella Eyre
Why Her Not Me – Grace Carter
I Gave It All – Aquilo
Bad Blood – Taylor Swift
Nightmare- Halsey
To the Hills – Laurel
Let Me Down Slowly – Alec Benjamin
Mother Tongue – Bring Me The Horizon
Fight For You – ALIUS, Rasmus Hagen
Don't Let Me Down – The Chainsmokers
Love Me Or Leave Me – Little Mix
Easier – 5 Seconds of Summer
Only Want You – Rita Ora
Now You're Gone – Tom Walker, Zara Larson
Power Over Me – Dermot Kennedy
Cross Me – Ed Sheeran, ft. Chance the Rapper

Fight For You – Man Made Machine
Love Again – New Hope Club
Say You Love Me – Jessie Ware

ACKNOWLEDGEMENTS

Jason, oh Jason.

If you got this far, I hope you enjoyed my brooding alpha-hole's story. Yes, he's cruel, yes, he's mean, but underneath that hard shell of his, is just a guy trying to find his place in the world. I hope you loved my misunderstood bad boy as much as I did writing him.

The support for this series has been none other than mind blowing. From the messages, to the beautiful edits, to the humbling reviews ... thank you to each and every person who has fallen in love with this bunch of cocky football players, your support is everything!

As always, there is a huge list of people I owe gratitude:

Andie, my editor and friend. You keep me sane and talk me off the ledge more times than I can count. I would be truly lost without you! Twink, thanks for being there whenever I need to vent, moan, or just roll my eyes. Nina, my alpha reader. Having you there to hold my hand through this release has been everything, thank you. My beta team: Becky, Bre, Jamie, and Tami, thank you for your honesty and help tweaking Jason and Felicity's story. Ginelle, my proof-reader extraordinaire, your eagle eye continues to astound me.

To my L A Cotton promo team – I bow down! Your constant support is amazing and I feel lucky to have you all in my corner. Virtual hugs and smoochies! My Indie Girls, you know who you are. Thanks for always being there when I need to vent or just chat about what's working and what isn't.

To my readers / spoiler groups – thank you for bearing with me and continuing to engage and support my writing and publishing journey. It's nice to have somewhere to come and talk books or just life. And to the bloggers, reviewers, and bookstagrammer who have supported the series, thanks doesn't really seem enough!

And finally, to my family. For giving me the time and space to 'get on with it'. I'm a workaholic, but I'm working on it. Promise.

Until next time,

L A xo

ABOUT THE AUTHOR

Reckless Love. Wild Hearts.

Author of mature young adult and new adult novels, L A is happiest writing the kind of books she loves to read: addictive stories full of teenage angst, tension, twists and turns.

Home is a small town in the middle of England where she currently juggles being a full-time writer with being a mother/referee to two little people. In her spare time (and when she's not camped out in front of the laptop) you'll most likely find L A immersed in a book, escaping the chaos that is life.

L A loves connecting with readers. The best places to find her are:

www.lacotton.com

Printed in Great Britain
by Amazon

41919318R00228